The Cava Queen

The Cava Queen

by

Amanda Meheux

First published in 2011 by Raft Publishing,

23, The Island,

Thames Ditton,

Surrey,

KT7 0SH

United Kingdom.

www.amandameheux.com

Cover design by Simon McMahon

The Cava Queen

ISBN 978-0-9571039-0-0

Formatted by www.bookformatting.co.uk

Printed and bound in Great Britain by TJ International Ltd, Padstow, Cornwall.

About The Author

On account of her love of pocket money, from the age of 12, Amanda Meheux's list of jobs would make a Careers Officer weep - Shelf Stacking, Egg Frying, Sandwich Making, Leaflet Dropping, Jean Selling, Wine Serving, Liniment Packing, Leg Waxing, Skin Fixing, Face Painting, TV Presenting, Wok Wiggling, Cauldron Stirring…

Throw a conman, cancer, wanderlust and magnetic attraction to all things weird and wonderful into the mix, and what you have is great anecdotal fodder and research for what will hopefully be her last career of choice – writing.

Based on her personal mantra that life is too short and precious to waste, she spent a couple of years in sunny Spain attempting to transform her varied experience and vivid imagination into a novel that would hopefully make people smile. After what turned out to be a rather protracted period of honing her procrastination skills to the max and making lots of excuses, now, much to the relief of her long suffering friends and family she has finally managed to finish her first piece of fiction - *The Cava Queen*

…long live the bubbles!

Acknowledgements

I'm clutching the award to my bosom; rivulets of mascara streaming down my face as I tearfully acknowledge everyone that has helped me get this far...
Just in case this doesn't happen, better get a few quick thanks in now...

All of my fabulous Sitges friends who ensured my two years in that glorious part of the world were happy, fun-filled, inspiring and very, very sparkling – Amanda & Ady, Mark & José, Cheyenne & Juan Carlos, Kevin, April & Dan, John Wedge, John Senior, Pascal, Stephen & Wayne, Sammy, Shaun, Rando, Mathias & Javier, Barry & Wayne, Olga, Nicky, Angela, Jane, Emma, Tutu, Ramona, Renu, Jonathon, Michael & Gregg, Pablo & Ben, Peter & Rico, and of course Doug x

My mum, for always uttering those immortal maternal words, 'you can do it'. As you quite rightly said, 'If you can beat the Big 'C' this is easy.' Love you xx

Sue Smart for editing, and re-editing, and not seeming to mind at all.

Sharon Cullinane for butt-kicking, Bergerac reds, and in advance for what you're going to have to do now.

Simon McMahon for rising to the challenge.

And you, for buying it!

Cheers x

For Peter and Neville, brighter than the fireworks on *Fiesta Major*, you always lit up the *pueblo,* and whenever I look up at a star-studded Sitges sky, I like to think you still do.

And for my dad, you light my path daily and are cradled in my heart.

ONE

'Alexandra! Where on earth are you?'

'Mum?' I mumbled through lips as dry as parchment.

'Everybody is here waiting for you!'

'Ugh?'

'Where are you?' Her voice hit a note that could shatter a greenhouse.

'I don't know,' I whimpered pathetically, although however hazy my location, my condition was a definite; in the early stages of the hangover from hell. Having thought I was dreaming about a ringing phone and then realising I wasn't, I was now half hanging out of a strange bed having ejected the entire contents of my handbag whilst rummaging around for the damn thing. My head was pounding, acidic bile was slowly creeping into my mouth and I was surveying a heap of clothes, some of which were certainly not mine. This was not looking good.

'Mel, talk to Alex, I can't get any sense out of her at all.'

Any momentary relief I felt at being passed over to my best friend was short-lived as she was obviously in no mood for niceties. 'I hope for your sake you've been bloody kidnapped,' she snapped. 'We've been calling you for hours.'

I squinted at my mobile phone and sure enough there they were. Twenty-four missed calls.

'So come on then, what future dinner party anecdote are you involved in this time? The blasted dial tone sounds like you're out of the country. Please, please, please tell me I'm wrong.'

As I hauled my upper body back onto the bed and flopped onto the pillow I heard a loud grunt and a tattooed arm thudded onto my naked stomach. I peered cautiously to my right. The owner of the

1

arm had dishevelled pink hair and the bright shards of sunlight that were blazing viciously in through the gap in the curtains were bouncing off his extensive body piercing.

Suddenly it all started to come back to me…

'I'm in Spain, Mel.'

I heard a sharp intake of breath and then she hissed: 'You stupid cow, we organised you afternoon tea and cocktails. At this very moment forty people are guzzling Freixenet and waiting for the guest of honour to turn up. It's your bloody birthday, how could you?'

'Oh my god, I didn't know…'

'It was meant to be a surprise! Your mum is going to be devastated.'

'Yes but…..'

I didn't get a chance to launch into a lengthy explanation as there was a loud beep and my mobile insensitively died. I tapped it desperately but it was no use, all communication with Planet Pissed Off had now been cut and my only hope of getting home and rectifying the situation would involve Doctor Who turning up in his Tardis.

I rubbed my eyes and slowly took in my surroundings. I was in a single room, spartanly furnished and incredibly chilly. Outside I could hear the burble of voices and clanking of china. I could feel the veins on my temples pulsating and my bladder was about to burst so I gingerly eased the arm from my belly, slid out of the bed and grabbed a navy towel that had been left on a chair. I wrapped it around myself and shuddered. Cold damp cloth on still warm skin will never be a sensory high. Turning the door handle as gently as I could, I peered out into the hall. The bathroom was right ahead. I darted across, closed the door and sighed.

In what could only have been twenty-four hours I had lost my job, got on a plane, missed my fortieth birthday party, and by the look of it, just ended three years in the sexual wilderness with a bisexual twenty-something called Zane.

Quite rock 'n' roll really - only I so wasn't.

TWO

The day before, when I had a job, my feet were on UK turf, my liver was in pretty good shape and my friends and family were looking forward to seeing that look of surprise on my face…

The minute I walked through the door of Beverley Herman's mock-Georgian mini-mansion on the outskirts of Manchester I just knew it was going to be one of those days.

'I thought you presenters were always a lot smaller in real-life,' my subject matter sniffed, obviously horrified that yours truly, Alexandra Chapman – health expert, lifestyle guru and presenter of the TV makeover show *Sort Your Life Out* - the person who was meant to be the answer to her prayers, came in similar packaging to her own. Granted I wasn't bedecked in enough gold to wipe out a small third world country's debt, my hair wasn't bleached and savagely back-combed to within an inch of its life, and I hadn't taken style tips from a lap dancer. In stark contrast; my curly red locks had never been subjected to blow drying and hair-straighteners, my somewhat eclectic wardrobe was a Lycra-free zone and at five-foot-ten (and a half) inches I towered above her five-foot-four. BUT we were both reasonably curvy size 14s, and this was clearly a matter of great concern to an obsessive dieter, who had obviously thought that my love handles were simply due to the camera adding its obligatory twelve pounds.

Wrong!

Those babies were the direct result of a penchant for chips with chilli sauce and mayonnaise, total reluctance to get my butt down the gym and lashings of ice cold cava. Not forgetting the ironic truth that love handles will always get worse when you ain't getting any loving. But of course, despite not exactly walking my talk, I

3

still had the audacity to 'sort out' everyone else's life - and get paid for it.

Today it was Beverley's turn. The entire life of this mother-of-two revolved around the calorific content of anything that might pass her lips. Her place of worship was the local slimming club, her bible – the latest fad diet book. I was on a mission to give her a healthier outlook and a little confidence boosting makeover. In the name of cheap daytime telly, I set about re-organising her calorie-obsessed world and she fought me every inch of the way.

When I suggested she tried flesh-toned *Spanx* knickers with tummy control to avoid a visible panty-line and refine her silhouette, she refused so vehemently that you would have thought I was asking her to move into a convent and don the habit. Her reaction to my sensitively delivered comment that less garish make-up would make her look younger, was to snatch a black kohl pencil from her make-up bag and proceed to demonstrate in no uncertain terms that she laughed in the face of *au natural* and preferred eyes that looked like she had gone a few rounds with a heavy-weight boxer. My little protégé yawned continually through the yoga teacher's session despite the promise of lithe limbs and boundless energy, and by the time we got to tackle the rudiments of a balanced diet, I was ready to shove the plate of hummus and crudités down her throat, and batter her into submission with a bottle of olive oil.

Nothing I could do or say seemed to be able to break through her protective veneer; she was buried under a mound of self-doubt. And yet, despite her prickly façade there was a part of me that couldn't help warming to her. Not that she would have noticed; she was far too busy being prickly, and I was far too busy trying to get the job done. Miraculously we managed to survive the afternoon without causing each other physical harm and by 5 pm it was *a wrap*. The crew packed up and disappeared. Beverley retreated upstairs, leaving me sitting in the kitchen alone waiting for a cab to take me to the airport. I was sadly doing a mental toss-up between a BLT or crayfish and rocket as my choice of crap sandwich for the journey home when Beverley re-emerged wearing a pink Lycra tracksuit I had suggested she chuck out earlier. The girl certainly had *chutzpah*. I couldn't help laughing.

'Boy oh boy did I want to punch you earlier,' she stood with her arms crossed, glaring at me.

'The feeling was entirely mutual,' I replied with a smile still playing on my lips. 'Why the hell did you even apply to go on the show if you didn't want to play ball?'

'I didn't,' she shrugged. 'My best friend Tanya saw the ad somewhere online and put in an application on my behalf. I can't believe you chose me.'

'Somehow, I'm thinking this lack of self-esteem isn't going to be banished by swapping to soya milk and doing headstands. How about this for an idea? Go and get a job, woman. Get out there, occupy yourself.'

'I wouldn't know where to start.' She nodded over to a framed picture of two stunning blonde-haired girls. 'I had my twins at nineteen. Heidi and Alice were my job. Now they've buggered off to London, and I hardly ever see them.'

'Well, maybe now is the time you find something for you?' I paused. 'Then you wouldn't have all this time to obsess about weight.'

'Laurence doesn't want me to work; he says I don't need to.'

I raised an eyebrow, 'Laurence is your husband I assume?'

She nodded.

'Okay, maybe financially you don't need to, but there are other reasons people work – for a sense of purpose, helping other people, or simply because they just love what they do. If you don't want a job, then volunteer, get a hobby.' I threw my arms up in the air, swung around on the swivel barstool for extra theatrical impact and bashed my knee against the kitchen counter. 'Ouch!'

'Do you love what you do?' Beverley ignored my buffoonery and fixed me with the type of stare that Clint Eastwood, back in his spaghetti-western days, would have spent many an hour trying to perfect.

'Sometimes,' I replied unconvincingly. I wasn't ready for a counter-attack so I attempted diversionary tactics. 'Have you ever fallen off these barstools? They're quite precarious aren't they?'

'Do you really think you help people?'

'Have I helped you?' I looked at her enquiringly, well, beseechingly really. Surely she had gleaned something constructive from the past few hours.

'Most of it seemed a bit pointless.'

Obviously her superficial bullshit detector was firing on all cylinders. 'That's telly I'm afraid,' I shrugged. 'You and I having a nice sensible chat doesn't make great viewing, and dare I say if they could have thrown you and me into a cage and let us fight it out, they would have loved it.'

'So why do you do it?'

'It pays.'

Now it was Beverley's turn to raise an eyebrow. 'And you think getting a job is going to do *me* wonders?'

'Touché.'

'Ah ha,' she laughed. 'Miss Bloody Sort Your Life Out isn't that happy with hers.'

'I have a job that most people would kill their granny for. It pays my bills, allows me to go off on little jaunts, and as there isn't anyone else that's going to do that for me, I am eternally grateful.'

Now who was going on the defensive?

The doorbell rang.

'That'll be the cab,' said Beverley, darting into the hall.

As I started to gather up my things, my mobile rang. Much to my surprise it was my agent Rae Stray. She never rang her clients on Friday evenings as she was usually holed up in Soho House with some producer or other media bigwig getting absolutely smashed. I grabbed the phone and answered.

'Hi Alex, how did today go?' Her voice sounded a little too high pitched and I could hear the predictable sound of 'bar babble' in the background.

'Can you hold on a moment Rae?'

I winked at Beverley, 'I'll be back in a couple of weeks to see if you've taken any of my advice.'

Beverley smiled, 'Yeah right.'

'You'd better,' I careered down the path with my bags, 'although I have to admit, you shouldn't throw that pink jogging suit away. It's so you.'

'Everything is going back in the wardrobe.'

'Good job too. What do I know anyway? Bloody lifestyle experts. Shoot the lot of them.'

The taxi driver, a rather weasel-like individual, looked at his watch impatiently and held the door open for me; I fell onto the back seat still shouting.

'And another thing Beverley, when I weigh myself, I even take off my nail polish.'

I heard a burst of laughter.

As we pulled away, another car pulled in and a tall guy with slightly receding hair jumped out. This had to be Laurence. I glanced back at Beverley. The change was instantaneous and dramatic. Laurence had walked straight past her and taken her laughter with him. She looked utterly despondent and very alone. My heart went out to her and I felt tempted to stick around and take her out for a drink, but I had a plane to catch. I sighed and held the mobile back up to my ear. 'Sorry about that Rae, just on my way to the airport.'

'Sounds like you had a good time.'

'Not the easiest of days, but it went okay in the end.'

'Good, that's fantastic,' she responded unenthusiastically.

'What's up Rae? You sound a little odd.'

'Oh, Alex, I hate telling you this the day before your birthday, and there's no easy way to say it. But I just want to get it out of the way. Utopia Productions have dropped you. They're not going to renew your contract for the next series.'

'But why?' a million worries started ricocheting around my brain; my rent, my bills, my cleaner; my whole bloody life was totally dependant on my renewed contract.

'It's all about the money Alex, they're getting squeezed by the TV channels because advertising revenues have gone down, you know how it is...'

'So, is it just a case of taking a little cut?' I interrupted with more than a healthy hint of concern. 'Surely there must be something you can do?'

'Well, no, that's what I was just about to move onto,' she said slowly, 'they are hiring someone cheaper...and younger...' her voice trailed off.

'What?' I screeched, 'Who?'

'That's not relevant Alex,' she muttered.

'Wait a minute Rae. It's Gina isn't it?'

Gina Black was Rae's latest signing, a mouthy twenty-two-year-old WAG whose only claim to fame was being spotted on an almost daily basis staggering down Sloane Avenue with enough designer shopping bags to make a Tibetan sherpa turn and run for the hills.

'Utopia felt she would bring a fresh new energy to the show...oh yes John, I'll have another Merlot. Thank you. Sorry Alex where were we?'

'Fresh new energy?' My torch paper was well and truly lit. 'What the bloody hell has she got to contribute?'

'Look we're very confident that Gina and her team will...'

'Her team? One minute ago it's a budget issue, and now she has a team?'

'Alex, calm down, they're just adding a more surgical element to the show. It's what people want. Anyhow I'm sure we'll find you something else. I mean there is a new series of Celebrity...'

I didn't even give her a chance to finish.

'I am categorically not doing any of that shit, and before you even go there, do not insult me by suggesting the unmentionable.'

'But, it pays brilliantly and there are so many perks.'

'I am NOT going on a shopping channel.'

'Well, I think at the very least we should change your age on your CV, maybe 34?'

'What? Are you out of your mind? How can I just drop six years, and why the hell should I?'

'You're obviously very upset, so we'll speak on Monday. Sorry to ruin your birthday weekend.' The phone went dead, but not before I heard her say to her drinking buddy, 'Thank god I got that out of the way.'

Bitch!

'Well, Happy Birthday to me,' I muttered as I stared at my phone in disbelief. Now that was a curved ball I hadn't expected.

'Here you go, love.'

The cab came to an abrupt halt. I was so preoccupied I shot forward and bumped my head on the seat in front.

'Is it a special one then?' The driver nodded at me through his rear view mirror.

'I beg your pardon?' I stopped rubbing my head and started to gather my things.

'Your birthday?'

'My fortieth, it's tomorrow.' I just hoped he hadn't got the gist of the entire conversation.

'Flying off somewhere nice then are you?'

'No, flying back to London. I'm having lunch with a mate tomorrow and then dinner with my family on Monday.'

'That's a bit sad isn't it? I mean you're only forty once aren't you? I'd be flying off somewhere exotic if it were me? Better have a word with your bloke love, or are you one of those career women?'

The smug look on his face when he turned around told me everything. He'd heard the lot and was now having a lovely time at my expense.

'Could I have a receipt please?' The habitual request of the self-employed fell instinctively and very curtly from my lips.

'Yeah I suppose every bit's going to help now isn't it?' the cocky little weasel sniggered as he turned and ferreted around in his glove compartment for a card.

Not waiting, I flung open the cab door and pulled my bags out. He wound down his window and looked up at me, 'That'll be thirty-seven pounds please.'

I resisted the urge to slap his face, gave him two crisp twenties, waved away the half-hearted attempt at returning my change and thrust another fiver at him - as if rewarding this little creep was going to make me feel any better. 'So, where did you go for your fortieth - the pub?'

'Nah; Barbados with the missus,' he chuckled.

'Good for you,' I turned briskly on my heel and marched towards the terminal. Boy oh boy did I need a drink.

THREE

I stared up at the departures board despondently; the Heathrow flight was delayed by two hours, 'Shit, shit, shit,' I murmured to myself, this was just adding insult to injury.

'Bloody typical!' Somebody else was obviously as pissed off as me; I turned around to see a rotund and rather sweaty little man in an ill-fitting suit, 'I wish I'd got the blasted train,' he grumbled. Misery loving a little company, I was well up for a bit of a rant. Public transport, petrol prices, trains, boats, planes, anything really. It was good to vent – for a while! But here was a person who had obviously had a worse day, well, life than me. Just as it seemed that he would never run out of steam, he suddenly pointed up to the board and said: 'You could get to bloody Spain quicker than London.' He then wiped his coat-sleeve across his head, which was now dripping with perspiration, threw me a disgustingly lewd look as he proffered a well-worn business card just in case I ever fancied a drink in town and then stomped off. 'I'm going to go and give someone merry hell,' he shouted back at me, 'see you on the plane.'

'Not if I can help it,' I whispered, my teeth clenched in a fake grin. When I was sure he was gone I screwed up the business card and threw it in the bin. Just to give you an indication of the sad state of my love life – this was about the closest I had gotten to a suggested date in a long time. Oh yeah, it was thin pickings out there.

But little did I know then that The Sweat Ball and The Weasel were unlikely emissaries of destiny. Along with the engine trouble which had kept our London-bound plane stuck on the tarmac, and that little matter of being sacked, if it hadn't been for the jibes about my lack lustre fortieth birthday and that podgy little finger pointing up at the departures board, I would never have checked my laptop bag for my trusty passport, wandered to the BA ticket office and bought an extortionate business class ticket to Barcelona. But I did, and as I walked through departures with a spring in my step and the prospect of Gaudi, Zara and tapas, mental clarity washed over me like a warm Iberian breeze. The universe was sending me a very clear message. Go forth and have a wonderful weekend it said. Why not? I thought. I had a couple of changes of outfit in my bag and basic toiletries, anything else I needed I'd just buy.

After grabbing a few spare pairs of knickers, some jogging pants and t-shirts, two paperbacks, travel size hair products and a Spanish phrase book, I sat down with a coffee and went to do a general ring around regarding my absence over the weekend but before I had the chance, I noticed that my flight was boarding. I threw my phone into my bag and ran to the gate. I would call everyone in the morning. Mel would be fine about cancelling lunch, she'd done it to me enough times, and I'd be back in time for dinner on Monday.

At this point, as you may have realised, that old adage about best laid plans going horribly wrong could not have been further from my mind. What possible trouble could I get myself into? A little bit of culture, shopping and sitting in cafés contemplating my navel fluff over a glass or two of rosé - I was guilt-free and fancy-free.

Once in the air I snuggled back into my seat and started to drift off. Travelling was my comfort zone as I had been born with a wandering spirit. Apparently when I was eleven months old, I made my first bid for freedom. Armed only with one of my mum's stiletto shoes and a bundle of pound notes grasped tightly in my chubby little hand, I desperately tried to crawl through a gap in the privet hedge with my captors in hot pursuit. But just as I got a tantalising glimpse of the world outside, a vice-like grip around my waist pulled me back. As I howled to the universe in noisy protest, my dad burst out laughing and my mum took a picture. It was an omen, a sure-fire sign that I was destined to always have one eye on that hole in the privet hedge. By the time I was six-years-old, my dad and I would have the same kind of conversation every time I wandered out to play.

'What are you doing today then?'

'Running away.'

'Anywhere nice?'

'Maybe India or Africa.'

'How about taking your brother along?'

'No, he'll get travel sick.'

'Will you be back for tea?'

'Depends…'

'I think we're having sausages and chips.'

'Can I have salad cream with mine?'

'I'm sure we can organise that.'

'And peas?'

'Of course! Give my love to the elephants if you see any.'

As I walked out of the door I was handed a little blue bag full of supplies – biscuits, pencils, a bright red notebook, tissues and a plastic container of orange squash – everything a young explorer might need. I never strayed far. I grew up in an era when parents didn't have to watch their children's every move. They knew the extent of my wanderings would be limited to the corner shop to buy a quarter of rhubarb and custard sweets, the local park to bug the life out of the older kids and a visit to our seventy-year-old neighbour, Mrs Crawley, whose husband Colonel Crawley, had died many years before of a rare tropical disease that you weren't allowed to talk about. They had spent most of their early married life stationed in Africa and India at the height of the British Empire, and her walls and shelves were bursting with all manner of strange artefacts - African masks, old spears and statues of women who to my childish delight, were not wearing bras. Her floors were covered with Indian rugs, and above her sofa hung a piece of beautifully embroidered cloth with small sparkling mirrors. I had never seen anything like it before and was totally entranced.

I would while away hours looking through her collection of grainy black and white pictures, and listening to her stories of riding elephants with Indian princes and sipping gin and tonic whilst watching the sun go down over the African savannah. The only thing she left out - which I was to find out about years later from my Great Aunty Dolly who was a past master at wheedling information out of people - was Colonel Crawley's penchant for local ladies of the night, which I have a strong suspicion contributed hugely to his final demise.

Whether or not Mrs Crawley wanted her uninvited Saturday guest I don't know, but I like to think we had a mutually beneficial relationship. She instilled in me a love of the exotic, and I helped her to keep her memories alive. With my imagination fired and my belly full of home-made chocolate cake, I would go home for tea, get out my notebook and recount the entire afternoon's stories as if they were my own. My parents couldn't get a word in and would sit, eyes glazing over, while I embellished and exaggerated every last detail. I loved those Saturday adventures.

A gentle nudge brought me back to the present. A stunning looking flight attendant was there with his trolley, 'Would you like chicken or fish madam?'

He had eyes like liquid amber and the kind of lips that if they were the universal norm, no woman would ever have to risk a cosmetically induced trout-pout again.

'I think I'll have the chicken please,' I sighed as he folded down my table and placed down my tray with the words I had been longing to hear, 'Drinks madam?'

'I'll have some white wine please.'

'Isn't he gorgeous?'

I looked at the pint-sized blond guy sitting next to me as he craned his neck to get a better view of the Latino flight attendant's disappearing butt.

'He's probably going home to a wife and screaming kids,' I smiled impishly although it was blatantly obvious this wasn't the case.

'No way sweetie, she's as pink as a nun's nipple.' He held his hand to his chest in mock horror, 'And I'm no exception, I'm Bart.'

'Alex, lovely to meet you.'

'I thought it was you' he squeaked, 'we all watch your show in

Sitges.'

'Sitges?'

'Just outside Barcelona, it's so beautiful. I live there. It's the gay capital of the Med darling; a poof's paradise. So, where are you off to?'

I explained the bizarre circumstances surrounding the trip, leaving out the 'sacked' part. Bart shrieked and called over the flight attendant, 'Forget the wine and let's have champagne! We have a birthday girl here! I fly for BA too,' Bart winked, 'they will look after us don't you worry.'

I certainly wasn't worried and felt totally in the birthday spirit when a half bottle of champagne was plopped in front of me. For the next hour Bart and I chatted and managed to finish another three half bottles, which left me feeling quite pissed. Just as we were coming in to land, he shocked the life out of me.

'Look, why don't you come to Sitges tonight?' he looked at me expectantly, 'The thought of you wandering around Barcelona trying to get a bed for the night is freaking me out. Plus, it's your birthday for God's sake, why aren't you doing something showbizzy and glamorous?'

'I can't imagine anything worse personally. Anyhow, I'm distinctly 'D' list darling.'

'Not in Sitges you're not. All the gay boys LOVE you.'

Well, what could one say to that? I felt my ego puffing up at an alarming rate. I mulled it over for precisely five seconds.

'I could, but do you know any hotels?'

'Oh you can stay with me tonight and if you want you can find one tomorrow.'

'But I couldn't possibly, you don't even know me and you've already been so kind.'

Bart looked at me and shook his head despairingly. 'Look girl, you came for an adventure. Trust your instincts. You'll love this town. It's full of people who aren't interested in the rat race and just want to live life to the max - all barking mad, but hearts of gold. I've got a spare room and you look quite house-trained. Plus, I am going to get such brownie points for turning up with you.

Whaddya say?'

I threw my arms around his neck and kissed him on the cheek.

'You're my guardian angel! I'd love to come.'

'That's highly unlikely if you're relying on me.' He screwed up his face in disgust. 'Haven't been down that road since the age of sixteen, scarred me for life it did. No wonder I'm gay.'

I punched him on the arm. 'We're not that bad you cheeky bastard.'

'You ever tried a little sister action?'

'Absolutely not,' I laughed.

'Got a man in your life?'

'Oh don't you start,' I groaned, 'I'm going through what you might call a bit of a dry spell on that front.'

Bart patted my leg and sighed, 'They're all bastards. You're better off with a cup of tea and a crumpet love.'

He had a point. At that precise moment, if I had to choose between a toasted crumpet and a bit of 'crumpet', I'd have been reaching for the butter and Marmite.

FOUR

By 11.30 pm we had pulled up outside Bart's apartment block in a quiet dark street in Sitges. Bart paid the cab driver. He had whizzed me through the airport so fast, I hadn't been to a cash machine for euros. He waved away my apologies. As I stood outside his door I looked up. It was a clear night and the sky was full of stars. I wondered which one was mine. Or should I say, which ones were mine. On account of one particular birthday when nobody had the foggiest idea what to buy me, I received four certificates from some scam outfit called The Star Registry saying I owned four different stars. Last year I adopted a llama, a dolphin and a couple of donkeys. I was hoping for a Polynesian isle this year.

'What you grinning at?' Bart unlocked the front door and started moving the bags into the lobby.

'Just happy, and bloody knackered, I've been up over twenty hours.'

'Well you better wake up,' Bart winked. 'As far as the Spanish are concerned, your birthday has officially started. We're going out.'

Before I had a chance to complain, Bart grabbed my bag and gestured for me to follow him 'Come on, I've got an attico on the 3rd floor and there isn't a lift.'

Bart seemed to spring up the stairs. I wheezed and panted and kept stopping for breaks. My heart felt like it was going to jump out of my chest. Finally I staggered into his flat, which seemed to be crammed into a space no bigger than my lounge. It was minute.

'We'll be quite cosy here - the Spanish aren't big on size – in more ways than one.' He gave a camp squeal and indicated for me to follow him.

17

Two steps later I was in my room - a box by most people's standards. The single bed had another rolled underneath, although if you wheeled it out there would be no floor space whatsoever. At one end of the room was a canvas Ikea wardrobe and at the other was a glass door, leading out onto a small balcony with a washing machine.

I threw my bag in the corner, took off my coat and sat on the bed. I could feel myself drifting off, but was shaken out of it by two towels sailing through the air and thwacking into my face.

'There you go. Come on I'll show you around *Bartingham Palace*,' Bart leaned into the room and grabbed my hand.

Space-wise, the lounge was a total triumph. Somehow Bart had managed to fit a two-seater sofa, armchair, dining-table with four chairs, coffee table and tall cupboard into a few square feet and still have room to move around. There was a plasma screen television on the wall and up-lighters stationed behind the furniture gave the room a lovely soft glow. Everything was oatmeal and ivory, with pale wood and lots of textured cushions in neutral shades. It was lovely.

There was a tiny American-style kitchen with a breakfast bar at one end, although god knows how you could cook a meal in there. There was only a two-ring hob with a narrow oven and I couldn't even see the fridge.

He led me through the glass doors at the other end of the room, and I found myself on a small terrace with another table and chairs. I looked around at the mass of other balconies that seemed to surround his. Most lights were still on and you could hear people rattling on in Spanish. The air was thick with the pungent smell of garlic and every balcony was festooned with drying laundry.

'Now come and see the rest.'

I followed him back through the lounge and into a small hall with two doors and a spiral staircase.

'There's the bathroom; only a shower I'm afraid, but the water's hot.'

'It's great.'

'And here is the centre of my universe – my bedroom.' Bart did a little pirouette and held his arms aloft.

Thankfully it was bigger than his spare room, and again the décor was tastefully done. He had simply carried on the neutral theme from the lounge.

He patted the bed and cocked one eye at me cheekily, 'If many more land on here I'm going to have to install runway lights.' He gave an ear-piercing shriek and pulled me to the bottom of the spiral stairs.

'Up you go and unbolt the door; I'll get us a glass of cava.'

'Can I have water please?' I shouted as I hauled myself up the stairs and opened the door. I emerged onto an amazing roof terrace the size of the entire flat. Lush plants and cactuses surrounded two huge bamboo sun beds.

The view across the rooftops was breath taking; to my left I could see the entrance to a small harbour in the distance and the sea was shimmering with the light of the moon. A church stood majestically in front of me and to my right, a long promenade fringed with palm trees stretched off into the distance.

'Fabulous isn't it?' Bart appeared with two narrow glasses of sparkling cava, 'It's why I bought the place.'

'It's stunning,' I stared at the glass in my hand and decided to keep quiet. He'd either not heard or decided to ignore me.

'Just wait until you see it in the daylight, it's beautiful,' he sighed, 'and it's meant to be a glorious weekend.'

A glorious weekend in the middle of February - that was enough for me. I was happy to finish my cava, go to bed and wake up ready to take it all in, but Bart was having none of it. No sooner had I taken my last sip than he grabbed my glass and pointed downstairs.

'Off you go, you've got five minutes to do that girlie thing, I'll sort us some stuff, and then we'll grab a quickie at El Cabaret.'

I changed out of my trousers and shirt and donned a black jumper and black jeans tucked into high black boots. I grabbed my handbag and went into the bathroom. I peered into the mirror. Shit I looked rough; not surprising after over twenty hours without sleep.

After splashing my face with cold water, I plastered on some lipstick, some extra mascara and sprayed on some perfume. I couldn't be bothered to do another thing.

When I came out, Bart was walking out of the lounge door, 'I've left you a little something on the table – it'll make you feel better. Mind you girl, I have to say, it's amazing what a little slap can do.'

I flopped down onto the sofa, threw my handbag on the table and looked, then I saw it – a rolled up note sticking out from under my bag. It was fifty euros. Bless him, how considerate can you get? I folded it in two and put it in my purse.

'Did you find it?' Bart walked in wearing a dazzling shirt that I couldn't help but feel was more suited to a Caribbean setting.

'Yes, thank you so much, I'll give it back to you tomorrow.'

'Oh don't be soft, look at all this, you mucky cow – where's the note? I'm not letting all this go to waste,' he started wiping the surface of the table.

Somewhat confused, I retrieved the fifty euros from my bag, which Bart grabbed with a raised eyebrow, 'You had that away a bit sharpish, I'm going to have to watch you,' then he rolled it up again and bent down and started snorting the little pile of white powder that he had accumulated. The penny dropped. I gasped and started laughing.

'I thought you'd left me the money!'

He wiped his nose and shook his head, 'Oh my god and you work in showbiz? You're a disaster! Come on Dorothy; let's hit the yellow brick road.'

Walking down Bart's stairs was infinitely easier than dragging oneself up them. No wonder the lad had so much energy – doing that a few times a day would give you a cardio workout and buns of steel. Or kill you.

We walked and chatted on about nothing in particular until we reached a little wooden door in a small alley; Bart pushed it opened and I walked into a long thin bar that was heaving with guys. A clock on the wall showed two-thirty. As if it wasn't late enough already, we had lost an hour on the time difference.

'Ooh look it's Bart the Tart,' the tallest of the three barmen shouted. 'Just got back?'

'About an hour ago,' yelled Bart as he pushed his way to the bar.

'Look who I found at Manchester Airport. Alex from *Sort Your Life Out* and it's her birthday!'

All eyes turned. Within seconds Bart had disappeared and I was surrounded by an entourage of gay men all clamouring to buy me drinks. I still couldn't quite bring myself to admit to my recent demise so I revelled in the attention and hit the cava.

'On the house,' the tall barman refilled my empty glass the minute it touched the bar, 'I'm Cam.'

There was something slightly androgynous about him - blond streaky hair and the most exquisite bone structure. He was quite beautiful really. Another barman came over; he was dressed in baggy white clothes and had a heavy wooden beaded bracelet on his wrist. He looked almost childlike, very ethereal with huge blue eyes.

'This is Aaron,' said Cam. 'He's a Buddhist – this week, aren't you darling?'

Aaron had obviously heard this before and gave a long-suffering smile. 'Don't mind him, he wouldn't know inner peace if it hit him in the face.'

'And that miserable bugger over there is Simon.' Cam giggled and pointed to a dark haired guy, again with amazing blue eyes.

'Get lost Cam,' he shook his head and came over, 'Nice to meet you. Are you here long?' He had a gentle Welsh accent and was sexy in an understated sort of way.

'Just the weekend, it's my first time here.'

He smiled a knowing smile and walked down to the other end of the bar.

All of a sudden Bart reappeared at my side and whizzed me around the bar, giving me the low down on virtually every person in the place.

'That's Fred and Pierre – he's French, typical Gallic pessimistic type. Over there that's Evie, you see her, the lady dancing in the corner? Those four over there – all BA staff, and that is Stephan who,' he dropped to a whisper as we looked over at yet another beautiful olive skinned guy with long dark curly hair, 'you will probably get to see as Stephanie this weekend.''

'He's a transvestite?'

'Don't EVER call him that. He is a drag queen.'

'There's a difference?'

'Oh sweetheart what are we going to do with you?''

All of a sudden the video screen at the end of the bar burst into life. Julie Andrews was blasting out 'Do Re Mi'.

'That means it's time to drink up,' Bart knocked the vodka he was drinking back in one. I followed suit with my cava as I took in the surreal sight of about thirty blokes all singing along to *The Sound of Music*. Jesus this was a weird place.

'We'll be at Organic,' hollered Bart as he manoeuvred me through the crowd and out of the door.

'Organic?' I was puzzled, 'What's Organic? I thought we were going home.'

'It's a club, you'll love it.'

'I've been up forever,' I whimpered.

'What do you want, a medal?' Bart laughed. 'Or some coke?'

'No! No coke. But I need to get to a cash machine Bart; I haven't got a single euro.' Not having money in my pocket was crucifying me. I was starting to feel totally out of control.

'Oh for god's sake, you're a birthday princess. You don't need money,' he frogmarched me along.

Organic was down a side street leading to the sea. A girl on the desk waved us through dismissively. We walked through a set of double doors and into a haze of dry ice and smoke. A seething mass of semi-clad male bodies was gyrating to the sound of loud garage music. I really wasn't in the mood for this, but I was at the mercy of my drug-fuelled host. I just hoped and prayed Bart would slow down soon. He thrust a twenty-euro note into my hand. 'Vodka and tonic and get whatever you want; I'm just nipping to the loo.'

No doubt to powder his nose again.

I pushed my way to the bar and ordered his vodka and some water for me. I waited around for about ten minutes and there was still no sign of him. I walked to the other side of the club and looked around.

'Happy Birthday!'

I spun around. There in front of me was a group of guys in jeans and T-shirts. A youngish guy with the most amazing reddish pink hair was beaming at me, 'We were on the same flight, recognised you by your hair. You're that bird off the telly aren't you?'

'Yes,' I beamed. This was amazing, but just as I was settling into my new role as a gay icon; he only went and pissed all over my glitter ball.

'You're my mum's favourite, and my gran's. They watch you all the time.'

My Kylie moment was over.

I'm Zane, and this is Froggy, Dean, Daniel and Jim.'

'Lovely to meet you. You guys here on holiday?'

'Yeah, we're here for Carnival,' they all chinked glasses and knocked back their drinks

'Go on Froggy, your round mate.' Daniel looked at me. 'D'you want one love?'

'No thanks I'm fine.'

'Not surprised, the way you're nursing that vodka, drink it woman.'

'This isn't mine. It's my friend's. He should be around here somewhere. I've lost him.'

'Where did you last see him?'

'He went to the loo.'

'Christ, it's all going on up there tonight,' said Jim.

I turned to him and mouthed, 'Drugs?'

'And the bloody rest.'

I obviously looked like a startled rabbit, because Zane patted my head and said, 'Ah bless her.'

'You'll have to get used to that in the clubs 'ere love,' piped in Jim grinning. 'Your first time is it?'

'Yes,' I suddenly felt very naïve.

Froggy, whose physical appearance I'm afraid to say, left you in no doubt as to his nickname, reappeared with five vodka and Red Bulls.

'D'you want me to go up and see if I can find him?' asked Zane.

'No, no…it's fine.' I shook my head, 'You don't mind me

hanging out with you, do you?'

'Of course not babes, it's your birthday,' he winked.

Two seconds later a vodka and Red Bull was put into my hand. I gave up trying to behave and drank it. Then I drank Bart's and god knows how many more? Then everything became a blur.

FIVE

Having no recollection of the night's, or should I say, morning's events was disconcerting to say the least. The phone call from Mum and Mel had brought me back to earth in a very big way and now here I was – in a strange bathroom in the middle of a small Spanish town whose name I couldn't quite remember. I attempted to isolate the moment Zane had somehow gone from weird looking lad to David Bowie, but courtesy of my vodka and Red Bull induced Booze Goggles, I'd obviously hurtled back to my first teenage crush and his bisexuality had just made him all the more appealing. Good grief, I had inadvertently become a cougar. Or was it sad old trout? I caught sight of my reflection in the bathroom mirror. My hair had virtually dread-locked and red-veined eyes stared back at me from a lightning white face. Any self-respecting trout would recoil in horror at the comparison.

I found a bottle of mouthwash and swilled some around in my furred up mouth, gargling noisily. There was a loud knock at the door.

'Alex, are you in there?'

I stood there with my cowardly heart thumping. There was nothing for it; I couldn't stay in the bathroom forever. I decided to brazen it.

'Any chance of a strong black coffee,' I shouted, 'and a bucket of water?'

'Ooh, hark at her,' a high-pitched camp voice rang out, 'Any sugar Your Ladyship?'

'No thanks.' I pulled the towel around me and opened the door. As I emerged Daniel, Froggy, Dean and Jim provided a welcome committee in the hallway. To my horror a clock on the wall said it was ten-past-five.

'Bloody 'ell you look rough.' Jim screwed up his face and minced into the kitchen, followed closely by Froggy and Dean who both looked slightly traumatised by the sight of a half naked woman in their midst. I padded nonchalantly into the bedroom.

Daniel poked his head around the door, 'I'll leave you two love-birds to it then shall I?' he sniggered and shut the door behind me. Zane was lying on his back with his arms outstretched on either side, but this was no 'come hither' look. He was comatose.

I picked up all my things and nipped back into the bathroom, had a quick shower and reluctantly got back into my smoky clothes. I cleaned up my face with some soap and toilet paper and reapplied some make-up into my smarting skin. These boys were gay – where was the face cream?

Then, with as much dignity as I could muster, I walked into the kitchen to face the music.

'Ooh that's better,' cried Dean, 'I thought we were going to get a flash of your lady-bits for one horrible moment back there.'

I followed them onto the terrace and sat self-consciously down at the table. It was covered with the remains of what looked like a marijuana induced munch fest - half-eaten sandwiches, packets of biscuits, empty crisp bags and dirty ashtrays brimming with cigarette butts.

The way they were all studying me you would have thought I was the missing link; there was an awkward silence. Obviously gay icons were meant to be worshipped and adored from a distance, not crawling out from a gay guy's bed – however bisexual he professed to be. I'd broken the rules.

'Um,' I began, 'I don't know where the hell I am and can anyone tell me what happened to Bart last night?' I gave them a pathetic look.

'Don't you worry about your friend Bart, he was having a whale of a time,' quipped Froggy, raising his eyebrows in such a way he resembled his amphibious namesake even more. 'You two had a quick chat and then he disappeared into the night with a young Argentinean guy.'

'He didn't happen to mention where he lived did he?'

They all looked at each other and shook their heads.

'Don't you remember?' said Daniel incredulously.

'I arrived in the dark, I've got no idea.'

'Well, Sitges isn't that big, I'm sure you'll find it,' said Dean unconvincingly.

'Yeah, if you go out of our door and turn left you'll be in the centre in about one minute,' said Jim earnestly.

'Thank you, I'll be fine.' I smiled, knocked back my coffee and grabbed my bag, 'I don't suppose anyone has a charger for a Sony Ericsson?' I added hopefully.

They all shook their heads, 'Bye love,' they all chorused as I walked to the front door, 'see you on the telly.'

'Remember go left,' shouted Jim, at which point the bedroom door opened and an extremely hung-over Zane emerged, looking, if it were possible, even less desirable.

I winced inwardly, and gave him a pathetic wave as I slammed the door shut and ran down the stairs. I allowed myself a quick smile as I imagined the ribbing he was getting now from the others who all obviously thought having sex with a woman was on a par with eating live slugs.

I rummaged in my handbag for my sunglasses as the brilliant winter sun hit me straight between my aching eyes. I was on a narrow street full of little shops. I turned left and wandered past a little delicatessen selling all sorts of goodies; my stomach churned. I was starving, but still euro-less and I also had to find some way of ringing home. The reality of that situation was kicking in. Somewhere in the UK a whole host of friends and family were gathered and bandying around phrases like 'bloody typical' and 'how could she do this to her poor mum?' Oh yes, my name would be officially mud. I felt awful. Maybe I could catch the next plane back and turn up, albeit late. But I had no idea where they were, my phone was dead so I couldn't check my messages and as for having anyone's phone number in my head – forget it. Plus the fact I had taken my passport out of my handbag and left it at Bart's place which at this point in time could well be on the moon for all I knew. Yup, I was in shit, but first things first, I needed money.

Thankfully I spotted a bank opposite. I nipped in and, after three attempts, I managed to extricate two crisp fifty-euro notes from the cash machine. This was no mean feat. The machine only offered instructions in a very weird language. It wasn't quite Spanish and reminded me of French. This was obviously Catalan, but for the time being, it might well have been double Dutch. The important thing was that I was now in possession of local currency. I felt a bit more secure and set out in search of coffee and carbohydrates.

Walking along the street I found myself in a small square. Straight ahead there was a café packed with people. I took a chair outside, not wanting to inflict my smoky clothes on anybody else, but as I looked around me, I noticed that everyone was smoking. There wasn't a single table that didn't have a full ashtray and a Marlboro Red haze floating above it.

Fortified by a couple of espressos, one large slice of pizza and a gallon of *agua sin gas*, I hit the road again and started to look for Bart's apartment. I gathered my bearings. His place must be behind the church. This was the easy bit, just walk down towards the sea; eh voila – there it was, it's yellowy spire standing out against the bright blue sky.

The next bit was a nightmare, after walking up windy cobbled street after cobbled street there wasn't a single landmark I recognised. I started to get that sick to the pit of my stomach feeling. What the hell had I done? The daylight was fading fast and so was my energy.

Despondently I stopped at another little café and ordered more water. I was so dehydrated it felt like I might shatter into little pieces if anyone so much as bumped into me. I don't know what was greater, my headache, the fear I may never find my way back to my luggage, or my increasing sense of shame for my sluttish behaviour. Funny isn't it? I have always been of the opinion that women should be as sexually liberated as men, and if you want a one-night stand and it does nobody any harm, who cares? But maybe it was turning forty? No matter how much I tried to persuade myself that I'd been rather 'avant-garde', I just felt a bit cheap.

After asking for directions to the toilet in French, the waiter pointed me towards a dingy little corner at the back of the café. I walked through the flimsy shutter doors and groped around for the light switch. I found it at waist level and a dim yellow light flickered tentatively on. I jumped as I saw three of me in the grubby mirror. Jesus - I was so exhausted I was starting to hallucinate.

After a couple of seconds my eyes came back into focus, I sat down on the seat and glanced down at my crotch and could have sworn I saw something move. I froze. If I wasn't mistaken there was a little black speck lurking down there. Actually not one; loads! I let out an involuntary squeal. Oh my god – it couldn't possibly be. Somebody banged on the door.

'One moment *por favour*,' I had progressed to *Spanglish*.

I pulled up my trousers and tried to stop myself crying. I could feel my throat tightening - a sobbing session was imminent. I quickly did my best to clean the seat, washed my hands and opened the door; a gloomy looking Spanish woman looked me up and down and grunted as we squeezed past each other.

Did I look like a woman with unwelcome visitors? My mind went into paranoid overdrive.

I returned to the table, and quickly paid my bill. I remembered seeing a pharmacy up at the square. How could I do this? I had managed to spend over twenty years without a single sexually transmitted condition. Now in a moment of drunken stupidity…! I fished my phrase book out of my handbag, jotted down a few sentences and made my way back to the square.

Thankfully I found the pharmacy immediately. I went to the counter and took a deep breath, but before I could get a word out, the solemn-faced pharmacist pointed back over to the door and started to serve a woman behind me. I looked around in total confusion, and then I heard a beep and looked up. A number was flashing in a box suspended from the ceiling. I saw another lady pull a ticket from a machine near the entrance.

I marched over and pulled a ticket. I wandered around the aisles scanning the shelves desperately; maybe I could spot the necessary stuff, pay for it and be out of there without an ounce of embarrassment. But try as I might to find a package with a picture depicting my condition, it was a fruitless search. Suddenly the buzzer went again, my number was flashing furiously.

I went up to the counter and removed my piece of paper. I cleared my throat, leaned over and began to read very quietly, *'Tengo cangrejos. Quiero medicina.'*

The man looked quite bewildered, *'por los cangrejos?'*

'Yes, sorry...*si.'*

'Comiste cangrejos?'

I frowned and shook my head. I didn't understand what on earth he was saying. I'd told him I had crabs and that I needed medicine – what was so difficult about that? He repeated what he said and pretended to eat something.

'No – tengo cangrejos.' I couldn't get more graphic. Surely he must know what I was talking about.

He looked perplexed so I held my hands up by my ears and opened and closed them like pincers.

He turned his back on me and started muttering.

There was a loud snort of laughter behind me, 'Put your castanets away for fuck's sake.'

I turned and was greeted by the sight of Cam, the barman, doubled-up with laughter.

Everybody started to look over.

'It's not funny,' I hissed indignantly.

'Oh it is,' he screeched.

'I was trying to tell him....I think I've got....' I faltered.

'It's okay. I know what you're trying to tell him.' Cam composed himself and patted my arm, 'It's just they don't use that English slang here.'

'I only had this,' I waggled my phrase book at him.

He shook his head and went and whispered to the pharmacist, who threw back his head and bellowed, *'ahhh – ladillas!'*

At this point every person in the pharmacy looked at me and simultaneously took a step back. The chemist gave me a look that said 'You are a cheap common English whore' and asked for twenty euros. I blushed from my toes to the ends of my hair and fervently wished for the grim reaper to turn up with his scythe and obliterate me from the face of the earth.

'Come on, coffee time I think,' smiled Cam as I stuffed the box into my handbag.

As we turned to walk away, we bumped straight into Stephan the drag queen, who had obviously witnessed the entire charade.

'You really ought to be more careful dahling,' he looked so thrilled; anyone would think he had been given the secret of immortality. I felt my body temperature rise to a level that could possibly cause spontaneous combustion.

Cam dragged me down to a café and ordered a couple of coffees with Baileys, which although you may think that was the last thing I needed, actually made me feel a little better. Well, momentarily, as suddenly I gave into the tears that had been threatening to come out for the past two hours.

'I lost Bart ... and I don't know where he lives ... all my stuff is there and I stayed with these guys, and ... I've missed my surprise birthday party ... and my phone's dead, and now I've got lice ... ' I gabbled on.

'Hey, come on,' Cam stroked my tear-stained face, 'I know where he lives; I'll take you there now.'

I followed Cam, taking note of everything we passed. We walked under some railway tracks and emerged in an area that Cam called *Poble Sec*.

'Don't you remember walking under here?' Cam asked with a look of disbelief on his face.

'Nope, I was too bombed.'

Two minutes later we were ringing the bell. The entry phone crackled.

'I've got your lost soul here,' shouted Cam. The door buzzed and we climbed the stairs.

Bart opened the door.

'Why didn't you use your key, you little tramp?' He pursed his lips in mock disapproval. 'I don't think much of your taste in men, or should I say - boys,' he shrieked.

'I haven't got a key,' I looked at him quizzically.

He spun me around and put his hands in my back pocket. Out came a key and a piece of paper. It had his address written on it. My mouth opened in horror. I had it all along.

Bart shook his head. 'Don't you remember? I gave it to you last night, when you insisted on going home with that monstrosity.'

Cam put his arms around my shoulders. 'Don't be too hard on her, she is very tired, very emotional and....'

'I have crabs...' I blurted it out.

Bart looked horrified, 'How on earth?'

'Don't worry, she has lotion,' Cam reassured him and when Bart's face still registered abject horror, he went for the sympathy vote, 'and she's just missed her surprise birthday party in the UK, so don't be too hard on her.'

Bart darted to one of the kitchen cupboards, re-emerging with a bottle of bleach and a whole host of other cleaning products which he shoved in my hand. He pointed to the shower room, 'There are plastic razors in the cupboard, don't come out till it's over,' then nodded at Cam, 'You fancy a drink on the terrace?'

They disappeared, no doubt to discuss what a bloody disaster I was. I grabbed my towels, went into the bathroom and gingerly removed my clothes. I would probably have to burn these now. I took a deep breath and looked down. The sight that met me made me gasp out loud. There in my knickers were loads and loads of pieces of navy fluff.

Zane's towel! Oh no no NO!

I had conjured up the whole thing in my paranoid, guilt-ridden, hung-over little head. Any sense of relief I should have been feeling disappeared into a quagmire of mortification, embarrassment and utter disbelief. How in heaven's name could I have been so stupid? I had a quick shower, donned my new jogging pants and T-shirt and wandered up to the terrace.

'That was quick,' Bart looked at me quizzically.

'It was navy towel fluff,' I muttered.

'Pardon?' screeched Cam, who then proceeded to piss himself

laughing along with Bart who I thought was going to hyper-ventilate. 'Navy blue crabs? You stupid tart!'

'I'm not an expert on pubic lice' I said loftily. 'How would I know what the bloody things look like?'

Eventually the pair of them regained their composure and I finally managed a smile.

'Well, what a birthday that was,' I buried my face in my hands.

'Still is!' Bart pointed at the open wine bottle, 'Drink?'

'My dignity has gone out of the window, might as well finish off my liver for good measure,' I flopped onto one of the sun-beds. There was quite a chill in the air; Bart threw me a blanket which I gratefully wrapped around my shoulders.

'Please tell me you're hanging around for a bit longer,' Cam was still wiping his eyes, 'you're good entertainment.'

'I'm too scared to go back now. I'm going to get murdered by my mother and my best friend may never speak to me again.'

'Missing your party is quite impressive,' grinned Bart impishly.

'I would never have *knowingly* stood up the NADs,' I whined miserably, 'really I wouldn't!'

'The NADs?'

'Nearest and Dearest,' I smiled. 'Poor buggers! Knowing Mum and Mel, it would have been forty-everything all the way.'

'Forty embarrassing pictures?' laughed Cam.

'Oh yes,' I winced at the thought of it. 'There would have been forty cupcakes, forty balloons, forty guests. I could have arrived a fashionably forty minutes late, doled out forty kisses, downed forty glasses of cava, and then staggered home for forty winks then everyone would have been happy.'

'But you didn't know. That's the thing about surprise parties. Nobody bloody tells you!! I bloody hate surprises!' Cam lit a cigarette and puffed away thoughtfully.

'I think I do now,' I smiled ruefully, 'but enough of that, have either of you got a Sony Ericsson charger?'

'I'm sure there's one in the cupboard in the lounge, I've got every make you can imagine.' Bart shook his head, 'I can't bring myself to throw them away.'

'Brilliant, I'll call home tomorrow and face the music.'

'Think it might be quite loud music, Alex,' winked Cam.

'Full orchestral manoeuvre darling,' I took a sip of my wine. 'My mum is not going to take this lightly that's for sure.'

SIX

Don't you worry; tomorrow will be a bright new shiny day were words uttered to me on a regular basis throughout my childhood by Nodge – AKA my gran - who lived on the top floor of our house. Nobody knew where the strange nickname came from, but she looked exactly like you would imagine a 'nodge' to be. She was all tiny and crumpled with soft squishy finger tips that could sooth a troubled brow in an instant, and she was always there providing a welcome haven every time I managed to land myself in yet another pile of deep shit with my parents. Usually, if I thought I could get away with it, I would incite my brother to commit criminal acts on my behalf, but most of the time I was quite capable of incurring the wrath of the big ones all on my own. My childhood was jam-packed with naughtiness, but the heinous crime that springs immediately to mind was The Great Trifle Disaster of 1976.

Every Sunday for as long as I can remember, about twenty or so friends and family descended on our house for that shining example of British cuisine - the Sunday roast. My dad would do his bit for the kids by making newspaper cones and doling out a bloody great bag of pic'n'mix sweets from Woolworths, then the men and a few of the more racy aunts would disappear down to The Porcupine pub for a few pints and a strenuous session of darts. This would act as a precursor to the card-playing marathon that would take place later in the afternoon. Sandwiched in between these two sporting extravaganzas was of course the lunch - an anxiety-ridden affair for my poor mum who just didn't feature synchronisation of hot food and hoards of people in her list of natural talents.

Her preparations would begin on a Saturday afternoon, and her lamentations around two-thirty on the Sunday afternoon when the potatoes were done, vegetables reduced to cellulose skeletons, meat carved and ready to go, Yorkshire puddings turning to charcoal in the oven, sugar-pumped, screaming kids running around her ankles - and of course - not a beer-swilling, dart-throwing guest in sight.

I can only assume that the reason she put herself through this culinary torture every weekend was the adulation she received for her glittering finale – the desserts. After the lunch plates were cleared away, she would proudly totter through the door clutching her latest concoction to a resounding chorus of 'ooohs' and 'aaahs'. Everybody, including me, knew that my mum was never happier than when she was playing at being The Confectionary Queen.

But, for reasons best known only to a seven-year-old, in the early hours of one Sunday morning, I made a very bad decision. I crept into the kitchen to get a glass of milk and opened the fridge to be greeted by the sight of a trifle, which appeared to have been loosely fashioned on the Parthenon. Chocolate fingers and maraschino cherries were performing a delicate balancing act as they formed pillars around a mound of whipped cream, toasted almonds and multi-coloured sprinkles. This was a trifle not to be trifled with.

Unfortunately for me, I noticed one small tantalizing gap between a chocolate pillar and the edge of the bowl. As if in a trance, I grabbed a teaspoon from the drawer and proceeded to excavate creamy custard from the sugary depths of my mum's work of art. I moved gingerly onto the jelly and sherry sodden sponge, and then joy of joys, I found even more cherries. Everything was going swimmingly well, until, with its foundations weakened, one section of the trifle subsided, causing a knock on effect rather like dominoes. Suddenly what was once a magnificent Greek temple was now more like Pompeii after the volcano.

As I gazed in horror at my handiwork and tried to work out how I could blame the entire mishap on my brother, from out of nowhere loomed a shadow - my heart sank - I had been rumbled. I slowly looked up into the unforgiving eyes of my dad. A collapsed trifle meant a hysterical wife, which in turn could jeopardise his weekly darts session. My backside felt the force of his disappointment and I was dispatched up to my bedroom to give some serious consideration to what I had done.

By the time Mum came into my room giving me the look that all mothers specialise in, you know - the one that says *you have wrenched my beating heart out from my chest and shredded it with a cheese grater* - I had created an elaborate story about how I thought my brother had attacked the trifle earlier and how I had been trying to mend it. This apparently wasn't the reaction she was looking for - an outrageous lie with no hint of remorse. I was stuffed. She reeled off a list of punishments that included the cruellest one of all – no playing outside. This sent me running upstairs to Nodge, who received her now sobbing grand-daughter with open arms and just sat and listened while I manipulated and dramatised the truth into a version I found more acceptable and that of course, made me appear angelic to the core.

Now I don't know if Nodge truly bought into her *bright shiny new day* philosophy. It can't be easy to maintain a positive attitude with bunions the size of mandarins. But her words have always lingered on in my memory and, as I wandered around Sitges in the warm winter sun, energised by a good night's sleep and lowered blood alcohol levels, I could see what she meant. Yesterday's dramas had faded away and I was bathed in a sea of vibrant colour. Everything from the striped awnings above the café tables to the vases of bright red peonies throbbed with life. The sunshine made everything better: hair shone, eyes glistened and smiles were wider. This was a far cry from dull grey London. I sat down outside The Buena Vida Bar in a small bay called *Playa San Sebastian*, ordered a salad and a bottle of water and turned my face to the sky. But there was no way I could truly relax until I'd phoned home. I took a deep breath, grabbed my freshly charged mobile from the table and dialled. She answered immediately in a voice so flat it made my heart bleed.

'Mum, it's me. I am so sorry I missed my party. I had no idea you guys were up to anything,' I gushed rather desperately.

'How could you Alexandra? It was your fortieth; of course we were going to do something. Just disappearing like that, you could have been dead for all we knew.'

I held the phone away from my ear while she vented her frustration, then eventually she calmed down, mollified by one singular possibility, 'Have you met someone? Are you having a romantic weekend?'

'No Mum, it's a long story but I just wanted to get away for a couple of days.'

'Always running away, Alex. What's happened?' Her voice was weary, 'God I wish you'd just settle down.'

'Nothing is wrong Mum,' I lied, 'I just did something spontaneous. Please don't worry. Now, c'mon tell me all about my party. Did everyone have a good time?'

She chatted on for about ten minutes, every now and then pausing to remind me how much I had disappointed every one of the thirty-eight other guests, Mel, and of course, herself, and then she threw me.

'By the way, I borrowed your back massager, hope you don't mind. I know it's new but my back has been dreadful, especially after carrying all your presents up those stairs of yours this morning.'

'My back massager?' I was confused.

'That pink one. It was on your kitchen table. Mel said it was a back massager.'

Bitchy gesture more like! One of my oldest school-friends Penny Johnson had sent me my birthday present early as she was going to be away skiing in Aspen. My jaw had dropped when I opened the box and found the all singing, all dancing, beaded pink wand with a charming note attached – *Hopefully this will be one relationship you won't fuck up!*

'It was a present from Penny.' I shrieked a little too hysterically whilst thanking the Lord that I had screwed up her caustic little note and thrown it on the fire. I was certainly not going to have a vibrator conversation with my mother. The possibility that my friends may have totally given up on the idea that 'one day my prince would come' and were now sending me battery operated replacements so that I could 'come', was a concept that would cause my Mum untold trauma.

'So? I'm sure she won't mind me using it. How wonderful of her to be so good to you after all these years, she's such a lovely girl – happily married, those lovely children…'

I felt sick. I didn't know what was worse, my Mum disappearing back down to Hampshire with a vibrator, or the fact that after thirty years she still thought the sun shone out of Penny Johnson's butt. I said goodbye and put the phone down. I hadn't mentioned the job situation as this would have just given her more to worry about. It was probably best to leave it till I had fathomed out Plan B.

And that was why I was here – to sit, still my over-active mind and work out where the rest of my life was heading. Did I even want to be in telly? The biggest joke was that I never really even wanted to be a presenter; I just sort of fell into it by accident - like everything else really.

In the madcap way that you do at eighteen, I reached the decision to forgo my dreams of going to university to study English, travelling the world as a journalist and finally living on some foreign shore writing novels, and I ended up doing an HND in beauty therapy instead. The notion of spending my life ripping out superfluous hair and finding the answer to wrinkles had never even crossed my mind, but a friend whose parents were insisting that she follow path in economics had decided to rebel and somehow I got swept up in the whole process. She needed a buddy to go with, so being a good supportive little pal; I went to Beauty College too.

It certainly wasn't that taxing from a study point of view, so yours truly had a fabulous two years partying her way around the south coast of England and after college I was offered a job in Kenya. So off I trotted, happy in the belief that there were benefits to this beauty lark. One year and some amazing memories later, I returned home, set up a salon with a boyfriend, lost him, lost it, set up another one, and then realised that not only was I not a business woman, I hated being caged within four walls. My artistic side was crying out, so I gave it all up and in true Dick Whittington style, packed up my lipsticks and headed for the big city. There began my life as a make-up artist. I did some great jobs and did some shit jobs, one minute I was working on an advertising campaign in

Barbados, the next I was doing test shots in Bermondsey. Variety was the name of the game and it eventually led me to television.

My not so glittering screen debut was as a make up artist on a morning show in the early 90s. One minute I was making up the presenters behind the scenes, and the next minute being thrust in front of the camera because the producers were short of an item. Waif-like, clad from head to foot in black and brandishing a make-up brush whilst earnestly extolling the benefits of bronzing powder as if it were the cure for cancer, I took to telly like an alcoholic to vodka.

This led to a whirlwind of 'expert' appearances on daytime magazine shows, where my expertise knew no bounds. I was advising on everything from the latest hydrating, non-creasing eye shadows to such life enhancing subjects as how to flatter a less than shapely calf with clever use of a stiletto heel and 60-denier support tights.

Trouble is, being in front of the camera can be quite addictive and it is all too easy to get it out of perspective. There is something glamorous about being picked up by a driver to go to work and arriving at 'the studios'. All of a sudden you are being wheeled around to countless commissioning editors and producers who keep telling you that you are The Next Big Thing. The danger being that you actually start to believe that you are. So, you positively rain ideas on every bigwig who promises you the moon and convince yourself that you are a victim of coincidence every time a new daytime face fronts a show identical to the one you proposed months before. Then suddenly you wake up and realise that you're never going to be The Next Big Thing and your daily rate is going down quicker than this winter's hemlines. All you are doing is drifting with all the other telly flotsam and jetsam in the backwaters of cable television. Until, like yours truly, you get dumped.

I had to find a new direction. Maybe now I was away from all the usual distractions I could figure out a new wall to lean my ladder against.

'Alex Chapman! I don't believe it...'

There in front of me was Marcus Jenkins - fashion stylist,

professional gossip and easily one of the most unpleasant little queens in London. His ladder was purely of the social climbing variety.

'What on earth are you doing here?' he asked with no intention of listening as he plonked himself down in a chair in front of me and waved at the waiter. '*Dos vinos blancos por favor.*'

'Not for me Marcus, I'm not drinking today.' The irritation I felt at this uninvited invasion of my personal space was written loudly and clearly across my face.

'Oh darling it's not for you, my friend Bubbles will be here any minute, ooh look! There she is,' he started waving at a rather amply proportioned woman in dark glasses, who was shuffling along the pavement. 'Hello darling, over here.'

Bubbles air-kissed Marcus and collapsed in a heap on the chair. She grimaced as a glass of wine was placed in front of her, 'I am so fucked! No more booze!'

Yesterday I would have been there with her sharing in her hangover pain. Today my body was a temple. I sipped my water and wished them both away.

'Bloody women,' hissed Bubbles whose lank dark hair was hanging limply around her sallow face.

'Oh don't mind her, girlie trouble,' Marcus waved his hands dismissively. 'Bubbles this is my friend Alex – she's a fellow TV presenter. She has her own show on the Style Channel.'

Had her own show. I held my counsel; Marcus would have a field day if I told him the truth.

Bubbles looked suitably unimpressed, took a huge swig of her unwanted wine and burped.

'Yes, Alex and I met on - what programme was it darling?' Marcus's voice couldn't be any louder if he tried.

'QVC selling incontinence pants wasn't it?'

Bubbles snorted as I smiled sweetly at Marcus who simply brushed the jibe aside. 'Very funny Alex, it was Richard and Judy actually - bridal makeovers - the gowns were fabulous. I got all the top designers involved…' Marcus twittered on about his prowess at cadging posh frocks from ageing designers whose work, shall we say, probably last graced a catwalk in the early 80s. He was part of a clique that featured very regularly in the social pages of *Hello* and *OK* magazines - a ubiquitous hotchpotch of bitter old queens, fading actresses, wannabe WAGs and ex-soap stars, whose addiction to the limelight ensured their presence at every tawdry social event where there just might be a camera. No quiz show was too tacky, no opening night too dire and no reality show too humiliating. These guys were clinging on for dear life, and none so much as Marcus who merely existed on the periphery. This was a world I was determined not to be a part of. That being said, I had saved the edition of *OK* where I had been photographed at an envelope opening, sorry, art exhibition.

'What are you doing in Sitges?' Bubbles yawned lazily and stretched her arms over her head.

'Probably filming some fantastic travel programme,' piped up Marcus, puffing viciously on a menthol cigarette. 'I was up for Wish You Were Here once but they gave it to that Craig Doyle - bastard!'

'Oh Marcus, how long ago was that? Get over yourself.' I smiled and looked at Bubbles, 'I'm just trying to get some peace and quiet for a change.'

Marcus leaned over the table, 'I've always thought we could be a perfect partnership, we have that natural synergy,' he flashed his nicotine-stained teeth. 'How d'you fancy doing holiday cover on *Good Morning*? We'd be fantastic.'

I stared at him disbelievingly. We had about as much natural synergy as oil and water, and as for doing holiday cover on *Good Morning* - the poor sod was delusional.

'Well you have come to a bloody strange place to get peace and quiet,' said Bubbles. 'It's Carnival time, it will be carnage.'

'I'm flying home tomorrow.'

'And miss a week of fabulous mayhem! Really, Alex, you're getting boring in your old age.' Marcus lit another cigarette.

I decided that boring and old were two words I didn't need to explore any further, so changed the subject. 'What are you doing here Marcus?'

'I have been coming here for years on and off, whenever I need a bit of sea air,' said Marcus loftily.

'A little se -*men* more like, dunno why he just doesn't move here and have it on tap,' snorted Bubbles who was methodically tearing a paper napkin into narrow strips.

'Yuk, too much information,' I winced.

Marcus leapt up, knocked back his wine and attempted to straighten his twisted Levis. 'Okay, I'll leave you two girls to enjoy the sun. I have a date tonight and I need a little siesta, lovely to bump into you Alex, see you later Bubbles.' He did a little round of air-kisses and disappeared in a cloud of Dolce and Gabbana.

'How do you two know each other?' I picked at what was left of my salad.

'We met at St Martin's Fashion College years ago and thought we knew it all.' Bubbles took off her glasses and shrugged, 'We designed stuff that was big in the club scene for a while in the 80s, and then we went so avant-garde we alienated ourselves. All our more commercial mates were being snapped up by the high street and we just got left behind – a couple of self-indulgent fashion dinosaurs. Marcus did his stylist thing, and I became a dominatrix…. drink?'

My mouth must have dropped open at this casual statement. I nodded dumbly at the suggestion of wine.

'Anyway, I won't bore you with all that. I live here now in beach side bliss.'

I would hardly have found tales from behind the whip boring, and felt a little disappointed that Bubbles had clammed up. A pale English waiter deposited two large glasses of white wine on the table and put the bill in front of me. 'I'm finishing my shift, d'you mind?'

Bubbles made no movement towards her bag, so I picked up the tab. My ten euro lunch had leapt to nearly thirty euro. But hey, it was my birthday weekend, so I let it wash over me and decided to be sociable. 'What made you come here Bubbles?'

'I suppose you could say it's my spiritual home – a bloody great circus, bursting at the seams with talented but wasted oddballs.'

I smiled. 'It does seem to be a very captivating place.'

'What do you know about it?'

'Nothing really.'

'Well, drink up. I need to lose this hangover, so I am going to walk up to the *Terramar* and watch the sun go down. C'mon, I'll give you a history lesson en route.'

SEVEN

Bubbles had lived in Sitges for three years and she was a mine of information regarding its heritage. Apparently this once small fishing village was turned into a ritzy resort in the 18th century when *Los Americanos* - the Spaniards who made fortunes in the tobacco industry in Cuba, returned and began building elaborate summer homes. Before long, the Barcelona elite followed suit. Money never being a guarantee of taste or ethics, one particularly tacky individual decided to display his wealth by covering an entire ballroom in elephant hide. Ironically it was now a Buddhist monastery.

At the end of the 19th century it all got a bit more risqué when modernist painters, sculptors, and poets started to meet in Sitges. Picasso came here to hang with his buddy – local artist Santiago Rusinol and even Dali dipped his toes in the water. This put Sitges on the map as far as tolerance of the bohemian lifestyle was concerned - liberals, rebels, homosexuals – all were welcome, but what really drew the artists was the quality of the light. By the time Bubbles and I reached the *Terramar*, a grand old hotel at the end of the *paseo* - the long seafront promenade that stretches on for the entire length of Sitges – where the earth (*terra*) meets the sea (*mar*), the legendary light was coming into its own. The sky was turning a deep shade of pink. We sat down on a rock to watch what promised to be a spectacular sunset.

'I never tire of this.' Bubbles started scrabbling around in her handbag, 'Ah there you are.' She produced a huge joint from one of the side pockets.

'The sunsets or the spliffs?'

'Both,' she took a huge draw and slowly exhaled. 'Want some?'

I gave into the 'girl that just can't say no' part of me and had a couple of puffs. It was strong.

'What the hell is in this?'

'Just weed, tobacco's bad for you.'

'Not in this town, by the sound of it, this whole place is built from the proceeds of tobacco. No wonder they all smoke so much.'

After another few puffs I felt my lips involuntarily twitching and I looked at Bubbles. She was bathed in yellow light and had a sort of holographic quality to her. I tried to maintain a serious conversation.

'So Marcus said you've been having girlie trouble – nothing serious I hope? I had to have keyhole surgery on one of my ovaries last year.'

Bubbles stared at me strangely, 'My girlfriend dumped me if that's what you mean. The cow went running off with a Spanish chick from Valencia.'

I pondered this for a second - then the penny dropped. Through my hash haze I was suddenly gripped by a panicky lesbophobia.

Men, men, men! If I said the word once I said it a thousand times. I stood on the rock, pointing out passing men who I thought were hot. It didn't matter if they were old, young, short or tall, on Rollerblades or carrying walking sticks – they were all sizzling to me.

Bubbles sat staring at me quietly. Eventually she decided it was time to take charge of this man-crazed, spaced-out twit.

'I think we ought to find some place you can lie down.'

Lie down? I grabbed my bag, 'Gotta go. See you later. Byeee…'

I could feel Bubbles staring after me as I staggered over the rocks. Somewhere beneath the stoned exterior, my more sensitive interior logged the fact that I had just offended someone pretty badly and it would have to be sorted, but for the time being, I had only one aim in life: I had to go in search of a shop that sold chocolate. Lots of chocolate…

*

'… let me get this straight, this afternoon you got yourself stoned with Bubbles, clocked on to the fact she's a lesbian, ran away and left the poor cow sitting at the *Terramar*, then ended up in that expensive chocolate shop on *Calle Angel Vidal*?'

'Yup,' I poured sparkling *Vichy Catalan* into a tall glass with an avalanche of ice. I was sitting in a deserted El Cabaret with Cam, filling him in on my latest exploits, 'I had the munchies.'

'Well it definitely wasn't the rug munchies,' Cam raised an eyebrow and grinned, 'Bubbles is renowned for her sunset spliffs, been the downfall of many a young damsel. You're certainly cramming in the Sitges experience aren't you?'

'Probably a good thing I'm flying back tomorrow, although I'll have to change my ticket, I booked a return from Manchester. Wonder how much I'll get screwed for that little oversight?'

'Line 'em up barman,' there was an icy blast of cold night air as two of the guys I recognised from my first night, staggered through the door. They nodded in my direction and ordered their drinks. There was a large mirror behind the bar, I glanced into it and caught sight of one of them waving his hands around like pincers. I swung around and glared at him, but Cam was already on the case.

'It's just idle gossip boys, c'mon you've been here long enough to know that the majority of what goes out on the Sitges tom-toms isn't true, particularly when Stephan is involved. Alex, Fred and Pierre are usually such nice guys and I'm sure they're very sorry.' Fred turned and looked at me apologetically, 'We're only messing about.'

'That's okay, luckily I'll be gone tomorrow,' I gave Cam a grateful smile, 'and then you can find someone else to gossip about.'

'You seem to understand Sitges already,' Pierre looked thoughtfully into his beer for a second, 'maybe you should come and live 'ere?'

'Live here, that's a bit random,' I laughed.

'Lots of people travel back and forth from the UK, Bart and all the other trolley dollies come and go. Probably wouldn't fit in with your hectic filming schedule though would it darling?' Cam quipped.

Before I had a chance to finally immerse myself in a full-on confessional, Simon and Aaron burst in causing Cam to scurry around the bar clearing glasses and straightening bottles.

'You still here, Alex?' said Simon.

'Only till the morning. In fact, as much as I hate to be a party pooper, I think I should bid you boys goodnight and make it back to Bart's before I get myself into any more trouble. It's been lovely meeting you.' I jumped off my stool and as I was about to put my coat on my eyes were drawn to a snapshot stuck on the shelf. A garish looking woman who looked oddly familiar was dressed head to toe in red sequins and had a pint glass in her hand. Aaron caught me looking and sniggered, 'That's Scarlett.'

'Is she local?'

'You could say that,' he handed me the picture and started nodding towards Cam.

'Crikey, are they related?' I peered at the picture closely. 'Someone needs a make-up lesson, that's bad slap.'

'Who needs a slap?' Cam came diving over and grinned as he saw the picture in my hand, 'Ah, so you have met my alter-ego?'

'That's you?' I screeched, 'I thought it was your ugly sister.'

'Hey, I don't look that bad,' he snatched the picture back and clasped it protectively to his chest.

'Well you're never going to win that crown off Stephanie next Sunday unless you come up with something a bit better than that,' shrugged Simon.

'What crown?' My ears pricked up at the mention of Stephanie.

'The Carnival Drag Queen Crown,' Cam put the picture back on the shelf and sighed, 'I'll beat him if it kills me.'

'Well I could make you look ten times better than that,' I sniffed.

'You could?' Cam lent over the bar, 'And what makes you say that?'

'I was a make-up artist for years.'

'Doesn't mean you were a good one though,' Cameron raised an eyebrow.

The irrepressible show-off in me won over. I opened my handbag and tipped out the contents of my make-up bag on the counter. Ten minutes of rubbing, smudging and blending with a black kohl pencil later, Cam was gazing at himself in the mirror with his mouth open, 'Look at my eyes, they're huge.'

'Add a pair of false lashes and some glittery shadow to that and you'd give Liza Minnelli a run for her money,' I smiled.

'Okay, I have a proposition for you,' Cam carried on preening. 'How about you stop all this nonsense about leaving tomorrow, come and stay in my spare room for the next week, in return, you make me up for Carnival?'

I stood and thought about it. I had a changeable ticket and the thought of being around for Carnival was tempting. Apart from the half-day filming with Beverley in a couple of weeks, I was jobless, and in anticipation of the surprise party, Mel and Mum had cancelled my restaurant booking for the next night weeks ago. Sod it, why not? 'Deal,' I clapped my hands, 'and Bart can have his place back to himself.'

Suddenly there was a clamouring of voices all asking if I might be able to fit them in for an appointment. I looked at Cam.

'I don't give a shit, just make sure I look fabulous next Sunday – I want that crown.'

'Can you make me look like Marilyn Monroe?' Fred piped up.

'Of course,' I tried my best to look affronted at the mere suggestion that I might not be up to the job.

'Looks like you're staying a bit longer then,' Simon glanced up from the glass washer machine.

'I suppose I am.'

'I'll come and grab you tomorrow around eleven,' Cam was standing at the end of the bar having a cigarette, looking totally ridiculous with his blackened eyes.

'Have you got stuff to take that off?' I pulled on my coat and paid my bill.

'A bathroom cabinet bulging with Clinique, darling.'

As I walked out of the bar, I heard a remark concerning other things bulging. I rolled my eyes and laughed; they would find sexual innuendo in a Billy Graham sermon in this joint.

EIGHT

'Welcome to Fairy Towers, the Temple of the Lonely Homo,' Cam made an expansive gesture with his arms as we gazed up at what was the nearest to a tower block I had seen in Sitges.

'Erm, what floor are you on?' I still hadn't quite got over the horrendous climb up to Bart's apartment, and Cam and I were loaded up with all my stuff.

'Eleventh,' he turned to me and smiled, 'fabulous view.'

'Oh god, I hope there's a lift.'

There was, and despite being particularly antiquated, twenty creaky seconds later the lift deposited us outside his front door. Cam turned and looked at me with a serious expression, 'I have one thing to ask you before we embark on our journey of domestic bliss – are you tidy?'

'Yes, yes, of course, especially in someone else's home,' I blathered.

'Great,' he said as he threw open the door, 'cos I'm not.'

My eyes widened like saucers at the scene that greeted me as I walked into the apartment. There didn't seem to be an inch of space that wasn't covered with stuff. Whether it was a screwed up pair of jeans, an empty CD case, or a pile of magazines – it was everywhere. I gasped and looked around for somewhere to drop my bags.

'It's a fright isn't it?' Cam looked vaguely apologetic for a second, and then he laughed, 'I believe life is too damn short to keep a tidy house.' He kicked a couple of beach towels out of the way and put my bag down, 'C'mon, I'll show you to your quarters.'

I followed him along the hall, gingerly treading over yet more rubble. I was amazed. On the few times I had seen him, Cam was always immaculately turned out. It reminded me of some of the people I used to see making their way to work on early mornings in many parts of Asia. They would stand waiting for buses outside little more than corrugated iron shelters where there was no physical evidence of electricity or clean water and yet they all looked as fresh as daisies with perfectly pressed clothes. Cam did not have the excuse of a Third World existence, although the apartment definitely had, shall we say, a refugee feel about it.

He pushed open the bedroom door with a certain amount of difficulty. This room hadn't escaped the litter deluge. He bent down and picked up a collection of gym bags, all overflowing with clothes. He pondered them for a second then threw them in to the hallway. 'You're staying in the Carnival closet,' he pulled a mischievous face as I went past him into the room.

There were feathers and glittery frocks everywhere. High platform boots galore in every colour of the rainbow were strewn over the floor.

'Is that a bed I spy before me?' I nodded in the direction of a particularly large pile of crap in the corner of the room.

'It was last time I looked. Make yourself at home sweetie, just move whatever you want and I'll make us a quick coffee.'

I chucked my stuff on the floor and decided the clear up process could wait. I wandered out and nosed around. In direct contrast to the rest of the apartment, the bathroom was sparkling. I walked into the kitchen, it was the same. Cam looked up and saw my confused expression.

'No matter how untidy this place is, you'll never find a germ in my kitchen or loo.'

'That's a relief,' I looked out of the window; the view was magnificent, even more impressive than Bart's.

He opened the fridge and swore as he shook an empty coffee packet, 'Oh bugger, just Uncle Peter. C'mon. Let's go to Mont Roig for a coffee and a *Bikini*.'

I looked puzzled, 'Uncle Peter? A *Bikini*? It's more confusing than Spanish.'

'*Tio Pepe* means Uncle Peter,' he pointed to an unopened bottle of *Tio Pepe* sherry, the only inhabitant of his fridge, 'and as for a Bikini – you will see, my darling.'

Cam disappeared into the spare room and emerged with a carrier bag full of glittery clothing; 'I need to make a new Carnival outfit. I'll use some of this stuff and jazz it up a bit, but we'll have to go shopping.'

We made our way back into the centre and within ten minutes we were sitting around a table drinking *cortados* – short milky coffees with a kick, and tucking into *Bikinis* - the greasiest but most delightful cheese and ham toasted sandwiches I have ever tasted – an unfortunate name for a snack that could ensure a certain amount of reluctance to don a bikini if you allowed them to become a habit.

'Isn't it lovely here?' I gazed up at the high glass ceiling of what appeared to be a very popular meeting place for both the Spanish and a whole host of different nationalities, who I couldn't help noticing were predominantly gay men.

'Service is a bit hit and miss, sometimes you can wait twenty minutes for a coffee, oh look there are Fred and Pierre,' Cam pointed towards the door.

They waved and found themselves a table. Fred was as blond as Pierre was dark, and they were both snuggled up in bright yellow padded jackets.

Cam gazed thoughtfully into his coffee. 'They're nice guys, only been here two months. I wonder how they'll find living in Sitges? They've been through a lot.'

'In what way?'

'Pierre was diagnosed as HIV positive about twelve years ago and nearly lost the battle a couple of times.'

'Wow; that must have been tough on both of them.'

'The most amazing thing is that they had only been together a couple of weeks before Pierre found out.'

'And Fred stood by him, how amazing! Is he okay?'

'He's not HIV positive if that's what you mean, but it's taken its toll. He started to suffer from anxiety attacks if Pierre was out of his sight for too long. So they left Paris and came here in the hope that a change of environment and slower pace of life will help the pair of them.'

Our conversation came to an abrupt end when Cam suddenly spotted a dark haired guy in the corner of the café. 'You see him over there? That's Enrique. He's from Buenos Aires. We've been flirting for months.'

The brooding object of Cam's quite evident desire wandered nonchalantly past the table, pausing for effect and nodding at Cam, before he strutted out of the restaurant like some wannabe Marlon Brando.

Fred came over laughing, 'Put your tongue back in Cam, for god's sake.'

'I can't, he's gorgeous.'

'Okay loved-up, what have you got in your bag?'

'Shirley Bassey meets Rue Paul,' I raised my eyebrows at Cam and smiled warmly at Fred.

'Have you got a pink boa? I need one of those for my outfit,' Fred started rummaging through the bag and dragged out a mangy old string of sad fuchsia feathers and exclaimed, 'Shit, wrong pink, I wanted more of a baby pink.' He then tipped the whole bag onto the floor and kept foraging through.

I looked around; nobody was turning a hair at the sight of this butch looking guy sifting through women's clothes as if he were searching for a ratchet in a toolbox. Carnival fever was obviously catching and Fred was having a very bad attack. He eventually gave up and went back over to Pierre who had his nose buried in a newspaper.

Cam finished his coffee, gathered up his stuff and then whizzed me around Sitges at the speed of light. We had to source a list of props that Valerie Singleton would have been proud of – everything from washers to cling film, and more make up for me. My existing cosmetic bag was a bit lacking in the drag department. To add a bit of extra tension, we only had forty-five minutes before the shops closed.

'Don't you just love this?' squealed Cam as we charged into yet another Euro store – bizarre places which sell piles and piles of the cheapest crap imaginable. 'Oh my God, look at these!' He was holding up a pair of false eyelashes that must have been three inches long.

'Put them in the basket, mine are far too tasteful,' I was totally distracted by the sight of rows and rows of Tupperware containers that were all less than a euro.

'C'mon, you're in the wrong department,' shouted Cam adding a packet of gold metal pan cleaners and clip on hair braids in every fluorescent colour under the rainbow to his hoard. I happily acquiesced and grabbed a royal blue lipstick.

By 1.45 pm not only had we Carnival shopped, I had managed to buy myself some new clothes and girlie necessities as my existing supply was getting a bit thin on the ground. We dragged everything back to the apartment. As I was looking through his buys, I found a pale pink boa.

'Did you buy this for Fred?'

He nodded.

'You are too sweet.'

'And I bought this for you,' he threw a tube of pink glitter over me.

'Hey, I don't do pink!'

'Have some of this then.' A shower of blue glitter rained down on me and I was encrusted: my hair, clothes and face. Everything was a great sparkling mass.

'You bastard, this'll take forever to come off.'

'Oh shut up, you miserable old cow, it's Carnival time.'

I had to laugh; Cam and I were getting on like we had known each other for years. I flopped down on a chair and gazed out of the window.

'Everything okay?'

'More than okay Cam, everything is very okay indeed.'

NINE

The next morning I woke up determined to do something nice for Cam to show my appreciation for how lovely he was being to me. It didn't take me long to come up with an idea, so I got straight down to it.

By midday I had finished. For four hours I had been creeping around Cam's flat while he slept, organising his chaos. I had quietly picked up all the debris and taken it into the lounge, after dusting, sweeping and polishing everything in sight, then sat gazing at the piles I had created. Every CD was in its container and stacked in the CD holder I had found buried under the sofa, a neat stack of unopened letters sat on the table, next to a mountain of magazines, I had found and washed fifteen ashtrays and they now sparkled on a shelving unit along with books that had been retrieved from every corner of the flat and had been categorised into sections. But the pile I was most fascinated by covered most of the coffee table; there must have been at least a hundred pieces of artwork. From exquisitely detailed sketches to delicate watercolours, they were fantastic.

I heard the click of Cam's door, my heart started pounding. He walked in to the lounge with his mouth open. 'What have you done?'

'I just thought it might be a nice surprise, are you mad?'

'Mad? You're the one who's bloody mad, you wonderful girl. This is amazing - look at my books, my music, oh shit - bills – didn't need to find those.' He wandered around grinning. Then he noticed the artwork on the coffee table and his expression clouded over, 'Oh god you found that rubbish.'

'They're not rubbish, they're brilliant.' I picked up a pen and ink drawing of the church, 'If this is all your handiwork, you're even more talented than I thought.'

He snatched it back and slapped it back on the table. 'Let's find a bin bag for this lot.'

'No, you mustn't, there's an empty drawer. I'll put them in there.'

I grabbed the pictures and placed them carefully in the drawer. Cam watched me silently with a strange expression on his face, and then walked back into his bedroom. I chewed my lip anxiously; I had obviously poked my nose in where it wasn't wanted. I just hoped I hadn't upset him.

Any worry on that front was totally without foundation as ten minutes later he emerged, showered and smiling, 'C'mon, get ready. It's a beautiful day, so I am going to treat you to a fish lunch on the beach front to say thank you for doing all this,' he waved his hands around the room.

'Anything you say, boss.'

As we wandered along the *paseo,* excitement got the better of me, 'I can't wait until Sunday,' I squeezed his arm, 'you're so going to win.'

'We'll see,' he sighed.

As we settled ourselves down at the Santa Maria restaurant for lunch, basking in the winter sun, Cam's phone rang. He handed it straight over to me. It was Fred saying he had another four friends interested in having their make-up done, 'You'll probably earn a few bob out of this,' said Cam.

'I could certainly do with it. My overdraft is at an all time high.'

'Don't they pay you much on the box?' Cam had finished ordering drinks and a seafood platter and was now rummaging around in his pockets for his Marlboro Lights.

'They didn't pay me too badly but it's very sporadic and I'm very good at spending. Not, I might add, on anything sensible like a mortgage; I prefer plane tickets. I dread to think what size my carbon footprint is. Anyhow, there's a spanner in the works now.'

He looked quizzically at me.

'They haven't renewed my contract, I've been sacked,' I smiled sadly 'that was partly why I ended up on a plane to Barcelona.'

'Oh my word, you managed to keep that a bit quiet,' he leaned back in his seat puffing on a cigarette, 'not that it's anyone else's business. What are you going to do now? Other irons in the fire?'

'No,' I started fiddling with my napkin, 'I'm sure my agent is hoping I'll acquire a well publicised drug habit or start shagging a married politician.'

'I'm sure we could rustle her up a little scandal here. Wouldn't have to try hard would we? Look at the potential,' Cam's eyes gleamed with wickedness.

I laughed. 'To be honest I've been getting a bit fed up with telly lately. It's about the right time to say goodbye. My main concern is losing the regular income.'

'Anything else you'd like to do?'

'I've got lots of ideas but have absolutely no idea, if that makes any sense?'

'It's a common phenomenon in Sitges. This place is a bit like a service station. You pull in for a while and work out what road you're going to take and then bugger off,' he shrugged, 'or you stay here and help everybody clsc do it.'

'So is that what you did? Came here to sort your own life out and then got caught up in everybody else's crap?'

Cam either didn't hear me or pretended not to. It was the second time I had seen him so uncomfortable that day so I carried on chattering, 'I do it too. I can't help myself. Don't get me wrong, I'm not a total martyr to the cause, but I'm easily lured into another person's drama.'

'Avoidance tactics darling, we all do it, now where are those drinks?' Cam swivelled around and looked at the door just as the waiter emerged with an ice bucket. After he poured the pale sparkling fluid into the glasses, Cam raised his glass to me, 'To your fabulous new future, whatever that may be?'

I smiled and chinked his glass, 'To freedom, to health and to you Cam. I am exceptionally happy to have met you.'

Cam gave a faint smile, leaned over and kissed me on the cheek, 'Likewise.'

In the way of old friends we sat in comfortable silence, gazing at the sea until the food arrived. I looked on in awe as Cam pushed a platter groaning under the weight of what looked like half the inhabitants of the entire Mediterranean Sea towards me.

'Jesus,' I said as I stabbed a piece of white fish, 'does anyone ever finish this?'

'Rarely, but I have a good go,' Cam shovelled about four pieces of fish onto his plate. 'Don't let this skinny frame fool you. I can eat like a horse.'

Well, maybe not a horse, but Cam's appetite could probably shame a Shetland pony. I managed two bits of fish and a few prawns and Cam nearly cleared the platter. When the waiter came, he asked for the rest to be put into a bag with all the scraps.

I gawped at him incredulously.

'It's not for me,' he said, 'but I do know where it will be really appreciated.'

We left the Santa Maria and went for a wander along the *paseo*. Long jetties made entirely of rocks jutted out into the sea dividing the beach into sections. Cam explained how these now empty strips of beach evolved into little sub-cultures during the summer. One section smack bang in the middle, right outside a beach-side restaurant called Picnic, was the gay beach, and when we reached the end of this beach, Cam started to clamber over the rocks, gesturing for me to sit on the stone bench that marked the beginning of the jetty. Suddenly he stopped and tipped the bag of fish leftovers onto a flat piece of rock. He came back to the bench and sat down.

'Just watch,' he whispered.

Suddenly small furry heads started to peer out from amongst the rocks, and then, very tentatively, a group of cats emerged and started to grab pieces of fish. There must have been about fifteen of them.

'Wow, they live there?' I was amazed.

'Yes, there are different little communities of stray cats all around the town, each with their own 'pussy patron' that feeds them,' he laughed.

'Feline-thropists,' I mused.

'Are you trying to out-smart-arse me Chapman? C'mon, *siesta*-time. It's my night off and I'm taking you out and about tonight. You are going to need all your stamina.'

I groaned. I had a feeling Cam was a guy who could party long and hard.

TEN

'So you're still here, are you?' hissed a voice in my ear as I stood in a bar called Air, waiting for Cam to come back with the drinks. I spun around and did a double take. Stephan was now Stephanie – fully made up and dressed to kill in a clingy black dress. He really was quite something: legs that most girls would kill for, a mane of dark curly hair, back-combed and sprayed to perfection, and dark smoky eyes, which at this moment in time, were narrowed to slits as he looked me up and down. 'So you think you'll be able to help Cam win, do you? He doesn't stand a chance.'

I felt myself bristling but before I could reply, Cam returned from the bar.

'Hello Stephanie, how are you? Being nice to my friend I hope.'

'Of course I am dahling. See you Sunday,' he turned and walked off, after shooting me a look which could have withered an oak tree.

'What did Stephanie say to you?' asked Cam.

'Nothing,' I murmured.

'Bullshit, Alex, I could see the venom spilling out of his bitchy little gob.'

'He said you didn't stand a chance on Sunday.'

'I probably don't, but we're going to try aren't we?'

'Yes,' I hugged him.

Cam and I managed to stay out all night, drifting from bar to bar, drinking and dancing without a care in the world, until eventually we ran out of energy and decided to make our way home. We wandered along in peaceful silence. The first signs of daybreak began to appear; a few early birds were warbling in the trees and old Catalan men with fishing rods were walking jauntily towards the seafront, puffing away on their cigarettes in the dim light. In spite of the unholy hour, I felt inexplicably awake. By the time we reached the beach bar Picnic, the sun was up and the sea was a crystalline blue. 'God, doesn't it make you want to jump in?'

Cam looked at me as if I had lost my marbles. 'We would have hypothermia in minutes. It's February you silly mare. C'mon let's get you home before you do anything rash.'

Once we were back at Cam's, we sat on the balcony sipping ice cold *Tio Pepe*.

'I cannot believe I am drinking frigging sherry at 7 am.'

'Me neither, you're a bad influence,' Cam said loftily, pouring himself another.

'Me!' I feigned shock. 'Actually I think it's a bad combination of the two of us – a sort of Molotov cocktail effect.'

'That would make you Molly and me Toff,' Cam screeched with laughter. A Spanish woman sweeping her balcony looked up and shot us a menacing look, muttering under her breath and attacking her tiles with even more gusto than before.

We decided not to upset her any further and resumed quiet conversation. Cam told me all about his life, from his ex-lovers to his love of liver and bacon, but when I touched upon why he had come out here, he clammed up and changed the subject. I left well alone and finally at about nine o'clock we called it a day and started to tidy up. As I popped the sherry schooners in the sink I couldn't help but smile.

'What are you grinning at?' Cam rubbed his eyes and yawned.

'If it wasn't for Harvey's Bristol Cream, I probably wouldn't be the person I am now.'

'You can't throw things like that into conversation then disappear to bed.'

I laughed, 'According to family folklore my mum conceived me whilst under the influence of a few too many sherries.'

'So that made you into the alcoholic you are today.'

'Well I was referring to the fact I was an Aquarian but maybe there's something in that too,' I kissed him on the cheek. 'Sweet dreams Toff and thank you for such a lovely day.'

'My pleasure Molly,' he smiled and we toddled off to our respective beds.

I pulled down the blackout blinds in my room and snuggled down under a pile of blankets and threw my coat over me for good measure, and started to doze off. Me, myself and I. Forty-years-old, making new friends and taking life as it came at me. If that was in part due to a few glasses of sherry, what else could I say but *Cheers!*

On her twenty-first birthday, after half a bottle of the said sherry and a little too much birthday cake, my Mum-to-be threw caution to the wind and didn't ask my Soon-to-be-Dad to pull out. Instead they lay there in post-coital bliss, unaware that they had set my embryonic wheels in motion. Little did they know as they snuggled up and planned the black, white and red Greco-Romanesque testimony to bad taste that was destined to be our sitting room for the next eleven years, that a particularly hardy, long-distance sperm had nearly completed Operation Egg. And when my dad popped down the chippie for a couple of saveloys a few hours later, he had absolutely no idea that he was attending to the dietary needs of his newly pregnant wife.

One month earlier and they would have spawned a studious, conscientious Capricorn, a month later and they would have been blessed with a sensitive day dreamy little Pisces. But the cosmos had bestowed upon their first-born the perfect excuse - to never dance to the beat of anyone else's drum. As I grew up I was thrilled to find out Aquarians were *visionary, humanitarian, original* and *inventive.* Of course I chose not to linger over *contrary, perverse, stubborn* and *unpredictable*, the not quite so attractive attributes of your average water-bearer, but they were there. Just ask Mum - She Who Was There to Ruin My Life.

You see, what she didn't quite get was that despite my lofty attitude towards my potential world-changing destiny, when it came to my physical appearance, like any other kid on the block, I was desperate to blend in. Genetics deemed that I was to be a head taller than other children of my age with a mane of unruly red hair. This in itself gave me automatic entry to the 'Sore Thumb Club', but my well-meaning mother elevated me to executive status by using me as a muse for her enthusiastic - but by no means polished - attempts at dressmaking. Just the sight of her brandishing a tape measure and her latest pattern for something normally seen on a member of a cruise ship cabaret act was enough to send me looking for an escape route. While other kids toddled off to school in normal clothes, I was a vision in psychedelic Crimplene. I wore so much man-made fibre that the air positively crackled with static around me. Had I ventured too near a naked flame, I would have gone up like a Hindu funeral pyre.

Consequently, I dreamed of being like Catherine Winthrop – a classmate who was everything I wasn't: petite with shiny blonde swingy hair and honey brown legs set off beautifully with long white cotton socks and black patent shoes – those alone filled me with deep-seated envy. In stark contrast to the outlandish outfits, my mum's views on the shoes were draconian. From the knees up I was Austin Powers, look down and there they were, my long, skinny, blue- purple legs merging into pale blue ankle socks, topped off with clumpy brown Startrites. This was a fashion statement that was never going to catch on. Well, maybe in refugee camps.

In my eyes, my mum's sole *raison d'etre* was to humiliate me, so I engaged in many forms of personal protest. I utilised every method I could think of to destroy my clothes, threw my shoes in other people's dustbins, and generally tested her patience on a daily basis. My dad became the referee and my younger brother and sister just looked on in amazement as my mum and I engaged in all out warfare. How she didn't end up being convicted of infanticide and ordered to spend the rest of her days languishing in Holloway Prison was a miracle.

But there you have me - a delicate blend of nature and nurture. One sherry-fuelled afternoon of passion, the subsequent planetary alignment and a mother who just wouldn't put the sewing machine away.

ELEVEN

Sunday night had finally arrived and I was exhausted. For the past forty-eight hours, I seemed to have done nothing but paint faces and slosh cava down my throat. It had all passed in a haze of hairspray and lip-gloss. I had been doing the sort of make up I hadn't done for years - artistic and over the top. *Cirque du Soleil* meets *Priscilla Queen of the Desert*. My ego had never been so bolstered. These weren't petulant models, jaded and fed up with having their faces plastered twenty times a week, these were guys who had been turned into glamorous divas and all they wanted to do was gaze at themselves. The louder the squeals, the broader my grin became, particularly when I spun Fred around to face the mirror, and there in his reflection was a very startled, if a little square-jawed Marilyn Monroe. And when Cam walked in and gave him the pale pink boa, you'd have thought he'd just won the lottery.

I, on the other hand, looked like shit. My face was grey and pale, my voice sounded like I'd been eating gravel and in contrast to the flamboyant, colourful, excited Scarlett that I had just spent the past two hours creating, I felt like bloody Cinderella. But it was worth all the effort, Cam looked spectacular. I couldn't wait to see Stephanie's face.

'Oh my god you're fabulous.'

'I know, thank you.'

'Not you, I'm talking to me,' Cam was staring awe-struck at his reflection in the mirror.

'Here you go,' I held out a bustier and matching headdress made entirely of wire, red and gold thread and red velvet hearts. Cam and I had designed and made the whole outfit in three days. He slipped the bustier over his red sequinned sheath and I helped him attach the two-foot-high head piece on top of his pillar box red curly wig that hung down to his waist.

He looked like an exotic burlesque bird of paradise; I grabbed my camera and took a few shots whilst he fluttered around the room.

'You have got to win, you look great.'

'Now you'd better do something with yourself,' Cam winced as he looked at the shadow that used to be me. 'What are you going as?'

'A frazzled make-up artist,' I scowled at him.

'Ooh touchy,' he blew me a kiss and high kicked out of the door. I sighed and opened a plastic bag containing tight black dress, some fishnet tights and high black shoes. Horrendously cheap and tacky – the whole lot cost me the princely sum of fifty-two euros. But from what I had seen of the other revellers over Carnival, this was the norm.

I plastered my face with 80s style make-up, donned some fake lashes, and put on a massive black wig that had been left hanging around. I found a long pair of green satin gloves in Cam's dressing up pile and finished off the effect with some fake emerald costume jewellery. I looked somewhere in between Morticia from the *Addams Family* and Joan Collins in her *Dynasty* days. There was a pretty good chance I could win the bloody drag queen crown myself.

When I came out of my room, Cam was like a child with a new toy.

'My god you are a girl. Look at that cleavage.'

Despite feeling a bit self-conscious, I loved the sense of freedom that comes with dressing up - permission to behave totally outside my usual box. It felt fantastic and I couldn't wait to be part of Carnival. I grabbed my new partner in crime, 'C'mon Scarlett, let's get out there and show them how it's done.'

Outside the streets were heaving with people; everyone was dressed up, already drunk and partying hard. *Carnaval* - as the Catalans call it - runs simultaneously with Carnivals all over the world. In places such as New Orleans, Rio de Janeiro and the Caribbean, there were currently thousands upon thousands of other people plastering on the slap, donning the costumes and nursing their throbbing livers all in this excessive build up to Lent. I was sure that, just like me, the majority had absolutely no intention of honouring the religious aspect of Carnival and would not be giving up a damn thing for forty minutes, let alone forty days.

It took us half an hour of pushing to reach *Calle Espaltar* - the street where El Cabaret was hidden away, but we couldn't cross the street to the bar as everything was blocked and the ground was literally shaking with the vibrations of loud Latin American music that was coming from the direction of the beach. I looked over the heads in front of me and gripped Cam's arm with excitement, the first Carnival float was looming up on us.

'It's the queen,' Cam shouted above the deafening music.

'It's wall to wall bloody queens,' I screamed back as I watched the spectacle before me.

About thirty gyrating women dressed as colourful bug-like creatures with sparkling antennae were leading the way for an enormous float weighed down with huge glittering green foliage and massive satin flowers. There, at the top, was the queen bee herself, hips flicking in a rhythmic sideways frenzy, a headpiece that defied gravity and a smile that said it all. Tonight was her night, tonight she ruled, tonight was a night she would tell her grandchildren about. Somewhere in the future, when the years had rolled by, and her beauty gently faded she would look at her pictures and remember the night she was the Queen of Sitges.

Cam turned to me and shrugged, 'Quite pretty, but you can't beat the real thing.' He gave his fake boobs a squeeze, pouted for effect and grabbed my arm, 'C'mon, to the bar, I'm gasping.'

'How the hell are we going to do that?' I nodded towards the army of gold and black Egyptian guards that were now blocking our path and the tractor dragging an immense barge complete with Cleopatra and her entourage of shaking, rattling and rolling slaves.

'We run.' Cam dragged me into the middle of the procession, his false nails digging into my hand, as we danced our way over to the other side of the street and the heaving madness of El Cabaret.

Simon did a double take as we pushed our way past a group of hairy-legged nurses in bright yellow wigs that were blocking the entrance to the bar. I had painted him as a devil earlier that evening and to my horror he was sweating so much, rivulets of red and black paint had dribbled onto the shoulders of his t-shirt. By the time we reached the bar two huge plastic tumblers of cava were ready and waiting. 'You both look amazing,' he grinned. Before we had a chance to reply, he whizzed off to serve a frighteningly realistic Baby Jane Hudson and one of the ten or so Madonnas in the bar that evening.

Cam knocked back half his cava.

'Nerves kicking in?' I smiled. 'What time does it all begin?'

'Three o'clock,' he swigged the rest of the glass and lit a cigarette, and nodded towards the door where Fred, in full Marilyn regalia was asking one of the *nurses* if they did mouth to mouth resuscitation. 'Somebody seems to be conquering his nerves. This is his first night out on the town without Pierre.'

I hung over the bar to ask for more drinks, my feet were already killing me and as the night had barely begun, I was going to need some serious anaesthetising. By the time Cam, Fred and I left the bar at two thirty, I felt no pain. Out on the streets there was no respite from the incessant pounding of loud music, it was coming at us from every direction, one great mass of shrieking party people. The three of us linked arms and made our way to XXL. As soon as they saw Cam, the doormen waved us into the crowded club. We diverted straight to the Señoras for a quick make-up check. Despite the number of 'ladies' occupying the mirror, until I walked in, it had been a distinctly oestrogen-free zone.

I covered Cam's lips with a sticky red gloss that was flecked with gold, sprayed a fine mist of glitter above his head and made sure his enormous false lashes were on tight. He took a deep breath, re-adjusted his crotch, winked at me and purred, 'Show time.' He then turned on his heel, breezed out of the door and slunk sexily towards the dance floor. I was gob-smacked at the way his body language and posture had totally changed since he had donned the outfit. Having just caught my own reflection in the mirror I decided to give it some serious diva. I stuck my boobs out, sucked in my tummy and attempted to wiggle my way behind him. Within ten seconds, I had knocked over two drinks and got one of my stiletto heels caught in some Gothic horror's fishnets. So much for sex kitten! Cam disappeared off to the side of a small stage and I was alone, well, until I heard a huge belch behind me and turned around. There leaning against a pillar was a very drunk Fred.

'Now that's not very Marilyn,' I slid my arm through his as the lights went down, 'Jesus nor is that!' A portly Spanish man, drenched in sweat staggered onto the stage and took the microphone, he made an announcement in lightening speed Catalan, and then for the purpose of what was probably half the crowd, he switched to broken English.

'Welcome to XXL, now time for de laaavely Carnival Queens to come to stage and you people to vote de best, most beautiful, most sexy lahdeeees.'

I burst out laughing. He was so sleazy. 'He's letting the side down,' I whispered to Fred, who was now hiccupping, 'he must have had a gay-style bypass at birth.'

'*Hic*, that's 'cos he's straight. He owns half of Sitges, including this club. *Hic!*'

Like a Virgin came blasting out of the speakers and the same Madonna who had been at El Cabaret burst onto the stage miming totally out of synch. Before our wannabe starlet had even reached the halfway point, the crowd had booed her off. The same went for Celine Dion, Tina Turner and Cher. It was like an exceptionally bad episode of *Stars in Their Eyes*.

'And now we have de sexy, de laaavely, de beautiful Scarlett...' obviously not a natural orator, Sleazeball had given everyone the same introduction.

Cam came onto the stage and my stomach lurched; I couldn't bear to see him humiliated. He grabbed the microphone and nodded at the DJ who grinned back. Suddenly a tune I recognised from Cabaret began in the background and Cam cavorted around the stage huskily singing *Mein Herr*. Not only could he sing; he could work an audience. The crowd loved it and whooped and cheered him on. When he took his final curtsey, he was bombarded with single red roses.

Fred and I were jumping, screaming and hugging each other when I felt a tap on my shoulder. I turned and there was Simon, grinning, 'He was something else wasn't he?'

'He'll be thrilled you're here,' I threw my arms around Simon who seemed a little thrown by my exuberance.

'I've left Aaron managing with a couple of the locals; I'll have to get back in a short while, but I couldn't miss this.'

'He's gonna win,' hiccupped Fred.

'Let's see what Stephanie is going to pull out of the bag, here she comes.'

'And now, we have de fantastic, de wonderful, de magnificent winner of last year's Carnival crown, de beautiful, de talented, de hot hot hot - Stephanie...' Sleazy had extended his repertoire.

Cam appeared at our side breathless and beamed when he saw Simon. We all turned to the front and watched as Stephanie glided onto the stage, arms outstretched, wearing an outfit so elaborate, it outshone that of the *Carnaval* Queen we had seen proudly fronting the procession earlier. This was full on Rio Glam. Feathers, diamante and sequins – it had it all, and when Gloria Estevan and the Miami Sound machine started telling everyone to *Get on your Feet,* nobody seemed to notice that Stephanie was even worse at lip synching than his earlier competition; he simply dazzled them into submission. I could see how he had been the ruler of this overly rouged roost for so long. But tonight it would all change. Cam had more talent in his little finger than Stephanie could dream of, and as for the outfit - expensive, yes, but certainly not creative and original. For me there was simply no contest – Scarlett was the undisputed star of the evening.

Cam went up to the stage as Sleazy revved up the crowd and got them to show their appreciation for each person in turn. There was a couple of embarrassing silences and a few slight smatterings of applause as the earlier acts took their bows. But as Scarlett stepped forward the noise was deafening. Stephanie's lips twitched angrily for a second and then he regained his composure, threw his arms up in the air and struck a pose worthy of a Hollywood starlet. The crowd cheered, they clapped, they paid him homage – but it wasn't as loud or as long. I caught Cam's eye and chewed my lips nervously. He closed his eyes tightly as Sleazy came forward and took a deep breath, 'Laaaahdies and gentlemen, I am pleased to announce that the winner of this years Miss XXL Carnival Queen Competition is...........once again de beautiful Stephanie.'

There was an initial silence, which turned to boos as Stephanie came to the front of the stage and accepted his sash. He turned to the crowd and looked down at them disdainfully. He waved his sash over their heads and cooed 'Thank you dahlings.' As he flounced off in search of sycophants, I looked at Cam who was utterly crestfallen. As soon as he came off the stage he was surrounded by throngs of people all eager to tell him he had been cheated. Although reassuring, it didn't help the fact that he had lost – again, and by the time he reached us, his disappointment had turned to anger.

'That Jorges is as bent as they come.'

I looked at him quizzically.

'The tubby little Spanish twat who judges this sodding fiasco every year.' Cam grabbed a drink off a table next to him and downed it in one, spluttering, 'Christ, I hate Bacardi.'

Simon patted him on the back and muttered something about next year. Cam swung around and barked, 'There will be no next year; this is the last bloody time I do this.'

I looked around the club; Fred had disappeared. I left Cam saying goodbye to Simon and checked everywhere, even asked the now tear-stained Madonna to check the men's toilets for an inebriated Marilyn, but it was useless, he was nowhere to be seen.

I went back to Cam who was staring despondently into a large vodka and tonic, 'You okay?' I rubbed his back.

'Yeah, just a bit fed up, stupid isn't it?'

'Nope, you put a lot of time and effort in, and it was so blatantly fixed, it's disgusting. Have you seen Fred?'

'No,' Cam knocked back his vodka. 'Have you checked

everywhere in here?'

'Yeah, I'm just a bit worried, he was wasted.'

'C'mon, maybe he's staggering home, we'll find him.'

As we headed for the door we were intercepted by a jubilant Stephanie, 'Aren't you going to congratulate me, Scarlett?'

'If you can take any pride in winning that farcical pile of shite, then yes I congratulate you, for being even more sad than I gave you credit for. Now excuse us, we have to go.'

Stephanie glowered at Cam, then looked at me and sneered, 'Well if it isn't our little make-up artiste? You don't even drag up well do you, dahling?'

'If I were you, I'd get yourself some stronger panty-hose Stephan, your tackle's hanging out.'

Stephanie raised his glass of cava, and for a moment I thought he was going to launch it at me, but Cam took my arm and pulled me out of the door.

'You're brave; Stephanie hates any reference to Stephan. They're two different people.'

'Don't like either of them.'

We wandered along the streets in the direction of Fred's apartment. Everywhere was littered with the remnants of Carnival; soggy streamers, plastic cups, discarded bits of costume. I even spotted a lonely red patent sling-back. Luckily we didn't have to look very far before we stumbled across a very forlorn looking pink bundle huddled up in the doorway of an estate agent up on the *Calle Major*. Fred looked up at us as we walked towards him, his teeth were chattering as he kept trying to light a cigarette, 'I forgot my way home, so I just thought I'd sit here and wait for Pierre,' his voice trembled. We sat down on either side of him, Cam lit his cigarette and popped it in his mouth and I put my arms around his shoulders.

'How are you feeling?'

'I've lost my handbag with my keys in it.'

'Where did you last have it?' I had gone to a parallel universe. I was having a lost handbag conversation with a guy.

'In the club I think.'

I jumped up, 'I'll go and check, will it still be open?'

'Yes someone will still be there, but I'll go,' Cam went to stand up but he had taken his shoes off and I could see two angry looking blisters.

'No, don't worry it will only take me a couple of minutes,' I hurried off down the road. When I got to the club, it looked deserted, but when I pushed the door, it swung open. I walked into the darkened bar area, there wasn't a soul in sight. I looked over to the pillar where we had been standing and as my eyes adjusted I could see something pale underneath a table. I went over and bent down – sure enough, it was a pink satin clutch bag. I picked it up and went to leave, when all of a sudden I heard a groaning sound. I turned towards a gloomy corner of the bar and saw Jorges sitting on a chair, his head thrown back as a familiar feathered headpiece bobbed up and down between his legs. I froze as he let out a guttural moan and before I had a chance to creep away, Stephanie turned around and his face registered total shock as he realised he had an audience, then abject horror as he realised it was me.

'Hey, who's there? You want to come and join the party?' Sleaze was sitting with his limp dick hanging over his open fly. I turned around and walked quietly out of the door. If the situation between Stephanie and me had been bad before, I had a feeling it had just progressed to all out war.

TWELVE

'Thank you very much for choosing to fly with British Airways, we hope you've had a good flight.'

The cold damp air hit me the minute I got off the plane at Manchester Airport. It was late morning and I had flown straight in from Spain to go to Beverley's to record our final recap show. There hadn't seemed much point in coming home straight after Carnival so I had hung out with Cam and Bart for another week, giving me the time to look around Barcelona and the surrounding area. The weather had been beautiful and the winter sun had given me a healthy glow which I could feel literally fading away as the grey March day enveloped me. Even just stepping back onto English turf was making my heart heavy and I spent the cab journey staring sadly out of the window.

Beverley greeted me at the door warmly this time, and I actually felt quite pleased to see her. Even though her pristine abode was yet again a mass of grubby cables and recording equipment with strange men in musty old waterproof jackets making themselves coffee in her kitchen, smoking in her garden and leaving the toilet seat up in her downstairs loo, she was much more relaxed. 'Enjoy Spain did you?' she piped, 'I didn't know that's where you were going when you left here.'

'Nor did I Bev,' I sighed as I followed her into the kitchen. She flicked on her Gaggenau coffee maker and nodded towards a neat little row of demitasse cups on the shelf above, 'D'you want a coffee?'

'I would love one, thank you.'

'So that was a bit spontaneous wasn't it? What made you go?'

'It was my fortieth birthday the next day.'

'Get away, I don't believe it!' I was just about to gracefully accept a compliment on my youthful appearance when Bev added, 'It was mine too!'

'Oh my god, you were born on Valentine's Day too? Doesn't it suck to be us?'

'And how!' The cups clattered loudly as they hit the marble work surface, 'Hateful state of affairs; the crappiest day of the year to be born apart from Christmas Day.'

'I'm not so sure, I think I'd have rather lived with the 'we're just going to get you one big present' syndrome.'

Beverley slid me a steaming coffee and sighed, 'I have to say, I didn't give a bugger about birthday presents in my teens. All I wanted was a two-foot high slushy card, with padded satin heart and a single red rose from the latest crush. I used to send myself flowers sometimes, how sad is that?'

'Very,' I smiled as I sipped my coffee. 'All I wanted to do was jet off to some far and distant culture that had never heard of *Hallmark Cards*. So what did you end up doing for your fortieth?'

Beverley's face clouded over, 'We went to the same bloody Chinese restaurant that we go to every year on my birthday, and I got the same perfume, the same voucher for a spa visit and a couple of grand in cash in an envelope to get myself something nice.'

'I got a vibrator from one of my friends; does that make you feel any better?'

'It would be more fun than my bloody husband I'm sure,' she grabbed a dishcloth and started to wipe away barely perceptible damp rings that the coffee cups had left on the counter.

More self-deprecation was obviously needed so I stepped it up a gear. 'Remember that call I got when I left here last time? They were giving me the sack, *which* is the real reason I got on the plane,' she spun around and went to say something but I held up my hand to silence her, 'and if that wasn't bad enough I missed my surprise fortieth birthday party on the Saturday, slept with a twenty-seven year-old guy, thought I had pubic lice, and ended up pissing off both the local lesbian dominatrix and the bitchiest drag queen this side of the Atlantic.' As I jumped down from my stool and curtseyed, Beverly looked at me in amazement, 'You didn't!'

'Nah; just thought I'd tell a few lies and cheer you up. Of course I did.'

Her mouth was still hanging open in shock when we got called through to the lounge where the crew had set up for our final chat, 'Just say it's all been fabulous, you are going to throw away the scales and from now on it's going to be happy, healthy Beverley all the way,' I winked at her, 'then you and I are going out for a birthday drink.'

Beverley was a dream, and after a few retakes purely for the benefit of the neurotic producer, it was done. My television career was officially over and I felt strangely elated. We wandered back into the kitchen chatting and I stopped in my tracks at the sight of a crop-topped, hipster-clad, fake-tanned chicken bone with jet black hair extensions perched on a stool filing her false nails.

'This is my friend Tanya,' Beverley sounded strangely awkward, 'Tanya this is Alex.'

'Best friend actually!' the chicken bone squeaked. 'I've just come to pick up the shoes you said you'd lend me Bev.' Beverley murmured something and then disappeared; I felt a jab in the ribs and turned to Tanya who was leaning towards me in a conspiratorial fashion.

'I just wish Beverley could be happy with being a bit on the cuddly side. I mean, men are meant to like that aren't they? I would put weight on if I could, but I just can't. No matter how much I pack away – chocolates, biscuits, cakes – I just stay exactly the same as I was when I was seventeen. It's been like that since we were best friends at school - Beverley always trying to lose weight and me always eating. I can't help it that I am naturally thin. I've never even been on a diet....'

This self-absorbed drivel continued until Beverley walked back in carrying a shoe box; at which point Tanya cut off mid-sentence and hit Beverley with a smile as fake as her tan, 'Alex was just saying you've done really well,' she cooed. My face must have registered total shock as Beverley shoved the box into Tanya's hands and said curtly, 'We just have to finish up here. Have a good time tonight.'

As Tanya tottered out into the wintry afternoon with one last animated swoosh of her man-made mane, a tall, expensively clad, forty-something man with receding dark curly hair swaggered through the front door - Laurence! He had a mobile in each hand and obnoxious written all over his high-rise forehead. I was no more impressed with Beverley's husband than I was with her best buddy.

After cutting at least five deals without pausing for breath so as to leave us in awe of his pulsating business acumen, his attention was abruptly taken away from the world of carpet tiles and drinking water machines by Haley - our nubile nineteen-year-old researcher who wandered into the kitchen to say goodbye. The sight of her bra-less and exceptionally pert boobs caused his eyes to shoot out on stalks. A man-eater in the making, Haley gave him a doe-eyed look and miraculously managed to make her nipples stick out like a couple of wing nuts. You could almost see all the blood from Laurence's brain draining directly into his penis as she shoved her hands into her jeans pockets, pulling them so low you could see the top of her black lace thong.

It was cringe-worthy; this was a man with teenage daughters. I immediately ushered Hayley out and said my goodbyes to a very awkward crew who didn't really know what to say regarding my recent demise. As I hugged each one to my bosom, there were a few mumbled *good lucks* and earnest promises of a 'get together' very soon but as I waved them off, I knew the likelihood of that ever happening was exceptionally remote. Life would take over, they would be onto the next production and I would be history. I walked back into the house. The tension in the air was palpable and a very stony-faced Laurence emerged from the kitchen grunting something about an important meeting and not being back until late. I looked at him coolly as he went past. His eyes met mine for a millisecond before he quickly averted them away. I had absolutely no respect or time for men like him, and it obviously showed.

Beverley emerged from the depths of her huge American fridge with a bottle of ice cold champagne, 'D'you mind if we have a drink here? I'm not really up to going out.'

'That would be lovely. You okay?'

She shrugged as she popped the cork and poured the champagne clumsily into two tall glasses. It bubbled over and a puddle of champagne spread across the black granite worktop. Unperturbed, she pushed a glass towards me, 'Different day, same shit. Cheers!'

I raised my glass to hers and chinked. She looked older than she had twenty minutes previously; her stress evident in every line on her face, her jaw was tighter and even her lips seemed thinner. I wanted to tell her to leave him, that if she could find the courage to just get out there and be on her own for a while she would experience freedom and a lightness of spirit. Her kids were grown so why stay? But these were my thoughts based on my experiences and observations. She wasn't asking me for advice, and when it came to marriage, I was in no way qualified to give it. So I reached over, grabbed her mobile phone and tapped my number into her contacts, 'We're Aquarian soul sisters darling, and rather than slice our thumbs open and mingle blood in an act of everlasting sisterhood, I thought I'd give you my number should you ever need it. Far more civilised.'

'You're alright you know, a bit bloody barking, but alright.'

'Why do I get the impression that coming from you, that's high praise indeed?'

She grinned and poured more champagne in our glasses, 'How do you feel about being forty?'

'I've never really given it a second thought to be honest. I think my friends and family are more concerned about it than me.' I took a sip, 'They think I've left everything *too late*.'

'What exactly?'

'They would all be a lot happier if I was happily settled down with The Man of My Dreams and cultivating a herb garden in Dorset.'

Beverley gave a derisive snort and downed a large mouthful of champagne.

'I have no responsibility and it freaks them out – no children, no mortgage and no proper job - well, I certainly don't have that anymore, do I?

'I still can't believe they sacked you.'

'It's alright, probably a good thing in many ways.'

'D'you pop happy pills or something?'

'What makes you ask?'

'You're just so bloody carefree.'

'Not always Beverley, we all have our days.'

'Well, I envy you. At least you can take whatever road you fancy.'

As I sipped my champagne, I tasted cava and my mind went back to a very nice beachside lunch under a glorious blue sky with a newly discovered kindred spirit.

'You look miles away,'

I smiled, 'I was Beverley, but not that far.'

THIRTEEN

'You're what?' Mel spluttered.

It was a couple of days later and I was back in London having lunch with Mel in Café Rouge in Chiswick. Her chic and business-like image ruined by the chip en route to her mouth, which was now suspended in mid-air dripping mayonnaise down the front of her slate grey Armani jacket.

'Moving to Spain,' I handed her a paper napkin and gestured to her chest, 'and you wonder why I hate lending you clothes.'

She dipped the napkin in her Evian and started rubbing aimlessly over her boobs. 'But what will you do there?'

'I don't know, I need to change direction but I don't just want to jump into something,' I swirled a piece of broccoli around in the hollandaise sauce that was covering my salmon and popped it into my mouth. 'I want some time to figure out what it is that makes me tick, and a sabbatical may be just the thing.'

Mel looked sceptical; this was a very alien concept to her more orderly brain. She pushed her cod in batter around her plate and decided to change the subject, 'How's your salmon?'

'Great, wanna try some?'

She speared a piece with her fork and chewed it slowly, 'It's lovely. Mine's a bit dry.'

I smiled to myself. Mel suffers from Menu Envy. Whenever we go out for a meal she always insists her food is crap and mine is fabulous, and I have to say, more often than not she's right. It started in our twenties when we were on holiday in Portugal. Inspired by a fabulous grilled squid I had at a beach-side shack in the afternoon, Mel decided to follow suit at a different restaurant in the evening. Their approach was a little more rustic. Whilst I was dipping into a fragrant *cataplana*, Mel was fighting back the nausea as her squid oozed a fishy slime that was threatening to take over her entire plate. We ended up sharing, and have been doing so ever since. Today was no exception; I pushed my plate into the centre of the table, 'I don't know why you just don't order the same as me and be done with it? You know I can work a menu.'

I watched her in amusement as she added a dollop of hollandaise to her stain collection.

'How are you going to afford to live there?' She sat back and shook her head, 'Have you thought this through?'

'What do you think I was doing out there Mel?'

'Partying?'

'Please don't mention the word party,' I winced. It was still a very sensitive subject. My mum had quite rightly made me send apology cards to everyone who had been invited.

Mel ran her hands through her dark hair and frowned, 'You don't know how hard it was to persuade your mum not to ring the police. What were you thinking Alex?'

'It was all very spontaneous.'

'Thoughtless.'

I sighed; I wasn't going to win this, whichever way I played it. Mel was a lawyer and arguments always had a habit of going her way. I gestured to the waiter for another couple of glasses of Sancerre, then thought better of it and asked for a bottle, 'Well, I'm glad I went, because I've found somewhere I think I really like. I fit in there.'

'Alex! You selfish bitch! I cannot believe you just said that. Do you know how much effort went into organising that party for you?'

'Of course I do, and I am so sorry I let everyone down,' I took a slug of my wine, 'but it wasn't like I did it on purpose. I just never thought in a million years that any of you would do something like that for me.'

'Why? We love you, why wouldn't we?'

'Because you're usually so wrapped up in your own lives. I can go for weeks and not hear from a soul, and yet the moment there's a crisis, it's 'Good old Alex' time. I have no problem with being there to help my mates, it's just that lately, that's all there is.'

'That is so unfair! We do see each other,' Mel's face was initially aghast but then it softened and she sighed, 'well maybe not as much as we should do.'

'Mel, I'm not laying a guilt trip on you. It's life. I lost you when we were twenty-five. You got married and had the kids; you went from strength to strength at work. That takes time and commitment. I'm proud of you and I love you dearly, but I can't just keep sitting on the sidelines. I need to get out there and work out what it is I want from life - my life, not everybody else's.' I said gently.

'I had no idea you were so lonely.'

'Oh for god's sake, I'm not asking you to feel sorry for me. I'm lucky I *can* go and do this. What's the alternative? Sitting in every night watching *Eastenders* and re-runs of *Sex and the City?'*

'How about going out on the pull with other single women?'

'Mel, do you even know me? I have nothing in common with women whose only conversation is about finding a bloke, or whining about their last one, and as for going out on the pull? How desperate is that? This isn't a whim. It's been building up for a while now. The final straw was losing my job. How long do you hang around in a life you are unhappy with before you do something about it? I'm just dealing with it, that's all.'

'And you think this place is the place for you?'

'For the foreseeable future – yes - as odd as this place is, I really like it. Its very camp, but I just have this feeling that this is where I need to go. And who wants to be in the UK at the moment? All you ever hear are bloody prophecies of doom and gloom.'

'Well it is serious Alex; this financial crisis is going to impact on us all.'

'There are bonuses to being me then?'

'Eh?'

'No job to lose, no home to have re-possessed and I certainly don't have investments.'

'Well, how are you going to survive over there then?'

'I'm owed around five grand by Utopia, another three or four for a few magazine articles and other bits and pieces. I'm going to sell my car, put the majority of my clothes on eBay and do a car boot sale. That will give me survival money and breathing space for a while. I'll work on ideas and ride out the storm living the simple life in the sun.' She didn't look convinced, so I threw in a little extra bargaining power, 'It's very cheap there.'

'You'll just spend double,' she sighed as she poured wine into our glasses. 'Oh my God, the Spanish make shoes – you're doomed. You never know, maybe you'll meet someone there,' she looked at me hopefully.

I raised an eyebrow, 'Mel, you're turning into my mother. I'm crap at it, remember?'

Mel had been witness to some pretty bad choices on my part over the years; the majority of my boyfriends ranged from mildly dysfunctional to the fully blown nut cases that most sensible women would body swerve. I was always willing to give them a chance, convinced that I could excavate positive qualities in them. This willingness to believe the best in people often had dire consequences, the most notable being a conman who, despite my worldly ways, managed to hoodwink me so effectively I lost the only property I had ever owned – but that is another story for another time. Every now and then a decent guy would come along but as a result of all the bad experiences, I had built my barriers so high they found it impossible to break through. Only the bad ones seemed to possess the right tools to do that. Mel could only look on in horror as I embarked on yet another foolhardy escapade with a good-looking twit who would bring me nothing but heartbreak, and then listen in disbelief as I managed to apportion most of the blame on myself. Now gradually over the years the gaps between relationships were getting longer, my barriers were virtually insurmountable and to all intents and purposes I was a confirmed singleton.

'You're just crap at keeping hold of the good ones. What about that South African plastic surgeon?'

'Mr Scalpel? I'd forgotten all about him. He was quite sweet really. He told Penny she needed an eye job – on her wedding day.'

'Should have kept hold of him,' Mel smirked; she hated Penny with a vengeance. 'I can't say the same about The Plank though, what a bloody psycho he was!'

I had to concede that Mel had a point with this one. I had an off and on fling with a guy who used to be a doorman at a nightclub we frequented in our early twenties. He was a member of the Territorial Army and used to run survival courses. Mel and I coined him The Plank after one spectacularly weird night when he suggested I went home, change into 'something comfortable' and meet him in the car park after the club closed. Assuming I was in for a night of unbridled passion, I turned up wearing black lacy underwear under a faux fur coat (it was the 80s okay!). Imagine my surprise when he led me over to a nearby building site, made me crawl under a fence and help him nick timber for his extension. When we did eventually have sex in the back of his van, it was somewhat disconcerting to know that what was really turning him on wasn't so much my lingerie, as his stash of illegal two-by-two plywood. It put a whole new perspective on the term *woody*.

'What in hell's name did you ever see in him?' Mel waved over to the waiter for the dessert menu.

'He was six-foot-six. The only time I want to look down at a man is if I'm on top.'

'Would you like to order coffee ladies?' I turned to see our young waiter blushing furiously.

'I think I'll have a nice big black one,' I winked at him.

Mel rolled her eyes, 'I'll have a Crème Brulé and a decaf cappuccino.' The minute he disappeared, she nudged me, 'You're appalling. He's probably got aunties your age.'

'Sitges is obviously rubbing off on me.'

'And while we are on the subject, why does my best friend want to move to a town that just so happens to be the gay capital of the Med? Is there anything you want to tell me?'

'Okay, you've got me, ' I grabbed her hand, 'the reason I'm leaving is I can't bear this any longer, I love you Mel and know you can never be mine, so I'm going off to Sitges where I can crop my hair, throw away the make-up, don the dungarees and start fixing cars.'

There was a thud as our coffees were plunked on the table.

'Actually I shouldn't joke; I do have a little situation to deal with when I get back there.' I told Mel about the afternoon with Bubbles.

'You're a prat,' she looked at me sadly, 'haven't you found anyone who has rocked your boat recently? It's been years since I've seen you even vaguely interested in anyone.'

'Nope.'

'There is a man out there for you, Alex.'

'Yeah – smack bang in the middle of a mid-life crisis and taking dating tips from Charlie Sheen.'

'You are so cynical. You just need to get out there and start flirting, get your *mojo* back.'

'Last time I saw my *mojo* it was wearing shoulder pads.'

'How about a younger bloke?'

'Well, I had sex with a bisexual twenty-something guy on my birthday. Does that count?'

'You didn't?' Mel's eyes widened in horror which spurred me on to totally freak her out.

'His name was Zane. He had pink hair and more body piercings than pores.'

'I think *you're* having a bloody mid-life crisis.'

'That's it. You're a genius. Thank you,' I gave Mel a huge smacker on the cheek.

'Pardon?'

'Mid-life crisis! How bloody marvellous! I'm Shirley Valentine without the bad perm and miserable husband.' I stood up and waved my arms around dramatically, 'Boldly the forty-year-old singleton strode forth into her future, the pages of her open book fluttering in the Mediterranean breeze...'

'Sshh!' Mel pulled me back down, 'You've lost the plot.'

'I know, fabulous isn't it?'

'You've always had a tendency to do this you know?'

'What?'

'Make me feel totally bloody boring when I'm trying to talk

some sense into you,' Mel smiled.

'You can't help being a straight-laced up-her-bum lawyer,' I cooed.

'And you're always going to be irresponsible-head-in-the-clouds...' she paused for second, 'what can I call you now – apart from exasperating?'

'Ah ha, and there we have it your honour, unlike your good self, the defendant doesn't have a title upon which to hang her hat. She is not a lawyer, tinker, tailor or candlestick maker. She is not a mother, mistress or a wife. She *was* a presenter, *was* a make-up artist, in fact, *was* many other things along the way. And now she finds herself at a crossroads – mid-life crisis or opportunity for change? I put it to you, your Lordship that neither is a crime in the eyes of the law.'

'And that's where you rest your case?'

'Yes. I am merely moving swiftly on before the rot sets in and I get all bitter and twisted.'

'I'm going to miss you,' she looked so sad.

'I'm going to miss you too,' I held her hand, 'and by the way, stroke of genius telling my mum that vibrator was a back massager, only trouble is she has taken it home with her.'

'No way!'

'Oh yes!'

'I was livid when you told me what that silly cow Penny put on that note. How dare she?'

Back on track, Mel and I spent a very happy afternoon, gossiping – well – bitching about Penny.

FOURTEEN

'That should do it, thanks Mum,' I pushed the storage unit door shut and padlocked it.

We were both covered from head to toe in dust and grime. It had taken us a week to pack up my flat, separating the essentials I would need in Spain from the other two piles – storage and excess baggage - all the stuff I would never look at, have a use for, or even think about again. We had raised nearly four hundred pounds at a car boot sale, sold my old Saab for a couple of thousand and I'd made about another thousand selling off all my smart clothes, bags and shoes on eBay. The rest I had donated to my local charity shop. I felt liberated and lighter of spirit – shame I couldn't say the same about a certain matriarch who wasn't enjoying the process one little bit and was being decidedly grumpy.

'Where are the men when you need them eh?' my mum brushed off a cobweb from her shoulder. 'If your dad had been around we would have done this in double quick time.'

The usual lump appeared in my throat at the mention of my dad: he had died three years before of a heart attack, and it still hurt to think about him. I looked at my mum, she was dabbing her eyes.

'Well, we did a good job, who needs them?' I regretted the statement the minute it left my lips.

'You do, Alex; I worry about you being on your own.'

'Mum, you've done so well over the past two days, do you have to start now?'

'I am your mother, I'm allowed to worry.'

I got it in the neck for the entire journey back to Hampshire, where we were going to have a Goodbye Do with the family, in other words a great opportunity for everyone to have a little nag at the renegade of the pack. But at least there was a chance I could swipe my vibrator back before somebody enlightened my mum as to its real role in life.

When we arrived, I dumped my suitcase in my old bedroom. It had been here I'd lost my virginity – not that you could, for a second, ever imagine this had been the scene of a passionate encounter. A far cry from the poster clad cavern of my teens, the room had been 'mummified'. Flounced and frilled to within an inch of its life. Everything from the curtains to the valance around the bottom of the bed was awash with pink roses. The carpet was now green and immaculate, I could remember pleading for a cream shag pile when I was about thirteen, and promising to vacuum it everyday to keep it clean. Within two months it was a mass of make-up stains and curling tong burns – just one in a long list of the casualties incurred when teenage girls Get Ready to Go Out.

Our usual destination was *The Rec* - a muddy sports field where the dilapidated old football huts provided the perfect spot to get down to a bit of serious flirting. Clad invariably in each other's clothes - never enough of each other's clothes if you asked my dad's opinion - we would hang out there for hours, giggling far too loudly at the boys' oafish antics and eventually copping off with the least puerile of the species for a marathon snogging session. This saliva fest was interspersed with trying to keep their grubby hands away from our bras and wondering what the hell was going on in their pants. And, if they were a good 'kisser', being only too aware of what was going on in yours.

I lay on the bed and stared at the Artex ceiling - the one thing that hadn't changed since The Big Event - and I went back in time. I was eighteen years old when I finally gave in to the amorous attentions of Simon Ward. I had kept him at bay for four months before I went on the Pill and put him on a fourteen-day countdown. Luckily for us, as the big date loomed, my parents decided to visit my uncle in Eastbourne for the weekend, taking my little sister with them. Simon gave my brother ten quid to bugger off, which he was only too happy to do. A whole ten pounds to treat his little hooligan friends to a few cans of *Hoffmeister* lager – with the added bonus that they could kick the empties around the pub car park. A perfect Saturday night!

Innocence and lack of experience on both sides didn't make my deflowering the most memorable experience. I think Simon had been furtively reading too many of his dad's dirty books and was disappointed there wasn't a blood-stained sheet to brandish out of the window. As far as I was concerned, the absence of such a messy trophy was just one less thing to deal with before Mum and Dad got home at teatime on Sunday. But with a little practice and dedication, and my parent's love of weekend jaunts, we got into the swing of things and spent the next two years honing our technique at every given opportunity.

Then as soon as I left college, I was offered the job in Nairobi and Simon's fate was sealed. Looking back, he was probably the one who ticked most of my boxes. He had a thing about redheads, loved travelling and had the best sense of humour of any man I have ever dated. But he simply came along too early. I was determined to fly the nest and Africa was a dream destination - safaris or Southampton? No contest. I left Simon and we slowly lost contact. Apparently he ended up in Australia where for all I know, he is probably married with four kids and a bald patch.

I looked around; it was disconcerting being back at home. Everything seemed so possible when I was in my teens. I had a head full of dreams and no real comprehension of where life was going to take me. Maybe it *was* a bit worrying that I still didn't.

My mobile phone buzzed. It was a text from Beverley asking how I was. I smiled. We had only known each other one month and yet I couldn't believe how fond of her I was after such a short time. I dialled her number.

'Hi there cosmic twin, how's it all going?'

'I can't believe it's the middle of March,' she wailed, 'I'm going to have to start fitting into my summer clothes soon.'

Beverley wasn't quite through with the weight fixation.

'Its five degrees today Beverley, don't think you should be digging out your denim cut-offs just yet.'

'I don't have any.'

'Thank fuck for that. Alarms should go off when anyone over the age of twenty-five starts pulling a pair over their ankles.'

'Only two more days,' she squeaked, 'are you excited?'

'Absolutely, and Beverley you were part of the process oddly enough. It was when I was chatting with you I decided to make the move. So thank you. Now all I have to do is get through the Family Do, then I'm off and running.'

'You lucky girl,' she sighed, 'Laurence is putting me through hell at the moment. He just keeps picking fights – when he's here that is.'

Could she really not be aware? This was the classic behaviour of a man that was up to something. We chatted about crap for another ten minutes until her twins Alice and Heidi arrived for a rare weekend home. We said our goodbyes and I thought about Laurence.

Married men are a particular sore point of mine. Not all of them, just the ones who can't keep it in their pants. Believe you me, over the years my friends and I have met quite a few of the following stereotypes.

First, we have Mickey the Martyr – he who has been hanging on in there stoically with his witch of a wife, because he is such a good guy. He has ignored his own needs selflessly until this moment, because you (lucky old you) have changed everything. All of a sudden he can see a brighter future; this is what real love is all about, blah, blah, blah! Mickey should be avoided at all costs. The right time for him to leave his miserable life will never arrive. You will be sitting at home alone, on every Christmas Day for the foreseeable future, gazing at the phone with only your cat and a couple of mince pies for company whilst he of course, is 'suffering' elsewhere.

Then we have Billy the Bullshitter. This one is a slippery toad with his wedding ring safely hidden away in his jacket pocket. He will treat you like a princess and say anything to get you in the sack. Should he succeed, he will make all sorts of promises and disappear into the night with your number and no intention of calling. The next time you see him, he will be pushing a heavily laden trolley around the local supermarket with his army of children and pregnant wife. You will stand rooted to the spot whilst he disappears at lightening speed into a freezer chest after a packet of chicken nuggets.

Lastly there's Terry Toe Rag. No fuss, no emotional shit, just sex. When you meet his wife, and you will, because he gets a buzz off it, you'll want to curl up and die because she looks SO nice, the sort of woman you could be friends with. What were you thinking when you caved in and slept with this ego on legs?

Oh yes! Married men are the bane of the single woman's life, which is probably why I haven't ever wanted to acquire one of my own.

That'll be enough cynicism for now Alex, back to the Family Do.

After attempting to hang a few things up in the wardrobe – an impossible task due to my mum's nostalgic collection of size ten 80s clothing in various pastel hues, I wandered downstairs to the ordeal that awaited in the kitchen – The Battle of the Control Freaks. In the smelly corner we had me and my rather pungent collection of Indian spices, and in the sweet corner there was Mother, waiting to take her relationship with egg whites and sugar to dizzying new heights.

Only idiots would attempt to cook Lamb Rogan Josh and Pavlova in the same kitchen on the same night when one person just can't stop fretting about the smell of curry wafting through her house, and the other one can't keep her sarcastic gob shut. But my mum still laboured under the illusion that this girlie bonding would be 'fun'.

I knew it would end in tears, and it did. About midnight, having cling-filmed up the serving hatch to the dining room, my mum stormed upstairs because I pointed out that the ambitious combination of Sharon Fruit, Banana and Guavas with a Kumquat Coulis and Caramelised Pumpkin might scare the living shit out of some of the family's more delicate palates, and that I was sure that the contestant on *Masterchef* only made it in desperation. Either that or he was obviously on drugs.

By the next morning all was forgotten and by midday the family arrived *en masse*. I steeled myself, pasted on my smile and circulated – a dumb-arsed wildebeest amongst a pride of hungry lions who took it in turns to come up and have a little bite. My godmother drew first blood.

'So Alex, you're still persisting with this bohemian lifestyle – you're not getting any younger you know. It will all catch up with you eventually darling. You need to put down some roots somewhere.'

'Maybe I'll put down roots in Spain?'

'They don't like us you know – the Spanish. They think we're terribly common.'

'Aunty Joan, I'm not doing *huevos y patatas* in Fuengirola, I'm moving to a very cultured, cosmopolitan little town near Barcelona.'

'Barcelona! Fuengirola! You're not Spanish so why live there? What's 'hwaybos epatatas' for god's sake?''

As I went to explain that it meant 'eggs and chips', she wafted off in search of another G&T. I sighed angrily. This was going to be a very long afternoon.

'Don't listen to her, she's only jealous!' My Uncle Bob slithered over and slipped his arm around my shoulders. 'What wouldn't I do to be young again eh?' I flinched as his fingers casually brushed against my left breast. I stepped away and glared at him, 'Well that just isn't going to happen is it UNCLE Bob?' I turned around and bumped straight into my sister, who gripped my arm and dragged me away hissing 'Don't leave me with him, he just pinched my arse and I've spilt bloody curry all over the back of Mum's new sofa.'

'So wouldn't be you,' I grinned 'I know what went into that sauce and it ain't going anywhere in a hurry.'

'It'll be you she curses then,' my sister laughed before darting off to rescue her three-year-old who was crawling towards the front door. It had been left ajar by the smokers who had congregated in the front garden and were currently flicking ash over my Mum's azaleas.

'Alex come over here and sit down with me,' a weak raspy voice found its way over Glen Campbell belting out *Rhinestone Cowboy*. I looked over to the corner of the room where my oldest surviving relative was propped up on an armchair, her lower limbs buried underneath a garish acrylic tiger-print blanket.

'D'you fancy a sherry Aunty Dolly?'

'Go on then – just to be sociable,' she winked. 'Has your mother got any cherries?'

'I'll see,' I laughed, 'I won't be able to invite you out to Spain if you're going to bastardise their national drink in such a horrendous fashion though.'

'Don't swear in front of Dolly, Alex, really!' Even though she was holding court at the opposite side of the room, Mum had ears like blasted satellite dishes.

I looked back at Dolly who shrugged and mouthed 'Just get the sherry.' I grinned as I walked off to the utility room that had been turned into the 'bar' for the day. In amongst the vast array of ghastly 'comedy' drinks that had been lurking in the drinks cabinet for decades I found not only a bottle of *Harveys Bristol Cream* and a jar of Maraschino cherries, but a cellophane bag of paper cocktail umbrellas. I toddled back over to Dolly who chuckled when she saw her pimped up sherry glass.

'You're a good girl,' she rasped in her South London accent, 'always been a bit nutty, but heart of gold.'

I hugged her and kissed her crinkled cheek, 'You were my inspiration Aunty Dolly. You always did your own thing.'

'Never had you down as following me into spinsterhood though Alex. I always thought there would be someone out there brave enough to take you on.'

'Aunty Dolly! Don't you jump on the bloody family bandwagon – I'm forty not ninety.'

'I'm ninety-three,' she said proudly, 'and I still haven't given up. There's a gentleman at the home called Leonard, who keeps flirting with me. He's only eighty-four. What do you think of that?'

'More's the point Dolly, what do you think of him?'

'He's a bit of a miserable old bugger. Always whining on about something - bit depressing really.'

'But what do you think he'll be like between the sheets?' I nudged her gently as she started to wheeze with laughter. 'D'you think he'll be a bit of a goer?'

'Are you alright Dolly?' My godmother came marching over just as the Maraschino cherry in Dolly's drink decided to lodge itself in her windpipe. I was pushed out of the way as Aunty Joan engaged Dolly in a very efficient Heimlich Manoeuvre which sent the cherry spinning across the room where it landed in a plate of Twiglets.

'What on earth were you saying Alex? You nearly killed Great Aunt Dolly?' Aunty Joan huffed as she puffed up the cushions behind Dolly, who rolled her eyes at me and sighed as Joan then proceeded to wrap the blanket around her legs so tightly, any attempt at escape would have been futile.

For the next two hours I wandered methodically around the room ensuring I spoke to everyone and feeling more and more like an alien with every passing conversation. They weren't bad people – they just didn't understand this little maverick in their midst.

But one person was so noticeably absent I had to keep stopping myself from looking for him. Social occasions were my dad's forte. He revelled in playing *mein host*. My brother had stepped into his shoes and was doing an admirable job of keeping everybody's glasses full but you just couldn't escape it – every corner of the house held memories of my dad. The last time we were altogether here it had been after his funeral, the memory of which sent me scampering up to my room at one point because I just couldn't hold back the tears. When I had composed myself and cleaned up my face, I went to go back downstairs and was halted in my tracks by the sound of sobbing from the bathroom. I knocked on the door and whispered 'Mum'. There was a muffled response and eventually she opened the door, 'You'd better get downstairs Alex; they'll be wondering where we are. I'll be down in a minute.'

'You'd better be, they're all revving themselves up for dessert,' I smiled sadly. Poor Mum, it was harder for her than any of us. She had a chap who she went out with from time to time, but despite being happy that she had companionship, it was still a little difficult for us to accept him into the family fold. Now on top of everything, I was buggering off too.

*

'Have a good trip darling,' my mum squeezed the air from my lungs as she hugged me in front of the departure gate at Gatwick. 'Send me some nice postcards.'

'You know there is utterly zero chance of that happening, but I will call. Now did you label up all my clothes and attach elastic to my mittens?'

'Stop being so facetious.' She suddenly looked very tearful, 'Why are you always getting on planes?'

'Because it beats trying to swim there,' I grabbed my bags, kissed her cheek, and then I remembered a little thing I hadn't sorted out, 'Mum, I couldn't find my – erm – back massager in your room, do you still have it?'

'Oh no, I hope you don't mind, but I loaned it to Rita, she strained her back gardening a week ago and it's really helping. In fact, I was going to ask where I could get a few more, they'd make fantastic Christmas presents for your aunts, and Shirley at the bank has an awful time with her neck, it would be perfect.'

I stood in stunned silence. Had my mum ever seen a penis? How in hell's name had she managed to conceive three times without ever taking it all in so to speak? Was her mate Rita equally as naïve or laughing at her? I proceeded to wimp out of the explanation, 'I'll find out Mum, but I think they're really expensive.'

'Maybe Boots do a cheap version.'

I smiled brightly and nodded, 'You never know.'

'I love you Alex, be careful.'

'I love you too Mum, don't worry, I'm a big girl and I'm doing the right thing, luck's on my side, I can feel it.'

Flight EZ5132 to Barcelona hit severe turbulence somewhere over the Pyrenees and the little girl next to me who had stuffed herself with a box of Pringles, a Kit Kat, a can of Fanta and a cheese and ham sandwich, threw up all over my legs. Can anyone tell me if that is a sign of good luck anywhere in the world?

FIFTEEN

When it came to finding an apartment, or should I say *piso,* the universe was definitely on my side and it couldn't have been timelier as I was starting to feel very uncomfortable at Cam's. While I was in the UK he had started to date Enrique. By the time I returned, the Argentinean diva had virtually moved into Cam's place and was making it only too obvious that three was a crowd. Despite protestations from Cam to the contrary, after five days of trailing around with the majority of Sitges seventy-seven property agents and getting very discouraged by the vast array of hideous rental apartments, I struck gold. I was sitting having a coffee at the Buena Vida Bar, when I glanced up. A man was draping a sign over a balcony - *PISO EN AQUILAR* - a front line apartment for rent? I shot out of my seat, and ran over to the building and caught him as he left. I pointed up at the balcony and then back to me.

He obligingly opened the door and took me upstairs to the first floor. As I walked into the apartment I gasped, there in front of me was a picture postcard view of the sea, and there to the right of the balcony was a huge palm tree. The property agent looked at me as if I were crazy as I ran about the apartment like a thing possessed. There was a small kitchen, two bedrooms, the hugest lounge and a balcony at the back with a washing machine. One of the bedrooms was en-suite and there was another bathroom just off the hall. I was stunned; it was so spacious. This was exactly what I wanted.

The rent wasn't the cheapest in the world, in fact it was exactly the same as I had been paying in London, but when he said he was showing it to another person later that day I high-tailed it to my bank and was back at the agency with a bundle of cash an hour later. After signing contracts and providing him with all the necessary details, unbelievably I actually had the key in my hot little hand three days later. I had kept quiet as I didn't want to jinx things but I was bursting to tell Cam so I called him and asked him to meet me at *Playa San Sebastian* for lunch. I bought a cold bottle of cava and found a couple of glasses in one of the kitchen cupboards then waited on the balcony. When I saw him approach I shouted down and he looked up.

'What the hell are you doing up there Moll?'

'Press *Uno Segundo* and you'll find out,' I trilled.

'Oh my God it's fabulous!' he screamed as he walked through the door, 'Don't tell me you've rented this.'

'Yep,' I said proudly as I prised the cork out of the cava bottle. 'Isn't it wicked?'

'And expensive I've no doubt; did you rob a bank this morning?'

'It was more than I wanted to pay, but look – I have a palm tree. I've always wanted a palm tree.'

'Oh that makes it worth it,' he said sarcastically, 'I never had you down as a tree hugger.'

'In honour of *Tio Pepe*, I'm going to call him Pete the Palm. He's going to look out for me, aren't you Pete?'

Pete's leaves rustled in agreement.

We went and sat on the balcony and people watched. The sea was crystalline blue and there wasn't a cloud in the sky. It was just too perfect. A tear trickled down my face. Cam looked over, 'Hey, you okay?'

'Yes, it's just that five weeks ago, I couldn't have dreamed I'd be living somewhere like this.'

'Destiny has called you, it was obviously meant to be.'

'If I can't find inspiration here, where can I?' I turned and looked back into the apartment. Most Spanish rentals were full of hideously dark and overly ornate mahogany furniture that were not designed for comfort. Here, the décor was minimalist with the occasional ethnic twist – perfect. Admittedly if you looked closer the cream sofa was fraying a little, and some of the tiles were chipped on the mosaic table, but I loved it, and with the view I had – who gave a shit?

That night Cam and an unusually animated Enrique helped me move my suitcases, and then zipped around to a local shop to get me a welcome pack of basic groceries and cleaning stuff. Cam offered to stay and help, but I declined. All I really wanted was a little space and time out. Plus, Enrique obviously felt he had done his bit and was getting more sullen by the second.

I waved them goodbye and spent my first evening unpacking, cleaning and rearranging everything the way I wanted it. After cooking my first meal – poached eggs on disgusting sliced white bread called *Bimbo*, washed down with a half bottle of cava, I decided to have a quiet night in – apart from the sound of the waves, the silence was deafening. All my music and books were en route from the UK and I had no Internet connection, so I flicked on the television and channel hopped. After watching twenty minutes of an ancient John Wayne movie dubbed in Spanish, the amusement wore off and I remembered that I hated westerns. I attempted to follow the news and finished off my telly-fest with ten minutes of a Catalan game show that was so dire I gave up the ghost, finished the cava and hit the sack. It was ten o'clock but thanks to the power of the bubbles I slept like a baby until three when I was rudely awakened by what sounded like someone banging loudly on my door. As I focused, I realised that it was indeed banging – right above my bloody head – and whoever my neighbours were, let's just say they were both exceptionally vocal. At around four, the screaming reached a pitch similar to that of a hundred people riding Nemesis at Alton Towers and then it all went quiet. Feeling a bit voyeuristic and embarrassed, I came out from under my pillow and after fidgeting for the next half an hour, I realised that I was now a member of the wide-awake club. I padded out to the kitchen to make a cup of tea but as there were no teabags or a kettle, I had two toffee-flavoured yoghurts followed by four slices of processed cheese.

Cam and Enrique's ideas of basic necessities were weird to say the least.

This unpalatable combination ensured that I tossed and turned until seven am, when I blearily dragged myself out of bed, donned my trainers and tracksuit and headed for the *paseo*, where I joined about twenty or so health conscious locals in their early morning trek to the *Terramar*. I jogged a little self-consciously at first, all too aware of certain bits of me jiggling round and my lungs threatening to cave in. But then realised I wasn't surrounded by the super fit and my twenty second bursts of jogging followed by five minutes of walking was absolutely fine – nobody cared. Some walked, some jogged, some cycled, some even hobbled but whatever our fitness level we all had one thing in common – the sight and sound of the sea, crisp spring air and the sun gently coming up in a pale blue sky. I felt energised, focused and a little self-righteous. Who needs an expensive gym when you can do this every day?

An hour and a half later, having pounded the *paseo* and watched the rock-dwelling cats for a while, I wandered home. Some of the cafés were starting to open, but all the shops were still shut. I smiled to myself. It certainly beat running around with the masses at Waterloo, clutching a coffee and wondering whether the Northern line was working. A tiny bar to the right of my balcony was open, so I nipped upstairs, grabbed some euros and ventured into its already smoky confines. I contemplated ordering a *bikini,* but decided against it as two bites of one of those would negate the benefits of my morning walk. So I joined the locals leaning against the bar and knocked back a couple of *café solos.* As I walked out of the door, I saw a couple leaving my apartment block; he was as stocky as she was willowy, and whereas he was balding, she had a head of heavily high-lighted hair that hung halfway down her back. Both were wearing dark glasses. I suppressed a smirk; these had to be the perpetrators of my disturbed night's sleep. I hung back a little until they had disappeared around the corner and then dived upstairs to shower and change. I stood shivering under the jet for a couple of minutes, expecting the cold water to get warmer but it remained resolutely freezing. I jumped out and felt the radiators – ice cold. I went and checked the boiler – dead as a dodo. The combination of being a technical and mechanical idiot and eternal optimist means that on occasions such as this, I always naturally assume that I have pressed something stupid and that all it needs is an injection of testosterone to make things better. I rang Cam and there was no answer. Bart was on a long haul trip somewhere exotic, so I turned up on Fred and Pierre's doorstep half an hour later. They were anything but thrilled to see me.

'You 'av woken us up because you 'av cold water?' Pierre stood at his door looking dishevelled and unshaven, but even so, somewhere between getting out of bed and answering the doorbell, he had managed to light a cigarette.

'It's eleven o'clock,' I cocked my head to one side and tried to give it 'cute girlie', forgetting I was dealing with a gay man. Pierre just frowned at me.

'Get back 'ere and finish what you started,' Fred's voice bellowed down from upstairs, 'and tell whoever it is to bugger off.'

'It's Alex,' shouted Pierre.

I blanched, 'I'm so sorry,' but before I had a chance to run away, Fred came bounding down the stairs with a towel around his waist and he started laughing, 'your timing's crap, we were just about to....'

'Don't go on....' I shrieked, 'I'm so embarrassed, sorry, sorry, I'm going now.'

Even Pierre grinned at this point and gestured for me to come in, 'I will put ze kettle on, it is all gone,' he sighed and looked down at his crotch.

'Nothing new there, what's up Alex?' Fred gave a huge yawn and wandered back upstairs.

'My boiler's playing up.'

'Is that all? We'll come and have a butcher's at it for you.'

'I was hoping you'd say that.'

Despite Fred and Pierre's heroic attempts at getting my boiler to work, it was obvious that a little testosterone was not quite enough. I decided that my best course of action was to go and see my agent, and based on the fact I knew the Spanish words for water, cold and hot, I was confident I could take on this little task.

A few *aqua's, frio's* and *caliente's,* supplemented with a couple of drawings on the back of a brochure later, even if my boiler wasn't, my agent and I were cooking with gas. I had managed to learn that the word for central heating was *callefaccion*, and actually understood when he said that *un hombre* would be around after siesta to sort out my problems. I was virtually fluent.

Spurred on by my linguistic prowess, I high tailed it around to my local supermarket to get some food that I actually fancied eating. I wandered around the store intrigued by everything on offer. Supermarkets in foreign lands are a culinary wonderland. I just get drawn in. How fantastic! There's some vacuum-packed, pre-cooked potato and pimiento tortilla! Wow! Must have some of that! A paella spice mix! Put that straight in the basket. Romesco sauce! What the hell is it? Who cares, it's cheap, I'll buy three!

It almost makes one forget that they don't sell Marmite.

Suddenly in the midst of turning my palate Spanish I had an urge to make something familiar. All I wanted to christen my kitchen was a bloody great vat of chicken soup. I found celery, parsley, carrots, onions, frozen peas, garlic, lemons, chicken stock, salt and pepper. Or should I say - *apio, perejil, zanahorias, cebollas, guisantes congelados, ajo, limones, caldo, sal y pimienta.* Impressed? You won't be for much longer.

My final ingredient was a chicken, so I made my way to the butcher's counter at the back of the shop where a corpulent old butcher with a bloodied apron was lovingly wiping his cleaver. I went boldly over and requested a large chicken '*Quiero una grande polla.*' He looked suitably impressed and decided I was worthy of a little chat.

'*Te gusta polla* ?'

Did I like chicken? Bless him; he was even trying to teach me some Spanish. I nodded enthusiastically '*Si, me gusta polla mucho.*'

'*Te gusta una grande polla?*'

'*Si, me gusta una grande grande polla,*' I got into the spirit of things and held out my hands like a fisherman bragging about his latest catch. At this point a Spanish woman who had been stacking shelves behind me launched herself behind the counter and started to hit my friendly butcher around the head. They screamed at each other for about five minutes, and then the butcher disappeared through a curtain and didn't return.

I stood with my mouth open, not really knowing where to look. The woman turned around to me with eyes ablaze, she thudded a partially plucked chicken complete with its head onto the marble surface and with one swipe of the butcher's prized cleaver she de capitated the poor thing, rammed it into a plastic bag and whacked it in front of me.

'Pollo, pollo!' She jabbed at the bag. *'Pollo, no polla!'*

I quickly put it into my basket and darted nervously to the till. A young girl chewing gum was slumped over the check out. She hauled herself up and called over a young guy who was cleaning the floor. She lazily lifted his apron and pointed to his crotch, then looked at me, *'Polla – entiende?'*

The penny dropped. *Pollo - chicken, polla – oh my God!* I cringed, hurriedly paid for my groceries and rushed back home. The filthy old git! I seethed as I unloaded my groceries onto the kitchen table but an hour later when the chicken was bubbling in the pan and the smell of garlic and onions had filled the flat, I was calm again. Even just making chicken soup, for me, is therapeutic. It's a labour of love, the ultimate recipe for nurturing people but the cook always has to have the first bowl because unless you look after yourself, how the hell can you look after others? More wise words from Nanny Nodge. By the time the doorbell buzzed at six-thirty, I had a cauldron of the golden nectar cooling down on the stove.

Pablo Hernandez-Cruz was exceptionally proud of his Catalan heritage. As I held the ladder whilst he fiddled around with my boiler, he waxed lyrical in broken English about the history of the region, the genius of Gaudi and Barcelona FC. Pablo Hernandez-Cruz was an intelligent good-looking thirty-two-year-old guy, he had it all going on – he also only reached my shoulders. But all *heightist* prejudice was being put to one side as I was currently at his groin level and my eyes were constantly being drawn to what looked like a prize marrow in his trousers. He caught me staring and grinned as I coughed nervously and looked away.

'*Bueno*, now I clean your pipes,' he started to climb back down from the ladder. When his face was level with mine, he stopped, reached out a slightly grubby hand and touched my hair, '*Muy bonita*, very pretty.' Then before I had a chance to react, he leapt down, grabbed his tool kit and walked into the lounge and started to bleed the radiators.

I felt a bit flustered, so wandered into the kitchen and started to fine-tune my soup, adding a little pepper and extra parsley. All of a sudden he was behind me leaning towards the pot.

'It smells *magnifico, que es?*'

'Chicken soup.'

'*Ahh sopa di pollo*,' he inhaled deeply. Not being one to hold back when it comes to showing off my cooking talents, I spun around and said, 'Would you like to try some?'

'*Si, si*, let me finish and I will try, *gracias*,' he disappeared into my bedroom.

After about ten minutes he came back into the kitchen carrying his tool kit, 'I will just put this in the car, *hasta pronto*.'

I found myself in the bathroom re-applying lipstick, spraying on perfume and generally tarting myself up. I looked at my watch. He'd been gone twenty-five minutes. Maybe he wasn't coming back – it was only a bowl of chicken soup. I sat on the sofa feeling a bit dejected. It had been nice talking to him and even though I had only been here in Sitges a week, little things like not being able to pick up the phone to Mel were starting to get me down – not that I would ever admit that to her at this early stage. Cam had disappeared into the obsessive wilderness with Enrique, and anyhow, it wasn't fair for me to rely solely on him. I made a mental list of things to do the next day. I needed a Spanish mobile and an Internet connection. I also needed to get out there and make some friends, beginning with an apology to Bubbles. Most importantly, I was here to work; the laptop hadn't even come out of the bag yet. I went into my room and grabbed it from under the bed and as I stood up the doorbell rang. I hurriedly shoved the computer back and pressed the buzzer, 'Hola, it's me Pablo.'

I let him in the main door and ten seconds later he walked into my apartment in clean clothes, carrying two bottles of wine, a bunch of flowers, a huge baguette and a carrier bag full of salad. My eyes widened in surprise. So this was suddenly a dinner party for two.

'For you,' he bowed and gave me the flowers, 'and now I will make salad, and you will make the table ready.' He marched into the kitchen and made himself immediately at home.

I was too shocked to be annoyed, actually quite thrilled if I was honest. Most of the men I have ever known are all too happy to throw themselves on the sofa and look at you expectantly when it comes to their stomachs and the only time they open the fridge is to get another beer. I pottered around and put some candles I had found in a cupboard on the table, put the flowers in a vase and opened the wine.

'Okay, *perfecto*,' Pablo put his salad in the fridge and came and sat on the sofa, I handed him a glass of wine, 'Thank you for all this, you didn't have to go to all this trouble, really.'

He smiled warmly at me, 'Maybe you think I am a little, how you say, cheeky?'

'A little,' I laughed.

'Well you are new here, so I thought I make you welcome, and if you wanted me to go, I sink you say so?' He raised his eyebrows enquiringly.

'If you had made me feel uncomfortable, yes I would have,' I flopped down on the other side of the sofa, 'but you didn't, so cheers.' We clicked glasses.

'*Salud*,' he said with a voice that made me think of runny honey.

We chatted and laughed, and eventually around ten-thirty, we sat down and had dinner. I raved about his tomato salad, he had three bowls of my soup, and we drank all his wine. You could cut the sexual tension in the air with a knife, particularly when he leapt up, grabbed my hand, and said 'Come I want you to feel something.' My mind jumped straight to the 'marrow', but he took me to the radiator which was piping hot.

'Well, who's a clever little lad then?' I regretted the words as soon as they came out of my mouth and it must have shown, because he looked me directly in the eye and said, 'You 'ave a problem with my height I sink?'

'No, no, I don't really, erm, well I'm very tall,' I gabbled, at which point he pushed me back until I fell on the sofa. I looked up at him and he grinned, 'Now you 'ave no problem, because,' he climbed on top of me, 'now it does not matter.'

It sure didn't and on the basis that if I wasn't careful, the Olympics would happen more regularly than my sexual trysts, I gave in gracefully. My earlier observations were not unjustified. The man had a *grande polla* in his pocket and it was definitely pleased to see me.

At three o'clock in the morning when I'd had 'my pipes' attended to in every conceivable place in the flat, I looked up at my bedroom ceiling and gleefully shouted, 'Right back at ya,' before diving under the covers for round five.

Things, alas, only started to go wrong in the morning, when Pablo Hernandez-Cruz zipped out, came back with croissants and coffee from the café, and awoke me with a kiss and five little words that I was not ready to hear – *I sink I love you.*

SIXTEEN

Any misgivings I had about banishing Pablo Hernandez-Cruz to the Land of One-Night-Stands were lost in the flurry of activity that followed me managing, tactfully, to extricate him from the apartment without giving him: (a) any false hope, and (b) any long lasting complexes. As fantastic as the nocturnal activities had been, this was all a bit quick, so I made a flowery cliché-ridden speech involving all my shortcomings (no pun intended, honestly), hugged him to my bosom and sent him on his way. Then after soaking for an hour in my first hot bath, I ran around the town like a thing possessed in search of life's little necessities and by the time all the Spanish were locking up their shops and wondering where to go for their *menu del dia,* I was staggering up my stairs with about twenty carrier bags and a brand new Spanish mobile.

I made myself some coffee with my new kettle and cafetiére, snuggled onto the sofa and rang Cam.

'Hola, guess who?'

'Alex,' he slurred, 'how are you darling?'

'Brilliant, how do you fancy coming over for lunch, I made chicken soup last night and there's a load left.' I babbled on about the butcher and my new acquisitions and finally dropped in that I hadn't been alone last night. That was the clincher. Cam arrived, thankfully minus Enrique, twenty minutes later. He looked bloody awful.

'Cam what's with the dark circles? You look like you haven't slept for a week.'

'I haven't, all he wants to do is talk and dissect everything I say over and over again. He comes in the bar and watches everyone I talk to, he accuses me of flirting about ten times a night, then we end up having a row as soon as we get home. Then sex, then more rows, then more sex, blah blah.'

'Then why don't you knock it on the head?'

'He's so sweet the rest of the time, and the sex is brilliant, talking of which…you little minx…who is he?'

'The plumber,' I nonchalantly walked into the kitchen and came out with two steaming bowls of soup.

'Not that Pablo guy?' Cam put half a slab of butter on a piece of baguette and dipped it in his soup, 'He's gorgeous.'

'How do you know him?'

'Oh half of Sitges knows him.'

'What?' I screeched, 'not another blasted bisexual!'

'He is straight you stupid cow. He looks after most of the bars and drives all of us poor little gay boys wild. Apparently he's got one like an elephant's trunk.'

'You can say that again.'

'You lucky bitch, give me a blow by blow account – I assume you blew him,' he cackled.

I gave Cam the nitty-gritty and my subsequent reaction to the five little words.

'Oh my God - more soup please – why do people get so heavy so quickly – and bread – it's scary – thanks darling, this is lovely.' He then sat back in his seat as the penny dropped. 'Before you say it, I know that's what I've done with Enrique, we're not talking wedding dresses or anything, but after we helped you, he went and got all his stuff last night.'

'Where did he put it, there's no room?' I laughed, and then added seriously, 'Did you ask him to do that?'

'Well I felt sorry for him, his flatmates were getting on his nerves and he was spending all his time at mine, so it just sort of made sense.'

'It's only been three weeks, are you totally sure about this? He's very territorial over you.'

'I know…' Cam's voice trailed off and he shrugged, 'we'll see.'

'Hey, I know what I need from you, a phone number for Bubbles. I need to do a little apologising.'

Cam tapped the number into my phone and kissed me on the cheek, 'You coming to the bar tonight?'

'Maybe, oh and Cam,' I looked up at him, 'can we keep the Pablo incident between ourselves? I'd rather it didn't go out on general release.'

'Of course sweetie, when you ask me to keep a secret, I do it, that's a promise.'

I hung off the balcony and waved goodbye as he walked up the street, then caught sight of my watch. It was nearly five. The day was evaporating fast. I cleared up the dishes and picked up the phone and called Bubbles, who answered straight away and sounded very bemused when I suggested a coffee a little later. We arranged to meet at eight o'clock at a café called La Granja. I decided to take a walk around the town and find an Internet café. I hadn't checked my emails since I'd arrived so it was probably about time I had a peek at my Inbox.

I found Internet access in the most unlikely of places – my local launderette. Sitting down in there with all those clean soapy smells and gentle whirring sounds made me feel quite cosy and nostalgic. I hadn't set foot in one since my college days. Granted this launderette was next to the fishmongers so the 'whiff *de la mer'* did fight a little with the soap powder but it was close and the computers worked, so I spent a happy half an hour bringing everyone up to date with my Spanish experience.

I had missed my early morning walk, so I decided to have a wander along the beach. As I neared a beach bar called Picnic, I spotted a vaguely familiar figure waving at me from a table overlooking the sea. I walked over and smiled at her quizzically. She had short curly dark hair and looked like she was in her mid fifties. She was wrapped up in a huge purple pashmina and had a pair of gold-rimmed reading glassed perched on her nose. She held out her hand and said in a strong Californian accent, 'Evie Goldstein, you're Alex aren't you?'

'Erm, yes,' I was still puzzled.

'We weren't officially introduced but I was at El Cabaret the night you arrived in Sitges,' she smiled broadly. 'How are you settling in? It's a lovely bay, and that apartment is so pretty, friends of mine rented it last year.' I must have looked a little horrified because Evie put her hand over her mouth and let out a deep throaty laugh, 'I'm so sorry my dear, you're new. Don't worry, you'll get used to this. This is such a small town, word gets around pretty quick.'

'It certainly does,' I shook my head, 'bit too used to being an anonymous Londoner I'm afraid.'

'With all your television experience I doubt you're anonymous,' Evie patted the seat next to her, 'Come and have a drink and we'll even up the score a little.'

Evie was a Jewish woman who had been born and bred in San Francisco. I was shocked to find out that not only was she in her mid-sixties; she was also a fully-fledged rabbi. She had led a very orthodox life in her earlier years. As she put it, while other women were burning their bras at Woodstock, she was at home making Matzo balls and keeping a kosher kitchen. She had stayed with her overbearing husband until her daughter had left college, then she divorced him in the early eighties and had turned her hand to all sorts of things when he refused to give her a penny. She had danced in nightclubs, cooked in restaurants, worked in women's refuges, even worked as a hairdresser without an ounce of experience, and then she had a brainwave, the ultimate slap in the face for her staunchly orthodox ex-husband - she joined the Reconstructionist Movement and was ordained a rabbi in 1991. She was fascinating. I was so engrossed; my peppermint tea was stone cold before I even thought to take a sip.

One thing intrigued me – what was a rabbi doing in Sitges? I couldn't imagine that she would have a large congregation here. To my knowledge, there wasn't even a synagogue. I asked why she came and wasn't quite prepared for the answer that she gave very openly and calmly.

'My daughter and grandchildren were killed in a car crash five years ago. I attempted suicide twice, was institutionalised for a short while and then decided what I needed was a total change.'

My eyes welled up immediately and a huge lump fixed itself in my throat.

'It's okay dear,' she leaned across the table and held my hand.

'I'm s-sorry,' I faltered, 'the last thing you need is an overly emotional reaction from a virtual stranger.'

'There's nothing wrong with being open about your feelings, Alex.'

'I just can't imagine what you must have been through.'

'It is the cruellest blow for any mother to bury a child, and crueller again to bury her grandchildren, but I have to honour their memory by living my life to the full and allowing them to live on in my thoughts and my heart.'

'You're quite amazing you know.'

'I'm their legacy,' she bowed her head slightly and looked at me from over her glasses, 'I look forward to getting to know you better, Alex; something tells me we are going to be great friends.'

I looked at my watch and jumped up, it was five minutes to eight. The last thing I wanted was to be late for Bubbles, even though I could have chatted to Evie all night. 'I've got to go, let me pay for the drinks,' I rustled around in my bag. She put her hand out and stopped me, 'Next time, Alex. Leave me your mobile number and we'll have some lunch.'

I hastily wrote down my number on a piece of paper and ran for my life. Luckily Sitges was a very small town and by the time I reached *La Granja*, Bubbles was approaching from the other direction. We sat down at a table by the door, 'What would you like?' I asked breathlessly, 'Apart from an apology for my stupid behaviour of course.'

'Cava,' she looked around the café, gave a bored sigh and started playing with the pleated cuffs of her bright red silk shirt. She wasn't going to make it easy for me that was for sure.

'Bubbles I am very sorry for being such an idiot, I'm not used to smoking and I was off my tits.' I gulped and hoped she wasn't going to cause a scene. A waiter placed two glasses of cava down on the table; she thanked him and turned back to me.

'D'you know what really pisses me off? Straight birds like you just assuming every bloody lesbian that comes into your body space wants to munch your goddamn rug. We don't just fancy any woman indiscriminately. As for you, you uptight cow, I'm not into redheads and absolutely hate freckles.'

We sat staring at each other in awkward silence, and then both smiled. I picked up my glass and chinked hers, 'Cheers,' I said before downing it in one. She followed suit. I gestured to the waiter who refilled our glasses, 'Now we've got that out of the way, shall we have another? Oh and by the way, it's your round, I'm not *that* sorry.'

'I'll buy you a whole bottle if you show me your tits,' she poked my arm and smirked.

'They're absolutely festooned with freckles, you'd be sick.'

'Yuk! Okay after this I'm taking you to another bar; you need to lose your stupid hang-ups pronto. You're living in bloody Sitges now. '

'Are you taking me to a dykey bar?'

'You also need to lose that word. I'm taking you to a bar frequented by women, yes!'

SEVENTEEN

I am and always will be *coiffurophobic.* You won't find it in the dictionary. It's my very own word that I use to describe my deep-rooted fear and mistrust of anyone wielding a pair of scissors near my hair. I can trace the origins of this phobia directly back to my first hair salon experience. We moved from London to Southampton when I was eleven and in order to give me a little extra confidence on my first day at the new school, my mum agreed to let me have my hair cut. It was time to say goodbye to the waist-length red locks and all the paraphernalia that accompanied them. No more ponytails, bunches, plaits and hour-long de-tangling sessions - I was going to have a shoulder-length layered hair and David Bowie was going to fall in love with me. I had it all planned.

When we walked through the doors of the Michael of Paris salon, I was overwhelmed with the grown-up glamour of it all. I didn't notice the rows of little old ladies under the dryers, tightly wound perm rollers revealing their pink and shiny scalps and the sad black and white pictures of people with ridiculous hairstyles that graced every wall, fighting for attention with the gaudy blue and pink wallpaper. The overpowering stench of ammonia was masked by the smell of sweet sickly hairspray and I was transfixed by the sound of the hair-dryers, the clinking of teacups and the girl who was manicuring a client's nails. Heavily made-up women with their heads wrapped in foil, glided around the salon swathed in blue nylon robes. I realised I would soon be one of these people. This little ugly duckling was going to emerge a swan. I was beside myself with excitement and quite relieved when Mum said she was going shopping and leaving me in the capable hands of Michael, who had insisted he look after me personally. Little did she know she was entrusting her daughter to a money-grabbing toe-rag who was just about to scar me for life.

The minute she walked out of the door I was robed up and led to a chair like a little lamb to the slaughter. I chatted on about my dream hairstyle but it was falling on deaf ears. Michael knew a potential wig when he saw one and he literally couldn't wait to start hacking away. He started from the back of my head and by the time he reached the front, it was too late. My hair was cropped close to my scalp with the odd pathetic tendril sticking out. I gazed at myself in horror, as the silver-bouffanted scoundrel carefully gathered up my tresses and high-tailed it to the back of the salon with his ill-gotten booty. By the time he returned, Mum was back and I was sobbing uncontrollably.

'I just did what the little lady asked for,' the smarmy hair-butcher shrugged helplessly as Mum tried to pacify me. 'Of course if the client is unhappy, we wouldn't dream of charging.'

'No, no, I insist.' Mum thrust a few pound notes into his hand and led me away, 'I should have known not to trust you on your own Alex, it was asking for trouble.'

The injustice was too much. Why didn't she shout at him? I decided to dole out my own punishment, so I ran back into the salon, found my prey and kicked him as hard as I could in the shin. He screamed at Mum to remove her little hooligan from his establishment. I wept all the way home and my dad wept when he saw me. I found a certain amount of solace in the fact he blamed Mum entirely and I spent the night snuggled up with him on the sofa whilst he watched *Starsky and Hutch*. As he stroked my shorn little head, I silently vowed to myself never to have my hair cut again, as hairdressers were now my sworn enemy and Michael of Paris had ruined all my chances of walking down the aisle with David.

But hair grows, memories fade and fashions change. I didn't carry out my Rapunzel pledge, even though the dread still exists every time I find myself with my head in a backwash basin praying that this time I have found a hairdresser who understands the word 'trim'. So when Tony of Sitges grabbed a handful of my hair in El

Cabaret and shrieked at my vast population of split ends, I felt the familiar knot in the stomach as I agreed to go to his apartment the next day for a 'little tidy-up'. As I walked across the dusty path behind the cemetery on my way to the port where he lived, I fingered my hair nervously, remembering every follicular disaster I had ever had: the fringes I hadn't asked for; the totally unnecessary perms that left me looking like an electrocuted poodle; the way the words 'layers' and 'volume' in my case meant hair wider than it was long; and the hairdresser who reassuringly made me look at the floor to see a mere few wisps of hair after he finished cutting, only to be caught emptying piles of my hair from his pockets as I left the salon.

But having reached the stage when combs were getting stuck in my hair and dreadlocks were looking imminent, braving the scissors was my only course of action. Before I knew it, I was there. I stood in front of the door for two seconds, then just as I was going to ring the bell, I heard a voice that sounded like Tony's cry, 'It won't go in.'

My hand wavered and then withdrew completely as the conversation continued and another male voice said, 'You'll have to try to get it hard again.'

I put my hand in my mouth to stop laughing but nearly choked when an exceptionally posh female voice yelled, 'Have you got any butter? That'll do it.'

What was this? Last Tango in Sitges?

'We've only got a tub of *Becel*, will that do?' The second male voice sounded like Kenneth Williams.

'He keeps trying to bite me.' It was Tony's voice. I jumped out of my skin as I heard a dog's shrill bark.

'He's just getting a little upset,' the woman's voice cooed.

'Christ! I thought he'd be a lot more enthusiastic than this.'

'It's quite often like this the first time but once they get used to it, you'll be able to hire him out and make yourself a tidy packet.'

I began to wonder if Spain had an RSPCA and decided to sneak away. As I turned to go, I tripped, my hand shot out to stop myself and hit the doorbell. Before I had a chance to run, the door opened and there stood a flustered looking blonde guy, 'You must be Alex. C'mon in. I won't shake your hand, you don't know where mine has just been,' he shrieked. 'I'm Tony's partner, Ian.'

'Sorry love, this is taking a bit longer than we thought,' Tony's voice bellowed from the lounge, 'but Barbara here has come all the way from Girona especially.'

'Best you stay in the kitchen, we're just getting Dudley relaxed - stage fright,' Barbara screeched out, 'but look, Tony, he's got the right idea, good boy, Dudley.'

'Oh look, he likes it.'

'You clever boy,' Barbara cooed.

I really didn't know where to look. Ian was holding his breath and clasping his hands in front of his chest. 'We're so proud; our little baby's growing up. This is his first time. We were so lucky to get Barbara, she's been doing this for years and she keeps us really involved which is nice. Would you like a cup of tea? I think this bit can take a while. You ever bred dogs?'

'Can't say I have,' I looked at Ian and tried to stop giggling. 'What type of dog is he?'

'A little Norfolk, ah look, here he is now,' a scruffy little beige dog careered into the kitchen and virtually nose-dived into his water bowl, lapping furiously.

'Look at him, he's gasping,' Ian pursed his lips and crossed his arms, 'How is my little stallion?' He bent down and picked him up. Dudley whined and looked down at his food. 'Of course we're hungry; we've been a busy boy.' He plopped him back down again as another creamy coloured terrier scampered through the door. 'Oh look, here's Milly. Good girl. Was Dudley gentle with you?'

Tony walked in and kissed me on the cheek.

'Hello love, we'll have a cup of tea and then we'll cut your hair.'

'Trim, Tony,' I said in a panicked tone, 'the word is trim.'

An hour later as I walked around the marina, I had to admit Tony had done a good job. My hair felt glossy and healthy and he hadn't felt the need to chop a foot off the length. I was happy, the sun was shining and I thought I would reward myself with a quick drink. I sat at one of the bars overlooking the boats and ordered a cava and some olives.

A movement on a large yacht caught my eye; a dark-haired guy was cleaning the windows. He must have felt me looking, as he turned around and grinned at me. He was gorgeous, slightly unshaven, dimples to die for, tanned, tall and much to my surprise, coming towards me. I looked up as he reached the table and shielded my eyes from the sun with my hand. This was more like it.

'Hola, a pretty lady like you should not be drinking alone. Can I join you and invite you for another cava?'

He seemed quite harmless, if a tad smarmy, so I accepted, and two hours later as the sun started to go down, we were still talking. As it turned out, my new friend Augustin was a bit of a playboy. He owned a couple of restaurants in the port and the boat he was cleaning was his pride and joy. It was a present from his father on his thirtieth birthday, as well as chairmanship of his multi-million euro business, selling Spain's famed Iberico ham all over the world, a fact of which he was very proud.

'My *jamon* is the best,' he cried as he slapped the table after our sixth *copa di cava*. 'If anyone can show me better *jamon*, I cut off my penis.'

'Very sure then,' I rescued a cava glass that was just about to topple over and shovelled a few almonds in my mouth as I could feel myself getting quite pissed. After the Pablo incident, I decided to avoid what could end up regrettable drunken behaviour, so I stood up, bent over and kissed him on the cheek. 'I have to go Augustin, it has been lovely.'

He shot up and took my hand, 'How can you go? I thought we could have dinner and maybe…' his voice trailed off and he looked over to the boat.

'Maybe another time,' I smiled.

'*Cariňa* you break my heart.'

I floated home in a gentle alcoholic haze. Shiny hair and a bolstered ego – that would do for me. It was still quite a novelty getting a bit of attention; very different to back in the UK where I hardly ever went out unless it was a few drinks after work with the crew or sometimes making up numbers at dinner parties with the recently divorced, perpetually single or socially unacceptable. Maybe I was getting my *mojo* back? I sent a text to Mel – *Tall Spanish playboy who's big in ham – sound any better than the midget plumber with the magnificent manhood?*

EIGHTEEN

In some ways living within walking distance to El Cabaret was brilliant. As it was out of season, it was full of locals and within three weeks of arriving in Sitges, I had increased my circle of friends ten-fold. My mobile phone now rang continually, rather than sitting silently in the corner of the lounge reminding me just what a Norma-No-Mates I was.

From the health, wealth and putting my life in order perspective; El Cabaret was a bloody disaster. It was just too easy to toddle over there for a night cap at around midnight, carry on drinking with the boys after hours, then end up in one of the nightclubs until dawn. I was turning into a creature of the night and whereas I used to be up with the lark and walking the *paseo,* you would be lucky to see me surface before 1 or 2 pm, when I would shower, don the sunglasses and stagger out to go and meet Evie, Bubbles or one of my other new found friends for lunch at one of the local Catalan restaurants or toddle over to the port to have a couple of cocktails with Augustin and his Spanish friends. I was living an indulgent ex-pat lifestyle and even after such a short time, this was eating away at my funds in a very dangerous fashion - not that I was sharing this little fact with the folks back home.

Since I had my landline and ADSL installed I was back in touch with the world at large and no-one was more pleased than Mum, who had settled back into her weekly routine of updating me on the lives of people I had never even met. I don't know what level of comfort I was meant to derive because Mrs Henderson had finally managed to find the perfect green tiles for her guest bathroom and even though poor Lola Spencer had been bed-ridden for three whole days because of a suspect egg mayonnaise sandwich at the

Nursery Garden Café, I wasn't going to have a sleepless night, but my mum was happy. The telephonic umbilical cord was back in place and she didn't have to resort to calling my mobile, an act of immeasurable danger as far as she was concerned. I had bought her one for Christmas two years before so we could keep in touch. For her it wasn't so much a gift as an assassination attempt, 'I'll end up with a brain tumour,' she'd said as she sliced the turkey. 'Why didn't you just get me another statuette for the garden?' I'd pointed out that I'd rather have a mother who could contact me in an emergency than a garden that resembled the Terracotta Army of Xi'an, so she reluctantly agreed to keep it, although to the best of my knowledge it was still in its box.

On the Wednesday before Easter I had a very strange call from her.

'So you promise you'll be there tomorrow daytime, Alex?'

'Yes Mum, for the umpteenth time, I'll be here, I promise,' I sighed wearily.

Whatever she had up her sleeve, today Mum was wired. 'It's just a little Easter present but I don't want you missing it.' She seemed so excited that despite having a deep-seated inner dread when it came to my mum's presents, I gave my acerbic little tongue five minutes off and played ball.

'I can't wait to see it, Mum, you shouldn't have gone to such trouble.'

'Just you be sure to call me the minute it arrives darling.'

'I will.'

'Oh, and can you thank Mel for me, it was lovely of her to get me those massagers. There's a really pretty pale blue one that I'm going to give your Aunty May. I thought it would match the wallpaper in her bedroom.'

'Oh, there goes the doorbell, Mum. Gotta go, love you loads, bye.'

I had resorted to utter cowardice on what Mel and I were now calling 'Vibratorgate'. Even though Christmas was eight months away, Mum liked to be organised on the present front and hadn't stopped harping on about them. So rather than have her wandering the Southampton high street brandishing a dildo, I had ordered ten various models online and had them delivered to Mel, who had re-packaged them into innocuous boxes with lots of colourful tissue paper. I was working on the theory that if my mum didn't know what it was, then neither would my aunts or her friends and in the unlikely event of discovery, I would just feign ignorance. Of course I was simply deluding myself and knew it was only a matter of time before all hell broke loose but for the time being this little saga was keeping Cam and the rest of the El Cabaret regulars highly entertained.

Maybe it was hearing Mum's voice that made me feel guilty, as the minute I put the phone down I decided to get down to some work and switched on the computer. Quite what I meant to achieve by this action who knows, but after staring at a blank document for ten minutes and coming to the conclusion that my creative genius was not going to emerge, I gave in to my inner lobotomy patient and clicked onto Games. Why don't they just eradicate that title from the software and replace it with something more honest? How about Procrastination Devices for the Creatively Challenged or Mind Numbing Time Wasters? But all that was just about to become a thing of the past because when I checked my emails there was one from a friend in Australia informing me that she was now on Facebook and suggesting that I join. Little did I realise that a new addiction was just about to be born.

I didn't know the meaning of the word 'procrastination' until this point. I spent the entire afternoon searching for friends and delighting in the whole voyeuristic process. I sent messages, I poked people, I found all manner of applications and quizzes – I was hooked. I then realised that my laptop had a microphone and integrated web cam so I downloaded Skype and proceeded to Skype anyone I vaguely knew who was online, revelling in the fact I was talking for free. I was like a child with a new toy. How had I never discovered any of this before?

Yeah I know – I had a life then. Eventually I gave up and decided to have a little siesta. By 1 am I was awake, full of beans and up for some fun, so as usual I showered, made myself up and wandered over to El Cabaret. I bumped straight into Fred and Pierre who were just leaving.

'Anuzzer night on ze town, Alex?' Pierre shook his head, 'People will start talking.'

'Let them,' I bristled, 'it's absolutely none of their business.'

'Hello treacle,' said Cam, who was working the bar on his own, 'Cava?'

'Why not?' I sat at the bar.

'Worked on any ideas today?' Cam raised an eyebrow at me. 'Approached anyone about work?'

'I really did try.'

'I'm going to start handcuffing you to the computer.'

'I've sat at the bloody computer all day. It's my head that's not working. How does one just alight on the perfect new direction in life?'

'A few less nights out might be a good idea.'

'I suppose you're right,' I begrudgingly admitted, then started to chat to some of the customers.

Everything was very convivial until the door opened and in stalked Enrique in a pair of Cam's ripped jeans and a sleeveless t-shirt. He glowered at me and went to the other end of the bar where he sat sulkily on a barstool, waiting for some attention from Cam. He finished serving some customers and loaded the glass washer before going over and pecking Enrique on the cheek. This wasn't enough obviously, as he spat something in Spanish at Cam and crashed out of the bar. Cam turned to me and raised his hands in disbelief.

'I've had it with him. C'mon, drink up then let's hit the town. He can fester in his own juices tonight and then find another sucker tomorrow.'

'Here, here,' I raised my glass. Cam locked up and we made for one of Sitges' most notorious late night haunts – *Raoul's*. When you first walk in, it's like walking into the bar in the first Star Wars film minus Luke Skywalker and Hans Solo but with plenty of strange-looking aliens and Wookies. The hair situation was a disaster. The older Spanish guys seemed to favour a curly mullet and the younger ones – well – all I can say is that when they look back and wonder why their teenage years weren't the sex fest they had dreamed of, they might want to throw the word shampoo into the equation. Why is it cool to be grubby? Someone enlighten me. Has nobody told them girls like a little hygiene? Hey boys, if that is what is going on with your hair, we certainly don't want to discover what's going on in your pants.

'Talk about thin pickings for you straight birds,' Cam winced as he looked around the club, 'they're all bug ugly.'

'I know,' I shrugged. 'All the good-looking ones are in the gay bars.'

We danced until dawn. Then we went back to mine and carried on. I made a huge tortilla with the contents of the fridge and then around 10 am when there was nothing edible or drinkable left, we both passed out in my bed. Our blissful sleep was brought to an abrupt end when we were awoken by the sound of my doorbell ringing furiously. I looked at my clock; it was 1.30 pm.

'What in God's name?' I muttered, then I remembered my mum's present. 'Must be the postman,' I slid out of bed.

'Tell him to sod off,' mumbled Cam. 'Oh jeez, what do I look like?'

'Road kill.'

I walked into the lounge and the buzzer kept ringing. 'Alright,' I yelled out of the balcony doors. The place was utter carnage. I don't think we had left a glass or plate in the cupboard.

I stumbled out of the door in my t-shirt and knickers. The postman was going to get an eyeful. I have to say at this point, if I had known what was waiting for me downstairs, I'd have got straight back into bed and pulled the covers over my head till Christmas.

When I opened the main door, looking like yesterday's breakfast, I was greeted by a sight that made my heart sink into my shoes. Dressed up to the max and giving it Jackie O was Penny Johnson, complete with enough Louis Vuitton luggage to sustain a transatlantic cruise.

'Shit! You look disgusting,' she barged past me carrying the lightest bags, leaving me with the two heavy ones. 'Don't tell me you haven't got a blasted lift?'

'It's good exercise,' I growled.

She turned and surveyed my thighs with a patronising smile, flicked her perfect shiny black bob and carried on upstairs. I struggled up behind her, my head throbbing and nerves fraying. My mum was dead - bloody Easter surprise indeed.

'God it looks like a squat.'

'We had a late night,' I threw her bags on the floor. 'Cam where are you? Penny has come on a surprise visit.'

'Penny!' Cam walked out of the bedroom in his underpants, 'Alex has told me ALL about you,' he yawned languidly.

'Well that's amazing considering the flaky bitch didn't even let me know her telephone number or address out here.' Penny went into one of her high-pitched and totally false laughs, 'But her mum rang me and asked me to come and check if she's okay, so here I am.'

'And I bet Alex is absolutely thrilled, aren't you darling?' Cam clapped his hands and walked over to the balcony. 'Isn't this the most superb view? The best in Sitges - everyone is so jealous. Oh well I'd best be off and leave you two alone. You've obviously got a lot of catching up to do.' He shot me an amused look, donned his trousers and left, leaving Penny and me alone in the devastation. I started to clear up, 'I think I have some coffee in the cupboard if you fancy one.'

'Well, if you get yourself cleaned up, I'll take you somewhere nice. Let's blast John's credit cards. You're probably broke as usual.'

'I'm not actually,' I retorted angrily.

'Oh don't take offence, Alex, let's not start the week with a row.'

'The week?' I whimpered.

'Yes, isn't it fab? John's taking the kids to his mother's for a week, so I am as free as a bird.'

'I'm just going to have a shower, make yourself at home, I'll finish this lot later,' I walked into the bathroom and looked at my grey face in the mirror. If this had been Mel, we would have been jumping around with excitement, hugging each other at every given opportunity. But this was Penny who would flinch if you so much as brushed past her. A whole week with the ice maiden, a whole bloody week of sarcasm and loaded comments - I was just going to have to make the most of it. She could be nice – sometimes.

NINETEEN

By the time I had finished in the bathroom, Penny had mine-swept the apartment and it was sparkling. Feeling immensely grateful for not having to deal with dusters and the vacuum cleaner, I decided to make an effort and at least make her feel a little more welcome. She had, after all, come all this way especially to see me. I walked into my bedroom where she was busily hanging her clothes in my wardrobe but before I even had a chance to bathe her in a little bonhomie, she machine-gunned my good intentions stone dead.

'I felt the mattress in the spare room and it's too soft for my back. You're obviously more used to sleeping in single beds than me - you don't mind, do you? It's only for a week.'

My jaw clenched and I had to bite my lip - she was now blithely chucking me out of my bedroom. 'No, Princess Penny, I'll be fine.' The jibe went totally over her head.

'Can we move some of your clothes in there? It's jam-packed in this wardrobe and my stuff will get creased?' Her lips curled with distaste as she looked at the crumpled bed, 'And where do you keep your spare bedding? Who knows what was going on in there before I arrived?'

'Cam and I are friends – he's gay,' I could feel red-hot anger surging through my body, 'and I haven't got spare bedding, I take it to the launderette, they do it for me in an hour.'

She brusquely stripped it off and looked at me. 'That's ridiculous, we'll get you another set this afternoon – I take it they do sell bedding around here?'

'Yes, but not until five o'clock – so cool it,' I screamed. 'Move away from the blasted bedding and stop being a bloody bully. You've turned up on my doorstep uninvited, you haven't even asked me how I am, you couldn't even be bothered to be polite to Cam and now you're picking holes in my home.'

'I came to surprise you.'

'Well surprise me and try getting off my back for a change,' I grabbed some underwear, jeans and a jumper and stormed into the spare room. I flopped down on the bed miserably. This was a bloody disaster. The phone rang. I marched out into the lounge and grabbed it.

'Hello darling, has your surprise arrived yet?'

'Yes Mum, she sure has, and she's still as bloody rude and thoughtless as ever. Next time, do me a favour and send me a bloody egg!' I slammed the phone down and turned around. Penny was standing in the bedroom doorway looking crestfallen.

'I'm sorry, Alex. I didn't mean to upset you.'

'You just can't help yourself though, can you? Look, I've got a hangover, so I'm probably a bit hyper-sensitive, but if you are going to be here a week then we have to have some ground rules – no nagging. This is what I came over here to get away from.'

'Okay, I'll try,' she came over and gave me the two-second clasp around the shoulders that constituted a hug. 'Shall we start again?'

'Yes, Penny, that would be nice,' I muttered, dialling Mum's number. 'Hi Mum, it's me, sorry for being ratty ... yes it was lovely of you to organise Penny coming ... yes, we're fine now. No, I'm not being horrible to her... yes it was my entire fault as usual...'

Ten minutes later we were sitting in the Al Fresco Café having salad and a bottle of wine that I ignored in favour of water for a while, then caved in because when Penny starts reeling off the list of the latest acquisitions, children's achievements and health spas she has visited in the past three months – it helps to be a little anaesthetised. When we left, just to prove an 'I'm not doing as badly as you think' point, I picked up the tab.

Now I wouldn't say the next couple of days were horrendous exactly but they were distinctly uncomfortable at times. Planet Penny is a perfect place where bank accounts never go into the red, bodies are always groomed, organic food is delivered weekly and one not only gets to buy three pairs of Jimmy Choos at a time, one actually gets to go to the types of functions where you wear such expensive footwear along with a posh frock. Some people who live on similar planets are adaptable and when mixing with those whose lives don't run quite as smoothly, are fantastic at showing a genuine interest in those around them, without having to continually bolster up their own sense of self-importance by bragging about their lifestyles. Penny is not one of those people. I was getting to the stage where I thought my face was going to remain in a permanent wince. Inevitably she gained momentum on the unpleasant front and really excelled herself on Saturday night when she got herself utterly drunk and started her usual bullshit – on my friends. Cam, Evie, Fred and Pierre came over to dinner and were regaled with every embarrassing and negative anecdote Penny could remember about me and then when she ran out of *let's undermine Alex* stories, she proceeded to give them her views on why they were all here – having never asked any of them a single question about themselves.

'Essentially you're all copping out aren't you?' Penny looked around the table, 'I mean you wouldn't have come here if you had been successful at home. John says that's the trouble with all ex-pats; they don't cut the mustard in their own country, so they run off and bum around in a less challenging environment. Excuse me, I need the loo.' She staggered to the toilet and slammed the door. We looked at each other in stunned silence until ten seconds later we heard the sound of her throwing up.

'Good,' said Fred, 'if it were me, I'd let her choke on it. Are all your mates like her?'

'No. I'm so sorry everyone.'

'What a sad girl,' sighed Evie.

'I sink she is very insecure person,' Pierre said balefully.

'And I think she's fallen down the toilet,' Cam stood up and nodded for me to go with him, 'just in case she's got her knickers around her ankles, you go first.'

Penny had passed out on the tiles and my entire bathroom was splashed with red puke.

'I'd be tempted to make her clear it up in the morning,' Cam groaned as we lifted her on to our shoulders and threw her on my bed. I put a blanket over her and went back and swabbed the decks. By the time I had finished, Evie, Fred and Pierre were getting ready to leave; they had washed up and put the remains of the *cassoulet,* salad *and tarte tatin* in the fridge. I apologised again, kissed them goodbye and went to join Cam who was smoking on the balcony. He lit another cigarette and gave it to me, 'Why do you put up with her? She's so different from you.'

'Nostalgia, habit, heaven only knows?'

'John this, John that, hasn't she got a mind of her own?'

'Let's just say she doesn't always use it to its best advantage. She has always been very spoilt and moved straight from rich parents to a rich husband who inherited all his money from his rich parents. They married very young, had everything straight away and have absolutely no idea what life is like on the other side of the coin, and they are turning their kids into carbon copies. Having me around makes her feel superior. She's a bad weather friend.'

'*Que?*'

'When things go wrong in my life, she is one of the first there, loves nothing better than bailing me out and showering me with *I told you so's*. She feeds off my misfortune in the same way a vampire drinks blood. But when things go right, like when I got the first telly job for instance, I don't hear a dickybird from her - *nada.*'

'So why is she still around?'

'In her own way, she makes me feel superior I suppose. I look at her and know that everything about her is not what I want to be, whereas my friend Mel, who I do admire, has it all but she's worked bloody hard for it and wouldn't pass judgement on another living soul.'

'Now SHE sounds great.' Cam poured more sherry.

'She is and she absolutely loathes Penny. I know the friendship should be six feet under; we've outgrown each other. I just haven't had the guts to have the conversation. And as for what she said to you guys tonight, I'm mortified.'

'Don't worry, Molly, we didn't take it personally and nor should you. People who haven't got the balls to do things like this always spout shit like that. She leaves in a few days, then, my advice would be to move again, change all numbers and don't even tell your mum.'

I laughed and hugged him, 'I love you Toffles. Hey, you haven't even told me what happened with Enrique.'

'Oh God, it was no big deal. I left here, went home and he hadn't been home all night either – probably holed up with his Argentinean buddies. I took the coward's way out, packed his bags for him and chucked them outside and then I double-locked and bolted the door. He eventually came back, shouted and tried to kick the door down for a while, so I put in earplugs, took a sleeping tablet and when I woke up he was gone. He's left two tearful messages and about ten threatening ones. He'll get over it.'

'So he still has keys?'

'Yeah, but he's not going to do anything.' Cam puffed thoughtfully on his cigarette for a while, 'Maybe I ought to change the locks?'

'I would,' I didn't trust Enrique as far as I could throw him. 'Do you want to stay here tonight?'

'No, I'll go back.'

'Call me when you get back and bolt the door.'

'Yes mummy.'

When Cam called safe and sound ten minutes later, I checked on Penny who was snoring loudly exactly where we had left her and I went to bed. Tomorrow Penny and I were going to have a team talk.

*

'I didn't say that!' Penny had her blotchy and pallid face in her hands.

'Yes you did and you cannot have one of these until you have rung all of them and apologised for being such a bitch.' I waggled the pain-killer container in her face and thrust the phone into her hands, 'Here are their numbers.'

She begrudgingly did as she was told, whilst I made her coffee and an omelette, which after initially refusing, she wolfed down before going back to bed, telling me not to make any noise. Relieved at not having to traipse around after her as she mindlessly went from one shop to another melting John's credit cards, I had a lovely afternoon wandering around in the sun looking at all the flower petal carpets that lined most of the streets in Sitges in celebration of *Corpus Christi*. Locals work all through the night so that these intricate and elaborate designs appear as if by magic the next morning. All that labour for a flash of beauty that only lasts a day. It was stunning. By the time I wandered back home around 7 pm, I was energised, relaxed and ready to deal with anything Penny could shoot at me – so I thought.

Maybe I was just lulled into a false sense of security by the canapés and cava she had prepared for me, and the hot bath with aromatic oils, and the profuse apologies for her behaviour the night before, but when we went down to the port for a drink and ran into Augustin, I made the stupid mistake of telling her I liked him. This was a red rag Penny just couldn't resist. Ever since I sat next to her on my first day at junior school with my stupid haircut and spindly blue legs, Penny Johnson simply had to have everything I wanted – first. Whether it was the skin-tight white FUS jeans, getting her ears pierced or snogging Steve Jordan, she just had to beat me to it, and Augustin was just about to get it offered on a plate.

'Things haven't been great with John and me on ... you know ... the sex front, for ages,' she whispered to me, as she watched Augustin go to the bar to get drinks. 'God, he's cute. What have you been waiting for?'

'I don't want to be too available.'

'Is he really your type? I've never imagined you with a Latin guy.'

'I'm finding out if he's my type – slowly.'

I found out that Augustin was not my type – quickly. When I nipped to the toilet ten minutes later, I returned to see him and Penny pull quickly away from each other. You could have cut the air with a knife as I finished what was left of my cava then with as much dignity as I could muster, I stood up and said brightly, 'Hope you don't mind but I'm not feeling that well and I want to go home.

Augustin, I'm sure you'll look after Penny.'

'Oh Alex, are you sure you don't want me to come with you?' Penny cooed. I shook my head and walked away. I knew that a self-satisfied smile would already be creeping over her smug little face. I'd really like to say that at this point I rationalised the situation and didn't let it get to me, that I shrugged it off as one of those things, but I couldn't. The minute I turned the corner all dignity dissolved and I burst into tears. Augustin was a player - more fool me for harbouring totally unfounded expectations because I'd been reading too much into every hug and compliment that he passed my way. As for Penny, however instrumental her role in this little bit of self-realisation, this was the final straw. I made a pledge that the conniving little cow was going to get her come-uppance, and the next morning when she rang the doorbell at 11 am - she did get it.

I hung over the balcony and looked at her.

'Oh Alex, I had the best time! Thank you for being so understanding last night. It's done my ego the world of good. Open the door and I'll tell you the gory details over coffee.'

'You actually think I want to hear them?'

'Oh god, you're annoyed aren't you? Oh Alex, he's not worth getting upset over, really, he wouldn't be right for you. I want better for you. Anyhow, let me in and we'll talk about it. I need to get changed.'

Up until that point I really was going to let her in and pick up her stuff, but thirty years worth of crap suddenly bubbled over and I flipped.

I got hold of one of the Louis Vuitton suitcases I had already packed for her and emptied it out onto the street before chucking it down. Penny looked horrified.

'Oops sorry, you'll need matching shoes and undies.' I hurled the contents of the next suitcase down. Penny's La Perla lingerie and Jimmy Choo's were strewn all over the street.

'Alex, this is not funny! You're over-reacting! Stop this!' The remaining two bags went sailing over the edge. 'You're crazy!' she screamed.

'You're damn right there, Penny, crazy for putting up with you for so long!' I shouted down. Quite a crowd had started to gather. 'You are a jealous, insecure, selfish bitch and I have had just about as much as I can take. You look down on everybody from such a great height and yet what the fuck have you done, eh? You married a bloke who has loads of dosh and about as much charm as a tub of margarine. Last night was just another golden opportunity for you to score points against me, and I hope it was worth it, because as far as our friendship is concerned - it's over! Do you hear me? OVER!!!!!! Now get lost and go home. Don't ever ring me or contact me again!'

As I stepped off the balcony and shut the windows, I heard her screaming something about me not telling John. I grinned. That was something she'd just have to sweat over for a while.

I could have been a bit more adult about it I suppose but in all honesty, I didn't feel one ounce of remorse at airing her rather expensive underwear in public. Sticking up for others had always been easy but when it came to doing the same for me, I was usually useless. This was quite liberating. I lay down on the sofa and slipped into the first relaxed sleep I'd had in a few days. I must have dozed off pretty heavily as by the time I woke up a few hours later the answer machine was flashing.

'Alex, what's all this I hear about your lesbian tiff?' Cam was laughing his head off, 'Stephan was on the street when you were chucking the stuff off the balcony. He's spread it all over town. Ring me.'

'Alex, this is Penny, just to let you know, not that you'd care, that I have managed to change my flight and I think you are pathetic. I can't help it if you can't get a man. If you are willing to let our friendship go because of a bloke then more fool you, and if you do tell John, I shall deny everything. Goodbye.'

'Alex, this is Mum, just ringing to see how you girls are getting on. I'm sure you're having a ball. Give my regards to Penny won't you. Love you darling. Bye.'

TWENTY

As May progressed, I realised there was a danger of me turning into a full on 'fag hag', so I took my 'tush' to The Bush, which even though it sounds like the perfect name for a lesbian hangout, is actually one of the three predominantly straight ex-pat pubs in Sitges. I ventured into this bastion of heterosexuality on a rugby international day and was pounced upon by a British builder called Dave - *Six feet two and eyes of blue, but when brains were handed out he was the last in the queue.* He was a normal affable sort of chap whose idea of a good night out was a game of darts or a meal at his favourite restaurant – a badly lit café run by one of his English cronies, where the quality of the food was matched only by the price. Cheap! The only way you could get the food down your throat was by drinking copious amounts of beer or local un-labelled wine, which led to me nick-naming this charming establishment *The Swig and Gristle.*

I felt relaxed with Dave because he seemed to be happy to have me as a friend but all this was to about to change. On one of our usual nights out, having dined on a piece of pork that was more fat than meat and swimming in a pool of *Bisto*, we had moved onto the glittering finalé – a doubles darts match with Bush regulars Viv and Knobby. They had managed to get a babysitter and were so full of Guinness they could barely stand. But however unsteady they were on their legs, when it came to chucking darts, their right arms seemed to have lives totally independent from the rest of their bodies. They were as steady as Ayers Rock in a desert storm. I, on the other hand, was crap. Much to Dave's mortification, we lost all three games, so he decided I needed another hobby and thereupon introduced me into Sitges quiz night culture.

Dave, Viv and Knobby were already in a quiz team called the Bristol Bayonets with Sidney, a local taxi driver who was able to complete *The Sun* crossword in the space of time it took him to eat a full English breakfast. But Dave was on a mission and by the end of the evening I had been hauled over to meet Telly Mark who installed Sky satellites, and his two buddies, Billy the Chip - a local carpenter and Veronica Luvvie who ran the English theatre company in Sitges. They had just lost a member of their team as he had sadly died alone in his apartment, having choked on a large piece of *chorizo*. I had an inkling that this would do the rounds as a cautionary tale to all future ex-pats heading for the Costas and resisted the temptation to start making quips about biting off more than one could chew. After bombarding me with questions for ten minutes and a short follow-up conference behind the pool table they came over and made it official – I was now the fourth member of the Shifty Shafters - a decision based purely on my previous TV form and knowledge of 80s soul.

As we went to leave, Viv came staggering up to me and threw her arms around my neck, revealing an expanse of sweaty armpit. The pungent smell of hops, coupled with imported cheese and onion crisps blasted me in the face as she burped then slurred, 'I think you're the best girlfriend Dave has ever had.'

I must have blanched in horror, as Dave came whizzing over and thrust a big beefy arm around my shoulders and bellowed, 'Not after tonight's performance she's not. I can't go out with a woman who can't chuck a double top.' Everybody roared. I went very quiet and maintained this silence as we walked the first five minutes home. A very nervous Dave kept doing that whistling thing where no actual whistle comes out; just short bursts of air, coupled with continually scratching his short-cropped blond hair. I decided to put him out of his misery, 'Girlfriend huh?'

'Well I thought we were dating?'

'We've been hanging out Dave. I had no idea that you - and what would appear to be half The Bush - assumed we were boyfriend and girlfriend.'

His head dropped down, 'So you don't like me then?'

'Of course I like you.'

'But you don't want to go out with me?'

'Well, it's early days yet. We're still getting to know each other. I'm one of those women who prefers to take things slowly,' my mind proved me a liar by flashing back to hanging upside down from my bed as Pablo Hernandez-Cruz proved that his tongue was as talented as his dick was huge. I tried to suppress a snort of laughter, which Dave took to be a sob. He clutched me to his chest and started stroking my hair, 'I can tell you've been hurt in the past. I'd never do that. You just take your time, love.' I was now shaking with hysteria and biting my hand, 'C'mon let it all out for Dave, that's my girl.' I could hold it no more and a wail escaped my lips that shook the street. Dave jumped back in shock, 'What in hell's name has some bastard done to you?'

'Nothing, just ignore me, I'm sorry,' I regained my composure and took a deep breath, this poor bloke was doing his best to be nice and I was being a prize bitch.

'C'mon let's get you home.' I let him take my hand and we walked back to my apartment, where he looked into my eyes and whispered, 'I think you are beautiful, can I kiss you?'

Instead of being firm but kind in my refusal, the pathologically nice and somewhat cowardly part of my nature came to the fore and I nodded dumbly. It was wet, sloppy and reminded me of kissing those teenage boys behind the sport huts in the days that I knew no better. Nowadays I did know a crap kisser when I came across one, and Dave – the poor lad – was the pits. I pulled away, my chin dripping with his saliva which I tried to subtly rub away with my sleeve, 'Well goodnight then.' I turned and unlocked the front door.

'I could come up if you liked, you know, just for coffee.' Dave nodded earnestly at me.

'I'm very tired, think I'll turn in,' I pecked him on the cheek. 'Thank you for a lovely evening.'

'I'll ring you tomorrow.'

*

'Well I think Dave sounds a good sort of guy,' said Cam as he carefully applied wax to my legs and ripped it off. We were having a girlie night in and were both sporting bright green face packs and oiled hair in plastic shower caps.

'Oh don't you start. I've had about ten emails from Mel extolling the virtues of 'normal' blokes. I think as far as she's concerned the Augustin and Penny incident just verified that my taste hasn't got any better.'

'There would have been three of you in that relationship darling - you, him and his ego. Whereas Dave...'

'...is dull and can't kiss.'

'Okay bikini line time,' he gently rubbed some Aloe Vera gel to my calves.

'Are you sure about this?'

'Just turn over, spread your legs and let's get it over with.'

'I hope that's not your typical bedside manner! Ouch!'

'Sorry, I haven't ever done this before, and the last time I was this near to a girl's fanny was the day I was born.'

'Have you really never been with a girl?'

'I've never even kissed one.'

'Ooowwwww!'

'Stop complaining, it's only a little bit of blood.'

'It'll be bruised for days.'

'So will your eyes if you don't shut up.'

'Bastard!'

'I'd be a lot nicer if I were you, I've still got the other leg to do.'

'I want my mummmmmmyyyyyyyyyyyy!'

*

'Are you alright? You're walking funny.' Dave and I were wandering up to The Bush for my first quiz night.

'I'm fine, just a little sore from running this morning,' I lied. Cam had crucified my bikini line and had lost the job as my personal waxer.

'I like a woman that keeps herself fit.' Dave nodded at me, 'You're in good shape, I can see that.'

'D'you wear contact lenses because I think they've fallen out.'

'Don't be so hard on yourself; you're perfect just as you are,' he held the door open for me as we arrived.

Why is it that the men you would really like to hear say those words never seem to say them? Instead of being touched by the compliment, which I couldn't help feel was verging on insincere, I just felt totally undeserving and uncomfortable.

'Right, a drink before we become sworn enemies,' I bought Dave a beer and got myself a cava. There were ten teams crammed into the pub, all hunched around tables eyeing up their competition. Everybody had to pay five euros to play and the winning team would receive the pot at the end, meaning each winning player would receive fifty euros. The tension was high.

I went off and joined my fellow Shafters. Telly Mark was our captain - which essentially meant he got to hold the pen. After the first few rounds, we had made it to second position, three points behind the Boston Stranglers: two married American couples who had an irritating habit of banging on their table and whooping every blasted time they got a question right. Despite Sidney's crossword prowess, the Bristol Bayonets were in ninth place, being spared the embarrassment of being last by the Fab Four: a team of British girlies in their early twenties who were obviously only there on the pull.

The final section came and the pressure was on. The Boston Stranglers had already used their double points on mountain ranges, now it was our double point section. At my suggestion we had picked food and we would have to get all the questions right to ensure beating them by one point.

The questions rolled out. What kind of wheat was used to make pasta? '*Durum,*' I whispered. What spice gave paella its golden appearance? '*Saffron.*' This was too easy. What kind of meat was Kleftiko? '*Lamb.*' It was in the bag. What exactly is a caper? '*Oh shit!*' I was stumped.

'You must know, think....' Veronica hissed.

'Knew we should have picked bleeding sport,' whined Billy.

'They're flower buds,' sighed Mark pompously, 'I used to pick them when I was travelling through Italy in my twenties. Really, Alex, I'm surprised you didn't know that.'

'Well, excuse me I'll swot up a bit better next time.'

'I just hope the rest of the answers are right,' Billy gave me such an evil look you would have thought I'd just suggested we eat his first-born on toast.

'Are you sure about that wheat question?' Veronica nudged me in the ribs.

'Yes.'

'Better be,' Billy was really starting to get on my tits.

'Jesus, it's just a bloody quiz.'

All three of them visibly flinched and looked at me in horror, and I got the feeling they would now have to have a meeting to discuss my eligibility as the fourth Shafter. My dedication to the cause was obviously questionable.

The final quiz sheets were handed in. Our American friends were grinning smugly. They had sensed a little unrest in the Shafter camp and were already spending the money but when Tom the landlord read out the final results, we had won by a single point. Ungracious in defeat, the Stranglers slid sullenly out of the bar without so much as a nod in our direction. We went up to the bar and collected the booty.

'Brains as well as beauty, eh?' Dave's arm appeared around my neck, 'That's my girl.'

'She didn't know that caper question; it would have stuffed us right up if Mark hadn't known the answer,' Billy muttered into his beer.

'Well you won so what's your problem?' Dave sprang to my defence and I snuggled into his armpit. Whether it was the warm glow of winning or the cava, Dave's persistence finally paid off. I agreed to go back to his place for a nightcap.

'Right then, do you want to sleep on the right or the left?'

After sitting on the sofa and having another not quite so sloppy kissing session, I had decided to do the dreadful deed. I led him into his bedroom and now he was standing there uncomfortably.

'Why don't you get us a drink?' I needed a little more loosening up and so did he by the look of it. I stripped off and slid into the bed, trying to ignore the pink floral printed quilt cover. Finally after what seemed an eternity, he came toddling through the door with a tray. He placed it down on the bedside table; I nearly fell out of bed. There were two steaming mugs of tea and a plate of Gypsy Creams. He mistook my shock for awe and beamed, 'You can't get decent biscuits here – my mum brings them over. She's great my mum, helps me with all the décor and stuff.'

'She must have chosen the bedding; you can tell that has a woman's touch.'

'Oh yeah, I've got matching towels in the en-suite too.'

My sarcasm had gone straight over his head and words cannot describe the rising sense of panic I was experiencing. I was just about to have sex with fifteen stone worth of mummy's boy. The Gypsy Creams and I had more sexual chemistry. I leaned over and grabbed my tea. I know, I know - any sensible woman with an ounce of common sense would have gotten out of that bed and ran for her life. What can I say? Once a people-pleaser always a people- pleaser!

'Go on, have a biccie,' he held out the plate. I obliged and took one. He sat on the edge of the bed and slurped his tea down with four of his prized biscuits. After checking I wasn't looking, he threw all his clothes except his underpants off, flicked off the lamp and jumped into bed giggling like a schoolboy. Then he literally leapt right on top of me, nearly expelling all the air from my lungs. As I lay there wheezing, he started to suck my nipples as if he wanted to remove them from my person, then after thrusting my legs apart and fiddling around for precisely ten seconds, he whipped a condom from under his pillow, pulled down his pants and spent thirty seconds fighting to get it over his penis which even in the dim light, I could see was strangely reminiscent of a mushroom. Before I had a chance to get even vaguely involved, he had pushed himself into me, not really noticing that it was as dry as the Gobi Desert down there and coupled with Cam's earlier handiwork, it was agonising. When I gasped in pain, the buffoon looked down at me and said, 'So you like my big cock do you?' and then proceeded to mash my face to a soggy pulp with his lips. I looked up and watched him heaving around on top of me with his eyes gripped shut and face so contorted you would have thought he was in a gurning competition. Every now and then he would grunt *'Tell me when you've come.'* I was tempted to point out that this may involve a little more participation on his part, but in all honesty, I just wanted it over and went off into a little world of my own. Finally I was brought back to reality by a noise that reminded me of a squealing pig. The eagle was about to land.

He switched the lamp back on and gazed down at me, obviously expecting me to purr like a kitten. I suddenly became aware of a half-eaten Gypsy Cream in my right hand. I quickly nuzzled his neck, put the biscuit in my mouth and slid my hand under the covers in an attempt to wipe away any tell-tale crumbs before he noticed. This was a first on the bad sex boredom stakes - Intercoital Biscuit Munching.

'Ah sweetheart, are you feeling all cuddly? I'll be back in a mo,' he whispered and strutted off to the bathroom. I heard the taps run and a particularly horrendous fart. If this was what having a nice normal bloke entailed, I wasn't sure I wanted one.

I lay there and pondered my dilemma. Should I persevere with Dave, try and gently educate him as to the finer points of the female anatomy? Would I be able to banish the floral sheets and biscuits to the back of my mind? Could I ever put myself through this again? Oh shit, what was I going to do?

Eventually he came back to bed and snuggled up to me, 'Night night sexy,' he murmured, and within three minutes he was snoring noisily in my ear.

I tried to doze off but tossed and turned. The pillows were hard, the sheets were full of biscuit crumbs and my ears were being assaulted by not only snoring but a beeping noise coming from the bathroom.

In the end I could take it no more, so I slithered out from his grasp and staggered to the bathroom where I found the source of the beeping – Dave's mobile phone.

Now, just as I never intended to be a no-show at my fortieth birthday party, I really didn't mean to do what I did next – initially.

I actually tried to turn the phone off but after fumbling around for a couple of seconds, there it was – the incoming text - coming in loud and clear.

100 more if u get her ladyship 2 let u in the back door.

It was from Knobby. For a millisecond I tried to persuade myself that this could be something to do with a building contract, but it wasn't. Shaking partly with cold but mostly with rage, I went straight to Dave's sent box and found his last text.

I win u lose. Shagged her senseless, she couldn't get enough of me, gagging 4 it.

With perfect timing, there was the sound of another bloody fart from the bedroom. I sat on the edge of the bath and went back through his texts to Knobby. There was plenty there to hang him - all vile and crude. Going back to the date of the first text, they must have started putting odds on me around the time I met him. To think I had been laying there agonising over how to knock this thing on the head without hurting this 'nice' bloke's feelings. It made me feel sick to the pit of my stomach to think I'd been the subject of a bet. All that fake flattery, pretending to be a caring individual - what kind of loathsome toad was he? Me? Gagging for it? I could feel my temper rising. One thing was for sure, he was not going to get away with a mere slanging match. I was far more imaginative than that.

First things first - I had his phone. I composed a new message...

As a result of Dave's unforgivable and inexcusably puerile behaviour I am now just about to delete you all from his phone, but before I do please read below to see just what a creep he's been and why I'm doing this....

I then cut and pasted a transcript of the text conversations between him and Knobby and sent it off to everyone in his address book, excluding his mum – I just couldn't bring myself to do that.

I then deleted all his contacts, messages and music files. Then with a final flash of inspiration I changed his language format to Russian. That would confuse him for a while.

I crept back into the bedroom and silently picked up my clothes. He was still honking away for all he was worth and it was all I could do to stop myself from inflicting grievous bodily harm. I placed his phone next to him and as I shut the bedroom door quietly behind me I noticed a glow coming from his study. Here was another glorious opportunity to cause mischief. He had left his computer on.

I quickly threw on my clothes and sat in his chair. I clicked on his screen; he had left various applications running including Facebook. My evil alter-ego positively leapt with excitement.

I went straight to his status and typed away...

Dave Hyde would just like to share something with all his dear friends. As you may know I have been living in Sitges for a few years and have now found the courage to come out as a gay man. I know you'll all support me in this. Words cannot express the relief I feel in finally being honest about who I really am.

In order to change his password and prevent him having access to his account, I had to enter his old one. Easy, he had shouted it out to me when he wanted to check Facebook at my place a couple of nights before. I typed in *Arsenal* and smiled to myself. I knew what I was doing was probably illegal but undeterred I removed the software for his phone with all his back-up records and then finally went through and changed his administration password, which was exactly the same. No computer and total havoc for Dave for a few days.

I tiptoed into the kitchen to retrieve my handbag and had my final burst of Evil Genius. Half a packet of Gypsy Creams were laying on the counter. I opened his cupboards and found two more packets plus Digestives and Jammy Dodgers. I didn't care for them at all but Cam loved them and the thought of Dave having nothing to dunk for a while brought me a certain amount of satisfaction. I popped them into my bag and disappeared into the night without a backward glance.

Apart from a very long apologetic text from Viv who had obviously not been privy to the bet and was furious with Knobby, I heard nothing. But after a couple of days, the inevitable confrontation occurred. Cam and I were meandering around town and just happened to wander past The Bush. Dave sailed out of the door.

'You bloody bitch, how could you?'

'How could she? I think you'd better look in the mirror yourself, you prick,' said Cam, who despite finding my revenge amusing, was furious with Dave.

'Keep your nose out of it, gay lad.'

'Word on the street is that you're one of us now!' Cam quipped. The Facebook story had whizzed around Sitges at the speed of light. Radio Cam had seen to that.

Dave's face darkened, so before things got out of hand I stepped in, 'Behave yourself, or I won't give you your password.'

He went quiet and just stood there glowering at Cam.

'One hundred Euros.'

'Ugh?'

The stupid twit thought I wanted money.

'1-0-0-E-U-R-O-S. Quite an appropriate password don't you think?'

'I'm sorry Alex,' he muttered almost inaudibly and for a moment I glimpsed a flicker of shame on his face.

'Oh just go back behind the bike sheds with all your friends,' I nodded towards the line of moronic faces staring out of the pub window and spun on my heel. As we turned to walk away, Cam went to say something but I stopped him, 'Don't bother Cam, he's not worth it.' I shot Dave a superior look but to be quite frank, I might just as well have blown a raspberry and flicked him the 'V'. It felt like school-days all over again.

'Feel better?' Cam put his arm around my shoulders.

'I'll get over it,' I hugged him back. 'D'you know what? I would never have been seen dead in a pub like that in the UK. Isn't it weird what we ex-pats do on foreign shores?'

'C'mon, let's bugger off to Barcelona and see a movie. There's bound to be a bit of Almodovar showing somewhere. Change of scenery would do us both some good I think.'

So off we went to immerse ourselves in a little culture. Nothing like an arty farty Spanish film with sub-titles to make you feel all grown-up again.

TWENTY ONE

In Spain it's legal to own three marijuana plants for your own use and totally acceptable to wander around the streets smoking a big fat joint. Unless you are buried in the depths of rural or provincial Spain you can pretty much find somewhere to drink alcohol at any time of the day or night. During my early morning walks along the beach front in Sitges I would regularly see old fishermen setting out their breakfast of a fresh loaf of bread with some *jamon y queso* and a bottle of *vino tinto* even though it was only six-thirty. Quite often on the beach I would bump into groups of young people who had been up all night and were still smoking spliffs and banging their drums, and then I would sit in the nearest café and be greeted by the sight of four hairy-arsed workmen tucking into *patatas bravas* washed down with a few *cervezas*.

Anything goes really, after years and years of the oppressive Franco regime, the fiesta loving Spanish are officially 'up for it'. I got the impression that they would take greater offence if you hadn't rung your mother for a week than if you stripped off and had sex publicly – well, unless you did it in a church. Life is for living - do what you want, when you want. Why not? I loved their attitude – what a fantastic way to live your life.

But complications can sometimes set in when you end up not knowing that you are doing something that you wouldn't have wanted to do if you knew – have I lost you there? It's all to do with *slipping in*.

Now we all do it from time to time - I am a past master at the art. I have slipped in a pretty inventive collection of sex toys into a friend's suitcase just before she took off on her honeymoon; I used to slip extra sandwiches and cake into the bag of an emaciated old guy who used to come to a café I worked in when I was fifteen. I have slipped a live frog into a friend's sleeping bag and all you veggie friends of mine out there – did you honestly think my mushroom risotto tasted that good without me slipping in a bit of chicken stock?

Well it would appear that Evie is also a bit of a *slipper* on the quiet, as she demonstrated at her birthday bash in May.

I had arrived early with Bart and Cam.

'Make yourselves at home children.' Evie was dressed head to toe in so much orange, one expected her to break into a Hare Krishna chant and start dancing around the flat jingling bells. We sat out on the balcony in the warm night air, nibbling nuts and doing our bit to keep the Spanish wine industry afloat. Cam was chatting to Evie about dysfunctional relationships, and Bart and I were talking about non-existent relationships.

'D'you know the last time I had a boyfriend was three years ago,' Bart said glumly as he used his tongue to suction off a piece of almond skin that had attached itself to his front tooth. 'I'm getting too old for all this darkroom crap. Anyhow, I was hoping you would do something for me,' Bart leaned over conspiratorially. 'Would you suss out how Cam feels about me?'

My nod was less than enthusiastic, as I already knew the answer to the question. I knew Cam's type – strong, silent, masculine guys with buff bodies and preferably longish hair. Bart was camp, cropped and crying out for attention. 'I'll see what I can do Bart, but it's not a good time for him at the moment, you know, after Enrique.'

'Oh babes, that was weeks ago, time to move on.'

'Hi everyone,' Bubbles burst onto the balcony, trailed by a posse of very butch looking Spanish girls. She was wearing a leather corset that must have been a remnant from her dominatrix days. Her tits were literally exploding out everywhere.

'Oh my God, it's Madame Whiplash and the rugby team,' shrieked Bart, who pretended to hide behind my skirt.

'Hi Alex,' Bubbles wandered over and gave me a hug.

'Hi there Shrimp Lips,' Bart re-emerged from behind me and

nodded towards her pals, 'have they been fed recently?'

Bubbles ignored him and carried on talking, 'Got myself a new bird, she's the pretty one over there.'

'Pretty one – let me see,' Bart screwed up his eyes, 'nope you've got me there Bubbles.'

'Do people regularly get the urge just to come up and punch you, Bart?' Bubbles nodded over to the slightest of the women, 'Her name's Carmen, she's a fashion designer. We're going to try and come up with a range together.'

'You could always call it Designer Dykes,' Bart had one last dig before throwing himself at Cam who was just wandering back from the kitchen with a handful of glasses.

Pretty soon everybody had turned up and the party was buzzing. Cam and I smiled at each other as we watched Evie and an older guy called Giles leaning against the balcony walls, chatting. Every now and then Giles would glance away looking at some cute young guy's butt, then he would turn back to Evie and they would resume gossiping.

'You thinking what I'm thinking?' I said to Cam.

'Yeah, that could be us in twenty-five years,' he laughed.

'Nah it won't, but it wouldn't be so bad if it was, would it?'

'Yes it would,' said Cam emphatically, 'we'd be perming and colouring your bikini line rather than waxing it by then.'

'Eeeeeew,' I punched his arm, 'let's go and get some food.'

Everyone was tucking into Evie's buffet with great gusto. There was an ice-cold gazpacho with a serious kick to it, and I noticed that the chilli was distinctly 'herby'. By the time the chocolate birthday cake came around, everyone was so off their faces they wouldn't have known what their own tongues tasted like. The sound of high-pitched laughter filled the room. An older woman, resplendent in white with excessive gold accessories and bleached blonde hair came over to me and peered closely at my face, 'I know what you are.'

'A tart,' giggled Cam.

'I'm very good at this; I never get it wrong. You're a Leo aren't you?'

Now I started giggling, 'What makes you say that?'

'All that hair, it's a dead giveaway.'

'Is anyone here a Pisces?' I shouted above the din.

'Me,' Fred shouted back.

'Check that man for gills and fins!' Cam and I dissolved into fits. Undeterred the woman carried on, as far as she was concerned I was obviously lying or stupid, as I couldn't be anything other than her original diagnosis. Eventually I got bored, 'I'm an Aquarian.'

'Well, I'd never have said that,' she turned on her heel and left.

'You didn't say that,' I shouted after her.

'How could anybody get it wrong? You're so Aquarian,' Cam's eyes had started to spin. He looked like Kaa, the snake from *Jungle Book*. 'Shall I get us another drink?' He walked off without waiting for an answer. I flopped onto some floor cushions on the lounge floor and realised I was having trouble focusing. Suddenly from one of the bedrooms, much to my horror, out walked Bubbles, who had obviously just decided that clothes were an out-dated concept and was now totally starkers bar a minuscule thong. Followed by her fully-clothed entourage she jiggled and wobbled out of the door announcing to everyone that she was a lunar Goddess and she was going down to the beach to worship the full moon. Somebody shouted out, 'More lunatic than lunar Goddess.' This started me off. I wanted to tell Cam but I was laughing so hard I couldn't get up. Evie came and sat down next to me, her smile looked three feet wide, 'Hi honey, how you doing?'

'I'm smashed and Bubbles hasn't got any clothes on.' I leaned on her shoulder, 'What on earth did you put in that food?'

'A little absinthe in the soup and a bit of weed in the chilli - we used to do it at college. I thought it would make the party go with a swing.'

'Go with a swing! You've nearly killed everybody, look at them all,' I looked blearily around the flat where people seemed to have collapsed into piles in corners, on the sofa, in the hall. Fred and Pierre were in the kitchen, every now and then you would hear the words 'Brussels sprouts' and then they would dissolve into giggles.

'Come and get some fresh air,' Evie stood up and pulled me onto my feet. I followed her out onto the balcony and gazed up at a huge beautiful moon that was creating a shimmering path in the sea. The cooler air made me feel momentarily more lucid. I looked around and spotted Cam having an animated conversation with Bart, who was looking up at him adoringly. Next to them in the corner was a woman sitting on her own eating flowers out of a vase.

'Oh that's my friend Frieda from Frankfurt. She does that every time she gets drunk,' Evie sighed. 'Whenever I know she's coming to visit I have to hide all my potted plants next door. She ate a silk lily once.'

Evie left me staring at Frieda who had just started tucking into a purple Gerbera. Another wave of alcohol and hash started to wash over me, so I decided to make a move. I wandered out of the front door and floated down the stairs. When I reached the beach there was Bubbles standing at the water's edge, arms aloft, singing something unintelligible while her friends silently looked on. I carried on towards home, loving everything around me. I loved the sea, I loved the church, I loved the lamp posts, I loved the stray cats - everything was lovely. Absinthe had made my heart grow fonder. I rang Cam to tell him I loved him but he didn't answer, so I then must have proceeded to work my way through the contact list on my mobile phone.

When I finally surfaced the next afternoon I had a few messages.

'What the hell were you on last night?' Mel's voice screeched down the phone, *'I mean I love you too, but did you really have to call me at two in the morning to tell me?'*

'It's me Pablo. I knew you love me too cariña - when we see each other again?'

'Erm - this is John from Shurgard storage in Hanwell - glad to- erm - know you're happy with our service.'

'Hey Alex, it's good to hear from you. Are you drunk? Nothing changed this end, Laurence is still a bastard and I'm still counting calories. Ring me and tell me how you're getting on. It's Beverley by the way, byeeeeeee.'

'Hello Alex, Mum here. Of course I'll come and stay darling, how lovely of you to miss me that much. I've just booked a flight, so I'll see you on Monday morning at ten-forty five. I love you too.'

*

I sat staring at my mobile over my fifth cup of coffee at the Bodega Bar on *Player San Sebastian* and let it sink in. My mum was coming the next morning and I had less than a day to clean up my act. For starters - the seemingly impossible task of transferring the two hundred or so bottles that had been piling up on my back terrace over to the recycling bins. I had more clothes stacked up on the spare bed than I had in my wardrobe. The fridge contained nothing more than a mouldy onion and a few cans of beer. I looked at my watch; it was three-thirty. I had to get some muscle power, and as if in answer to my prayers, the phone rang. Pierre was in Barcelona and Fred needed occupying. Perfect. Within five minutes he was on my doorstep in organisational mode. In three hours it was done. I seriously contemplated marketing him as a Hunky Home Help and attempted to sell him on the idea, but as we sat out on the balcony with a couple of diet sodas all he wanted to do was watch the boys go by. 'Roll on summer,' he said as an already bronzed god waltzed past. When Fred left five minutes later and wandered up towards the church, I had a fleeting sense of foreboding.

Just before I went to bed that night in my new gleaming apartment complete with full fridge and colour coordinated wardrobe, Cam popped in on his way to work and went straight to the kitchen to get a beer.

'Jesus, I was going to ask what happened to you last night but obviously the full moon turned you into a Stepford wife.'

'More like all the bloody crap Evie put in her food. I was out of my stack, and so were you. Last thing I saw was you in a deep *tete á tete* with Bart.'

'Oh if only that was where it ended,' Cam shook his head. 'Why did you leave me?'

'Oh my God, you didn't?'

'Sure did and now her Ladyship thinks we are getting married.'

I roared, got myself an *aqua con gas*, and then sat on the sofa with Cam. 'He was trying to get me to find out if you liked him before the buffet knocked us all into orbit.'

'Alex, he worships me.'

'The question is, was it any good?'

'Can't remember,' he laughed, 'just woke up this morning and found myself staring at his little face. I nearly died - he had mascara smudged around his eyes.'

'Well you're a fine one to talk.'

'*That* is Carnival and *that* is different,' Cam leaned back into the cushions.

I giggled, 'This town is like one big college campus. We've all regressed to being students again. Off we go to each other's dorms with our bottles of grog, get pissed, smoke joints and end up in bed with people we shouldn't. If we do the walk of shame in the morning, everybody knows about it by midday. The only thing that has changed is we use mobiles instead of passing notes around the classroom.'

Cam laughed, stood up and ruffled his hair in the Balinese mirror above the sofa. 'Gotta go honey, you coming in tonight?'

'Nope, my mum arrives in the morning.'

'What?'

'You slept with Bart. I invited my mum over. Evie is officially toast.'

TWENTY TWO

'Maman!' A French girl next to me at the arrivals gate ran excitedly towards an elegant older woman in a cream trouser suit and Prada shades. Two seconds later my mum emerged looking very Miami housewife hits Vegas. Her travel ensemble consisted of a pale turquoise velour 'leisure suit', brilliant white trainers and a pink sun visor. Just where she had got her luggage I don't know, but I would imagine if you actually set out to find a three piece matching set, complete with vanity case in a floral print last seen gracing windows at the beginning of the twentieth century, it would prove a difficult task. I considered asking the French girl if she'd like to swap but before I had the chance, Mum had me in a bear hug and her trolley ran over my foot.

'Darling you look dreadful.'

'I think I have five broken toes.'

'You've got dark circles, and Alex, have you put on weight?'

'Lovely to see you too, Mum,' I pushed the offending trolley out into the sunlight, hailed a cab and told the driver to take us along the coastal road. Mum broke into a pretty incessant stream of her usual chitchat, 'I've got three hundred euros. Will that be enough? I've brought good old English teabags - bet you can't get those here, and chocolate digestives, I've got you a treat – a big jar of Marmite. You'll never guess what your sister did last week…' then she noticed the abundance of scantily clad women lining the back roads from the airport.

'Alex there seems to be a lot of girls hanging around these roads, isn't that a little dangerous?'

'They're prostitutes.'

'They're what?'

'You heard me - hookers.'

Suddenly she was fixated. 'I don't think that one was wearing pants, Alex, look at that one. Gosh, look, look over there, a car's stopping, she's getting in. He should be ashamed of himself, in broad daylight as well...'

Our cab driver gave me a bemused look in the rear view mirror. I was in no doubt that he had probably stopped off for a little light relief on the odd occasion.

I tried to steer her back to a little normality, 'Look Mum, the sea, isn't it beautiful?'

'Mmnn,' she was too busy craning her neck trying to get a better view of a delivery truck pulling up by a pretty Latino girl in minute yellow shorts.

'Well, the weather has perked up over the past few days so you might even get to sunbathe. By the way, how long are you staying?'

'Don't look so panic-stricken, Alex, only four days. I don't want you chucking me out like you did poor Penny.'

'Poor bloody Penny – my arse! Mum what did she tell you?'

'She wouldn't discuss it with me, just said that you two had a disagreement and you over-reacted. She's very loyal to you and obviously didn't want to bitch about you to me, but I could tell she was very upset. What made you do such a thing?'

'Well I have no qualms about bitching about her to you. She's a two-faced selfish little cow who has been pulling the bloody wool over your eyes for years, and what drives me nuts is that you always assume the worst of me.'

'Oh Alexandra, that's not true.'

'Yes it is, now let me tell you my side of the story.'

By the time we reached my apartment Penny Johnson was no longer on a pedestal. I spared my mum no details. She had committed a crime, so serious in Mum's eyes there would be no forgiveness. It wasn't so much that she had cheated on John and been vile to my friends, it was the fact she had buggered up a potential boyfriend for me. This was one thing Mum could not tolerate. It brought out the protective mother lioness in her.

'I'm never asking her to the Debenhams sale preview night ever again.'

Well sort of…

'What a pretty flat! What a beautiful view!' Mum wandered around opening cupboards and checking the place out as only a mother would do, surreptitiously running her fingers across surfaces which yesterday would have been thick with dust. She walked out onto the back terrace and gazed around her at all the other apartments that overlooked mine. 'I hope you pull the curtains when you're getting changed.'

'Oh I think they've all got better things to do than wait around for a flash of my butt.'

'Mmmn,' she had disappeared into her own little world. I could tell she was plotting. 'We could get you some lovely plants and ornaments for out here.'

The key word here was ornaments. Mum suffers from a condition common to many women of a certain age – *ornamentitis*. She just loves to fill any available space with crap. Extreme vigilance is necessary or else this crap can very easily creep into your life too. The real danger zone is when she goes on holiday because I know damn well she's going to come back and present me with a condiment set made of camel ears or something equally ghastly, and me, well I have a face that says it all. I've never been able to hide my reactions and would never make a good poker player. More often than not, Mummy's present-giving ends up with her feeling offended and me totally guilt-ridden. So it's best to avoid the situation completely.

'No Mum, plants are far too much responsibility, and you know I hate bloody statues or whatever glazed pottery things you're thinking of. If you want to get me a present, I'd really appreciate a new wok – normal simple metal kind, not enamelled with flowers.'

'But it could be so charming out here, you could sit outside in the summer and have drinks and read a book, and it would be …'

'Mum, have you forgotten the phenomenal view I have from the balcony? Move away from the terrace and come inside. I do my washing out there, I hang my clothes out there, as does everybody else if you look around you. I do not want to be sitting out there in the summer surrounded by underpants and beach towels. Come in and find me those tea bags. I'll make you a lovely cuppa.'

'Right, I'll sleep in here,' she threw her suitcase on the spare bed.

'No Mum, you can have my room.'

'I wouldn't dream of it, I'll be as cosy as anything in here.'

'Penny threw me out of my room,' I couldn't resist one more little poke.

'She would,' she muttered as she unpacked an array of pastel coloured clothing. She pulled out a box of PG Tips and chucked them at me, 'and to think it was me who suggested that little snake in the grass came to see you.'

I smiled to myself as I put the kettle on. Pathetic as it was, you have to remember that hearing my mum say anything even vaguely negative about Penny was a total novelty. Oh the joy - game set and match – Alex.

'Right what would you like to do?'

'I would like to have a good wander around and see where it is you're living, oh and Alex, I'm a little peckish.'

Now if Mum can run riot with her camera, be faced with an impressive sweet trolley or rummage around a bargain bucket, she is as happy as a pig in shit, so I decided we could do all three. Our afternoon consisted of lunch at a local patisserie, a mammoth walk from one end of Sitges to the other, taking in all the cobbled streets, the cemetery, the church and the beaches, and for my *piece de la resistance,* I let her loose in one of the euro shops. She was in her element and bought the worst presents imaginable for everybody except me – I got an expensive wok from a posh shop.

In celebration of my new culinary utensil, I cooked a chicken stir-fry for dinner and Mum hit the *rosado* whilst she rearranged her presents on the table, trying to work out exactly who should be the lucky recipient of the melon baller with a handle fashioned on a likeness of the Sitges church. By midnight, we'd eaten dinner, she was steaming and my sister was destined for a nasty shock when she opened her little gift. I suggested Mum go to bed. Suddenly we had a role reversal situation on our hands. She behaved like a spoilt teenager.

'I don't want to go to bed now, I'm not tired.'

'Mum, if you want to go to Barcelona tomorrow, you'll need an early night. It'll be a long day.'

'You can't tell me to go to bed. I'm your mum. I tell *you* when to go to bed.'

'You're too drunk.'

'I want to go out.'

'Oh Jesus!'

'Just for an hour, Alex, c'mon, we'll have more wine.'

'You've had enough.'

'Alex, don't be such a bore.'

So being the dutiful daughter that I am, I took my mullered mother to El Cabaret where, I have to say, she was a total hit. I sat back and watched as she gossiped with Fred and Pierre, made arrangements to get together with Evie for drinks and generally endeared herself to everyone in the bar.

'What on earth were you going on about?' Cam poked my arm, 'Your mum's great fun.'

'She's as drunk as a skunk.'

'Well they say the apple never falls very far from the tree,' a familiar but unwelcome voice rang out from behind me. I turned and there was Stephan.

'Well your mum must have been quite a character then - God only knows what she used to get up to,' I smiled sweetly.

His eyes flashed angrily and he went to spit something back but he obviously thought better of it because as far as Stephan was concerned, I was holding a trump card. I had never told a soul about what I had seen the night of the competition. Even Cam was unaware the reason he lost was because Stephanie had been servicing Jorges. My silence was more effective in unnerving Stephan than sending the information on the Sitges 'gossip express'. Anyway, by now it would have been yesterday's story and I preferred to keep it as possibly tomorrow's news – he hated the fact I had one up on him.

'Who's this then, another of your friends I haven't met? Hello, I'm Alex's mother. Haven't you got lovely hair?' Mum ruffled Stephan's curly mane. He shrank back uncomfortably.

'I'm Stephan, nice to meet you.'

'You sound very foreign, where are you from?'

'Croatia, have you been?'

'No but Alex has, she's been everywhere.'

'Yes, your daughter certainly gets around, Mrs Chapman.' Stephan's capacity for polite chit chat came to an abrupt end, 'Do enjoy your visit and be careful you don't catch anything nasty. Alex is always in and out of the pharmacy aren't you, dahling? Must dash. Ciao ciao.'

Cam and I glanced at each other; luckily Mum was totally oblivious to any undercurrents and she went wandering off again to chat to her new best friend Evie.

'He's usually over all this by now,' Cam shook his head, 'but he really has got it in for you. Mind you, you don't exactly keep the peace with him do you?'

'What's the point? I can't get on with everyone.'

'Just don't let it get out of hand - he can be very spiteful and I don't want you on the receiving end.'

'I'm a big girl,' I leaned over the bar and kissed him on the cheek. 'I'm just going off to the loo; keep an eye on Mum for me, will you?'

When I returned Mum was nowhere to be seen. I pushed my way through the crowd and spotted Evie who told me she had just gone outside for a little fresh air. I looked outside the bar door but she wasn't there. Cam came over and asked if everything was okay.

'She's disappeared.'

'She can't have done, she only walked out a couple of minutes ago.'

'Look, I'll go back to the flat and see if she's there, if she comes back, keep her here and ring me.' I legged it out of the door and ran home. It was empty. I rang Cam. There was still no sign of her.

'Okay, I'm going to walk the streets until I find her,' I said, trying to swallow my rising fear.

'I'll join you. Aaron can close the bar. Don't panic, she can't have gone far.'

Despite trying to remain calm, my imagination ran riot. The thought of something awful happening to her made me feel sick to the pit of my stomach. I vowed never to be sarcastic ever again, I would be the perfect daughter, I'd go shopping with her, I'd let her fill my whole flat with ornaments, I'd ask her to teach me her recipe for pavlova, I wouldn't leave the phone on the table and bugger off and make coffee when she was in mid-monologue ever again. I met Cam down on the street, 'What shall we do, split up?'

'You take everything left of *Raoul's*, I'll take everything right and the *paseo*.'

'Okay, we'll ring if we find her.'

We both went off in separate directions. The streets were still quiet as the season hadn't officially started yet. A few groups of kids were hanging out on the *Cap de la Ville* but essentially Sitges was like a ghost town. How could my mother just vaporise into thin air? I walked down every side street, looked around the church, scanned *Playa San Sebastian* and even walked up to the cemetery, but *nada*. Suddenly after thirty minutes of searching, the phone rang.

'I've found her. She's absolutely fine - meet you back at yours.'

I ran all the way back, arriving simultaneously with Cam and a very dishevelled, exhausted mum.

'I went for a little walk and got myself lost.'

'This is exactly why I bought you that bloody mobile phone, Mum. I was so worried.'

'Well I'm here now, aren't I?' She stuck her bottom lip out like a petulant little child.

'Mmmn; well get upstairs and go to bed, you drunken old moo,' I laughed with relief and we all clambered up to the apartment.

'Fancy a quick Uncle Peter?' I looked at Cam; sherry had become our ritual late night drink.

'Yeah, hit me with a schooner.'

'Not for me,' Mum had already donned a nightgown and was cleaning her teeth at the dizzy rate of what looked like about four brush strokes per minute.

'Funnily enough I wasn't talking to you; now go to bed.'

'Don't talk to me like that, I'm your mum,' she shut her bedroom door and I could hear the sound of gentle snoring within minutes.

'Here you go,' I passed Cam his *Tio Pepe*. 'Where did you find her?'

'Shagger Sands.'

'No!!!'

Shagger Sands was a name that Cam and I had given to the section of the beach that was a nocturnal haunt for those in search of a bit of anonymous gay sex It's a hive of activity between 2.30 am and when the clubs chuck out near daybreak.

'What on earth was she doing all the way down there?'

'Asking all the nice young men she bumped into, if they knew you and where you lived.'

'She didn't actually go onto the beach did she?'

'No, boy would she have had an education. Thankfully she'd managed to bump into Bart, who was just about to bring her back here when I found her,' he laughed, 'which worked out brilliantly for me. I just looked all hurt and said I couldn't possibly have a relationship with someone who hangs out down there. So I'm totally off the hook.'

'Poor Bart,' I sighed. 'I'm taking Mum to Barcelona tomorrow.'

'I'll come.'

'Are you sure? It means being here at eleven,' Cam's face dropped, he loved his bed and was dreadful at waking up.

'Will you ring me about ten-thirty?'

'Of course, now either bugger off or sleep here. It's four-thirty already.'

'Your mum might get the wrong impression, I'm going home.'

TWENTY THREE

'Is he still not answering?' Having sworn to never drink again, Mum was sitting at the table nursing her fourth cup of strong tea.

'No, I'll kill him,' I looked at the clock. It was five to eleven. 'C'mon Mum, drink up, we'll go and wake him up.'

We arrived at Cam's apartment block ten minutes later. I rang his bell but there was no answer. A Spanish couple came out of the building. I grabbed the door before it closed and just before I went in, I noticed something in the flowerbeds by the door. It was a smashed mobile phone. I recognised the multi-coloured striped casing immediately - it was Cam's.

The lift took forever but eventually we reached the eleventh floor. I bashed on his door and shouted his name but there was no response. My heart was pounding in my chest.

'Alex there's probably a simple explanation for this, calm down.'

'Mum I know something is wrong.'

The door next to Cam's opened and his old Spanish neighbour poked her head out. She looked frightened.

'*Donde esta Cam?*'

She pointed to his flat and waved her hands, '*Mucho ruido, muchos gritos.*'

'I think she said there was a lot of shouting and noise. Hey, wait a minute. I can get in through her balcony.'

'*Por favor! Cam es mi amigo!*' I left her gabbling on in Spanish and barged through and opened the doors. I started to climb onto the edge of the balcony.

'Alex, please come off there,' Mum looked horrified as I balanced precariously on the narrow ledge. Not daring to look down, I grabbed hold of the flimsy partition that separated the two balconies, closed my eyes and tentatively swung one of my legs around to the other side. It found the ledge and gripping as tightly as I could, I brought my other leg around. For one split second I couldn't find a foothold and my hands started to slip. Mum sprung forward and wrapped her arm around my waist. As my foot found the ledge, she pushed me and I fell with a bang onto Cam's balcony.

The lounge windows were open. I rushed in. The place was in chaos - the shelves were on the floor and the glass side-table was smashed into smithereens. I pushed the door open to Cam's bedroom and somewhere in the distance, I heard myself scream as I saw his body lying on the floor. His shirt was ripped to shreds and his face was black and blue and caked with blood. I shook him gently and he groaned, 'Enrique was here.'

'You stupid bastard, you never changed the locks did you?'

There was banging coming from the front door so I opened it and Mum rushed in. The neighbour peered in nervously and I thrust my mobile into her hand, *'Emergencia, emergencia.'* Even though it wasn't the right word, she obviously picked up on the vibe, dialled straight away and shouted *'Socorro'* Confident that she had indeed called the emergency services, I went back in and sat on the floor with Cam, where Mum was already stroking his head. Sure enough, ten minutes later, the flat was filled with ambulance staff and police. My frustration at my lack of Spanish had never been so monumental. Luckily the old lady could fill them in. As they started to carry Cam on a stretcher down the eleven flights of stairs, I looked at Mum who was still in a state of shock, 'I'm going to ring Evie and get her to come and pick you up from downstairs and I'm going to the hospital, okay?'

'I'll come with you.'

'They probably won't let more than one other person in the ambulance, Mum. You'll be better off with Evie.' I dialled Evie's number and she said she would be there in five. We took the lift and by the time the ambulance door was closing, I saw Evie careering through the gates and rushing towards Mum. I turned back towards Cam who was now a mass of tubes and leads. The ambulance man must have seen me starting to heave because he thrust a bag in my hands just before I vomited.

Cam had three broken ribs from being kicked, two black eyes, about twenty stitches on his forehead and scalp and mild concussion. His face was swollen so much he could barely talk. He had walked in and caught Enrique and a couple of his friends burgling his flat. They had thrown his phone over the balcony when he went to call for help. A fight had ensued and Enrique probably would have killed him, had one of the other guys not pulled him off.

I sat in my kitchen numbly bringing Mum and Evie up-to-date on the situation. The boys from El Cabaret had been brilliant support. Simon and I had stayed at the hospital all night and Aaron arrived at 7 am to take over so we could get some sleep. Before we left we were allowed to see Cam, who thankfully had stabilised and was conscious. When we suggested we contact his family in the UK, he was adamant we did no such thing.

'You have to respect his wishes, now c'mon, go to bed, it's nearly nine o'clock,' Mum rubbed my back.

'I'm sorry Mum, this isn't much of a break for you is it?'

'Don't be so stupid, Alex. Evie looked after me very well yesterday and she cooked a lovely chilli last night.'

I raised my eyebrows at Evie who shook her head and smiled. The idea of my mum on Evie's birthday chilli didn't bear thinking about. 'Thank you, I owe you one.'

'Alex, please, your mother is wonderful and it was my pleasure. She told me all about what you did. That was very brave of you. Actually, we thought maybe it would be a good idea if she extended her trip a little, maybe an extra three or four days?'

'I'd like that - very much.' Suddenly the thought of not having her around seemed unbearable. 'We need to change the flight.'

'We'll do it on your computer, now please go to bed, I'm back in charge,' Mum ruffled my hair.

'You don't know the first thing about computers.'

'I do, so do what your mother tells you and get yourself into that bedroom,' Evie said sternly.

'Are you two ganging up on me?'

'Yes.'

I awoke to the smell of cooking and the sound of laughter. When I emerged, Mum and Evie were in the kitchen cooking up a storm, doing a little fusion cuisine – essentially Californian Jewish meets South East London Church of England. Evie was preparing salmon with what looked like potato and courgette fritters, and Mum, predictably, was making dessert – a trifle. As I walked into the kitchen she was telling Evie the infamous 1976 trifle tale.

'….the little bugger sat there trying to blame it on her brother – she was caught red-handed and still thought she could fib her way out of it.'

'Okay, so shoot me.'

'Hello there,' they chorused.

'Has anyone heard anything from the hospital?'

'Yes, Aaron just called me. Cam is resting and they are probably going to let him out either tomorrow or the next day,' Evie thrust some bright green asparagus into a pan. 'Dinner will be ready in five, so relax and go and sit down, it was traumatic for you, too.'

I walked back into the lounge, sat down and looked at the table, 'You've forgotten the wine glasses.'

'No I haven't,' Mum came into the lounge wiping her hands, 'we just thought a night on soft drinks would be good for everybody.'

'Me, you mean,' I responded a little too quickly and defensively.

'Yes,' said Evie calmly, as she placed the food on the table.

I knew deep in my soul what was coming, as it wasn't anything I hadn't already been thinking myself. I steeled myself for the onslaught.

'This is a dangerous little town. Everything is there for you if you want to indulge and it takes great strength of character not to get drawn in. We all misbehave from time to time – including me,' said Evie. 'It's just that you do seem to be on a roller coaster ride at the moment. You're a party girl, always ready to go out at the drop of a hat, buy people drinks, listen to their life stories, stay out all hours and be everything to everybody. But where in all that equation is time for Alex? What are you doing for yourself right now?'

'Not a lot I suppose.'

'I was shocked when I saw you, Alex, you look dreadful, you've put on weight and did I see you smoking the other day? Is this what you meant by changing your life?' Mum sighed.

'You're right; I can't honestly remember the last day I didn't have a drink and as for the smoking, I know it's stupid.' I was tired and emotional and the tears started to well up, 'Oh my god, I'm an alcoholic!'

'Hey come on, stop that and eat. Your food's getting cold. Nobody is saying you have to be a nun, Alex,' Evie passed me a jug of Hollandaise sauce, 'just try to be a bit more moderate.'

TWENTY FOUR

I told Cam about the conversation the next day as I sat at his bedside, feeding him Mum's trifle with a little plastic spoon. His bruising was already changing colour and he seemed to be able to talk more easily.

'I think we all need to slow down,' he muttered. 'Maybe Molly and Toff should go into retirement for a while.'

'Yeah, like you're going out on the town sometime soon! Crikey Cam, I've turned into a stereotypical ex-pat. Living the dream and drinking myself stupid. Penny would have a field day wouldn't she?' I did an impersonation of the drunken tirade she'd treated us to around the dinner table.

'Don't make me laugh, it hurts my ribs.' Suddenly he grabbed my hand, 'Alex, thank you.'

'For what exactly?'

'Caring enough to come around and check on me.'

'I was coming around to kick your sorry arse out of bed.' I squeezed his hand.

'I still can't believe you nearly fell off that bloody balcony.'

'I'd have been a pavement pancake if it hadn't been for Mum. She saved my life. I keep getting these horrible flashbacks. Is there any news on that little shit and his friends yet?'

'Nope, the police checked their flat and they've cleared out.'

'Poor baby, I want to hug you but I think I'll hurt you.'

'You will,' he smiled. 'I suppose we're going to have to kiss goodbye to 'The Cava Queen' and start calling you 'Spider Woman' now?'

'The Cava Queen?'

'Didn't you know you had a nickname?'

'No I didn't!'

'We call you that because of your bubbly personality.'

'Bullshit! That is it, seriously Cam. I'm going to start behaving myself.'

Cam wheezed, at which point a nurse walked in and ushered me away. It was time for *Senor* Ferguson to take his siesta. I blew him a kiss and went back to the apartment where Mum was busy doing 'mummy' stuff. I had a pile of ironed clothes, sparkling windows, gleaming bathroom tiles - she'd even reorganised and cleaned my kitchen cabinets.

'Maybe you should stay forever, Mum,' I flopped back on my now puffed cushions.

'I think a week might be our limit, don't you?'

'Maybe two,' I winked at her, 'anyhow you have effectively organised me a mummy number two haven't you?'

'I've got to have someone to keep an eye on you.'

'She's amazing isn't she? I assume she told you her story.'

'Yes, it's tragic isn't it? I don't know if I could get through that and come out the other side like she has,' she gasped and let out a sob. 'Alex, I don't know what I would have done if you had fallen, my mind just keeps flashing back to you on that balcony.'

'Hey Mum, don't get yourself upset, I didn't fall. You saved me.'

'This is what I worry about when you keep gallivanting around. Say something happens and there is no-one there to help you, say you hurt yourself?'

I leapt up and gave her a cuddle.

'Mum, I have some very good friends who would help me if I were in trouble. I'm sorry I'm not what you'd like me to be, living around the corner and going to your Debenhams sale previews with you, but it's just not me.'

'Oh Alex, you're everything I want you to be. I'm proud of you. I suppose it just hurts sometimes to think you don't need me. You never have.'

'Of course I need you.'

'You don't Alex, whenever you had a problem you would run to your dad, he was the one who sorted them out and I always seemed to be the one who caused them. Since he died, you don't run to anyone. I suppose I had hoped you might confide in me for a change but all I see you do is take on the woes of the world. Who do you talk to?'

'I talk to everybody, you know that.'

'Really talk to?'

'It's an Aquarian thing. We don't feel the need to.'

'Utter poppycock! Don't hide behind that horoscope nonsense, young lady. I know you far too well to fall for that old twaddle.'

'You don't know me well enough to stop nagging me about bloody men, though. Most of them are a waste of space. I mean you're only with boring old *what's his face* because it makes you feel more secure when you have to go out with all your old married friends - who incidentally backed away in droves when Dad died and now have only allowed you back into the clan because you're with somebody.'

'Oh, Alex, don't be so hard on them, it's a generational thing.'

'That's a load of crap. It was even starting to happen to me, Mum. I'm the first person everyone calls to fill in the gaps and mop up the tears when it's all going wrong. Good old Alex, she's got nothing better to do. I can't tell you how many relationship break-ups I've been dragged into. Then they're either back with the old one or onto the next and suddenly it's easier and neater to have an even number at the dinner table, so the couples gravitate back towards each other with yours truly left kicking her heels.

'Alex, that is so negative.'

'That's my reality I'm afraid. I've seen you have more of a laugh with Evie over the past few days than I have in the past few years with any of your lot. Isn't it better having girlfriends, gay friends, fuck it – any friends that you get on with and actually enjoy talking to, rather than putting up with some miserable old sod who bores you to tears just because you want to fit in? Is it really so vital to have a bloke's arm to dangle on?'

'I don't know any different, it's what I'm used to.'

'And I have never been in your shoes so can we just beg to

differ?'

'Oh I don't know, Alex; I would love you to have someone in your life who is there for you, someone who will catch you if you fall.'

'Oh god we're back to the balcony again.'

'Alexandra, that is not funny.'

'Sorry.'

'For the life of me, I've never understood why you pick such dreadful boyfriends,' my mum shook her head and fiddled with a stray thread that was hanging from the sleeve of my 'cover a thousand sins' cardigan. 'Do you think sub-consciously you don't want to get overly attached to anyone, so it won't matter if you lose them?'

'Where are we going with this Mrs Freud? I assume we have been tossing this around with Evie?'

'I just don't want you to be lonely Alex.'

'I think it's you who's lonely Mum. I miss him too you know.'

Her eyes welled up instantly which initiated an identical reaction in me. We both flopped down on the sofa and bawled our eyes out for a solid ten minutes and then once our cathartic howl was over, we mopped ourselves up, made a great pot of tea, ate her stash of chocolate digestives and reminisced about my dad. This was the first time either of us had done it since he died. It was almost like mentioning his name and talking about him in past terms meant we were letting him go to an unreachable place. I honestly think there existed somewhere deep in both of us the whimsical pathetic belief that one day he was going to walk back through the door and 'make things better'.

'Did you ever regret marrying him, Mum? Ever thought you were missing out?'

'Not in the beginning, your father was a catch - tall, good-looking, caring, a real gentleman but I had my moments, Alex.' Mum gazed out towards the balcony, 'I never had the opportunities you had. I would have loved to have travelled more and maybe been a dress designer or even a model. Your life has been so exciting in many ways, but...' she turned back to me, 'I wouldn't have changed a thing, other than bring him back of course.' She smiled sadly, 'That's who you need to meet Alex, somebody a bit like your dad.'

'I think looking for a daddy replacement is a little bit creepy.'

'Evie told me yesterday you have to be careful what you wish for in Sitges, because you might just get it. Apparently it's quite a magical place in that way. Well, why don't you try it? Make a wish Alex. Wish this man into your life.'

'You're officially off your rocker.'

'Stop being so cynical and try it.'

'Okay just to shut you up, I wish with all my heart that the perfect man will arrive in my life before my bum sags even further - but Mum don't hold your breath - men like that don't grow on trees – particularly in this place.'

I went to bed that night and thought about my dad. Mum was right; he had been a bit of an old charmer really but most definitely a one-woman man. He had always loved the outdoor life and in his younger days he worked on the River Thames as a lighterman. What the hell is that, you might ask? Well, it's a long-dead trade. If he was still around he could tell you better than me but essentially lightermen crewed the barges that transported goods along the Thames from the Port of London, when it was much more of a working river than it is today. They were a very closely-knit bunch of highly skilled men who served a seven-year apprenticeship learning everything there was to know about the river before becoming fully qualified. Their expertise was legendary; they could navigate heavily-laden barges into tight mooring spaces using no more than their intimate knowledge of the tides, a long oar called a sweep and sheer muscle power. He loved it with a passion until one day, almost without warning, when I was eleven we were whipped away from my idyllic South East London life and taken to Hampshire where he had gotten himself a job at the Southampton Docks. Victims of technology, the days of the lightermen were numbered and Dad wasn't going to wait around for the final fall of the axe. But I knew that right up until the day he died he missed that part of his life – the healthy sweat of hard grafting, the fresh air and more importantly – the sense of freedom. That was the part of him I had inherited. My entire life had always been an exercise in maintaining that feeling. I was a restless soul.

Over the next couple of days, courtesy of a few shopping excursions with Evie, Mum underwent a complete metamorphosis and returned to England an ageing hippy complete with dangling silver pendants and gypsy skirts, much to the shock of my siblings who treated it as a slightly belated mid-life crisis, for which I, of course got the blame. Within a week of her return I got a call from my sister.

'What have you done to Mum?'

'Nothing - why?'

'She's burning incense sticks, taken up salsa classes and cancelled her holiday in Torquay because she wants to hang out with Evie in Seville. Hanging out? Since when has she said hanging out unless she's talking about her washing? Who is this Evie anyway?'

'She's just a new friend, who's a lot more bloody interesting than her usual mob.'

'Isn't she a bit old for all this?'

'She just wants to have a little fun, that's all.'

'You've brainwashed her, haven't you? A week with you and she thinks she's bloody Shirley MacLaine. Weren't you meant to argue all week and get on each other's nerves? That's what you usually do.'

'We've moved on, we're cool.'

'Jesus.'

'What?'

'That's exactly how she put it.'

TWENTY FIVE

Life has the strangest way of dealing you exactly what you need from time to time, usually when you least expect it. I needed to slow down and slow down I did, because no sooner had Cam's bruises started to disappear when we had to make another ambulance trip - this time with me in the hot seat.

Cam had been staying with me since the 'incident' and one Sunday night, when we were watching movies with the perfect accompaniment - *Super Pollo* and chips, he noticed that I was pushing mine around the plate.

'You alright Moll?'

'Feel a bit sick actually.'

'You look very pale, why don't you lie down.'

I did as I was told and Cam brought me some water - our tipple of choice for the whole of the past week. I sipped it and felt even more nauseous. Reluctantly Cam left for the bar, leaving me strict instructions to call him if I felt worse. Within an hour I was climbing the wall with a burning pain in my pelvis. I rang him and he was back within minutes with a Spanish doctor who had been in the bar. The diagnosis was immediate. I had acute appendicitis that could burst at any time. When the ambulance arrived and I was writhing around in the back of it with Cam holding my hand, I realised that the paramedic who was giving us strange looks was the same guy that had thrust the sick bag in my hands a couple of weeks before.

Despite the apparent urgency of the situation they certainly took their time in getting me to surgery and I had to lay in A & E for five hours with different doctors coming in periodically to check if I still screamed in agony and hit the ceiling if they pressed on my appendix and let go. Subsequently I learned the Spanish word for pain was *dolor*.

'*Mucho dolor?*'

And they learned a few new words too.

Namely – *you frigging sadistic bastards!*

Eventually at 7 am, they got me ready for my operation and started to wheel me down the corridor. As I said goodbye to Cam, I thought I caught sight of doctors and nurses smoking behind the admissions desk. I grabbed his hand in a panic.

'You're not going to die but just in case they open you up and find that your internal organs are irreversibly pickled and they decide to put you out of your misery, can I have your ashes made into a sherry decanter?'

'Bastard,' I whimpered and was whizzed away with the orderlies chattering on in Catalan above my head. I was momentarily petrified and had images running through my mind of Mum answering the phone to a tearful Cam who would have to break the news that my excessive Sitges lifestyle had finally got the better of me. I told myself to stop being a drama queen, said a silent prayer as they administered the anaesthetic– and the next thing I knew I woke up, albeit in *mucho dolor,* in a depressing hospital room with just a crucifix for company. I had various tubes protruding from my abdomen because, as I was to find out later, they had nearly left it too late and the appendix did indeed burst during the operation. I drifted in and out of consciousness and was brought back into reality when I heard a voice saying what sounded like 'Melaaaarnygreeefiss.' I looked up and a tubby male nurse was taking my temperature. I squinted in confusion at him. He smiled and walked out of the door but not before turning and saying it again, 'Melaaarnygreeefiss.'

I passed out again and slept, being woken intermittently by different nurses who poked this and adjusted that. The next day when I opened my eyes, there was Tubby with his strange unintelligible chant, shoving a bedpan underneath me.

'Melaaarnygreeefiss, now you sssssssssssssssssss,' he was obviously trying to tell me to pee, but instead of giving a girl a bit of privacy, he stood at the end of the bed grinning inanely at me. This in itself made my bladder constrict and then he totally guaranteed a dry pan when he pointed at himself and said, 'Me, Antonio Banderas, you Melaaarnygreeefiss.'

All Tubby had in common with Antonio Banderas was his mother tongue, and me - Melanie Griffiths? Here I was with drips sticking out of various parts of my body, a face etched with pain not make-up, my fanny thrust up on top of a metal bowl, badly chipped toe-nail polish, looking more like Linda Blair in *'The Exorcist'*, and Freaky Chops here thinks we ought to be gracing the cover of *'Hola!'* I wanted him out and I wanted him out now, particularly when I saw his hand in his trousers fiddling around with himself.

'Help meeee!!' I screamed for all I was worth, which made my innards feel like they were being ripped to shreds.

Tubby bolted and about ten minutes later a female nurse walked in. She totally ignored the fact I was crying and waggled the dry bedpan in my face, then she shoved it straight back again and walked out.

Great – a pervert and a sadist. I lay there snivelling and eventually managed a trickle, which was eventually whipped away by my stony-faced Florence Nightingale.

Later on that day, a bunch of flowers arrived from my mum, and much to my great relief, so did Cam and Evie loaded up with even more flowers and gifts. I told them what had happened earlier and Cam went to complain. Not surprisingly, 'Antonio Banderas', sensing he may have got himself into a little hot water, had got in first and complained that I was abusive to him, which would probably explain the female nurse treating me like I was the Antichrist. The best Cam could achieve was an assurance that he wouldn't be looking after me any more, as the nurse on duty was sure it must all be a simple matter of my drug-induced delirium.

'I'm sure it must be some sort of 'philia',' I said to Cam and Evie, 'you know, having a thing for post-operative women on bedpans.

'I'll Google it,' smiled Cam.

'What lovely flowers,' said Evie, smelling the multi-coloured floral explosion from Mum. 'Did you know we're going to Seville in the summer?'

'Yes, I think it's a great idea.'

'She's such fun and she'll get to meet loads of my friends there.'

'Really?'

'Oh yeah, we get together every year, a bit like a school reunion - there's some of the girls from my dancing days, a couple of fabulous artists - she'll have a ball.'

I smiled, 'Just don't let her smoke pot.'

'Oh, Alex, she's already done that.'

'I cannot believe this is the same woman who read me the riot act a couple of weeks ago. You have corrupted my mother - shame on you.'

Cam snorted, 'You should see your face.'

'Mum's never even smoked a cigarette in her life. Evie, you're a bloody rabbi, or would that be total hypocrite?'

'Oh lighten up, Alex. Your mum's a grown woman who spent her younger days bringing up a family, why shouldn't she experiment a little?' Evie chuckled.

'What next? Crack cocaine? Maybe a couple of E's with her morning coffee? Why don't you two forget Seville and go clubbing in Ibiza?'

'Alex, I think you're a little over-tired,' Evie rubbed my hand. 'Why don't you rest a little more?'

'Actually we should go, we don't want you over doing it,' Cam leaned over and kissed my forehead, 'and if you get any more trouble from Antonio, ring me and I'll be straight down okay.'

They left and I fell asleep immediately and dreamt of Mum dressed in exotic silken clothes, eyes kohl pencilled up to the max, reclining in an opium den taking long puffs from a hubbly-bubbly pipe while nubile servants rubbed oil into her feet.

Finally after four more days, endless visitors, and most importantly when I had suffered the indignity of proving that I could *peda* – fart, and *caga* – pooh, they let me go home.

TWENTY SIX

'Oh dear Moll, are those bikini bottoms meant to be a thong?' Cam yawned as I gazed miserably at my reflection in the mirror.

'My sabbatical has turned into a bloody flabbatical! That scar is so ugly!'

'That's allowable, you can't help that.'

'I bumped into Stephan yesterday and he asked me if I was five months pregnant.'

'Only the five?'

'Shut up you walking chopstick. Where did all these come from? I never signed up for a life-long subscription to thread veins.'

'Alex, do you really think the day before your period is due is a good day to try on your summer wardrobe?'

'It's boiling. Oh my God, I can't do this zip up.'

'Alex, either you put a track suit on, come in the lounge and have some drugs or I hit you, it's that simple.' Cam was lying on my bed with one of my pillows over his face.

'Okay, I'm sorry; I'm having a Bad Me Day.'

'That's an understatement if ever there was one. No wonder so many people get divorced if this is what living with a woman is like.'

'D'you hate it?'

'Wait a minute? Other possible symptom of PMT – tears! No Alex, I love living with you, it's quite simply the most fantastic experience of my life. It's sublime, wonderful ... put that shoe down,' he darted out of the door.

'I'd get off you know, if I killed you. PMT is taken very seriously nowadays.'

I covered up my shame with an over-sized grey T-shirt and sweat pants and followed him into the lounge where I flopped onto the sofa. Cam and I were now officially cohabiting. It was the perfect arrangement for both of us.

Cam was unhappy living at Fairy Towers as the place just held too many bad memories. I was eating into my funds and having half the rent and bills paid would take the pressure off. So I asked him and he jumped at the chance. We had been living together a week and things were settling into a nice little routine. Since coming out of hospital I had got into the habit of having early nights and every morning I was up at about seven-thirty and walking the *paseo*. By the time Cam arose around 1 pm I was at the table in the lounge, facing the sea, sketching out ideas for various businesses, reading endless articles about changing your life and even meditating in an attempt to work out where I wanted to go in life.

We cooked dinner at home every night and instead of partying, we spent most of the time on the Internet. Cam was trawling 'Gaydar' in search of that elusive someone whilst I continued my obsessive searching for long lost friends on Facebook and snooping on the on line lives of my godchildren Nat and Chloe – under strict instruction from Mel, who as their mother wasn't allowed to be their 'friend'.

Cam brought in some pain-killers and water.

I snuggled into the big taupe sofa, 'I wonder if she'll be on the *paseo* tomorrow.'

'Who?'

'Lady Red Shoes.'

Every morning on my walk I had seen the same older woman. She was probably around seventy or so, and everything about her was totally what I expect for a woman of her years. She wore blue and white patterned frocks; her grey hair was short and tightly permed and she even carried a little grandma basket with her but the one thing I had zoned in on were her shoes which were totally incongruous with the rest of her attire – they were bright red satin *espadrilles*, with laces that tied halfway up her tiny little calves. Whenever I went huffing and puffing past, she would be sitting on one of the stone benches that lined the *paseo*, stretching out her legs and smiling as she twisted her feet from side to side, admiring her shoes. I was sure there was a tale behind them.

'You'll just have to practise your shit Spanish and talk to her; nobody will be around that early to laugh at you.'

'I'll have a go – tomorrow morning.'

'But don't go encouraging *Guapa* man; I don't want him coming around here for tea.'

'I think the likelihood of him drinking tea is very remote.'

Guapa man was a scruffy old weather-beaten guy who used to sleep rough on the beach. He earned a living by making the most stunning sand sculptures – mermaids, dragons, wizards; all perfectly chiselled and intricately designed. Tourists would take pictures of his fantastic creations and throw coins in his hat, the majority of which would be spent at the local supermarket buying the cheapest booze he could get his hands on. No matter how quietly I walked past or whatever mini-detour I took to avoid him, he would always manage to spot me and throw himself into full-on *guapa* frenzy.

Now someone calling you *guapa*, if you are female or *guapo* if you are a guy is a compliment. It means good-looking or attractive, but when it is shouted by a leathery old toothless drunk with a whole host of lewd gestures, it does tend to lose its edge somewhat. The only time he remained quiet was when I was with Cam or one of the other guys, then butter wouldn't melt in his mouth, although one thing that remained consistent was the alcohol fumes emanating from his person that could probably knock-out an elephant.

But by far the most interesting local character I was fast becoming fixated with was a guy who lived in a cave in the rocks under the cemetery. He always looked reasonably groomed and was as fit as a butcher's dog. He had a unique take on exercise and could often be found hanging upside down on a nearby tree branch for an entire afternoon pretending he was an olive or chasing petrified tourists off the beach brandishing a huge stick. Whenever I saw a funeral car drive past, I knew that Caveman would be like a bear with a sore head the next day as apparently there would be hell going on in his abode all night, because it was there - so he used to tell whoever was willing to listen - that the devil came to collect his latest guest, and by all accounts he wasn't exactly standing there with a welcome cocktail and tray of canapés.

Whatever had made these two men the way they were, who knew? But they were an intrinsic part of the rich tapestry that was Sitges - a tapestry that now I wasn't spending my life in bars and clubs, I could spend time exploring.

I went to bed early and the next day I was fired up; I was going to power walk and power talk – that little lady didn't know what was coming. As usual I saw the shoes before I saw the rest of her, glinting wickedly in the early morning sunlight. This time there was no shy nodding and a muttered *bon dia*, I was on a mission. So at precisely 7.35 am a very sweaty and red-faced me plopped myself down on the bench next to my slightly startled and red-footed obsession. We began with the daily niceties. How are you? Lovely weather! Blah blah! Then I cut to the chase... *'Zapatos adorables'.*

Well the minute I mentioned the shoes, I had her.

This was a woman who knew a kindred spirit and within twenty minutes of infant school-level Spanish my instincts were proved correct – there was a tale and it was beautiful.

Her name was *Nuestra Senora de las Nieves* which means 'our lady of the snows', but she assured me I didn't have to be so formal and said I could call her Nieves, and she was more than happy to tell me the story of the shoes. One June morning, when she was six-years-old, her mother dressed her up in her clothes which were usually reserved for church and best occasions, and took her on the train to Barcelona. After coffee and cakes they made their way to *La Manual Alpargatera* in the *Barri Gòtic*. This was a new shop that specialised in making *espadrilles* and it was here that Nieves was allowed to make her first grown-up decision – amongst the hundreds of different styles that were on display, she was allowed to choose what she wanted. When she pointed to the most elaborate pair she could see, made entirely of red satin, her mother didn't flinch and those shoes came back to Sitges that very afternoon. Ever since then, at the beginning of June, Nieves makes the pilgrimage to *La Manual Alpargatera* and collects her red satin shoes - the only pair she will wear throughout the whole summer. She was very proud to tell me that they make *espadrilles* for *Senor* Michael Douglas, *Senor* Jack Nicholson and even *El Padre* (the Pope to you and me). As far as Nieves was concerned, all you needed in life was a good pair of shoes and great tomatoes - whereupon she produced a handful of cherry tomatoes from her basket and insisted that I try. It was love at first bite. They were the sweetest ones I had ever tasted; they literally exploded in my mouth. She grew these on her terrace and promised me that the next day she would bring me a bag. I bid her *adios* and hurried home. Cam was still sleeping, so I rang Mel, thinking that she would love this story but after five minutes of me twittering on, she cut me short.

'Alex, look I have to go, I have a meeting in an hour and I've got to pick up a prescription for Chloe, take the cat to the vet ... I haven't got time to chat. Sorry, bye,' the phone went dead.

I sat there for a while staring into space. I felt a sense of incredible sadness. The realisation sunk in that life still went on as normal in the UK. Everybody was still there getting on with his or her own stuff. This was my adventure that they weren't a part of. I had wondered why Mel hadn't jumped on a plane by now, the fares were so cheap and it was so close. I had just naturally assumed she would want to come and see what I was doing, where I was living, meet my new friends – but why should she? It wasn't she who had wanted to leave. Why the hell should she care about an old lady with red shoes on the *paseo*?

'Hey, what's up sunshine?' Cam wandered into the lounge yawning and flopped down beside me.

'It's not the same with Mel any more, I thought she'd want to hear about the shoes but she sounded really pissed off at me....'

'Have you spoken to her? Lady Red Shoes?'

'Yes.'

'That's brilliant, tell me all about it, come into the kitchen and

I'll make coffee.'

Later on that afternoon, I sent Mel an email telling her that I missed her and the kids; she sent one straight back saying sorry for being so snappy. Not exactly a huge resolve but you need to be face-to-face for that. I just hoped it wasn't that long before we were sitting in front of a cold bottle of something sparkling and getting back on track. This was one friendship I wasn't prepared to let fizzle out.

In the meantime, I had a new friend. Over the next week, Nieves and I got into a little routine - I would jog to the *Terramar*, and then on the way back, she would be sitting there with a little bottle of water and a few tomatoes for me. I actually found my Spanish improving and was touched when she invited me to go to a local Catalan haunt with her on the Friday evening. How could I refuse? When we arrived at the *Prado* at eight–fifteen, I realised to my horror she had brought me to something I had never attended in my life – bingo!

As it turned out, the evening was highly entertaining. Everyone seemed to have their own good luck rituals from genuflecting to standing on a chair and turning around three times. Before every game, for thirty seconds, the *Prado* was abuzz with strange activity. After a nudge in the ribs from Nieves who obviously thought I was wasting my money if I didn't have a pre-sheet routine, I somewhat self-consciously developed 'my thing'. I clicked my fingers three times before patting the top of my head four times, and Nieves nodded proudly. I was catching on fast. She was so impressed she invited me to the *Prado* the next night for a really big event – a Dominoes tournament.

The Spanish just love having a little flutter, and over the next couple of weeks, I found myself getting inextricably drawn in: bingo, cards, dominoes, lotto tickets. My little septuagenarian cohort and I were unstoppable. But whereas Nieves seemed to have an inexhaustible supply of good luck, no matter how loud the clicks and definite the pats, whether I did it with my right hand or my left, my little ritual was getting me nowhere fast – except a lot lighter in the purse department.

Cam brought it to my attention one evening when I was getting ready to meet Nieves at the *Cap de la Villa* for a quick sherry before bridge night at the Retiro.

'People are gossiping about you.'

'What now?'

'You've replaced excessive alcohol with gambling, you bloody addict. Plus, everyone thinks it's odd that you are spending most of your time with an OAP.'

'She's fun and it's interesting seeing another side to Sitges. I had a seventy-something best-friend when I was seven – this is nothing new. Anyhow, stuff everyone else, what do you think?'

'She's a bad influence – look at yourself, you've jumped three decades in dress sense.'

I looked in the mirror and had to admit he had a point. Nieves and I had been shopping and she had gone into raptures when she saw me in a floral frock – she said it was *muy femenino*. I now owned three little girlie numbers – all with matching bags and coordinating cardigans.

'You should be doing Prada not the *Prado* darling. How much have you spent?'

'I don't know,' I muttered.

'Yes you do,' Cam folded his arms across his chest; 'now spill how much?'

'A few hundred euros.'

'How many exactly?'

'Four hundred.'

'Fucking hell, Alex, that's half a month's rent.'

'I know, I just, well, I don't always understand the Catalan and Nieves makes my bets for me.'

'Right, you are going to tell your little partner in crime that you are pulling out of the circuit for a while. Come here and give me your handbag.'

I reluctantly handed it over and screwed up my face in anticipation of what was to come.

'Alex, there's a hundred and fifty euros in here!' Cam took one hundred and thirty and put it in his pocket then took all my cards out of my purse. 'Right, that's your limit, and if I find out you haven't told 'Lady - I encourage stupid English girls to get themselves in the Red - Shoes' that your gambling days are over, I'll tell her, and you know how brutal I can be.'

I nodded dumbly and went up to break the news to Nieves that our partnership was over. It turned out to be an easier task than I imagined because Nieves had brought along someone she wanted me to meet - her grandson, Pablo the plumber. I suddenly had a flashback to that fateful night and an image of him proudly presenting me with a plate of sliced tomatoes. It was obviously a genetic obsession. We both masked our shock and sat making small talk (bad pun alert) over an uncomfortable sherry and some forgettable *tapas*. When Pablo nipped to the toilet, I took the opportunity to sorrowfully explain to Nieves that I was now financially embarrassed and worried that my bad luck may rub off on her. She considered this possibility for a second or two, and then politely asked me if I would mind *not* accompanying her to the Bridge game as there was quite a big prize this evening and she wanted to give herself every possible chance of winning. Luckily, she assured me, Pablo was a very talented partner.

I nodded enthusiastically for all the wrong reasons, and then left taking my 'bad luck' with me.

When I walked back through the door at nine-thirty, Cam was in the bathroom shaving.

'Well done, Moll, I knew you had it in you.'

'More like *who* I've had in me.'

'Pardon?'

'Pablo the plumber is her grandson.'

'Oh bloody hell!'

'Can I have my money back now?'

'Maybe,' he winked at me in the mirror, 'when you've made me a pot of your splendiferous chicken soup.'

'I could teach you how to make it if you want.'

'Do I look like Gordon Ramsay? Remind you in certain lights of Jamie Oliver?'

'Maybe Nigella,' I laughed. They would be advertising skiing holidays in hell before Cam did anything constructive with a cooking utensil. 'Okay, I'll make you some soup.'

'Thank you mummy.'

TWENTY SEVEN

'D'you know that herrings talk through their butts?'

'Que?' I pushed my sunglasses up and squinted at Cam.

'According to Canadian researchers if you put your ear to the water in the presence of herrings, you can discern a raspberry type sound which indicates they are communicating with each other.'

'Well to me it sounds like herrings fart a lot, and Canadian researchers have far too much time on their hands. Whatever happened to curing cancer?' I flipped my glasses back down, closed my eyes and turned my face to the sky.

'That was so last century. Oh my God, listen to this,' Cam was flicking through his newspaper. It was a hot July afternoon and we were hiding out at *Bar La Bocana*, a tiny place right at the end of the port where all you had to contend with was the creaking of the halliards, the smell of paella and the occasional sighting of a good-looking nautical type. He took a slug of his beer and continued, 'Apparently Barcelona men have the worst quality sperm in the world.'

'Maybe that's why they're so short. Are you hungry?' I was starving. On account of the fact that half my wardrobe no longer fitted me, I had been exercising like crazy. In order to catch the cool temperatures, I had started jogging at six-thirty in the morning, not even Nieves was around at that time. 'How do you fancy a few mussels and some pan con tomate?'

'Lovely.'

'And cheap,' I smiled. 'Can't keep doing these lunches can we?'

'S'pose not. You come up with any ideas yet? Or are you going to start looking for work here Moll?' Cam looked at me enquiringly.

'Maybe it is time for a job, but what?'

'Your agent called this morning didn't she?' Cam put his newspaper down and stretched languorously, 'I've always wanted an agent.'

'Well you can have Rae,' I laughed, 'she's about as much use as a chocolate fire guard.'

'If she's that bad why have you stayed with her?'

'Laziness, cowardliness and I don't think anyone else would want me.'

'Don't be so hard on yourself.'

'There isn't a letter of the alphabet for the celebrity list I'm on.'

'What did she want anyway? Is she still trying to get you to go on that shopping channel?'

'Oh God, don't!' I groaned, 'It's the presenter graveyard.'

Rae had been trying to get me to go for an interview with some awful shopping channel for about a year. They wanted a presenter with a background in beauty to front their cosmetic shows. I couldn't deny it was reasonably good money but the thought of becoming a glorified on-air beauty consultant didn't appeal, even if, as Rae kept reminding me, I would have a free weekly manicure thrown in - perfect pinkies for fondling and pointing at crap products. The whole idea made me shudder.

'No, thankfully she seems to have forgotten that glorious opportunity.'

'What did she want then?'

'They are doing re-runs of *Sort Your Life Out* on some 'Just In Case You Didn't Catch It On The Thirty Five Other Channels That Have Already Shown It' channel which has created a flicker of interest in a crap TV guide which does a regular piece called *'Celebs and their Pets'.'*

'You don't have a pet.'

'I know, but Rae has told them I have a dog,' I shrugged. 'I rang Tony the hairdresser. He's going to take a quick picture with his dog Dudley this afternoon. I am now officially 'in love' with my Norfolk terrier. We're inseparable, don't you know?'

'What a load of bollocks! You should pretend you've adopted one of the stray *gattos*. We'll get you on the rocks surrounded by all the cats and get a snap of you cuddling the little chosen one - very Angelina and Madonna. I can see it now; Makeover Guru Alex Chapman tells TV Bullshit Magazine about her love for Sitges Pussy.'

'You could be very good at this, how do you fancy being my agent?'

We spent the next twenty minutes coming up with outlandish publicity stunts that would probably have me arrested and dissolving into hysteria. Eventually we calmed down and managed to give a very bemused waiter our order. Cam's face became a little serious.

'I don't think Fred and Pierre will last the summer.'

I nodded and smiled sadly.

'It's normal Alex, at this time of year everything changes.'

Cam was right. Between October and June you can't escape a soul in Sitges, all you have to do is literally think of a person and they walk around the next corner or are sitting in there in a café as you walk in. When the season kicks in around the beginning of July it is a totally different story, the town simply splinters off into little pockets of people who move around the town independently of each other and just don't interact for the next three months. The clever ones sub-let their apartments and bugger off, earning enough in three months to pay their entire winter rent. For others it's time to make hay while the sun shines - local ex-pats become reps, do airport runs, clean apartments or work in bars and restaurants. Everyone is suddenly a portfolio worker. Days off are a thing of the past, tempers rise along with the temperature and temptation abounds. If a couple is going to split – it happens at this time of the year when there are just too many cute guys and girls cruising around in search of a bit of summer loving.

Fred seemed to be flourishing. The town was small enough for him to feel in control and now it was all about the gym and the beach. He was even getting the confidence to go out and about in the evening without Pierre, who was going out less and less. When you did see them together they were sniping at each other continually. Physically, they looked totally different now - Fred had been working out and sunbathing obsessively and Pierre was grey and a little emaciated. I was seriously worried but if I broached the subject of his health with him, he would just brush it aside, and just lately he had stopped returning my calls. On top of which, according to the local gossip, Fred had been seen hanging out with a string of young guys.

'We are just going to have to let it run its natural course, Alex,' Cam sighed. 'Difficult as it is, they always shoot the messenger and you've spent quite enough time playing nursemaid in the winter, so just let it go and get on with your life.'

'I know, I just feel so sorry for Pierre at the moment. It's great that Fred has got over his anxiety attacks and got his confidence back, but did it have to be like this?'

'Who knows what goes on behind closed doors? It's their business and nobody else's.'

Cam had a point, so I shut up and tucked into the mussels. They were so fresh, the taste of the sea in a fantastic tomato and garlic broth. I mopped up every last drop with the crusty bread, finished my *aqua con gas* and leaned back against the café wall enjoying the sun on my face. Someone on a boat was playing old Gershwin tracks on a crackly tape recorder. It was summertime and living was easy, but all too quickly we had to leave, as Cam had to clean the bar. We paid up and wandered along the quayside. Suddenly I noticed Augustin's boat. I hadn't seen him since the Penny incident and wasn't really in the mood today. I looked straight ahead and hissed at Cam, 'Is there anyone on that big white boat over there?'

'Don't think so but there's a cute guy in that bar over there checking you out big time.'

I glanced over and saw a bearded blonde guy in khaki shorts, 'I don't do facial fungus!'

'You're too damn fussy.'

'Too fussy?' I bit back. 'A bisexual, a midget and a misogynistic mummy's boy with a mushroom dick! If that's me being fussy - God knows what I'd bring home if I dropped my standards.'

Cam whispered, 'He is still checking you out though.'

'Well his time would be better spent with a cut-throat razor and some shaving foam.'

'You are such a little moo, you don't deserve a boyfriend.'

'I don't want one. I'm so happy at the moment, why ruin it?'

TWENTY EIGHT

I love being naked. Not in a 'posing-in-front-of-the-mirror' or 'let's-join-all-the-other-nudists-on-the-beach-and-get-sand-up-our-arses' sort of way, and certainly there is nothing worse than being with a 'let's-leave-the-lights-on' person when you are in a 'let's-turn-them-off' mood. No, I'm talking more about those fantastic occasions when nobody else is around and you are totally free to stand around in your kitchen eating cornflakes, sit in your study checking emails or even just wander from room to room with your bits hanging out without a trace of anxiety that someone may walk in and catch you.

So, when I woke up with the larks, quails, or whatever early morning chirpy feathery things frequent this part of Spain in the summertime and read an early morning text message from Cam saying that he was staying over with a couple of his hard-partying tourist buddies, I bounced out of bed and luxuriated in my naked freedom. That is, until I threw open the shutters to my balcony.

Now what I expected to see at 6.15 am was a glorious unobstructed view of the sun rising gently over the shimmering Mediterranean sea. Instead, a mere twenty feet from my balcony, there was a man hanging off Pete the Palm wearing a bloody great pair of goggles and carrying a chainsaw. To say I jumped out of my all-too-visible skin is an understatement. As he turned and grinned, I gave a primordial howl worthy of a Neanderthal caveman, slammed the shutters closed and trapped one of my fingers in the process. I sank behind the sofa in a daze and stared at my throbbing digit. It was the bearded guy from the port.

I had just revealed myself in all my wobbling and scar-ridden glory to a tree geek – a straight tree geek. This was definitely not a fairy on top of the tree and somehow that made my embarrassment ten-times worse. I bandaged my finger and slunk around in the shadows until finally the whirring and cutting sounds abated and I could no longer make out his silhouette through the gaps in the shutters. Then, at 11.30 am, Cam sent another text saying that some of the boys were meeting at the Mont Roig café and I should go along. So, complete with huge dark glasses and a disgusting sun hat that Mum had bought me at the Euro shop as a parting bad taste gesture, I emerged from my front door looking like some thrift shop Mata Hari. The coast seemed clear so I paused for a second to study Pete, whose leaves had been given a crew cut and whose trunk was now adorned with what looked like huge condoms. The tree geek had made my tree gay. Suddenly I saw him wandering out of a café with a *bocadillo* and a can of coke. He looked over in my direction. I ran.

Sitges was hot and heaving, its narrow streets and shops crammed to the hilt with fun-seeking visitors and guest-weary locals. I fought my way through the crowds and eventually, drizzling with sweat, I made it to Mont Roig situated on what was now 'Cruiseville'. Here the oiled up, sometimes tragically over-styled tourists occupy the front line of street-side tables, either bitching about or lusting after whoever is wandering along - what in the winter is a quaint Spanish street - and in the summer turns into a catwalk full of posing peacocks.

I spotted my crew huddled around a table in the calmer and much cooler inner confines of the café. Usually our morning debriefing sessions consisted of just that - me sitting and listening to their tales of who had 'debriefed' whom recently. But if I thought this morning's incident was going to make me the runaway leader on the 'Have I got a story for you!' stakes I was to be bitterly disappointed. Not only did Aaron, Simon and even Cam not seem in the slightest bit interested in my pathetic revelations, they actually told me to sit down and shut up.

With just a hint of sulk, I broke my 'no booze in the daytime' pledge and ordered a *carajillo con Baileys* and listened to their conversation. Today's topic was a lot more serious than the usual gossip. It would appear we had trouble in paradise. Like many holiday destinations, along with the tourists comes the inevitable bevy of vagrants and opportunists all intent on making a buck wherever and however they can. Balcony doors left open to catch the sea breeze, handbags slung over restaurant chairs, wallets stuffed in a back pocket: it's all just too tempting and too damn easy. But now it had suddenly got nasty. Apparently there was a group of North Africans roaming the streets and they were violent. In the past week there had been three muggings and last night someone had ended up in hospital with stab wounds.

'We've got to be more careful,' said Simon. Simultaneously they all turned and looked at me.

'What?' I blustered indignantly.

'None of this bloody running around on your own, Alex,' Cam shook his head sternly. 'You have got to make sure someone always walks you home.'

'Particularly between 4 and 5 am,' added Simon.

I looked at him quizzically and he explained that apparently, for what would appear reasons of a purely social nature, all the police in Sitges had a coffee break between 4 and 5 am, thus leaving the streets a perfect playground for muggers and other assorted trouble-makers. It didn't take mega brains to work out that if you were going to take your chances and attack someone – this was probably the time to do it.

But despite promising them all that I would never go on a nocturnal walkabout alone, when I fell out of Organic at around 4 am the next morning, after falling off the wagon during an afternoon of swilling chilled rosé with Bubbles, a quick siesta, dinner with Tony and Ian and the inevitable round of the usual haunts, I had totally forgotten the dangers that lurked in the streets.

As I ambled towards the steps of the church, my only concern was that I was just about to do the equivalent of twenty minutes on a step machine. Okay slight exaggeration, but they were bloody steep and there were a lot of them. All of a sudden I felt the hairs on the back of my neck stand up, in tandem with an adrenalin rush that sent my heartbeat racing.

I swung around to see a man of darkish persuasion emerge from the shadows and start following me. The steps were now the least of my worries and I took them two at a time but I could feel him getting closer and knew that the quiet bit of the church was just around the corner – where it would be just him, me and a 100-foot rocky drop into the sea.

Now, you put 400 metres and a few fences between me and a reduced Armani frock and I would give an Olympic hurdler a run for his money but here, in danger of being robbed and maybe stabbed or raped for good measure, I still wasn't running. My legs were remaining resolutely leaden. My brain on the other hand was processing the whole scenario at an amazing rate of knots. Did I have a weapon? *No.* Would I use one if I had one? *Probably not.* Could I talk my way out of this? *Unlikely.* Had I wet myself? *Not yet.*

I decided that the contents of my handbag – thirty euros and a grotty old lipstick were not good enough reason to take a bashing, or worse. So I started to remove my handbag from my shoulder whilst desperately groping around for my apartment keys. The footsteps were getting louder; I went to turn around and fling him the damn thing then a miracle happened.

There in front of me, from a dark narrow alley, jumped a naked man. Yes, yours truly had managed to be in the same part of the universe as not only a bloody mugger but now a flasher.

As Naked Man threw his arms up and shouted something in unintelligible and almost certainly filthy Spanish, he noticed the man behind me and sort of fizzled up like a popped balloon. The equally shocked mugger screeched to an abrupt halt and suddenly my legs received the message from my brain to run like hell. Although I probably should have hugged him, I shot my saviour's now shrunken parts a disparaging look as I whipped past him and clattered down the cobbled alley that led to the beach. I heard shouting, then the sound of footsteps running behind me. The mugger hadn't given up. Even if I out-ran him I would never have enough time to unlock the front door and get in. As I reached the sea wall, I decided to separate myself from the object of his desire and launched my handbag over onto the sand, a great move if only I hadn't tripped over my feet and thudded down on to the pavement. As I lay sprawled out like a spatch-cock chicken, I closed my eyes and braced myself for a confrontation. Suddenly, I heard a deep Australian voice bellow out from above me.

'Come here you slimy little bastard and have a bit of this!'

I looked up, and there, standing above me brandishing his clenched fist was the tree geek. He dropped to his knees and touched my shoulder. 'Are you okay?'

I nodded and let him pull me up. I was shaking like a leaf.

'C'mon, let's get you indoors,' he nodded towards the apartment. 'It's over there isn't it?'

'You know it is.' I started to smart with embarrassment then remembered I hadn't managed to retrieve my keys before lobbing my bag. 'Oh shit – my handbag.'

'Wait there.'

Before I had a chance to protest he took off and left me shivering outside my door. Within a few minutes he was back, swinging my bag slightly self-consciously in his hand.

'Is this it?' he smiled.

'Thank you so much; I dread to think what might have happened if you hadn't been there.' I found my keys and opened the front door and looked at him. 'What were you doing here?'

'Oh, just stalking you,' he chuckled as he saw my eyes widen in horror. 'It's a joke. I was out for a walk. I've got a bit of jet lag and it's turned me into a raving insomniac.'

'That would have been too weird. Talk about the unholy bloody trinity - a mugger, a flasher and a stalker.'

His eyes twinkled mischievously.

'I wasn't actually referring to me. There was a real one by the church. Now, if you promise never to bring up the subject of my nakedness again you can have a coffee.' I was now far too hyped to sleep, 'Or you can just carry on roaming the streets in search of another damsel in distress.'

'Yes ma'am,' he saluted. 'You have my word as a gentleman.'

'You'd better be,' I said as I blithely walked into my home with this total stranger. I just didn't want to be alone. I made two black coffees, grabbed the bottle of Baileys and gestured for him to follow me out to the balcony. We sat down.

'I have a bone to pick with you.' His face was serious. 'It's not really my business but what the hell were you doing walking around alone so late?'

'Being a stupid cow,' I felt pretty sheepish, so decided to change the subject. 'And, whilst we are talking bones, I have one to pick with you.'

'Hey, what have I done?'

'I want to know what you have been doing with Pete.'

'Pete?'

'Pete the Palm,' I nodded towards my tree whose shorn leaves were swaying gently.

'Before I divulge such sensitive information, I feel it only right and appropriate that I tell you something about me first,' he leaned over and looked deep into my eyes.

I raised my eyebrows expectantly, 'Will you have to kill me afterwards?'

'Chainsaw oiled up and ready.'

'Let's hope it's worth it.'

'It's my name. I'm Stan, Stanley Berringer.'

'Ooh dear, poor you!'

'Hey, I come from a long line of 'Stanleys'.'

'Well maybe it's about time for a Stanley knife,' I held out my hand. 'I'm Alex Chapman.'

'Is that short for Alexandra?'

'Yes.'

'Lovely name,' he held onto my hand for a little longer than was necessary. I pulled it back but not before a fuzzy warm glow came over me. I snuggled into the chair and looked at the ocean.

'Okay, Stan the Man, spill the beans about Pete the Palm.'

TWENTY NINE

The blight of the Mediterranean Date Palm is the Red Palm Weevil – a prolific wee beastie who just loves to travel, namely by cadging free rides over to places such as Spain, stowed away in the trunks of imported palms from Israel and Egypt. They chomp away gaily, breed like – well - palm weevils, turning each palm into a Weevil metropolis and then fly around leaving their larvae in nearby local palms in order to ensure a slap-up dinner for about a million or so of their descendants for the next few years. And so it goes on.

Those in the know regarding these arboreal terrorists, live in a world where trees have passports and military terminology is used to chart the global movements of this little red beetle. Apparently there had been a flurry of Internet activity between the serious players in the palm world because to quote - *one had gone down in Marbella*. I cannot possibly pass on the opportunity to comment that probably quite a few have gone down in Marbella, but I'm not talking trees and this is a seriously cheap gag – move on Alex.

Where was I? Ah yes - now the battle had come to Sitges. My poor Pete the Palm - he who is consistent and sturdy and never answers back – was being eaten alive by weevils and drastic measures were going to be necessary to ensure his survival. On top of the usual plan of attack, namely injecting him with a lethal combination of chemicals and setting pheromone traps (Don't you just love it? Pheromone traps in this town!), Pete was going to be the guinea pig or should I say guinea palm, for a cutting edge kick-weevil-arse treatment from Australia.

Enter stage left – Stanley Berringer, leading entomologist and tree surgeon extraordinaire with his big box of *Entomopathogenic nematodes*. To a Red Palm Weevil the arrival of these lads is tantamount to the SAS crashing in through your window brandishing AK47s. The humble nematode, a simple roundworm, is biological warfare at its most effective. Though harmless to humans and plants, it produces a form of bacteria that will kill weevils in 24 to 48 hours.

Fascinating?

Well, I did ask, and Stan was only too happy to oblige with a passionate explanation of his chosen career path, which incidentally only stopped when the sun came up and he passed out on the chair. Now, this could be due to the jet lag catching up with him, the Baileys getting the better of him, or just that quite simply he had bored himself senseless. I decided it was a mixture of all three and sat studying him for a while.

Underneath all that facial hair he was probably quite good looking. He had dark dirty blonde hair that was longish and unkempt and his greenish eyes were surrounded by friendly creases. He even smiled in his sleep.

The early morning sun was getting hotter by the second. I took the cups and glasses indoors and put a pillow and a sheet on the sofa. I gently nudged him awake and he grunted a garbled apology as he followed me to the sofa where he collapsed in a heap.

I pulled the shutters closed and crept into my room. My last thought as I started to drop off was that having told Mum that men didn't grow on trees, that's exactly where I'd managed to find one.

A few hours later the phone rang. It was Cam who obviously had stayed out all night again, taken verbal Viagra and wanted to yak. I wandered into the hall giving occasional *ums* and *ahs*, and poked my head around the lounge door. The sofa was empty. I checked the balcony and tapped on the bathroom door. He was gone. No note, nothing.

I felt quite disappointed.

'You're not listening to a bloody word I'm saying are you?' Cam screeched down the phone.

'Sorry, it's just that, erm…'

'You've got someone there haven't you?'

'That bearded geezer from the port was here…' my voice trailed off.

'Kettle on now, I'm on my way,' the phone clicked.

By the time I jumped out of the shower, Cam was walking through the door. I was in the kitchen wrapped in a towel and he bounced passed me like a Mexican jumping bean.

'Tell me, tell me, tell me …'

'Coffee first – can you make it?' I gestured towards the kettle, 'I have the most horrendous hangover.'

Once I was dressed and we had a couple of steaming cups of coffee in front of us, I proceeded to tell Cam everything that happened the night before. He spent the majority of the time doubled up laughing but did threaten to ground me if I ever went walking alone again.

'So he's called Stan and you two spent two hours talking about worms?'

'Weevils and nematodes actually.'

'Didn't you find out anything about him?'

'He's Australian and he spends his life either hanging from trees or killing bugs.'

'Very TarStan.'

'Very funny, anyhow, I didn't want to interrogate him.'

'You interrogate EVERYBODY!' Cam shrieked. 'You are the Spanish Inquisition personified. You are the nosiest person I know apart from me of course.'

'Look, the chances are that I may never even see him again.'

'He works outside our balcony, stop being so melodramatic.'

'Coming from you - that's priceless,' I poked Cam in the ribs. 'He didn't even leave me a note.'

'God, you're needy. He probably left in a hurry with a hangover; give the poor bugger a break. Don't you worry; he'll probably turn up under your balcony with a bunch of roses and start serenading you.'

'Fat chance - he'd be too busy checking them for greenfly.'

Cam tried to entice me down to the gay beach, but I declined. One, my head was very delicate and two, I wanted to be around just in case a certain person came to check on Pete – and me of course.

During the afternoon, I had about twenty calls. Radio Cam had been busy. The flasher and mugger tale had been circulating around Sitges. The question on everyone's lips - how big was the flasher's dick? Bloody typical! The sad truth is that was probably the only detail I did remember. Despite feeling that I really ought to report it, there seemed no point in going to the police if the only description I could come up was *about three or four disappointing inches*.

For the rest of the afternoon and well into the evening, much to Cam's amusement, I sat on the balcony gazing out to sea like the bloody French Lieutenant's Woman, glammed up to the max with a book I wasn't reading and a bottle of wine I wasn't drinking. Every now and then somebody would pass and shout up. Bubbles offered to take me for coffee, Evie had just bought some new kaftans for her holiday and wanted my opinion and Nieves rattled off a story in faster-than-the-speed-of-light Spanish that I think involved the rather humongous basket of tomatoes she was humping up towards the cemetery.

Everybody seemed to pass by. Everybody that is, except him.

As I cleaned off my make-up that night I made myself a promise. IF I saw him again, I would hold back, play it cool. I knew deep down in my soul that I was cruising for a bloody great bruising with this one, and I wasn't about to let that happen.

THIRTY

I awoke the next morning like a woman possessed. I cleaned the apartment, did my laundry, went to the market, I even spent two hours in front of the computer (achieved bugger-all - but at least I tried), and by the time Cam emerged with the daily beach request, I was up for it. I just had one stipulation – no gay beach. I wanted to see cellulite and sandcastles, not six packs and budgie-smugglers (skin tight and rather miniscule male swimming attire – leaving *nothing* to the imagination!).

We wandered the entire length of the *paseo* and settled ourselves on the relatively quiet family beach. Cam, obviously exhausted by his last few nights' escapades, started snoring loudly the minute he lay down. I covered myself in sun block and people-watched.

A family arrived a few minutes later. There was about ten of them, all weighed down with beach bags, coolers, surfboards and a comprehensive selection of blow up bananas, dragons and rubber rings.

I glanced away for what could only have been a couple of seconds and then there it was - a mammoth erection. A majestic green and white striped gazebo encasing a selection of Formica tables, chairs and countless cushions had appeared from nowhere. One of the mothers was obviously the Martha Stewart of beach protocol and was busily organising a glittering array of Tupperware containers and snap-top plastic bags full of snacks. This whole day out was being executed with military precision. I could hear her on the phone now – *Okay Susie you bring the bread rolls and beers, we'll do lemonade and crisps and I'll get Paula to make tuna sandwiches*…I had a momentary flashback to my childhood jaunts.

Traipsing down precarious cliff-side paths in deepest Cornwall, in order to set-up camp at some virtually inaccessible inlet, only to find we had to share the five-foot square patch of sand with another family of idiots. This of course would become a 1-by-5 foot strip as the tide came in. There were always piles of sand-encrusted mackerel sandwiches and of course the perfect accompaniment - warm orange squash with unmistakeable plastic undertones. After a day of non-stop 'fun', usually involving Dad competing with the other dad for the 'Construct-Disneyland-from-Sand-Award'; and the highly prestigious 'Bet-my-kids-scream-louder-than-yours-when-I-dunk-them-in-the-cold-grey-sea-Prize-for-Sadistic-Fathers', we had to face the death-defying journey back up the cliff – now even more slippery with the lower levels being beaten by the waves.

Then the fantastic journey home, cramped up in the back of the car with siblings, cousins, buckets and spades, sandy shells and a couple of live crabs. Quite an ordeal when coupled with the rising temperature of sunburned skin and the sand that had taken up residency in every available body orifice. It was no wonder the beaches were so tiny – it was all up our bums.

Oh and joy of joys, the roads. Hundreds of equally sticky hot holidaymakers en route back from their 'deserted cove'. If we hadn't had that all important last pee in the sea and had indulged too readily in the warm orange squash, all that awaited us was the embarrassment of squatting in a ditch, partially shielded by Mum's skirt, as she got herself totally distracted by the not-quite-ready blackberries, and listening to Dad getting wound-up as he watched the lorry he managed to overtake half an hour ago, rumble by.

I was shunted out of memory lane by the sight of people staring and the realisation that Cam's snoring had reached such embarrassing proportions it was actually starting to drown out the sound of the ocean. I punched his arm.

'You sound like a tractor,' I hissed. 'Turn over and I'll put some cream on your back.'

'Well hello there!' The Australian drawl was unmistakable. I sucked my stomach in and looked around.

Stan was crouched down behind us with a beer in his hand.

'Well hello,' Cam sat up, 'you must be Bug Man.'

'Stan this is Cam – local wit and world-renowned raconteur, available for weddings, funerals and bar mitzvahs.'

Stan gave Cam an intrigued look and tentatively shook his hand.

'Good to meet ya, mate.'

He turned and smiled at me. 'Well I've slept like a dingo in the desert - right through until eight o'clock this morning – how about you? You okay?

'Brilliant,' I gave him a casual smile back.

'Please join us,' said Cam in a voice that seemed to have gone down a few octaves.

'Don't mind if I do, I'll just get my stuff.'

I grabbed my bag and hastily applied some lip gloss.

'Shit, he's fit. What's with the ice-maiden attitude?' Cam was peering at me from over his sunglasses.

'You asking him to join us,' I hissed, 'look at me.'

'He's seen you naked, you silly mare,' Cam shook his head wearily.

The sand crunched as Stan came back towards us. He threw his beach towel down on my side and flopped on to it. I was now turning puce with the effort of holding everything in and was planning my next body position - lying down on my back wasn't the greatest look for my boobs which were threatening to disappear under my armpits but if I sat up my tummy squished into soft rolls. If I turned over on to my stomach, he may notice that my bum closely resembles a landmass that could probably be seen from the moon or at the very least, cause a total eclipse. I decided that on my back, raised up onto my elbows was the least horrific and tried to ignore the taut toned bodies of four teenage girls who were sitting in micro bikinis in front of us.

'Sorry for passing out on you yesterday. I called out to you before I left, but no answer. I was going to come and find you but I was a bit nervous that you might be starkers on your bed,' he winked at me.

'Very funny,' my stomach was churning over. I felt like a bloody schoolgirl. I could see Cam smirking out of the corner of my eye and just hoped he wasn't going to say anything stupid. Stan took off his glasses and closed his eyes. It all went quiet. Cam gave my ankle a kick. I glared at him and nodded towards the sea, mouthing *swim*. He obliged immediately and trotted off to the water's edge, pussy footed around a bit then started to slowly wade out with his shoulders bunched up to ear level.

'Must be cold out there,' Stan opened one eye and nodded in Cam's direction.

'Oh, he's just a big girl,' I laughed.

'I gathered,' Stan muttered.

'You do realise where you've landed, don't you?'

'Meaning?' He looked at me quizzically.

'Sitges is the gayest place in the entire Mediterranean,' I frowned at him. 'Don't tell me you haven't noticed?'

'Well I've seen a few gay fellas,' he shrugged, 'but I...'

'Do I detect a little homophobia?'

'Maybe a little...'

I remembered my first encounter with Bubbles. Now that was pathetic. I was guilty as charged. I decided to borrow a line from her repertoire.

'Not every gay guy who meets you wants to jump your bones, you know.'

'I know, I know, and before you even go there, the fact I'm so uptight about blokes means there is some repressed inclination on my part – which, incidentally – there isn't - blah, blah, blah.'

'You've had this conversation before I assume,' I laughed.

'What conversation?' Cam's idea of a swim was merely to get wet and get straight out again. He shook the water out of his ears and sat down. He lit a cigarette. 'Sorry, rude of me to interrupt.'

I glanced at Stan, he grinned and shrugged. I took that as a green light and turned to Cam, 'Stan here has a little problem with gay guys.'

Cam's eyes twinkled, 'So a big butch boy like you finds us all a bit frightening? You do surprise me.'

'I'm alright just as long as you all leave me alone.'

'Well I suppose you're kinda cute for an old bloke, some guys might find you attractive.'

'Enough of the old fella, I'm only forty-nine.'

'Shit you need some face cream.'

'Blokes do not use face cream.'

'That's why you look so craggy, and that beard, pahleese…'

'It looks alright to me.'

'Glad you're so thrilled with yourself.'

'D'you wanna come for a swim.'

'No way.'

'Not you, Fairycakes, Alex.'

I sat up and nodded. Stan stood and pulled me up. I turned and gave Cam a triumphant little wave.

'Enjoy,' he winked and started to apply sunscreen.

'Somebody needs to buy those girls a few pies,' Stan muttered as we walked past the bikini babes. 'I like women with a bit more meat on them,' he gave me an appraising look. I went to do my usual and say something self-deprecating but thought better of it. In fact, my *mojo* and I positively swaggered down to the sea.

The water was beautiful. I paused for a second at waist level and then threw myself onto my back and floated around for a while.

'That's not swimming,' Stan appeared at my side.

I flipped over, 'I'm relaxing,' I circled him doing a hybrid of doggie paddle and breaststroke.

'You're going to need to build up an appetite,' he shook his head at me. 'When I cook, I cook big-time.'

'Eh? Is this some roundabout way of inviting me to dinner?'

'Yeah – at my apartment they've rented for me. D'you like prawns?'

'Love them,' I attempted to show off by diving underwater but swallowed a mouthful of sea water and came up spluttering.

'Alex Chapman,' he laughed as he thumped my back, 'you're such a bloody dag.'

'Dag?' I was still coughing

'It just means you're a bit goofy.'

'Nice!'

'Well, it was originally a lump of wool and shit hanging off a sheep's arse if you really want to know.'

'You obviously don't chat up women very often, do you?'

'Well luckily for you I'm partial to that 'mascara running down your face look' - especially when it's all mixed up with white streaks of sun cream.'

I never have been and never will be – a natural beauty.

As Cam and I wandered home on our own later that afternoon to get showered and changed for the evening ahead, I was still twittering about him.

'And you just dismissed him out of hand when I pointed him out in the port,' said Cam airily.

'I know, unbelievable isn't it?' I chewed my lip nervously, 'I quite like him, Cam.'

'He's very likeable.'

'But…' I paused.

'But what?'

'I meant what I said at the port, Cam, I'm happy now and men just have a habit of wrecking that.'

'Oh, Alex, just enjoy this for what it is. Don't let fear get in the way of what could be a very nice time.'

I hugged his sandy shoulders, 'You're right; I'm just being a wimp aren't I?'

'Yes.'

'I'm not jumping straight in the sack with him though.'

'Whatever!'

THIRTY ONE

Now during our short acquaintance you could be forgiven for thinking that all it takes is a few sherbets and I'll drop 'em. Granted, there was a link between booze and long-lost confidence - *mojos* can be difficult little buggers to retrieve.

When it came to Stan, I was absolutely determined to hold out for as long as was humanly possible and get to know him. I alternated water with wine, I sipped instead of guzzled. I listened more than I spoke, I did that extra button up and I wore the kind of comfy knickers that you just don't want to be caught in. But with the best will in the world the task was a difficult one as quite frankly, I was becoming obsessed.

He had insisted on cooking me dinner three nights on the trot and we had spent the entire time swapping tales from the travel zone. Stan was a typical globe-trotting Australian. As well as his work, he had also done loads of voluntary stuff for various charitable organizations. He had helped build a school in Botswana, lay water pipes in Ethiopia and countless other good deeds. This totally appealed to my idealistic if shamefully under utilised humanitarian beliefs, and on an attraction level, it was pure cat-nip. Cam could not get one ounce of sense out of me in the daytime as I spent my entire time wandering around clutching my mobile and checking my messages with a stupid grin on my face. When it came to flirting, Stan and I were winding each other up a treat - we were at boiling point.

So on night four, I cooked dinner at mine, complete with plunging neckline and some scanty La Perla undies. I ignored my water, was at my sparkling best and when I started to clear the table, it was officially 'game over'. A newly de-bearded and very hot-looking Stan followed me into the kitchen and nuzzled against my neck whispering a whole list of sexual profanities. At this point if God had come down from the heavens and told me that He would grant world peace if I could manage to ignore the fact that my fanny was a furnace, and just say 'no', I'd have feigned temporary deafness and sold you all out to the Four Riders of the Apocalypse.

Two smashed plates, a tray of broken glasses and a scattered bread basket later, we ended up on the lounge floor having sex – no let's get this right - fan-fucking-tastic sex. This was a man who knew the neighbourhood so to speak, and as far as his dick was concerned, it wasn't shaped like a mushroom, pierced or prone to first night nerves. It was perfect – utterly perfect. When we actually managed to get to sleep that night it was as peaceful and natural as sleeping on my own, well, until the five am toilet visit.

Ordinarily when sleeping solo, I might stumble out of bed in the middle of the night for a quick pee, I might even make it to the fridge in search of juice when it feels like my tongue and the roof of my mouth have been fused together – we all do that. But girlies – as you all know, it's a different kettle of fish when you have someone new in your bedchamber. In the early hours when you're sure your new lover is snoring away for all he's worth, you slide out of bed quiet as a mouse and head for the bathroom, then, having prepared the territory by throwing the sound-proofing wad of toilet paper into the loo, you exercise maximum pelvic floor control as you piss in a gentle stream rather than giving in to your usual relaxed *wushhh*. You quietly close the seat before flushing, as there is plenty more to do yet, and you don't want him to wake up before you have carefully wiped away the garish smudges of mascara from underneath your eyes. When you no longer look like Alice Cooper, you move swiftly onto the generous flooding with eye-drops if you have them to hand - please note at this stage that ear drops grabbed by accident sting like crazy and turn the whites of your eyes a dangerous shade of burgundy. A little tooth cleansing and mouthwash follows, and of course, if you have hair like mine, a desperate attempt to get rid of the 'fuck-knots and shag-tangles' without rendering yourself totally bald in the process. The final stage of this beautifying journey is the *foo-foo freshening* – turning your nether regions into a veritable oasis of gorgeousness. When you no longer resemble a heroin addict in a hurricane, then, and only then, can you flush the toilet and slip back into bed, giving it serious pillow Goddess. A foolproof plan – unless of course – you just so happen to have shagged an Australian tree surgeon who can hear woodworm whispering. Just when I was about to creep back into the bedroom, there was a bash at the door.

'Jeez Alex, I've been busting out here, put the bloody lip gloss away.'

I'd been busted.

Then to add insult to injury, on emerging from the open toilet door having just urinated like a cart-horse, and casually washed his dick with as much aplomb as rinsing a bloody cucumber, the bastard proceeded to laugh with my toothbrush still in his mouth and say, 'You didn't do too badly, most women take at least fifteen to do the secret clean up.'

At this point something deep down in my soul lurched. Nothing to do with my covert beauty session being rumbled, he had referred to 'other women' - a fact I wasn't ready to let invade the proceedings. So I went all out to make damn sure I didn't fit into the 'most women' category and managed to control my gag reflex to such an extent he claimed it was the best blow job he'd ever had – not easy when somebody hasn't quite washed all the soap off and you think any second you are going to literally start frothing at the mouth.

When he eventually left later that morning, after another two solid hours of platinum sex, I lay in bed and wondered why I felt so bloody sick to the pit of my stomach. I sadly acknowledged that my original diagnosis had been correct – I was cruising for a bruising. I had forgotten what it felt like to be so smitten by somebody this quickly, and I didn't like it one little bit. In the name of self-preservation I would have to cool this right down. So when his texts started rolling in an hour later, I ignored them. When he started calling around midday, I went and hid my mobile under a pile of washing on the balcony and took to my bed wearing earplugs. By the time Cam poked his head around my bedroom door at around five pm, I was laying on my bed staring blankly into space. He raised his eyebrows and I burst into a flurry of fear-ridden excuses as to why I probably shouldn't see Stan again.

'Oh for Pete's sake, a few dinners and a good fuck and look at the state of you.' He sat down on the bed. 'If this was me what would you be saying now?'

'Just go and have fun and enjoy it.'

'Precisely, and on that note, the object of your rather evident desire is sitting outside Phillip's bar looking into his beer with a face like a wet weekend. If I were you I'd clean yourself up and get down there, as four Dutch girls are out there giving him the eye.'

That was all it took, I was down by Stan's side quicker than you could pop a cork.

'I've been trying to get hold of you all day,' he said, looking me straight in the eye.

'I was ignoring you.'

'Why?'

'Because I'm pathetic I suppose.'

'Fair do's,' he smiled his crinkly smile. 'I'm taking you out for a slap-up dinner - no cooking tonight. That is, unless you've got other plans?'

'No plans,' I stroked his cheek. 'I need to go and get ready, d'you want to come up?'

'Nope, but you can send Cam down.'

'What for?'

'He bet me a few beers he'd get you down here in ten minutes.'

'He's dead meat.'

'Top bloke I'd say, he's got you sussed alright.'

'Where are the Dutch girls who were giving you the eye?'

'It's been just me and that old bloke over there for the past hour.'

'I'll kill the crafty little bastard.'

THIRTY TWO

Despite constantly reassuring myself that all I was doing was having a fling, I found myself doing all the stuff you swear you'll never do; I abandoned all my friends and spent my days and nights either with Stan or thinking about Stan. I would 'casually' wander past while he was treating a nearby tree, and literally dissolve into my flip-flops when he smiled at me. I was a total slush-bucket. It was a no holds barred, access all areas relationship; we could talk about anything, except when it came to previous relationships. We both admitted we were pretty bad at them and that was that. In all honesty it was quite a relief not to have to take him on a little journey down my series of romantic disasters, because no matter how I played it, I always came out looking like a right idiot. I assumed he'd had a few bad experiences, and did what every spiritual guru tells you to do - I lived in 'the present'. No past-relationship-post-mortems. Marvellous!

We did talk a lot about our upbringings. His dad had brought him up on his own since his mum ran out on them when he was three and they hadn't seen her since. When it came to his dad, Stan was full of admiration. It was from him that he not only had inherited his dreadful name, but his love of nature. They had spent most of their weekends going off on expeditions into the bush or deep sea fishing. He laughed when I told him about my imaginary treks to the jungle when I was little. As far as he was concerned I was exactly the sort of little girl he would have liked to played with.

Well now he could, and who was I to stop him? It's bloody amazing just how quickly those love handles disappear with a little concerted effort. I had more sex in a few weeks than I'd had in ten years - early morning, late night, mid-afternoon. Stan brought a whole new meaning to *siestas*.

We were lying on my bed, shutters drawn, escaping the sun one incredibly hot afternoon when the phone rang; it was my mum who had just arrived in Seville and had been briefed by Evie, who had it on good authority from her Sitges spies that I had been spotted with my arms around a good-looking man outside the Intermarché supermarket.

'Didn't I tell you making that wish would work? Tell me all about him,' her voice was so loud it echoed around the bedroom. Stan prodded me in the tummy and mouthed 'What wish?' I shook my head and he started laughing.

'I can hear a man laughing, is that Cam? No it can't be, far too butch. Oh my God it's him, isn't it?'

'Yes Mum, do you think you could go down a few decibels, apart from the fact that you are embarrassing the life out of me, the Pope has just sent a text from the Vatican to say you're disturbing his nap.'

'Oh sorry Alex, say hello to him for me, and I'll ring back when you can talk.'

Stan grabbed the phone off me, 'Hello there Mrs Chapman, I'm Stan. I'm not having you two talking about me when I'm not here. Whaddya want to know, and what's all this about a wish?'

I tried to grab the phone back but to no avail, I lay back on the bed and groaned.

'I told Alex to wish for a nice man, and it worked.'

'Oh I'm not nice, but last time I looked I was a man.'

'Erm, you are a straight man I assume?'

'Yes Mrs C, have no worries on that front.'

'And you're from New Zealand?'

'Oz – how could you even suggest such a thing?'

'We've got family in New Zealand.'

My mum's logic baffled me sometimes, undaunted she carried on her investigation, 'And so Stan, can I ask you what you do for a living.'

'I climb trees.'

Silence...

'I'm a tree surgeon.'

'You operate on trees?'

'Well, kinda, you see………..'

I spent the next ten minutes listening to Stan making my mum wish she had never asked the question. It was bliss; she couldn't have got a word in edgeways if she had tried. Eventually I decided to put her out of her misery and gestured for the phone back.

'Okay, hope that's put you more in the picture Mrs C, enjoy your holiday now, here's Alex…'

'Hi Mum.'

'Well he does love his trees, doesn't he?'

'Sure does.'

'D'you think he knows much about hydrangeas?'

'Quite possibly but let's not get him started. How are Evie and her friends?'

'Oh Alex, they are wonderful, I haven't stopped laughing since I arrived.'

'Wouldn't have anything to do with wacky backy would it?'

'Ohhhh, you know?'

'Sitges gossip is a two way street, Mum.'

'Well, you have to try these things don't you?'

'Well you behave yourself, and careful what else you decide to try eh?'

'Oh Alex, you're getting all protective.'

'Trying to protect myself from the embarrassment of having to come to Seville and bail you out of jail.'

'Really Alex, oh, everybody is ready to go out, Evie sends her love, bye darling, love to Stan and all the boys. Don't muck this one up. Byeee…' Click.

'Your mum smokes joints?'

'She's a late developer, frightful isn't it?'

'Nah, bet she'd liven up me old man a bit, do you look like her?'

'Not really, she's shorter, brunette with a splash of grey.'

He went quiet; I looked up at him, 'Was your mum a brunette?'

'Yeah,' he sighed and kissed my forehead, 'but enough of all that. I think we should hit the town tonight, let's hang with some of your friends – you must be missing them.'

'You're not going to go all homophobic on me?'

'Nah, I'm over it. As Cam said, a big butch boy like me ought to be able to handle a few poofs.'

'You can begin by losing the 'poof' word.'

'What do I call them then?'

'By their names would be good.'

After a lovely dinner of wild mushroom risotto, rocket and parmesan salad and a bottle of *rosado*, Stan and I went out and about on the streets of Sitges – it was madness.

We caught sight of Bart mincing around a group of young Italian guys in silver mesh vests and camouflage micro shorts down on Sin Street. A kerfuffle on the beach turned out to be Bubbles and Carmen having a fistfight, which then actually progressed to all out wrestling in the sea. Crazy the Caveman followed us into a beach side bar and just sat and stared at us until Stan started to get uncomfortable, so I decided to push him to his limits and dragged him to El Cabaret, which was absolutely heaving with guys. A very uncomfortable Stan indulged in a little uncharacteristic hand holding as we pushed our way towards the bar.

'Hey there you two,' Cam shouted across a sea of gelled and bleached heads, 'what can I get you?'

'Say 'outta here' and you're dead,' I hissed at Stan whose mouth snapped shut immediately. 'Cava and a beer please.'

'There you go,' Cam slammed the glasses on the bar, leaned across to kiss me, then turned to Stan who already had his beer to his lips. 'Thirsty or do I detect a little nervousness?'

'Don't you start Fairycakes.'

Every head within a ten feet radius turned and glared at us, 'Fairy is not a good word, either,' I muttered.

'Overly sensitive tourists,' Cam laughed and called Simon over. 'Come and meet my mate Stan.'

'Oh my word, the Cava Queen is back in town!' Simon shot over, shook Stan's hand and leaned over to give me a peck on the cheek, 'Very nice, you lucky girl,' he whispered.

We managed to last a couple of hours and then when Stan gave me a pleading look that said, 'can we go?' I nodded and finished my drink. The boy had done well, having endured being openly stared at, blatantly flirted with and not least of all, been subjected to a solid hour of show tunes which didn't exactly fit into his heavy rock orientated musical tastes. I did a round of air-kisses as we left Cam and the lads to deal with yet another influx of summertime revellers and the subsequent wave of excitement as Doris Day singing 'Whip Crack Away' burst onto the plasma screen above the stage.

As we wandered back to mine luxuriating in the cooler night air, I stopped in my tracks as there in front of us was Stephanie walking out of Bourbon's nightclub.

'What's up princess?' Stan gave a loud belch and hugged me to him protectively.

Stephanie turned towards us; her eyes glittered dangerously in the lamplight.

'So this is the man I've been hearing so much about, shame *we* didn't bump into each other a little earlier,' she looked Stan up and down then turned to me, 'I'd watch your back if I were you Alex, he's cute.'

'And SO not interested in you - we're off home, happy trawling, Stephanie,' I smiled sweetly and dragged Stan off.

'Jeez, she's a bit forward isn't she?' Stan turned and watched Stephanie strut off.

'He's a bit forward, Stephan is a bloke.'

'Fuck!!!!! Alex you're kidding me.'

'Nope.'

'Blimey, he's pretty convincing. I've never understood why they want to prance around in all that women's stuff. That is one thing you would never catch me doing – ever.'

'That's a relief.'

*

'Alex, Alex, hey wake up.'

I opened my eyes and blinked at Stan who was leaning up on one arm looking at me with one of his crooked smiles spreading across his face.

'Oh my God, I had a dream – actually no – my worst nightmare.'

'I'll say you did, you just thwacked me one and started shouting about Stephan.'

I let it register for a while then sighed with relief. I had gone back to the night at Organic and instead of Jorges, it was Stan that was sitting in the shadows with Stephanie busy at work between his legs. I told Stan the dream and filled him in on my on-going feud with Stephan.

'Crikey, so I've had my dick sucked by a fella in a frock.'

'Hopefully only in my dreams.'

'Well it wouldn't have happened in one of mine I can tell you.'

'Bet you would, most men wouldn't mind giving it a try,' I tickled him.

'Get outta here, shit Alex. You worried about losing me to the other side?'

'Losing you period,' the words tumbled out of my mouth before I had a chance to stop them.

'Sorry, forget I said that,' I muttered as I turned over. 'By the way, when do you leave? We might as well get that out of the way, as I seem to have raised the subject.' I tried to keep my voice steady but it quivered and gave me away as tears pricked the back of my eyes.

'Middle of September, back to Oz to see Dad, then who knows where the next sick tree is?'

The best I could manage was a nod. He snuggled into my back and kissed my shoulder, 'You've got under my skin you know.'

'You can probably get cream for that,' I made a weak attempt at humour.

'Seriously Alex, I don't know exactly how, but are you up for trying?'

'Trying what exactly?'

'Trying to make this work?'

I swung around and faced him, 'Please don't bugger around with my emotions just to bolster up your own ego.'

He leapt out of bed, 'Where did that come from? I'm trying to be positive about us here.'

'I've heard it all before and had it all thrown back in my face, every time I've made the stupid mistake of liking someone, it just goes wrong.'

'None of us can predict the bloody future, but if you're too scared to even try, then I'm barking up the wrong tree.'

'It's all about bloody trees with you isn't it?' I sniffed.

He sat back down on the bed and hugged me, 'I know it's all a bit quick, but I really think we have something, don't you?'

'Yes,' I mumbled, my heart beating so loud in my chest I could barely hear myself think.

'You're just going to have to give me some time to get a few things sorted out, and then we're going to have to do some serious thinking about how we do this,' he tilted my chin up towards him and kissed me, 'Alex please don't cop out on me.'

'I've waited this long – what's a bit longer?' I squeezed him tightly, snuggled into his shoulder and allowed myself to smile contentedly. Was this what feeling secure was meant to feel like? Was this what I'd been missing out on?

THIRTY THREE

It only took a few days before a third party started getting involved with our now official 'relationship'. Time to introduce my personal gremlin, an even more fearful version of me, who insisted on waking me up in the middle of the night and making uninvited appearances into my consciousness during moments that should have otherwise been blissful, and continually reminding me in a horrible, scared little voice that everything would all go pear-shaped. This was a side of myself I didn't have to face as a single person. I was an optimist, a positive person in every other facet of my life, but my past relationship history was still deeply ingrained in my psyche and I just couldn't seem to get rid of it.

Just to add fuel to this particular fire, I had a bit of a shock when Stan and I decided to brave the tourists and spend a day in Barcelona. I wanted to take him to the beautiful *Cathedral Basilica* in the Gothic quarter and as we approached the steps leading up to the entrance, I stopped dead and gasped. There in front of me, laughing his head off and sitting with his arms around an older guy with a goatee beard, was Pierre, whose face dropped like a stone the minute he noticed me. He jumped up and came over, 'Bonjour Alex, bonjour...er,' he held his hand out towards Stan.

'Hi there I'm Stan.'

'Pierre.'

'And that is?' I nodded towards the other guy who was now fiddling around in a tatty old briefcase.

'Juan Carlos, he is – erm - a friend.'

'I've been worried sick about you. Pierre what's going on?'

'I'm going to go and have a look around in the church, why don't you two have a catch up?' Stan could obviously sense a little tension in the air.

'We will be in ze coffee shop over zere,' Pierre pointed to a small café across the square.

'Will you be okay?' I kissed Stan on the cheek.

'Yes mummy, see you in a while, send me a text if you can't find me. Good luck, Pierre,' he walked away grinning to himself.

'Wow, Alex, who is zat man?'

'My boyfriend I suppose,' I blushed as I said it. 'Anyhow, come on. Is your – erm - friend coming with us?'

'You don't mind?'

'Oh Pierre, of course I don't mind, I am just relieved you're not unwell - you're not are you?'

'*Non*,' he lit a cigarette, 'come, Juan Carlos, meet my friend Alex.'

Juan Carlos stood up and dusted himself down. He beamed at me as he walked over and clasped my hand. *'Hola* Alex, *encantada.'*

'Encantado, Juan Carlos.'

We sat at an outside table and ordered coffee. I looked expectantly at Pierre, 'So how is everything?'

We did small talk for the first ten minutes and then I broached the subject of how they had met.

'Juan Carlos and I met at the hospital,' Pierre smiled warmly, 'we 'ave both been zrough ze same sing. When you 'ave such a close brush with death it makes you want to live life as fully as possible, and like me, Juan Carlos wants to make up for ze time we lost. We want to travel and explore ze world, and we are both city people at heart. Sitges is a village Alex. It is perfect for Fred, but not for me. You understand?'

I nodded, but I couldn't help but wonder, despite his summertime flings, when it came to the crunch, how well Fred would get on without Pierre. As if he read my mind, Pierre leant over and touched my hand.

'In our 'earts we 'ave both known it is over for a while; we just 'ave to make it official. Fred will be better without me, trust me Alex. After *Fiesta Major* I will be moving to Barcelona and Fred will stay in Sitges, he 'as many friends zere now.'

'Well, hopefully it will all work out for everyone,' I smiled. 'I hate to rush away but I'd better go and find Stan now. It was lovely to meet you Juan Carlos, keep in touch Pierre,' I stood up and kissed them both, then wandered thoughtfully over to the cathedral. Here I was beginning a relationship, while Fred and Pierre were in the process of ending theirs.

It won't be long whispered the gremlin.

I entered and spotted Stan standing away from the crowds, gazing at the vast number of flickering red candles that were bringing the ornate gold interior of the cathedral to life. It was an intensely beautiful spectacle. I stood and watched him for a while, not quite believing my luck. Suddenly he lifted his hand to his face and quickly wiped both his eyes. He looked up and caught sight of me watching; then walked over and pulled me to him, 'Everything okay with your friend?'

'I'll tell you the whole story later, how about you? Are you okay?' I looked into his eyes inquiringly.

'Yeah, of course, what makes you say that?'

'Could have sworn I saw you wiping away a tear, you big softie.'

'It's that candle smoke, gets in your eyes.'

As we walked away, I turned. As far as I could see, there wasn't any smoke coming from the candles. I smiled to myself and kept quiet. Obviously 'real' men didn't cry in public. While we wandered around Barcelona I told him about Fred and Pierre.

'Well, I suppose relationships do reach a point where you realise it can't go on, people change and have to face up to difficult decisions…there you go *senor*,' Stan jingled around in his pockets and thrust a handful of change at an ice-cream vendor, who couldn't hide his excitement. Generosity or stupidity – he didn't give a shit – this dumb *turisto* was paying him three times the going rate for an already extortionately priced Magnum on *Las Ramblas*.

'You pay them way too much you know,' I chided.

'Who cares? I hate pocketfuls of shrapnel, now where were we, oh yeah - difficult decisions,' he took a huge bite of his ice cream and went to speak, but was interrupted by the sound of my mobile ringing in my bag.

'Hold that thought – *hola*.'

'Alex, it's me Beverley.'

'Hey, how are you?' This was a surprise, Beverley and I hadn't been as good as we had promised at keeping in touch, and she sounded terrible, 'Are you okay?' I mouthed 'sorry' to Stan who shrugged and started taking pictures of a mime artist outside a café.

'No, Alex,' she let out a sob, 'Laurence is having an affair.'

'Oh Beverley,' I tried to sound surprised, but obviously wasn't hugely convincing.

'I know he's probably had loads of others but this is different.'

'In what way sweetheart?'

'IT'S TANYA!!!!! He's been shagging my so called best friend for the past fifteen years!'

'Fuck!'

'He sent me off to a health spa as a surprise and I came back a day early because I didn't feel well,' she wailed. 'Alex, he was in our bed with her, Alice and Heidi were in France with friends, so he had her in MY BED! THE STUPID TART WAS HANDCUFFED TO MY BLOODY BED!'

'What on earth did you do?'

'I ran downstairs and got a knife,' she sniffed.

'Jesus, Beverley you're not calling me from prison are you?'

'No, although I wish I had murdered the pair of them and thrown their bodies into the Rochdale Canal.'

'Probably better you didn't darling. So what *did* you do?'

'I chased Laurence out of the house.'

'Please tell me he was naked.'

'No, the bastard managed to put his underpants on and grab his car keys.'

'Bugger! What about Tanya?'

'She was still handcuffed, so I said I'd cut off her hair extensions if she didn't tell me everything. She sang like a canary. Fifteen bloody years Alex – the kids were toddlers when it started. She said it was my fault for being so absorbed in the girls, that Laurence felt lonely. And d'you know what? I realised something. She has been manipulating me for years. When ever I have started to feel good about myself, lost some weight, started exercising – she sabotages it. She either creates some drama to knock me off course, starts bringing around little treats for the pair of us, turns up late when we're meant to be going to the gym together, it's endless. She never wanted me to be confident did she? I'm sure she only put me forward for your programme to humiliate me.'

'Probably.'

'Well, I did have a little revenge. I told her I couldn't find the key to the handcuffs and called out the local locksmith to set her loose, after having taken pictures for the lawyers of course.'

'Bright move.'

'The locksmith is her uncle.'

'Pure genius!'

'I'm going to take that bastard husband of mine for every last cent, the only good thing is I'm too stressed to eat, but I suppose every cloud has a silver lining,' she laughed hysterically.

'Beverley you've got to look after yourself, where are the kids?'

'They're still in the South of France. Laurence is staying at Tanya's flat. She's welcome to him,' I could hear the hysteria turning to tears again.

'Beverley is there anything I can do for you?'

'Just be on the other end of the phone, I haven't got anyone else to talk to. My sister is in the middle of Africa saving a rare species of snake, and I married one,' She started to weep in earnest. 'All our friends knew and never said a word.'

'Beverley, can I say something?'

She let out a huge sniff, which I took to be a yes. 'This may not seem very apparent at the moment, and you might say that it's easy for me to say, but I think it may be the best thing that has ever happened to you. As far as that stupid cow Tanya is concerned, she might think she's won the lottery but all she has done is inherit someone who will do it again at the next given opportunity. You deserve better than that, and he didn't deserve to be married to you.'

'I just feel so humiliated.'

Stan wandered back and winked at me; I rolled my eyes and shook my head, 'You'll be fine Beverley, honestly. Focus all your energy into coming out of this as well and as whole as you can. Go for his jugular and if you need a break away from it all, ring me.'

'Thanks Alex, I'm sorry for off loading on you.'

'Beverley, don't be such a sap, we're cosmic twins remember.'

'Okay, bye.'

'Christ does everyone come to you in a crisis? What was that all about?' Stan slid his arm around my shoulders and kissed me on the forehead.

'A mate, well, a new mate...'

'A cosmic twin,' he smirked.

'Don't take the piss - Beverley was born on the same day as me and the same year – anyhow, she's having some problems.'

'It sounded quite intense.'

'I'd say! She has just caught her husband having sex with her best friend; apparently they've been having an affair for fifteen years behind her back.'

'Well, maybe there was a good reason for it. Maybe there is stuff you don't know about the situation.'

'Pardon?' I looked at him incredulously, his lofty attitude made my hackles rise, so I bit big time. 'I do know that running around having countless affairs and screwing your wife's best friend, isn't usually included in your average marriage vows.'

'So your advice is to go for the jugular, quite the little counsellor aren't we?

I jumped away from him, 'What's up with you? Don't be so sarcastic, believe you me, if you had met this guy, you would understand why I said that.'

'There are always two sides to these kinds of stories - that's all I'm saying.'

'Well let's give you a few other sides shall we? A few years ago I started dating a bloke who didn't think it was necessary to tell me he had a wife and a new baby – I found out when she turned up on my doorstep with the bloody pram. More recently I was virtually stalked by a friend's husband who wouldn't take 'no' for an answer, and just a couple of months ago a so-called best friend of mine, married with children, came out here and jumped in the sack with someone she knew I liked, now I don't know what goes on behind closed doors, and what kind of problems these couples are having, but you want to do married – do married. You don't want to be married any more, sort it out before you start affecting the lives of people like me who believe in a little honesty and integrity.'

He stood quietly staring at me, 'So this is all about you, is it?'

'No it's bloody not.' Yes it bloody was. I was incandescent. He carried on staring and I carried on ranting. 'This type of thing hits a raw nerve with me; I hate infidelity. Granted, there's probably a lot I don't know about Beverley's marriage, but I still fail to see how anything justifies what her husband and best friend have done. Maybe my past experiences mean that I am a bit overly sensitive, but what I do know is that Beverley is a good person who certainly didn't deserve this, and I hope from the bottom of my heart that she finds some way to turn this whole thing around.'

'So do I Alex, but maybe encouraging a bitter divorce battle isn't necessarily the way to do it.'

'I hope she takes him to the cleaners,' I muttered and walked ahead.

We wandered around Barcelona for the next couple of hours in virtual silence, both lost deep in thought. I couldn't believe how quickly the atmosphere between us had changed. When Stan said he was tired and wanted to make his way back to Sitges, I readily agreed, and when we pulled in at the station and I said I fancied a night in on my own, he didn't argue. We walked off in different directions without a backward glance. Six weeks – six short weeks and we were at this stage already.

The gremlin in my head shouted loud and clear – *Well done Alex, you've done it again.*

THIRTY FOUR

'So all he said was that there might be more than one side to a story, and you bit his head off?'

'It was the way he said it.'

'Calmly and objectively? What a bastard, how dare he have an opinion?'

'Am I in the wrong here?'

'A tad...'

I snuggled up to Cam on the sofa and great fat salty tears started to spill down my face. 'Mel's right, I always fuck up relationships with the good ones,' I wiped my face with one of Stan's t-shirts that I had been carrying around like a comforter since we parted company the night before. 'Cam, I went off like a Catherine wheel.'

'Hey, there's nothing wrong with showing your vulnerability. You are going to have to trust someone with your emotions eventually.'

'I trust you.'

'That's different, I'm your sensitive gay friend, always on hand with Kleenex and sherry, talking of which, have some more Uncle Peter, he does wonders for melancholic moments.'

I grabbed my *Tio Pepe* and took a sip, 'Drinking at this hour is not good. I'm lapsing back into my naughty ways.'

'Alex, it's nine-thirty in the morning, we've done it before.'

'Yeah, but we usually come in and carry on, not get up and start.'

'Bugger it, we are mid-crisis, it's allowed.'

I laughed, 'Most people would be administering hot sweet tea,' and then looked at him, 'Cam, why haven't you told me about those pictures?'

He went silent, leaned back against the sofa and closed his eyes.

'Look, ever since I saw your reaction when I found them, I have stayed away from the subject. I guessed it was painful and respected your privacy, but here we are talking about vulnerability and being open, and yet there is a whole chunk of my 'sensitive gay friend's' life that I know nothing about. Can't you trust me?'

'Of course I trust you, more than anyone else here; it's just a thing I don't talk about.'

'Try me.'

He poured himself another sherry and twisted around to face me, 'Okay, but please don't tell another soul.'

I nodded, and he carried on.

'I've always been good at art, ever since I was little, in the genes I guess – my dad is a frustrated artist who masquerades as a civil servant. He converted the garden shed into a studio and we used to paint and draw together most nights and weekends. My stuff was hung everywhere in the house, and he used to get a huge kick out of coming to the school and seeing my pictures on the walls. Every prize day I would win the art award, and it was just accepted that one day I would go to art college,' he paused and had a mouthful of sherry. 'Everything was going along swimmingly, great O-level grades, sailed through my A-levels and I was all lined up to go to The Royal College of Art in London, and then I did something that I can't regret or wish I hadn't done - I had to do it. On the night before I was due to leave, I told my parents I was gay.'

'And?'

'He, being my loved and adored father who I thought was liberal and progressive, reverted back to his Scottish Methodist roots and flew off the handle, ripped up the grant cheque and went and got drunk with his cronies down the pub. She, being what I now realise is a life-long doormat and coward, never said a word in my defence, just suggested that I see 'somebody that could help'. I left the next morning and went to London to see if I could get some sort of bursary or scholarship, but it was too late, they had already allocated their funding.'

'Oh Cam!'

'I tried to make it work for three months, living in a squat with what turned out to be three drug addicts and working all the hours known to man in a kebab shop in Kings Cross. It was a bloody nightmare. I couldn't leave anything at home because the druggies would go and sell it; there was no hot water or electricity. Eventually I was called into the Head of Department's office and given a warning. I was falling asleep in classes, my appearance was too unkempt and my coursework just wasn't up to scratch. I gave up, couldn't hack it any longer.'

'What did you do?'

'I worked in Heaven as a barman, affiliated myself to every gay rights issue I could, in order to give some semblance of meaning to my life, and numbed my senses with drink and drugs. Then, six years ago I came here on holiday and never went back.'

'How do your parents feel now?'

'I wouldn't know, haven't seen them for fifteen years.'

'Shit! They don't even know you're here?'

'Alex, if they can only be proud of what you can do and yet can't accept who you are, what's the point?'

I exhaled loudly, got up and walked over to the balcony doors. The sea was like a millpond and the beach already starting to fill with tourists. I turned to Cam, 'Are you ever tempted to see if their attitude has changed and if they realise what they did to you?'

'It's too late, Alex, the damage is done; they can't give me back the past fifteen years.'

I went to say something, but Cam interjected immediately, 'Don't say anything else, I cannot and will not be persuaded to contact them. As far as I'm concerned I'm an orphan. I've been adopted by the universe.'

'At least do something about your art, Cam; those paintings and drawings were phenomenal. When did you do those?'

'During the past six years, usually when I'm drunk and maudlin.'

'Well you should carry on; you're wasting a god-given talent.'

'Maybe. I'm going to have a quick shower then go and get us some breakfast,' he came over and gave me a cuddle and pressed his bristly cheek again mine. 'I'm glad I told you,' he whispered.

I pulled away from him and looked into his eyes, which looked glassy and red, 'I think you came here to learn forgiveness,' I said quietly and put my hand to his heart, 'even if it's just in there.'

For a second Cam looked like he was going to burst into tears, but suddenly he looked over my shoulder and shouted, 'I don't believe it.'

I turned around, half-hoping to see Stan, but instead there was a vision in purple and a vision in yellow trundling along the street dragging wheelie suitcases behind them. It was my mum and Evie, who both started waving madly the minute they saw us.

'What in hell's name? They're meant to be in Seville.'

'Yoo hoo darling! We thought we would come and spend *Fiesta Major* with you,' my mum was virtually unrecognisable. Her housewife perm had grown out and looked lighter, and she was tanned, wearing a glittery kaftan and -- if I wasn't mistaken – linen trousers. This was a woman who, only a few months ago, thought linen should be Irish and gracing the dinner table, and whose sense of style was purely 'Prêt á Polyester'.

'Put the kettle on,' shouted Evie, 'mummies one and two on the way up.'

'Alexandra, is that a glass of wine in your hand?' My mum looked horrified.

'Don't be silly Mum – its apple juice.'

'I'll buzz them in,' laughed Cam, who had totally regained his composure, 'and once I've hidden the sherry and performed my daily ablutions, I'll keep them busy while you ring you know who.'

'I suppose I ought to,' I shrugged.

'Yes, he's too good to let get away Mollie – even if he has got the most un-sexy name on the planet.'

*

'It was fabulous, we stayed at this amazing old *masia* with a beautiful pool and orange groves, olive trees, fig trees, the most stunning sunsets. Oh, Alex, it was beautiful.'

'Just like Torquay then Mum,' I smiled, 'How much fun did you have exactly?'

'If you're talking about spliffs darling, we shared one every night after dinner, apart from the brunch party, then I pushed the boat out and had one by the pool with Antonio,' she beamed at me.

'Who's Antonio for Pete's sake?'

'He's my Romanian poet friend,' said Evie, 'he thought your mother was a natural philosopher.'

I choked and spat a mouthful of tea over my lap, 'Okay Socrates, was this compliment sandwiched in between the joint and trying to get his 'quill' into your M&S full piece by any chance?'

My mum tutted and shook her head, 'Really, Alex, I don't wear full piece costumes any more – I bought some bikinis.'

I put my tea cup down before I dropped it. My mother was losing a decade a week. Sod HRT; just introduce your mum to the miracle of marijuana.

'So, Alex, tell us how you're getting on with this man – Stan isn't it?' Evie nudged my mum and they both looked at me expectantly.

'Well I'm flabbergasted the pair of you managed to avoid the subject this long.'

'Evie said you'd get defensive if we brought it up straight away.'

'Well, what can I say, it was all going brilliantly until I over-reacted to something yesterday and we had a bit of a tiff, spent the night apart, haven't spoken since, you know, the usual.'

'I knew it, didn't I tell you, Evie? She does this every time. I just don't know what you do Alex?' My mum had lost a little of her new found calm and starting screeching again. I found it oddly reassuring.

My mobile started to ring in the kitchen and was rescued by Cam who had wandered up the stairs wearing nothing but a pair of jeans that were more rips than denim.

'It's Stan,' he chucked it at me.

'Be nice Alex.'

I glared at my mum and answered it with my heart in my mouth, 'Hi there.'

'Hi,'

'Apologise,' my mum hissed.

'Wait a minute, we have an audience. Evie roll my mum a spliff will you?' I walked out onto the balcony. 'How are you doing?'

'Been better, how about you? Did I hear right, is your mum there?'

'Yes, a little surprise this morning, she and Evie have come back to see the *Fiesta Major* celebrations, although I think it has more to do with catching a glimpse of you. Not that there's much chance of that any more. I feel awful Stan, I'm so sorry, you didn't deserve one of my rants.'

'Alex, I was being a dick, you were only being protective of your friend, I'm sorry.'

'Am I forgiven?'

'Ah shut up, but we do need to get together and have a chat.'

I sat down on a chair, weak with relief, 'When?'

'Well I've got to head down to Villanova today and check on a few trees on the front, so how about later?'

'Okay, it's the big one in Sitges tonight - they have their *Fiesta Major* fireworks display, which by all accounts is utterly amazing. Why not meet us on the beach down near the church around eight? Everyone gets there early to get a good spot. I'll make sure we're well stocked with beers, then once the fireworks are over and you've suffered enough at the hands of Evie and Mum, we'll escape to a quiet beach with a bottle of wine and a blanket.'

'Sounds perfect....Alex,' he hesitated for a second, 'I do love you, you know.'

'I've got a horrible sneaking feeling I love you, too,' I clicked the phone off and turned around to see Cam, Evie and Mum all grinning inanely at me.

'We heard you say you loved him,' said Cam.

'And we get to meet him tonight,' my mum clapped her hands.

Evie was already grabbing her things, she nudged my mum, 'Come on we've got a picnic to prepare.'

'I'll do dessert.'

'I know dear.'

They disappeared out of the door chattering away about their menu. Cam shut it behind them, 'They're like the bloody Golden Girls.'

'I know. I don't think she's ever had a mate like Evie before. All her friends are so straight-laced.'

'She'll shake them all up a bit when she gets home then.'

'Scare the living shit out of them more like.'

'D'you feel better now?'

'Yes, thanks for the pep talk,' I smiled sheepishly.

'So, Bugman and Alex love each other,' Cam sighed and started to clear the cups and glasses away.

'It would appear so, and for the record, Alex loves Cam, too.'

'Cam feels exactly the same way,' he winked at me and walked into the kitchen. 'Oh shit the dishwasher's full. I'll unload it if you put away.'

'Okay,' I trudged into the kitchen; this was one job that Cam and I hated more than anything.

THIRTY FIVE

The beach was already starting to fill when Cam and I started to clamber over the sand weighed down with a cool box full of beers and wine and a couple of large blankets. We found a spot near the water's edge and spread out. Cam stood and looked around, 'Yes, this is a great place to be, we can see the church, prime location for the water display and the fireworks will be directly over our heads. Perfect!'

I tossed my shoes off and lay down excitedly. Cam had been winding me up about these fireworks for weeks. He assured me that they would be the best I had ever seen in my life. I closed my eyes and listened to the waves. I must have dozed off because when I opened my eyes and sat up, Mum and Evie had arrived and were laying out a veritable feast. Dusk was starting to kick in.

'Hello there sleepy,' my mum ruffled my hair and kissed me on the cheek.

'Here you go, this will liven you up,' Cam thrust a paper cup of cava into my hand.

I leaned over and grabbed a piece of chicken, 'Anyone got the time?'

'Alex there's a bloody great church clock behind you,' Cam laughed.

It was eight-thirty. I looked around, we were pretty wedged in, I grabbed my handbag and looked for my mobile phone – it wasn't there. I had put it on to charge earlier in the afternoon, and obviously left it behind. I had an image of it flashing furiously with countless messages from Stan.

Evie seemed to read my mind in a second, 'Do you think your young man will be able to find us?'

'He'd be thrilled to hear you refer to him as a young man, but actually I am a bit worried; I've left my mobile behind, so if he is having trouble, he won't be able to get hold of me.'

'You can use mine if you want,' Cam poured more cava into my cup.

'I couldn't tell you his number if you paid me a million quid.'

'You see, that's the trouble with mobile phones,' my mum clucked, 'they're making us all brain-dead, in more ways than one.'

I frowned at her, 'Okay I'm going to wander up onto the *paseo*, I'll have a better chance of finding him there, if he does manage to get here without bumping into me, I'll be up by Picnic.

I wove my way between the hoards of revellers, who were all getting quite tanked up. There was barely any space in between the blankets so I literally had to walk across everybody else's patch – not that anybody gave a damn. Finally I reached the steps. No sooner had I climbed up onto the side walk, when I heard Stan shouting my name. I turned and saw him running towards me. Something was wrong, he was dressed in trousers and a jacket and carrying a suitcase.

'Hey what's up?'

'Alex, I've been ringing you for the past hour,' he was out of breath. 'I've got to get back to Australia. It's my dad; he's in hospital. He's had a heart attack. Of all the days to forget my phone, I did it today. There was a message waiting for me at the reception when I got back.'

'Oh God, I'm so sorry, I left my phone at home by accident, too. How is he?' My eyes welled up, I had been in this situation before with my own dad, but at least I had been in the country, not the other side of the world.

'In Intensive Care, look I need to get a taxi, but they're not letting any cars down here, so I'm going to have to go up to the rank at the train station.'

'We'll go up via *Espaltar*, it'll be quieter there.'

'You don't have to come Alex; you'll miss your fireworks.'

'Blow the fireworks.'

'Just come as far as the train station, honestly my head is

spinning and I have more calls to make and...'

'Hey, it's okay, come on,' I said gently and took his hand.

We virtually ran all the way to the station and when we arrived, there was one solitary cab. Stan threw his bag in and hugged me. 'I'll call,' I felt dampness on my cheek, he was crying.

'Just get there,' I started to choke up, 'go.'

The cab pulled out of the station, he gave a half-hearted wave and was gone. I stood rooted to the spot for a few minutes, tears flooding down my face at the prospect of what he was going to have to face. A Barcelona train arrived and hundreds of people started to pour out of the exit, all going down in the direction of the *paseo*, I had no alternative but to join them as if I left it much later I would never get back to Cam and the others, who must be wondering where the hell I had got to.

After what seemed an eternity I finally made it back to the beach and had the shock of my life when, as I got closer to the blankets, I noticed that the last person I wanted to see was sitting next to my mum and nibbling a handful of crudités. It was Stephan.

'Alex are you okay, where's Stan?' My mum looked up, 'We found Stephan here wandering around alone, so we asked him to come and join us. He said he saw Stan earlier and he looked distressed. What's happened?'

I glanced over at Stephan, who was luxuriating in my obvious discomfort, and Cam standing behind him, mouthing 'I didn't ask him to join us.'

'His dad has had a heart attack; he's on his way back to Australia as we speak.'

I could see by the look on my mum's face she was hurtling back in time in the same way that I had. I gave her hand a reassuring squeeze.

'Christ is he alright?' Cam gulped.

'He's in Intensive Care. I just hope Stan makes it back in time. Where did you see him?' I asked Stephan who was sipping red wine from a plastic cup.

'I have a friend who is staying in the same apartments, and I was leaving as your boyfriend arrived. He seemed very upset when they gave him the note. In fact he was in such a state he dropped it, so I picked it up, just in case it was important,' he stood up, rustled around in his jeans pocket and produced a crumpled piece of paper, which he thrust into my hand.

I couldn't help gasping as I read the words. Suddenly all the street lights went out and the beach was thrust into darkness. There was a huge explosion as the first firework shot up and illuminated the sky. Stephan's face was triumphant as he brushed past me to leave.

'You didn't know?'

I sank to the floor and Cam crawled over. I held out the paper, he read it and his face dropped, 'Alex, I don't believe it.'

I was too numb to react, too shocked to speak. The fireworks may have been the best I would ever have seen in my life, but I didn't see a single one. I just sat staring blankly into space with the words on the note rolling around in my head: *Mr Berringer. Your father is in hospital. Please can you call your wife urgently!*

THIRTY SIX

It took a while, but eventually I felt my heart calcify into a hard little lump. After three days of alternating between anger and tears, all that was left was a dull ache. Even the weather was mirroring my mood. On the morning after *Fiesta Major*; after having run off and spent the entire night alone in a Catalan bar where nobody kept asking me how I was feeling, I stumbled home as the heavens opened and hit Sitges with the worst storms they had seen in decades.

As the torrential rain and vicious winds blasted every last trace of the summer excess away from the town, sending it cascading into the sea, I lay on the sofa and refused to see anyone. I switched the mobile off and Cam crept quietly around me as I listened to my gremlin. *Told you so, told you so, what were you thinking?*

Then on day four, when I was confident that I had safely locked my vulnerable self away behind a bloody great impenetrable wall of steel, I emerged along with the rest of Sitges into the cooler, brighter air and took a sigh of relief that the sticky, cloying heat and madness of summer had disappeared. I wandered around and reacquainted myself with the sheer beauty of the town. The colours seemed to seep into my being, a transfusion of utter bliss. I hit the market and filled my basket with mounds of vibrant fruit and vegetables, symbolically, it was time to detox.

'You do know that your mum is leaving tomorrow, don't you?' Cam looked at me quizzically as I filled a huge cauldron with cheap tomatoes, and started washing the twenty jars I had bought for my home-made *passata* or as the Spanish say, *tomate frite.*

'Yup,' I smiled at him,' we can have her and Evie over to dinner tonight. I think pasta would be a good idea,' I nodded at the vat of tomatoes. 'I need to apologise for running off the other night.'

'Your mum and Evie are just worried that's all. You still haven't told me where you went.'

'I ended up in this dodgy little Catalan bar where nobody kept asking me how I was and didn't give a shit that I kept grizzling into my glass.'

Cam gave my arm a squeeze.

'D'you know what pisses me off most? You don't realise emptiness is there until someone comes along and fills it. Now I just have to get back to where I was before. I told you, men cause me trouble. Always have, always will.

'You haven't turned it on yet have you?'

'What, the gas oven?'

'You know bloody well I'm talking about your phone.'

'I can't face it.'

'Alex, life is going on out there. You're not the only one going through a crap time. Bubbles is walking around with her own personal black cloud because Carmen dumped her, Fred and Pierre have finally made the break, and I haven't met the man of my dreams this summer, either,'

'Just be glad you didn't.'

'You're going to have to front it up with him at some point. He has no idea you know.'

'Cam, he lied to me.'

'He didn't lie; he just didn't tell you the whole story.'

'That's a pile of crap and you know it. All that bollocks about not discussing our pasts, he's probably got a sucker like me in every bloody port and countless kids of every colour and creed dotted all over the world.'

'You don't think there is any chance Stephan faked that note?'

My blood ran cold for a second, and then I shook my head, 'No, funnily enough, I think this is the one thing I have to be grateful to him for. No matter how nasty his motives were, he actually did me a favour. I'm fine now, really. It was just exactly what we said in the beginning – a summer fling.'

Cam held my phone out towards me and pressed the 'on' button,

'You'll be alright checking your messages then, won't you?'

I sighed and dried my hands before taking the phone. There were a series of shrill beeping sounds as three days worth of unanswered calls and texts hit the screen - thirty-two texts and twenty-one voice mails.

'Oh Christ, there's loads,' I groaned.

'Off to the sofa with you, I'll make tea.'

Most of the messages were the usual - invitations to go out, *Vodafone* leaving unintelligible messages regarding special offers, a couple from Beverley and then inevitably the ones I was dreading.

'Hey Alex, Stan here, just got back from the hospital. He's bearing up, but they want to operate on his heart when he's stronger. I'll call you tomorrow. Love you. Bye for now.'

'Alex, where are you? It's Stan?'

'Alex, please call me on this number, I'm worried.'

Tears pricked the back of my eyes. It was so good to hear his voice.

Cam came wandering in with a tray, 'Everything okay?'

'I'm going to have to call him aren't I?'

'I think you should.'

I looked at the time. It would be late evening there. I grit my teeth and dialled the number. Luckily it was him who answered.

'Oh Alex, thank god, there you are, how are have you been?' His voice sounded disconcertingly close.

'Erm, fine, how's your dad?' I answered in flat wooden tones.

'We'll see, hopefully he'll have the operation soon, then we can get him back on track.'

'Who's 'we'?' I just couldn't help myself.

'Pardon?'

'We – who exactly is 'we'?'

'I don't know what you're going on about. Oh wait a minute Alex, shit, that's what I wanted to talk to you about. Alex, you have got to listen to me.'

'So it's true then – you are married, you do have a wife?'

'Yes but, it's…'

'Over,' I cut in, and then promptly cut him off.

Cam was staring at me open-mouthed, 'Talk about brutal.'

'Best not to let him explain his way out of it, just in case I feel tempted to forgive him.' The phone rang again. I switched it off and looked at Cam, 'I am nobody's bit on the side. Come on, we've got fifty tomatoes to peel,' I smiled brightly and wandered into the kitchen. He looked at me warily, but decided to hold his counsel. By the end of the afternoon we had twenty jars of rich and fragrant *passata,* the whole apartment was filled with the smell of tomatoes and garlic. I decided it was time to touch base with a few people.

I called Beverley first. Her drama was far larger than my drama. I couldn't even begin to imagine what she must be going through. She was surprisingly stoic about it all. It had only been a week, and yet she said she had already seen lawyers and the wheels were already in motion. I told her about Stan.

'They're all bloody bastards,' she sighed, 'What a shame Alex; you sounded so happy during the past few weeks.'

'It's okay, Bev, I'll get over it. But, I'll tell you something, I am seriously swearing off them now. It's just not worth it.'

'Hey, maybe I'll take you up on your offer and come and see you soon?'

'You are welcome any time you want.'

I also did something that was long overdue – I called Mel.

'Not another bloody arse-hole,' she screamed, 'why didn't you call me before?'

'Well, it only happened four days ago.'

'But you usually call me the minute something like this happens. I didn't even know you had a man. How long is it since we last had a chat?'

'Shall we just say too long and leave it at that?'

Mel had been manic over the summer - two snatched holidays which were in her words, 'more stressful than relaxing', made worse by her total inability to turn off her Blackberry. I pointed out that the entire British judicial system had been operating successfully for many years before her arrival and would continue to do so, however badly and unjustly, long after she was dead and gone, so maybe it wouldn't have slid into total chaos during her three-week absence. She did the 'I know, I know' thing that essentially means 'I'm ignoring every word you're saying' and then had to go because - yes you've guessed it - her Blackberry was beeping furiously. Still, we had actually conversed for fifteen minutes and she had promised to try and come over to see me.

And then I rounded off the catching up by nipping out and having a quick coffee with Fred and Bubbles. Granted it was surrounding myself with more 'walking wounded', but Cam was right, I wasn't the only one having problems, and what better way to forget my troubles than to utilise one of my old tried and tested techniques - immersing myself in everybody else's.

By the time Evie and Mum arrived for dinner, I was feeling better; even so, they handled me with kid gloves. We banned the phrase 'plenty more fish in the sea', my mum pledged never to mention men again and Evie decided that a little 'pain' in the *passata* was a good thing as it was the best she had ever tasted.

Buoyed by this culinary praise, the next morning I decided to run it past an expert – literally. At seven-thirty I ground to a halt when I saw Nieves sitting on her usual bench on the *paseo*. As I held out two jars of blood red *passata,* I noticed that she was wearing sensible brown shoes. She nodded at her feet and said sadly, '*Alex, es finales del verano.'*

And 'then smiled broadly when she saw her present, 'Ah muy bien - una poca sol en un tarro.'

I hugged her, yes it was the end of summer, but the fact that in her eyes I had captured a little sunshine in a jar lifted my spirits. There was significance in her incidental metaphor. Creating something positive out of a negative, that is what I would do, but my optimism was just about to suffer a setback. On the way back from my run, I nipped into a supermarket to pick up some bits and pieces, and my credit card was refused. I felt like some petty criminal, particularly as my personal nemesis Stephan walked in as I was handing all the goods back.

'Oh Alex, this summer has cost you dearly hasn't it?' He was glowing. As far as weeks go he was having a great one at my expense.

I had no comeback, not one equally caustic remark was lingering on my lips. So I ignored him and high-tailed it back to the apartment. Feeling slightly sick, I nervously went online to check my bank balance, hoping there had been some mistake. There hadn't. I was so seriously in the red that I wouldn't even be able to pay the next month's rent. I had been so busy being 'loved up' I hadn't paid any attention to my finances. Even though Stan had been generous to a fault, I had reciprocated with lavish dinners, expensive wines and of course – new outfits, underwear, lotions and potions – the whole *enchilada*. Coupled with the little gambling phase with Nieves, I was up shit creek without a paddle.

I confessed up to Cam immediately.

'Don't panic, Alex, what about these ideas you keep working on? You must have something there?'

'What ideas Cam? I'm no nearer to knowing what I want to do than I was when I arrived. I need a bloody hand grenade up my butt. I sit down with good intentions, try to focus myself, and then after ten minutes I go and make a coffee. Then I check my emails, and then I stare into space for ten minutes. I decide I need to research something and get lost in cyber-space for an hour. Of course by that time my coffee has gone cold, so it's back into the kitchen, oh dear, I'm hungry now, let's make some grub. Back to the computer, might as well see what's doing on Facebook while I eat. Wait a minute, I've been meaning to tidy under my bed for weeks…why don't I do that while I think about my future? Oh there's the phone…Hi Bubbles, lunch? What a great idea! See you there in five. I'm a bloody disaster.'

'You're just easily distracted, come here and give me a hug.'

I rested my head on Cam's shoulder and looked despondently at the floor.

'I'd say get a bar job, trouble is they all go on skeleton staff here at the end of the season.'

'Actually there is something I can do,' I gave a resigned sigh.

Desperate times called for desperate measures. There was only one thing for it. I rang Rae.

THIRTY SEVEN

'Okay Alex would you pick up the pencil on the table in front of you and sell it to us please? See if you can keep going for two minutes.'

I looked down the camera lens at the producer talking into my earpiece, put on my cheesiest grin and took a deep breath.

'Isn't it amazing to think these little fellows have been around since the mid-1500s? I mean, where would we be without this graphite and wood wonder? The humble pencil is etched in our history. Think of all those amazing sketches that Leonardo da Vinci did with his pencils. During the civil war pencils were standard issue for American soldiers– imagine all those romantic love letters. Well you can also own one of these fabulous pencils for just £9.99, and if you call in the next ten minutes we'll throw another nine pencils in nine glorious jewel colours. Just LOOK at the FANTASTIC shape of this pencil. Have you ever seen anything quite so beautiful in its simplicity? Eight inches of cold hard graphite just waiting to make out with your paper, how can you resist? It is gorgeous. Can you see how its nib just glides over my notepad here leaving a perfect pencil line? Imagine yourself, just you and your pencil on holiday in Tuscany, sketching sunflowers whilst sipping Chianti.........'

'That was fantastic Alex; you really brought that pencil alive. It was poetry.'

Gold-plated, zircon encrusted bullshit actually, I thought as I stared glumly into space.

'She was great, wasn't she?' Rae was sitting next to me as Marjorie Hargreaves, the American head of the shopping channel, paced excitedly around her office.

'I really think you can do big things here at *Gotta Have It*,' she gave me a manic grin, punched the air and screamed, 'GOTTA HAVE IT…'

'…*or I'll Die*,' I obligingly rolled out the company slogan and bit my lip as she whooped with delight.

'I just knew she'd be perfect for you Marjorie,' gushed Rae who had inside information and had primed me for the 'pencil' part of the audition. Did you really think I was a leading expert on pencils? Pahleese!

'If I'm not mistaken, that's one of our Charlene Collection two-piece suits in Summer Coral that you're wearing Rae. It looks simply stunning.'

'I just love it, Marjorie, and machine washable too.'

Rae couldn't be serious. She looked like fluorescent pink salami.

'Don't you worry, Alex, you'll get a wardrobe allowance from Charlene. We love our presenters to fly the colours so to speak, and there is an emerald cowl neck jersey in the autumn collection that you will look darling in,' she boomed. Marjorie was a vision in another of Charlene's signature colours – bright yellow. I am not the greatest fan of colours that remind me of childhood crayons, particularly when they come in stretch jersey.

'Oh clothes, too, how lovely! Isn't that lovely, Alex?' Rae nudged me in the ribs in an attempt to dislodge the pained expression I was wearing on my face.

'Yes, yes, very good,' I nodded. 'Thank you very much.'

I think I was still in shock. Since I called Rae, things had moved frighteningly quickly; within five days I was back in the UK and in the process of selling my soul to the devil. But as Mel kept reminding me, I would pay off my overdraft and it wouldn't have to be forever. I had just completed my second audition – a mere formality according to Rae, and it looked like the job was mine.

I listened as Rae and Marjorie discussed the ins and outs of my contract. While I 'relocated', to ensure I could be close to the studios, the shopping channel would be willing to pay for me to stay in the dingy bed and breakfast in Vauxhall that had been my home for the past two nights. A depressing prospect as the view from my window was a grey tower block bedecked with satellite dishes, a sight so grim and soulless I hadn't wanted to open my curtains in the morning.

I started to daydream of a picture postcard sea view and a palm tree called Pete. I dreaded calling Cam with the 'good news'. This was going to mean that unless he could get another lodger pronto, he would lose the apartment. Letting a friend down was troubling me more than my financial position. Boy had I been irresponsible.

'So that's all sorted then. Alex we look forward to seeing you here on Monday morning for product training, and then at eleven am on Tuesday we'll launch you onto the airwaves with a new cosmetic line we're very excited about, it's called 'Feed Your Face'. It's everything you could ever want from a product line.' Marjorie's eyes glistened in an almost evangelical way, pure passion emanated from every pore. Obviously for Marjorie, selling crap was a spiritual experience.

Rae had to catch the five-thirty seven to Orpington, so we bade Marjorie farewell and went to Starbucks for a quick post-mortem.

'You could try and be a little more grateful,' Rae glared at me over the rim of her skinny latte, 'there's a bloody recession hurtling towards us as we speak, people are losing their jobs and homes, and you've just walked into a very well paid little number.'

'Of course I'm grateful and I suppose you should be too.'

Rae's head shot up, 'I beg your pardon?'

'You don't do this for love Rae, you do it for commission.'

She didn't have an answer for that one.

THIRTY EIGHT

I suppose it's quite soporific in a way. Almost like sitting on a train or in a restaurant half-listening to two women having a chat about nothing in particular. I'm sure this is what the viewers were experiencing while watching the thrice-daily *Beauty Hour with Alex Chapman* on *Gotta Have It*. For me it meant filling time soliloquising about memories of my first face cream, the day I looked in the mirror and realised 'less was more', interspersed with lightly veiled threats of sagging skin and lipstick bleed if you didn't get on that phone RIGHT NOW as there were only 3742 items left.

The UK had all the promise of the coldest October yet and the papers were full of credit crunch doom and gloom. I had been working for the shopping channel for two weeks. Talk about slow death. My overdraft was going down but so was my zest for life. My Say-It-All face was giving me away. Marjorie had pulled me in twice for pep talks regarding my lack of enthusiasm for encouraging people to spend their hard-earned lolly on cheap make-up and nasty smelling creams, supposedly all the more fabulous because they came in complimentary clear plastic *pochettes*.

I really tried, but no matter how much I focused on the idea that there were people out there, for whom *Gotta Have It* was a saviour as they couldn't make it to the shops, I kept dwelling on the fact that the majority of the callers were not housebound due to some awful health problem or successful career women making the smart choice. They were ordinary women falling for the 'buy one and get all these other things free' gambit, cranking up their credit cards and ordering stuff they didn't really need as some form of consolation for a life less lived. Surely given the current global situation, people should be doing a little re-prioritising, not desperately looking for miracles in a jar?

I was having a severe ethical crisis. A fact I couldn't really share with the NADs for the following reasons:

Mum: thrilled that twenty times a week she could actually see me on screen and check that all my limbs were in place.

Mel: the ultimate pragmatist; any mention of slight discomfort before my bank balance was well back in the black would probably push her to the end of her tolerance levels and I just wasn't ready for that.

Cam: it was because of me he was looking for a new apartment.

Beverley: was currently dealing with a divorce after twenty years of marriage and being betrayed by her so called 'best' friend.

And of course, the one person on whose shoulder I would like to have buried my head was certainly not nearest and most definitely not dearest. Enough said.

This was a definite case of Put Up and Shut Up. I wasn't dealing in drugs or selling children, it's just that I wasn't exactly doing anything useful either. God, I aggravated myself sometimes. I was either one of those people who was destined never to be happy, or hopefully a person on the verge of a breakthrough regarding the meaning of life.

What I wasn't going to be was the person who ran away as usual. I had gotten myself into this mess, and I was going to damn well get myself out of it.

My accommodation situation had to be resolved. Living out of a suitcase is only bearable if you are on holiday, so I spent a few evenings trailing around looking at apartments in the area. The thought of signing a one-year contract wasn't sitting easily with me as I hadn't even finalised the work one yet, but I went through the motions hoping something would jump out and grab me. Finally I found a small garden flat in Stockwell that wasn't going to break the bank. The neighbours were all quiet single professional women, and it would be available within a month, when the owner was going to return and okay her prospective tenant. Apparently she was living somewhere in Spain.

The irony of this situation didn't escape me. As a result of what can only be described on paper as a seven-month glorified holiday, achieving nothing more than debts and a broken heart, here I was back in the UK on the verge of moving into an apartment that was smaller and even more expensive than my previous London abode, with the same prototype neighbours and a job that was making me feel like a disciple of Lucifer. On top of which, I was going to be funding somebody else's lifestyle on a sunny foreign shore. Nice one Alex.

I decided to cheer myself up, so organised a little Friday night in London with Mel and Beverley. They had both heard a lot about each other, so it was about time they met. Mel was a member of Soho House, so we arranged to meet there at six for a few drinks.

It was weird walking back through the hustle and bustle of Old Compton Street surrounded by all the gay bars and shops; I couldn't help but think of Sitges, so I sent Cam a text telling him where I was. He texted straight back, *Go into Balans and see if a waiter called Oliver is there. He's a summer fling!! Say hi from me! Have fun with your friends Moll, miss you, Toff.*

I laughed and checked the time. I still had fifteen minutes, so I wandered up to Balans restaurant and poked my head around the door. A beautiful guy with cropped blonde hair and huge brown eyes came straight over, 'Can I help you?'

'Is Oliver working tonight?'

'That's me,' he looked intrigued.

'Cam from Sitges says hi,' I laughed, 'I'm his ex-roomie and official messenger.'

'You must be Moll,' my eyes widened in surprise as he grabbed my hand and pulled me in, 'quick glass of wine?'

'I would love one but I'm meeting friends up the road in five, maybe another time.'

'So what on earth are you doing back here? I thought you and Cam were Sitges' very own Will and Grace. He adored living with you. Weren't you seeing some tree doctor?'

The last question caught me totally off-guard and I must have looked shocked.

'Oops sorry, obviously a raw nerve,' he pulled an apologetic face.

'S'okay, it was just a summer fling,' I managed a fake smile. 'Anyway, I have to rush.'

'Please send Cam my love. He's such a great guy. Shame he doesn't live here,' Oliver shrugged and held the door open for me. As I left he touched my shoulder and said, 'I'm sorry about your man.'

I gave him a clumsy Spanish style kiss on each cheek and looked at him sadly, 'So am I, Oliver.'

It sure was a small world, I thought as I walked up the narrow wooden stairs to Soho House. When I signed in at reception they told me that Mel was already up in the bar. Despite her face brightening up when she saw me, I couldn't help but notice how tired and strained she appeared.

'Hello trouble,' she jumped up and hugged me, then stood back and looked me up and down. 'You look different. Your hair's lighter, you're thinner.'

'They're particularly flattering jeans, I have a tan and if you feel my hair it's like straw, but I do have fabulous nails,' I waggled my recently manicured hands in the air. 'How are you babes?'

'I'm great.' She flopped back down onto the sofa and looked up at me, 'Just a bit knackered.'

'You're at burnout point if you ask me; can't you slow down a little?'

'I wish,' her voice trailed off and she poured me a glass of wine. 'What time is your friend arriving?'

'I told Beverley to meet us here at six-thirty, so we had a bit of time first.'

'We'd better get gossiping then,' she smiled. 'Did I tell you I've been ostracised by the Yummy Mummy brigade at the school?'

'No,' I laughed, 'which one did you upset?'

'All of them, it was bloody marvellous.'

Mel and I were stilling giggling like a couple of schoolgirls when I felt a tap on my shoulder. I turned around and there was Beverley looking just as wonderfully Barbie as she was the last time I saw her.

'Hey, you made it. Did you find your hotel okay?' I jumped up excitedly.

'Yes, I'm staying not far from here, The Sanderson, d'you know it?'

'Yes, it's lovely. Beverley meet Mel,' I moved to one side and let Beverley sit in the middle, 'I'll just go and order some more wine.'

Beverley put her hand out and stopped me, 'There's a bottle of Verve Clicquot on the way, I've had some good news today and this is my first night out in months.'

Mel and I looked at her expectantly.

'I know it's tacky to discuss money but I've just found out I'm worth rather a lot.'

'What does that feel like?' I whimpered.

'The settlement came through today,' she smiled, 'so I'm celebrating - big-time!'

'That was quick. I would have thought he would have strung it out as long as possible.'

'He wouldn't dare rub me up the wrong way,' Beverley said triumphantly, 'I have far too much on that man. Seriously, he's got money stashed everywhere, properties galore, boats. He may not have been good for many things, but the lad could sure turn over a bit of cash, and a lot of it isn't exactly what one would call 'at risk' from the current crap the banks have put us all in.'

'Plus those pictures must have exercised a little extra leverage,' I explained to Mel what Beverley had done. She roared.

'I'm sorry,' she wiped her eyes, 'I shouldn't laugh, but I can just imagine her face when her uncle walked through the door, had you covered her up?'

'No bloody way!'

'What a cow,' Mel looked at me, 'can you imagine if that had been you and me?'

'Frankly no, but one thing is for sure,' I hit her arm playfully, 'you would have stabbed me.'

'And made a good job of it!' Mel turned to Beverley, 'Sorry, we shouldn't joke.'

'That's okay, it's nice. How long have you two known each other?' Beverley sipped her glass of champagne.

'Over twenty years; it's hard to believe I could have put up with her that long,' Mel winked at me.

'Watch out, I'll ring Penny and reinstate her. She is my oldest friend remember.'

'Don't get me started on Penny,' Mel growled.

'Well, she was given the red card a while ago now.'

I went to the 'Ladies' while Mel filled Beverley in on the demise of Penny. When I walked back in, she looked up chuckling, 'How many bags did you throw off the balcony?'

'Four. Two big and two small - all Louis Vuitton of course,' I smiled wickedly as the memory of her clothes flying around the street came back.

'Shit, remind me never to piss you off.'

'You're okay Beverley; it'll take her thirty years to react,' laughed Mel, 'unless you're a bloke. She's always been pretty vitriolic when it comes to nuking bad boys.'

'That's true,' I sighed.

'Maybe I need to take a few tips,' said Beverley before disappearing off to the loo.

'Beverley is lovely isn't she?' said Mel. 'I'm ashamed to say I would have judged her on her appearance if we'd met somewhere else. I would have taken one look at her hair, her false nails and – oh you know what I'm talking about, and I would have simply dismissed her as someone I wouldn't get on with.'

I had to laugh, in stark contrast to Beverley's head-to-toe Versace, veil of fake tan and mounds of make-up, Mel was bare-faced, pale and sporting her classic black work suit with a white shirt. If you threw my distinctly BoHo sense of style into the mix, we were a very different trio – outwardly.

'She's a good soul. Hopefully this will be the beginning of a whole new life.'

'What new life?' Beverley sat back down.

'E.O.E!!!!!' shouted Mel and I in unison.

She looked suitably confused so we explained our little code; it stood for Earholes-On-Elastic and was usually muttered mid-gossip if we thought someone was eavesdropping.

'I like that,' she nodded, 'I'll have to use that.'

'We're the only others who know what it means,' I pointed out.

'Well, it'll just have to be with you two then. Ooh I feel like I'm in a gang.'

'So, Alex, tell us about the job,' Mel asked trying to be enthusiastic.

'What can I say?' I shrugged, 'It's a job.' I didn't even have the heart to muster up a few 'Marjorie' anecdotes.

'I used to buy stuff off those channels all the time,' said Beverley, 'when Laurence was out and I was bored.'

'Stuff that you didn't need and probably only used once or twice?'

'Pretty much.'

I died a little more on the inside.

'Alex Chapman, you're back!' My heart sank a little further. Marcus Jenkins came swooping over from the bar. 'I haven't seen you since Sitges. Doing the shopping thing now so I hear? Very brave I must say,' he couldn't cover his glee. 'I can't imagine Channel Four are going to come knocking on your door in hurry.'

'We haven't been introduced, I'm Mel,' she shot her hand out.

'Marcus Jenkins – presenter and stylist to the stars,' he tittered.

'So what are you working on at the moment Marcus?' asked Mel.

'Oh, this and that,' he waved his hands about theatrically.

'That usually means bugger all in my part of the world,' piped Beverley. 'Cheers!' she raised her glass as if to dismiss him. 'Sorry was he a mate?' she asked as he turned huffily on his heel and walked away.

'Was he hell?' I snorted. 'Thank you girls. He's such a poisonous little wretch.'

'Did you hang out with him in Sitges?' asked Beverley.

'No, he just visits there occasionally. The people I hung out with were lovely, and so was Sitges.' I sighed, 'It'll be a shame to go back and pack up.'

'When are you doing that?' asked Mel.

'First available weekend - I'll have to do it soon because Cam will be either moving out, or hopefully moving someone in.'

'What about this weekend? I'll come and help you,' Beverley's face split into a grin. 'I never did visit and I'd love to see it.'

'I've got Monday off, so I suppose it's possible, why not?' I shrugged. 'Might as well get it over and done with.'

'We could get an early plane tomorrow and be there by midday.'

'And fly back Monday evening.'

'Yay!' we clinked glasses, I looked at Mel; she'd gone very quiet. 'You could come too you know.'

'Nah, it's impossible, I can't.'

'Can't or won't. You never did come out to see me.'

'I was busy, Alex,' Mel suddenly sounded defensive.

'Well, come now, I'd really love you to.'

'Oh, Alex, it's the kids, and my job.'

'Can't your partner look after your kids for one weekend?' asked Beverley. 'If I think of all the times I missed out on having a good time because I was the one that always stayed at home. And look where that got me?'

'Work?'

'Pull a sickie,' I looked at her, 'go on, you never go sick.'

'Oh, I don't know, let me think about it.'

'Well don't take too long, because we need to book it. And I'll go without the pair of you,' laughed Beverley who was getting a bit giddy with excitement.

'Well?' I looked at her quizzically, 'Are you in?'

'Let me go and make a call,' she disappeared outside. Beverley and I watched through the window as she paced around the street.

'I think it's a 'yes' - she looks quite happy. Wait a minute; unless my lip-reading is letting me down, I just saw a definite 'thank you'. I think she's coming, Beverley!'

I was right, and after a jolly old dinner at Balans to get the girls in the mood, with Oliver catering to our every need – well, not all of them – we went back to Beverley's hotel and booked our tickets online with Easyjet. On the way back to mine I called Cam.

'Hey Toff, Oliver says hello, and guess what?'

'You're pissed and I'm not there,' he mumbled; I'd obviously woken him up.

'But I will be tomorrow with Mel and Beverley.'

I heard a rustling of sheets and the light click on, 'You're what? What time?'

'We arrive at eleven-thirty, if we all wake up on time and get to Victoria by seven. Is that okay?'

'It's better than okay.'

'How's Pete the Palm?'

'Missing you.'

THIRTY NINE

'Are you sure you're not Jewish?'

'Beverley please don't start her off, she's desperate to associate herself with a more exotic lineage,' Mel howled with laughter as I poured more chicken soup into their bowls.

'Thank you, Beverley; you can officially be my NBF, as Mel has obviously just resigned from the position.'

'What about me?' Cam stuck his bottom lip out petulantly.

'You're something they can never be, you're my Toff,' I kissed his forehead, 'and you must be special to have persuaded me to cook bloody chicken soup the minute I walked through the door.'

'I was hankering after it, sorry you. For the record Mel, I think Alex is very exotic.'

'You little creep,' snorted Mel.

I had to laugh. Mel had been driven mad over the years with my theories about my ancestry. I was convinced that somewhere in my DNA was the ancient blood of the nomads, even though the bit that contained the ability to ride across the dusty plains on magnificent steeds must have been filtered out over the years, as the one and only time I have been on a horse – a sweaty polo pony in Lahore – I had a panic attack and nearly fell off. Give me a steering wheel as opposed to a set of reins any day of the week.

Nevertheless during my schooldays I buried myself in books about women who travelled against all odds. Mary Kingsley, Freya Stark, Marianne North - bold, sassy, intelligent women, who often went where no men dared to tread. When my history teacher set a school project on the origins of our names I found out that Chapman was derived from *Chapmen* - 16th century merchants who travelled selling amongst other things, *chapbooks* – small educational pamphlets.

Instead of cruelly pointing out that we hailed from the loins of what was in essence, a travelling salesman, my mum and dad allowed me to fantasise about the gypsy-like quality of my ancestors. These *Chapmen* had the reputation of turning up in the right place at the right time with the right thing in the back of the wagon. Whether they were sharpening knives, providing herbal remedies or bringing news from court, they were lively, entertaining folk who brought things to a community, rather than took from it. I liked that image, as it was the essence of the true nomad.

Now here I was en route back to the UK and a job I hated - nothing very nomadic about that. I looked out to the sea which was turning an intense shade of pink - yet another beautiful sunset.

'Isn't it fabulous?' Beverley came over and hugged me.

'It is lovely Alex, better than bloody Chiswick High Road,' Mel grabbed her camera and took what must have been her thirtieth shot of the view.

'I know, and pretty soon some other lucky person will be living here,' Cam and I looked sadly at each other. He had decided to reduce his outgoings and get a much smaller apartment in the cheaper *Poble Sec,* so that he could live on his own.

'Anyhow, let's not dwell on that. What would you like to do now?' I clapped my hands together.

'I'm pooped,' sighed Mel.

'I'm up for it!' squealed Bev.

I looked enquiringly at Cam.

'I'm not working, so I was going to go out and about for a wander,' he said.

'I have a suggestion. Why don't you go out with Cam, Beverley, and I'll stay here with Mel?'

'I couldn't do that,' Beverley looked horrified.

'Why? Don't you like me?' Cam poked her in the ribs.

'Of course I do, it's just that...' she looked at me for reassurance.

'It's just that what?' I grinned, 'Look Bev, get out there woman. I am more than happy here, I've got packing to do remember, and

Mel,' I turned and looked at her settling herself down on the couch, 'will be asleep quite soon. We've got another two days here together, and this is Sitges. We can pack quite a bit in, believe me.'

'If you're sure,' Bev bit her lip, 'I just feel so terrible leaving you.'

'Loosen up and go have an adventure. If anyone deserves one, it's you. Just watch out for Stephanie.'

'Who?'

'I'll protect you. Now go and get your gladrags on, we leave at ten,' said Cam.

'But that's ages away,' replied Beverley.

'You're a woman aren't you?' Cam raised his eyebrows.

'Oh yeah,' she sighed, 'better get going then.'

She disappeared into my bedroom. 'Thanks Cam, you don't feel abandoned do you?' I looked at Mel who had already dozed off.

'Absolutely not! I'll take Beverley on the grand tour. She'll have a great time'

'Of that I have no doubt. Now, if I were you I would start getting ready.'

'Uh?'

'You're a gay man aren't you?'

'That's a point.'

I covered Mel with one of the sofa throws and cleared the dishes away. I was on the balcony when Beverley and Cam emerged, both looking and smelling fantastic. Beverley was a vision in leopard print, and Cam had gone for all black.

'Isn't she a doll?' he clasped her to him proudly.

'Are you sure you'll be okay?' asked Beverley.

'I will be when you bugger off, now go have fun,' I smiled. They didn't need telling twice and were out the door in an instant.

'Now I've got a Molly and a Dolly,' Cam's voice drifted up as I watched them wander off in the direction of the church. Beverley was in for a riotous night.

'Well, Pete, nearly time to say goodbye,' I looked at my beloved palm tree.

'Who's that you're talking to?' Mel wandered out wrapped in the throw and sat down next to me.

'Pete the Palm.'

'Oh,' Mel shrugged it off as if catching me talking to trees was the most natural thing on earth.

'Let me just go and get a jacket, it's getting quite chilly.'

'We wouldn't be doing this in London right now, would we?' yawned Mel. 'It's lovely here - so peaceful.'

I came back with a pot of coffee.

'Thanks for pushing me into coming this weekend,' said Mel as she cupped her coffee, 'I think Beverley is really going to enjoy it, too.'

'I'm looking forward to seeing her chill out this weekend. And you for that matter, you're wrecked.'

'I just don't know how much longer I can keep going, Alex. I always seem to be chasing my tail. If it's not work making outrageous demands on my time, the kids always need something. Never have blasted pets, you spend your entire life at the vets, running out at some ungodly hour because you've forgotten to buy cat food, or driving bloody miles to get frozen mice for the snakes.'

'What in god's name ever possessed you to say 'yes' to snakes?'

'Absolute guilt - I spend my life over-compensating because I work such horrendous hours. You want a snake, Nat? Buy five. Chloe you fancy a llama? Why not? John, you want a blow job? Fuck off I'm too tired. That poor man is a bloody saint!'

'He worships the ground you walk on, Mel.'

'Say he gets fed up and decides to have a little fling on the side? He might find some single bird with no responsibilities who worships the ground he walks on for a change. I mean it's not as if the kids are his.'

'Oh, Mel, he loves those two as if they were his own. He wouldn't have agreed to look after them this weekend otherwise. Don't get yourself unnerved by what's happened to Beverley.'

Mel's first marriage had ground to a halt after eight years and she had met John, a graphic artist, a couple of years later. He was one of the most patient men on the planet. Nothing fazed him, and even though I had a sneaking feeling he would have quite liked to have a child of his own, he totally respected Mel's need for a career and threw himself wholeheartedly into being a great stepfather to Nat and Chloe.

'I must make more time for him. Christ, I can't remember the last time we had outrageous sex. It's all been a bit 'once a month, nudge in the back, roll over, legs open, groan-groan and finished in five'.'

This prompted me to tell her about the horrendous Dave episode, and we started giggling so hard we nearly choked on our coffee.

'Was Stan any better?'

I went quiet.

'Sorry, Alex, I didn't mean to upset you, it's probably still a bit raw isn't it?'

'I just don't think about him, Mel. I can't afford to do that. Part of me really thought it might work, and the other side just didn't believe it could. I'm useless - we've said it time and time again.'

'Alex, it wasn't your fault.'

'I've just got a natural homing instinct for bad ones. He was up that tree you know,' I sighed and remembered the sight of him when I thrust open the balcony doors. I looked out to sea and told Mel the whole story, but just how much of it she heard I don't know, because my reminiscing was halted by the sound of her gentle snoring. I nudged her awake and led her into my room, where she collapsed gratefully on the bed. I contemplated going to bed too, but sleep had been eluding me for weeks. The only benefit to this insomnia was that I had been staying up until the early hours writing my journals. My childhood, my travels – whatever I was in the mood for, it just felt good to let it all out. At this moment in my life it was all that was keeping me sane. It would be nice to have something to read back through when I was older. Maybe I'd turn into a bit of a Mrs Crawley. Maybe some weird little child would come knocking at my door on Saturday afternoons in search of a story and a piece of cake.

I pulled it out of my handbag. Maybe if I wrote about Stan now I could finally let go of him.

Beverley and Cam came crawling in at dawn and found me

curled up on the sofa clutching a dirty old t-shirt.

'What the hell is that?' Beverley pulled a face.

'Oh, Alex,' Cam shook his head, 'where did you find that?'

'I found it shoved down the back of the sofa just as I was falling off to sleep.'

'It's Stan's,' Cam explained to Beverley, then turned back to me. 'No matter what you say, you're not over him. What's this?' He leaned over and looked at my notepad that was open on the floor.'

'Nothing, it's just my journal. Please, it's nothing,' I went to grab it.

'It's okay, I won't read it,' Cam picked it up and clapped it shut, 'but I did see my name there,' he raised an eyebrow at me.

'I was writing about Sitges; just trying to exorcise a few ghosts.'

Beverley sat down and clasped me to her bosom; even though her clothes stank of cigarette smoke, I could still smell her perfume, 'You smell of chocolate.'

'It's *Angel*. Laurence said it smelled like cat piss on me.'

'Was he ever nice to you?'

'Now I think back, not really - only when he wanted something. Was Stan nice to you?'

'Well, I thought so at the time,' I smiled wryly. 'Anyhow, let's not think about them. Take it from me, you're going to turn a few heads this weekend - they'll love you here.'

'All the straight boys on Sin Street couldn't take their eyes off her,' said Cam.

'Well, if Brad Pitt came up to me now and wanted a bit of action, I'd have to say 'no'. I'm knackered. He dragged me everywhere last night, Alex.'

'Morning,' Mel came staggering out of her room. 'Oh my god, have you two only just got in?'

'Yep, we're dirty stop-outs,' said Cam.

'Why don't you two get some sleep, then we can go for a walk down to the *Terramar* later.' I couldn't get through the weekend without a wander along the beach.

'C'mon, you can share my bed,' Cam pushed Beverley out of the kitchen, 'but no funny business.'

'I'm having the best time,' she sighed and then disappeared.

'I can't believe her make-up is still perfect. What time is it?' asked Mel.

'Six-thirty.'

'What! It's Sunday! I'm going to back to bed,' she stomped back off into the bedroom and I passed out on the sofa. It was so nice to be home.

FORTY

'What shall I wear? I don't do walking,' Beverley was totally serious.

'Well you've got plenty of jogging suits, just wear some trainers instead of your usual Betty Boop numbers,' I shook my head. 'You do have trainers?'

'Of course I do.'

Beverley did indeed have trainers - they were pink, white and gold - and even though Mel and I wouldn't be seen dead in them, they suited her to a tee. We all set off and when we walked to the other side of the church, they both stopped in their tracks at the sight of the palm-fringed *paseo* stretching out in front of them.

'That's the *Terramar* at the end,' I pointed out as we walked down the steps.

'Shit, I'll die,' whimpered Beverley.

'Don't be such a wimp,' laughed Mel skipping down the steps like a child. 'Cam doesn't know what he's missing.'

Cam had opted to stay in bed, and would be there until early evening. It was now two-thirty and the late October weather was glorious. Bev and Mel were fascinated by the sand sculptures. *Guapa* Man had excelled himself – angels, priests and even a medieval knight on a stallion formed part of an elaborate sand tableau and as an added bonus, we were treated to every vulgar gesture in his repertoire.

When we reached Picnic, we bumped into Nieves. I introduced Beverley and Mel, and much to my surprise, Beverley started chatting to Nieves in pretty good Spanish.

'Where did that come from?' I squawked as we wandered away.

'I did a Spanish 'O' Level and used to come to Spain on holiday every year - Marbella of course,' she glanced down at her trainers and grinned.

'She puts you to shame,' laughed Mel.

'She certainly does.'

Even though it was October the sun was shining and a few brave sunbathers were on the beach. Three young girls clowning around doing headstands and cartwheels caught our attention. They were absolutely lily-white and wearing mismatched bikini tops and bottoms.

'I just couldn't,' said Mel.

'Me neither,' sighed Beverley.

'Why not?' I laughed. 'Stop taking life so seriously.'

'Easy for you to say,' Mel raised one eyebrow in my direction.

'Who gives a shit what people think?' I walked down the stairs to the beach, whipped off my jacket and threw it on the sand, and then started to pull off my T-shirt.

'What the hell are you doing?' shouted Mel as I removed my trainers.

I ignored her, pulled off my jogging bottoms and did a very clumsy cartwheel. 'Look at this, white flabby skin AND black knickers with a turquoise bra! The Fashion Police will be here any second.' I sped off towards the water's edge and started to splash in the surf.

'You're barking,' squealed Beverley.

'Scaredy-cats!' I pealed and attempted another couple of cartwheels. A few people had stopped on the *paseo*. They weren't aware I was a woman trying to make a very valid point; they were watching a deranged lunatic who had lost the plot. Suddenly I had company in the asylum. Beverley screamed 'Sod it!' and started to disrobe, followed by a more reluctant Mel who still felt the need to fold her clothes. They came running down the beach shrieking with laughter. We whirled around like dervishes for twenty minutes and then collapsed giggling on the sand.

'I've never laughed so much in my life;' wheezed Beverley, 'look at the state of me.'

'At least you've tanned up and your underwear matches,' said

Mel, 'we're the white ones who got caught out with the comfy knickers and favourite bras. Oh god, look at my stretch marks.'

Beverley was wearing a very nice pink and black bra set that looked hugely expensive, even if it was now encrusted with sand.

'You're looking quite racy there, Mrs Herman,' I wanted to reel the words back in as her face fell. 'Oops, sorry Beverley.'

'It's okay, it's Samuel now, Beverley Samuel,' she smiled. 'Beverley Herman wouldn't have done this.'

'And now comes the fun part, putting all our clothes back on over all this sand,' groaned Mel.

'Killjoy,' I poked her arm.

'It is getting a bit nippy,' shivered Beverley.

'C'mon then, there's a hotel bar up by the *Terramar*. I need to introduce you to *carajillos.*'

'Who's he?' said Mel.

'A good friend, short, comforting, and oh so addictive.'

*

'I quite like your mate *cara* – what d'you call these?'

'Just say coffee with Baileys,' I grinned. Languages were not Mel's strong point. She usually resorted to speaking English in a sort of comedy French accent like something out of *Allo Allo.*

'I still can't believe I was running around a beach in my knickers,' sighed Beverley. 'I'm starting to feel embarrassed now.'

'You want to hear embarrassing, ask madam over here about her Chinese trip,' Mel ruffled my hair affectionately.

Beverley looked at me expectantly.

I laughed. 'A few years ago I was stuck on a remote corner of the Great Wall of China with chronic food poisoning. No Imodium tablets, no toilets within a ten-mile radius, just me and about thirty other people.'

'Oh my god, what did you do?' gasped Beverley.

'Let's just say that the Dutch accountant who held onto my arms as I performed my bodily functions whilst dangling precariously over the edge of the three-hundred-foot drop didn't keep in touch.'

'I'd have died,' she screamed.

'It was probably quite therapeutic. I'd just come out of yet another disastrous relationship.'

Beverley looked at me quizzically.

'You can't really focus on emotional shit when you're dealing with the real thing,' I grinned.

'D'you always do that when you finish with someone?' asked Beverley.

'What? Pooh off a wall?'

'I think Beverley is referring to the running off at any given opportunity,' Mel groaned.

'I just find it easier to put things in perspective from a distance. Nobody ever really gets that about me,' I punched Mel's arm, 'do they?'

'Ouch! You bitch!' She retaliated with a swift leg pinch.

'I've never had what you two have, even with my mum. Right up until the day she died, we never had a nice conversation - she was always moaning at me. It's probably why I got married so young.' Beverley's eyes welled up. 'My sister and I have never got on, and my so called best-friend was having an affair with my husband.'

Mel and I discreetly exchanged glances. Whatever life had thrown at us we had always been there for each other. Salt and pepper, fish and chips, Alex and Mel – we met in our salad days and would be there in our twilight years. I couldn't imagine my life without her and I knew it was likewise. It broke my heart to think Beverley had never found that sort of enduring friendship. As I put my arm around her, Beverley's chest started to heave. 'I met Laurence when I was sixteen and was married by eighteen. This is the first time I've ever really been on my own. What am I going to do?'

'Anything you want, Beverley.'

'I don't even know what it is I want,' the tears started to roll down her face. 'I feel so bloody lost.'

'It's going to take some time,' said Mel gently, 'but pretty soon you'll be dating some amazing bloke, building a new future.'

'Or,' I shot Mel a look and turned back to Beverley, 'you might actually start to enjoy having the freedom to do exactly as you please. The kids are adults now - you're your own woman.'

'I've only ever slept with Laurence,' Beverley sniffed. 'I'm just so inexperienced. Sad isn't it?'

'Better than having experienced half the toe-rags that we have,' said Mel.

'But you were married quite early too weren't you?'

'Let's just say that I was quite busy at college,' Mel smiled. 'Alex didn't have the total monopoly on morons.'

'I just don't think I'm as strong as you two.'

'Yes you are. You've just got to get out there and test yourself a little.'

'I'm too scared.'

'Aren't we all in one way or another?' Mel looked at me pointedly.

'I don't know what you're talking about,' I steeled myself, but luckily Beverley created a diversion.

'Would you like to change your life, Mel?'

'At the moment - yes I would.'

One would think that having narrowly avoided a few Mel home truths I would have kept my gob shut, but no, I just couldn't help myself. 'She should delegate a bit more at work, get home at a reasonable hour and spend more quality time with the kids, so when she does want to do something for herself at weekends, she doesn't feel guilty. She should also go buy herself the sexiest underwear on earth, a couple of porn films and drag John's butt into bed a bit more regularly. She used to be brilliant at cooking and making stuff, but it's all gone by the wayside. It's just work, work, work,' I winked at Mel. 'Maybe somebody else has forgotten who they are too?'

She laughed, 'Thanks for that Oprah. You should do this for a living.'

'I did - remember - but it was a crock of shit most of the time.'

'You inspired me,' said Beverley.

'Really?'

'Not with all the smoothies and yoga, but the sheer fact you came here to do something about changing your life. I admired that.'

'Not that it got me very far,' I laughed, 'BUT, if I hadn't, I never would have met Cam and all the other fantastic people I know here, who incidentally, you are going to get to meet at dinner. Plus we wouldn't have been sitting here in this spot right now would we?'

'No I suppose we wouldn't,' grinned Beverley.

'So,' I lifted my coffee cup, 'I suggest we drink to you Beverley Samuel, and your new life, wherever and whatever it may be.'

'Here, here!' agreed Mel.

We ambled back along the *paseo* looking at all the houses and apartments.

'I like that one,' said Beverley suddenly and pointed to an old colonial style building that had been left empty for years.

'You've just picked my favourite,' I leaned on the gate and looked up at its grand but decaying exterior. 'I'm sure houses are just like people. This house should be loved and nurtured, poor thing's lost its *alma.'*

'What's an *alma?'* asked Mel.

'It's Spanish for soul,' said Beverley wistfully.

'So what would you do with it, Alex? How would you put a little *alma* back into the place?' Mel joined me at the gate.

I thought for a second. 'I'd like to see it as some sort of academy that represents the spirit of Sitges, as it used to be.'

Both of them turned and looked at me quizzically, so I explained all about the creative and bohemian side of Sitges, about the artists drawn to the incredible light and how people used to view Sitges as almost a place of healing.

'I could do with some of that,' sighed Beverley wistfully.

'I think a lot of people could,' I smiled, 'particularly with all the crap going on out there at the moment.'

'I can't stand all that Wavy Davey personal development shit,' groaned Mel as we walked away.

'No, more practical than that - dancing, art classes, cookery classes, whatever! The kind of things that people can lose themselves in, that helps them to de-stress. Remember the stuff you used to do at school? There's something very therapeutic about throwing paint at a bloody great canvas.'

'I'd like to know how to give someone a great blow job.'

Mel and I spun around and looked at Beverley, 'Hopefully you weren't doing *that* at school!' quipped Mel.

She laughed weakly, 'He had an affair for fifteen years with my so-called best friend – and who knows how many more besides – I can't have been that good can I?' She gazed sadly out to sea. 'Seriously, if I've only slept with one man, how the hell do I know what's good and what's not?'

'Oh Beverley, I am going to get one of my illustrious friends to give you a few tips. Bart would love to share his expertise with you,' I hugged her.

'He's gay?'

'Of course, go figure. Hey, maybe we should teach all that stuff as well?'

Mel shook her head at me. 'Earth calling Chapman – you have a JOB now - IN THE UK.'

'Did you have to bring me back down with such a bang?' I said petulantly.

'That's MY job,' she smiled.

FORTY ONE

'Aren't we meeting your friends at eight o'clock?' Beverley, Mel and I were leaning on the balcony watching the world go by and Mel was anxiously checking her watch. 'It's eight-fifteen.'

'Chill, we're in Spain. Hey, there they are,' I pointed to the church. Fred, Bubbles, Evie and Bart were wandering along chatting. They caught sight of me and waved.

'Where are we going? Is it a long walk?' asked Beverley, looking down at her high black stilettos.

I pointed down to Josep's restaurant next to The Buena Vida Bar.

'I love this,' sighed Mel. 'No cabs, no underground. I can't believe you can just walk everywhere.'

'Then stagger back,' laughed a very fragrant Cam as he emerged from his bedroom. 'Don't you three look fabulous? A redhead, a blonde and a brunette – it's like the Witches of Eastwick. If I was a straight bloke I'd…'

'Promise us the earth, get into our pants, then piss off,' I laughed. 'C'mon let's get down there, I'm bloody starving.'

Everyone was on form and the wine and conversation flowed, and when I thought Beverley was drunk enough not to die of embarrassment, I asked Bart if he would teach her the art of the perfect blow job. You would have thought I had asked him to choreograph Madonna's next world tour.

'Of course, Beverley, I would be honoured; I've got more tricks up my sleeve than a high class ho.'

'Why didn't you ask me?' Fred looked offended.

'Or me?' Cam joined in, 'I'm her first gay friend, so she told me last night,' he pursed his lips at Beverley.

'You two don't brag on about how fantastic you are at it as much as he does,' I laughed.

'We could do a triple act,' winked Bart lasciviously. 'I can see it now – The Fabulous Fellatio Brothers!'

Beverley looked petrified, 'Erm, how practical is this 'lesson' going to be?'

'Don't panic love, we're all mouth,' Cam grinned as the rest of the table groaned.

'Alex came up with a good idea for a school earlier.' said Beverley, 'Tell them about it, Alex.'

It was like lighting a rocket. The minute I finished outlining our dream school, they were all throwing in their ideas, which of course all got a bit ridiculous for a while.

'We could do it in drag.' Bart was beside himself with excitement, 'I could be the Head of Giving Head - Dr BJ! I can see it now - Nana Mouskouri in a white coat - lashings of red lipstick and thick black glasses.'

Fred joined in, 'I could run art classes dressed up as Tracy Emin or Frieda Kahlo. Damn, has there ever been a pretty female artist?'

'You're more Marilyn Monroe-Does-Sticky-Back-Plastic,' I turned to Cam, 'I think art classes would be a great idea, don't you?'

'Mmn,' his eyes flashed warning signals at me so I immediately backed off.

'We could run a Kitsch Kitchen with the Dancing Rabbi? Cookery lessons with a little spiritual sustenance on the side,' Evie enthused.

'Yeah and bugger all that bloody nonsense about blow jobs,' said Bubbles. 'Bondage for Beginners with Bubbles – Don't take all that Lip, show him your Whip.'

Cam had a sensible moment, 'Dragging up everyday would be a drag.'

'Spoilsport,' Bart stuck his bottom lip out.

'He's right Bart,' I laughed, 'believe you me if I didn't look like a boiled egg without a bit of slap, I wouldn't be getting my mascara out everyday.'

'Where would we do it?' Fred puffed on his cigarette.

'That colonial place on the sea front.'

Everyone cooed in agreement.

'What's the real essence of this school Alex?' asked Evie thoughtfully.

'Losing yourself in a little creativity, art, dance, dressing up, cooking, whatever!'

'What could we call it?'

''The Academy of Performing Tarts' would just about sum it up, but sod the name for the time being, the baby hasn't even been born yet,' I smiled. 'It's a pipe-dream anyway.'

Then my sensible best friend totally floored me, 'I think you ought to do it.'

'What?' I looked at Mel incredulously.

'You're all wacky and mad enough to make it work.'

'But Mel, I have a job,' I echoed her previous comments.

'Shut up Alex and listen. People would love it. It's the perfect antithesis to all those holier-than-thou retreats. I would far rather come and learn how to belly dance, bake bagels and get all trussed up in thigh length boots, than meditate in a rain-forest eating lentils.'

'You'd have to drum up some funding and find out if you're allowed to use it for a school. It's probably owned by some wealthy Catalan family that will drive a bloody hard bargain,' Cam lit a cigarette thoughtfully.

'It won't be easy that's for sure,' nodded Bart.

'I'll do it,' announced Beverley.

We all stopped in our tracks.

'What exactly?'

'Fund it. I have the money, I have nothing to do and when it comes to bargaining – I'm Jewish - the Catalans won't know what's hit them.'

'Beverley, you're pissed, let's talk about it later,' I nudged her in the ribs.

'I am deadly serious,' she looked at me and grinned. 'I want to change my life and boy oh boy am I going to do it. That is, of course, if you'll help me Alex.'

'Bravo Beverley,' clapped Evie.

'See what you've started,' I looked over to Mel.

'Maybe you should start thinking about how you wriggle out of that contract with the shopping channel,' she said smugly.

'I haven't signed it yet.'

Mel leaned over and kissed my cheek, 'Alex that is the brightest thing you've done in ages.'

'Wait a minute; you're freaking me out now. You are actually encouraging me to knock this job on the head?'

'Alex, you stink at it. I watched it last week and the misery is written all over your face. Why not leave with a little dignity before they sack you? But maybe wait until things are a little more concrete,' she nodded over to Beverley and the others who were still gabbling excitedly, 'although at the rate she got that divorce sorted out, I doubt that this will take very long. Your friend Beverley is a lot brighter than she gives herself credit for.'

The conversations carried on back at the apartment. Mel, Beverley, Cam and I sat bunched around the dining table, plotting and planning and scrawling over enough paper to redecorate Buckingham Palace. By three in the morning we were all exhausted and, for the first time in a month, I slept like a baby. The next morning Beverley was still adamant she wanted to do it, so I rang Nieves who was a leading authority on anything to do with Sitges and the wheels were set in motion. Sure enough, she knew someone who knew someone who owned the house. Within an hour Nieves rang my mobile; the owner was interested in talking and his lawyer would meet us at the property at four o'clock that afternoon. This was cutting it fine as we had to be at the airport by seven in the evening, and I still hadn't packed up my stuff.

'Don't worry about that for the time being, Alex,' Beverley walked into my room as I was hurriedly stuffing things into boxes.

'Cam has to be out of here within a couple of weeks.'

'No he doesn't.' She smiled smugly, 'I'd like to pay for another few months rent so that we can come and go, if that's alright with you?'

'Alright with me, of course it's alright, but...'

'But what?'

'I'm just worried that, well, you can't keep spending all this money, Beverley. We don't even know how much they will ask for the property,'

'Will you stop worrying Alex, I have a good feeling about this, and as for the money – believe you me, it's not a problem. When I said millions, I didn't say how many did I?' She leaned over and whispered in my ear.

My mouth dropped open in shock, 'Good grief! Was Laurence money-laundering by any chance?'

'Who cares?' She flung herself down on the bed and stretched luxuriously, 'I think I could quite get into this independent lark.'

I laughed, 'Sitges has worked its magic on you already. Two short days and look at you. You're a changed woman.'

'Absolutely,' Mel came walking though the door crunching on an apple.

'Was that an example of what I think it was?' Beverley looked at me and I nodded. 'E-O-E!' we both hollered.

'Guilty as charged,' smiled Mel and flopped down next to Beverley.

The house was magnificent and must have been built to house a very large family and servants. There was a ballroom downstairs, a humongous kitchen, countless bedrooms and four large reception rooms. The grounds could easily accommodate a pool and eating area that could be set in a beautifully landscaped garden. The potential was there, it would be outstanding when it had been restored to its former glory.

The owner had been waiting for someone who didn't intend to knock down the place and erect an apartment block. The old Catalan lawyer was utterly charming. He apologised for his client's absence and explained that the original owner of the house was a patron of the arts and that its current owner had always dreamed of seeing it being used for creative pursuits and was thrilled at our plans for its future. But he was not prepared to sell to us.

Obviously we were confused but the lawyer sat us down and explained his client's proposal. If we agreed to sensitively restore the building to its original condition, we could have a 99-year lease, rent-free, if, and only if, we continued to use it to help and encourage an artistic community in Sitges. If we thought we could be responsible stewards of the property the wheels would be set in motion immediately. There was another proviso. Because I was the one Nieves could vouch for, I had to be one of the lease-holders. We excused ourselves and had another look around the property. Despite me playing devil's advocate for ten minutes and throwing up every negative I could think of, Beverley was adamant. 'All we have to do now is renovate. I was willing to buy the bloody place.'

We stood staring up at the shabby façade.

'What an amazing opportunity to do something so fabulous.' I smiled. It really was starting to look feasible. We said goodbye to the lawyer and walked out onto the *paseo*. Caveman was sitting on a rock on the beach. He was wearing a wetsuit and a colourful knitted hat. I caught his eye for a moment and smiled. As usual he just seemed to look right through me.

'Who's that?' asked Mel.

'Another of Sitges' local characters; he lives in a cave in the rocks near the church. Harmless really, just a little crazy I suppose.'

'Bless him,' sighed Beverley. 'D'you think he needs some money?'

'I wouldn't go over there waggling your purse around,' I laughed, 'he takes great exception to that, and I would hate to see you being chased around the beach by him and one of his sticks.'

Beverley looked horrified.

'Actually I'd love to see that,' Mel slid in between us and linked arms. 'Now can we go and have a last drink on the seafront before we have to return to wet, grey, polluted old London?'

'We'll go to the best bar in town – our balcony,' I rang Cam and told him to put some cava in the freezer.

'I'm going to come back next week and start the ball rolling,' said a newly forthright Beverley as we chatted to Cam. 'Mel, if I have any problems with the contracts can I get you to liaise with the Spanish lawyers?'

'Of course. I'm not really up on Spanish property law but I'll certainly keep an eye on things for you.'

'I know a couple of architects over here, so I'll see what the planning permission involves,' said Cam.

'I'm not very helpful really, am I?' I felt a little useless.

'Pardon?' said Beverley. 'It was requested you were put on the lease. It was your idea. What use is a school without a syllabus? It's your creativity and expertise that will pull this together. This is just about providing you with a space to do it.'

'How about builders?' asked Cam. 'Your average Spanish workman needs a stick of dynamite up his arse to even lift a hammer?'

'No problem,' said Beverley, 'I know a fantastic Polish guy called Mr Smollensky. He was a friend of my dad's and he has done all Laurence's renovation and building. I'll fly him over from the UK and see what he thinks. His guys don't need long lunches and siestas; they will sleep on site, and even work through the night if necessary.'

'How many of these hairy-arsed Polish demi-gods will we be importing? Rough trade with a sweaty builder in the middle of a dusty construction site – we could sell tickets.'

'Not hard to work out which one of the guys in Village People you fancied,' Mel laughed.

'Just love a hard hat,' Cam grinned devilishly. 'So, when do you expect to get this place open by?'

I looked at Beverley who shrugged, 'Hopefully the renovation will be predominantly cosmetic.'

'Well, why don't we aim to open in time for Carnival in mid-February?' I suggested.

'Don't you think that's a bit overly ambitious?' Cam looked dubious.

'Nope, let's aim for Christmas Eve,' said Beverley.

'Now you are talking out of your backside,' Cam shook his head and poured some more cava.

As Cam walked us down to the cab, I gave his hand a squeeze, 'It's great you haven't got to leave the apartment just yet, isn't it?'

'Yeah,' he sighed, 'talk about a stay of execution.'

'Plus you haven't said what role you'd like to play in the ministry of mayhem yet? Doesn't the idea of running a few art classes appeal?'

'Not at the moment,' he shook his head. 'Anyhow, I think Fred would be brilliant, he used to sculpt and he needs a focus, it would be perfect for him.'

'But...'

'No Alex,' he cut me dead then softened his tone, 'I have a job. But if this madhouse brings you back here then bring it on, that's all I can say.'

'She'll be back,' laughed Beverley.

I smiled happily, and just hoped it wouldn't take too long.

I had no reason to worry. By the following Monday, Beverley had called, the lease was ready to sign and she was going to totally bank roll the whole place for the first year to give it a chance to get off the ground. She suggested I parted company with *Gotta Have It* as soon as possible. Before I had even broached the subject of money, she rattled off a suggested salary that was on a par with what I was getting paid in London. I argued that it was all too much, but the more I was getting to know Beverley, the more I realised arguing was useless. I just said a quick 'thank you' to the universe for allowing us to meet and applied myself to the job of getting sacked – it had to be done.

Where's the fun in resigning?

As luck would have it, the products I had to promote the next day were so dire it made what I was about to do very easy indeed, and I think I will continue to chuckle well into my dotage as I remember the shocked face of Valdene, the spokesperson for *Feed Your Face*, and the sound of the producer screaming down my earpiece as I cheerfully pointed out that the anti-ageing cucumber eye gel stung like fuck and the cleanser had distinct undertones of ammonia and formaldehyde. As panic spread like wildfire, I had just enough time to indulge myself in a Force Ten rant about bored housewives desperately seeking the answer to life in a pot of cheap cream before I was escorted from the studio during the commercial break.

I had a gloriously happy week going from daytime show to

daytime show explaining my actions to bemused presenters and was tickled pink that my antics were on You Tube getting a ridiculous amount of hits. Even Zane re-emerged; dark haired and toned down, with a little story about his 'night of passion' with the renegade presenter. Not exactly Demi Moore and Aston Kutcher, but, hey – it was all good press coverage for the Academy. I returned to Sitges a hero. Rae was reeling in shock as suddenly I was flavour of the month and the offers were rolling in. Much to her horror and my utter delight, I turned down every single one of them.

FORTY TWO

When you're waiting desperately for exam results or a much needed holiday, six weeks can seem to stretch on forever. When you are trying to pull off the total transformation of a ten bedroom dilapidated beach side property, the same six weeks shrink. We hurtled towards our completion date at the speed of light. It was frenetic and not without its disasters, but miraculously enough, we did it.

When I arrived back from England at the beginning of November, things were already under way. Beverley had returned with her finances in place and a lorry load of belongings. As is the way of Sitges, Cam managed to find her a three-bedroom apartment on the seafront within a day, and she was fully installed before the ink had time to dry on her one-year contract

Hot on her heels was Jacek Smollensky and a truckload of Ottos, Wladimirs, Jozefs, Krzysztofs, Stanislaws and other names too difficult to pronounce. To ensure that his workers had full stomachs, he had also brought along his wife - Lidia Smollensky – a giant of a woman with hair the colour of buttercups and teeth to match. When we were first introduced, I couldn't help scanning the immense collection of gold jewellery adorning her rather large personage to see if I could spot an Olympic medal for shot-putting. From a safe distance though, I had a feeling she would have anyone straight in a headlock if they even slightly pissed her off.

Despite our ridiculously short time frame, Jacek seemed totally laid back about the magnitude of the job. Miraculously there were no signs of damp but they would have to re-wire the entire place, knock out the existing kitchen and bathrooms, and install new state of the art replacements. Next on the agenda was re-plastering and

273

painting walls and ceilings, sanding, re-staining and varnishing the floors, replacing rotting window frames, making sure the fireplaces were in working order, and providing heavy duty back up for Bart's mate Ben, a local landscape gardener who was going to re-design the grounds around the house and organise the construction of the pool and pool house.

Whilst the Polish contingency got down to a bit of hard labour, the Sitges chapter immersed themselves in pursuits of a more decorative nature. Most days in amongst the plaster and paint you could find Fred and Bubbles wandering from room to room, brandishing swathes of material and flashing their doorknobs. Bart was always ready to offer a helping hand, but his motives were not entirely born of a passion for interior design and he spent many hours feigning an avid interest in electrical wiring, much to the horror of Jacek who, periodically, checked all the rooms to see if Bart was distracting his otherwise diligent workforce.

Whilst Jacek was busy dealing with his problems, Lidia went to war with the belligerent

Catalan shopkeepers. Her main problem being the sausages - the local *butifarra* just wasn't up to the Polish *kobassa*. How could spicy *chorizo* be any match for a nice hearty *krakowska?*

Talk about the Battle of the Pork Swords! I hadn't realised sausage people took their sausages so seriously.

Nieves rose to the challenge and took Lidia under her deceptively tough wing. She frogmarched her new and physically imposing charge around the local markets where they manhandled the produce with such a look of disdain, the poor traders would virtually give their goods away just to get rid of this strange, mismatched pair. Such was the power of Nieves' influence that Lidia became a huge fan of the Catalan dietary staple – *pa amb tomàquet.* Bread and tomatoes - it was cheap, easy and filled up her boys. What more could an economy driven Polish mother hen wish for?

Back in Colour Swatch and Door Knob Land, we had decided that the Academy was to be a mixture of eclectic and contemporary. We wanted it to be bright and fun, but not so overpowering that the décor detracted from the beautiful surroundings. Somewhere along the line Fred and Bubbles got in touch with their Inner Pretentious and had to be reminded on a regular basis that it wasn't their money they were gaily spending. Eventually they got the message and both proved their worth by scouring the streets and the few junk shops that existed in the area, and coming up with finds that were then customised into stunning pieces of furniture and light fixtures.

We couldn't have kept my mum away if we'd tried. She flew out in early December armed with her trusty sewing machine and set about the mammoth task of making curtains and drapes, along with Bubbles who furthered Mum's burgeoning knowledge of The Life I Never Had a Chance to Lead by enlightening her on subjects such as the intricacies of lesbian love, what to do when your client is hyperventilating because he can't get his rubber mask off and how tea tree oil works wonders for septic body piercings.

I spent countless hours glued to the computer, writing press releases and creating course structures. I still couldn't come up with a name though.

The town was ablaze with gossip. Apparently we were setting up everything from a boutique hotel to a brothel. Nobody had the foggiest idea what we were doing, and that was the way we liked it. Even Caveman had taken to hanging around the beach in front of the building. He would sit for hours gazing at all the comings and goings.

By the middle of December most of the structural work was done and we bade farewell to twelve of the Poles. At the little gathering we held for them, they got themselves shit-faced on vodka and beer, then gave a spontaneous demonstration of Poles Dancing. It wasn't rhythmic and it certainly wasn't pretty. Kylie would have hung up her hot pants for good if she had caught sight of her latest dribbling and drooling disciples stomping to 'Spinning Around' as if they were killing an army of cockroaches.

The next day as the truck pulled away, I noticed a lingering look between Bart and 'One of the Wlads' as we called them, and judging by his subsequent tragic mood, I assumed that Bart's attention to electrical detail had eventually paid off.

We had ten days to go and the chips were down. Jacek and the remaining eight workers painted the subtly textured plaster walls a simple ivory. Fred and Cam dangled from high ladders nailing in curtain poles and hanging beautiful curtains in pale aqua, deep red and gold. The pair of them had made ornate chandeliers with wire and hanging faux jewels. Trucks were arriving daily with desks, tables, chairs, free-standing wardrobes, wrought iron beds, and box upon box that had to be emptied and a home found for all the contents. Evie and Mum were having a whale of a time organising and stocking the kind of kitchen I had dreamed of all my life. High tech meets rustic. It was perfect and could easily accommodate ten students eager to bask in a little Evie-style wisdom and waffles.

The main reception rooms, which were now the dance studio, the dining area, the lounge and the art room, all had high ceilings that glimmered with gold flecks and either a fabulous view of the sea or the garden. Amazing artwork filled the walls – Fred had been very busy. There were framed posters of past Carnivals, stylised images of drag queens and vibrant modern paintings. It was full-on camp glamour and it captured the spirit of Sitges perfectly.

We kept seven rooms as en-suite bedrooms and the other three were office, consultation room and a make-up and hair salon.

Finally, three days ahead of schedule, it was done. Jacek, Lidia and the rest of the guys left to drive all the way to Poland to spend Christmas with their relatives. Lidia and Nieves shared a tearless goodbye, each giving the other a respectful nod in honour of their mutual ability to strike terror into the hearts of anyone with anything to sell.

We all breathed a sigh of relief and decided rather than obsessively plumping cushions and moving various *objets* just a little to the left or right, we would give ourselves a night off. At this point, Beverley flopped down onto one of the sofas in the lounge and announced she wanted a long hot bath, and a gin and tonic. She was shattered, and on top of everything, trying to deal with the news that the twins had opted not to offend either parent and were going to spend this Christmas period with friends. 'This is one of those occasions I miss having a man around,' she sighed wistfully, 'I could just do with a bit of attention.'

'You could do with a bit of a shag you mean,' Cam laughed and gestured for me to follow him to the kitchen. I closed the door behind me and looked at him quizzically. He outlined his plan. It was magnificent in its simplicity.

'Where are her keys?'

'Over there on the hook.'

'Keep her talking,' Cam bent down and grabbed a long screwdriver from a tool kit that had been left lying around. 'Cupids arrow,' he winked at me.

Within twenty minutes Cam came waltzing back through the lounge door looking terribly smug. He looked at his watch, 'C'mon ladies, time to get your butts out of here.'

We locked up and wandered along the *paseo*. Beverley's flat was close to the church, so we kissed her goodbye and dragged ourselves up the steps.

Five minutes later as we walked into our apartment the phone was ringing.

'My bloody boiler's broken down, can you believe it?' Beverley wailed miserably.

I winked at Cam, 'Don't worry, darling, I know a great plumber who will be with you in minutes, just pour yourself a drink, put your feet up and put some lippie on.'

'What? Why do I have to put lippie on? Alex....'

'See you tomorrow Beverley.'

I laughed and got straight on the phone to Pablo, who got over his initial frostiness when I mentioned that there was a new lady in town who desperately needed his help.

Happy that a good deed had been done, and that there was a strong chance Beverley would now get some 'attention', I went to bed and Cam went to work. The next day Beverley looked utterly knackered but had that special glow about her. When she started humming 'I will always love you' for the fourth time, I cornered her in the kitchen and made her spill the love beans.

'I had five orgasms,' she squealed. 'I've never had five

orgasms.' At which point Nieves came wandering in hissing something about Ben the gardener, who had planted flowers where she wanted to grow tomatoes.

'That's your lover boy's granny,' I muttered to Beverley, who immediately went puce.

'I'm going to kill the bitch,' Ben bellowed as he stormed through the door, flicking his shoulder length surfer blond hair out of his eyes.

'Six pack's looking good, Ben,' I nudged Beverley in the ribs. She obligingly nodded and murmured in agreement.

The compliment totally stopped him in his tracks. 'Really?' His tone softened and he struck a pose that seemed to flex every muscle on his bronzed naked chest, 'I've been working out.'

'Ben, you work out everyday in the garden; don't tell me you go to the gym as well?' I cooed.

'Four times a week,' he twisted into a new pose. Ben was a very pretty and hugely narcissistic gay guy – of course he went to the bloody gym.

'Now tell me, how has Nieves been upsetting you?'

The preening stopped and his bright blue eyes blazed, 'I caught her pulling out my plants by the roots. You didn't tell me you asked her to grow tomatoes.'

'I didn't Ben; she just took it upon herself.'

'Well she can just take it upon herself to take herself and her tomatoes and bugger off as far as I'm concerned.'

Nieves stormed back into the kitchen and hurled a stream of abuse at Ben, who flew back at her in exceptionally base Spanish.

'Your turn,' I smiled at Beverley who was away with the fuck fairies.

'Ugh?' She shook her head, 'Sorry, I was in a different world.'

She went straight back there, so I ushered a still squabbling Ben and Nieves out into the garden to negotiate planting rights and boundary fences.

When I had divided out the horticultural territories to both their satisfaction, I marched back into the kitchen to find Beverley giggling in a sexy girlie voice on her mobile.

'He wants to take me to dinner tonight,' she clicked the phone off and beamed, 'shall I go?'

'Hello? Of course you should go.'

So of course, she did go, and again the next night and judging by the way she went legging it home at three o'clock the next day after a text that brought a blush to her cheeks, I would assume they had gotten another quickie in that afternoon. I decided there was no need for her ever to know that Pablo had dipped his toes in my pool so to speak. Cam was sworn to secrecy, once warned, Mel would never let the cat out of the bag, and I was sure that Pablo would be discreet. Some things are best left in the past where they belong, and this was definitely one of those things.

FORTY THREE

'Alex,' the sound of Beverley's voice made me jump. 'What are you doing here on your own?'

'Doing my Christmas Eve thing,' I was sitting in the main entrance hall, basking in front of an open fire, gazing at our mammoth tree dripping with baubles and trinkets that I had collected from all over the world, allowing myself the only present I truly treasure - remembering every person and place which means something to me - re-living every memory and wishing them well.

'Whaddya think?' Beverley pirouetted in front of me wearing a beautifully simple black dress with a stunning pair of low heeled black suede shoes she had picked up that morning. 'I didn't have time to do my hair, does it look okay?'

'Beverley, it looks fabulous! Thank god Tony made you lose all that back combing.' Her hair was tousled and natural and she was wearing half the amount of make-up she usually plastered on. She looked ten years younger.

She rushed up to the mirror, 'Pablo prefers me like this, too, and...' she paused for dramatic effect, 'we spend so much time in bed, I simply don't have the time to fuss about.'

I smiled to myself. What a difference three short little days can make? I went up and looked at her reflection, 'Well, Mrs Inexperienced, somebody must be having a very good time, or else he wouldn't be coming back for more would he? Talking of Pablo, where is the little stud muffin?'

'He's spending the evening with Nieves and the rest of the family,' she smiled bashfully, 'and then he's going to join me later. Why was I getting myself in such a state?'

'Because you're human, and you've spent half your life with

someone who sapped your self confidence.'

'Pablo thinks I'm beautiful,' she grinned, 'he even likes my bum.'

'There's nothing wrong with your bum.'

'It's over forty years old.'

'Do me a favour and allow yourself the luxury of not worrying about anything for five minutes will you?'

'Why don't you worry about stuff, Alex?'

'Of course I worry about stuff,' I leaned my head on her shoulder, 'but I try not to make it a full-time occupation. It's better to enjoy the rainbow today and not get too caught up in what might be in that supposed pot at the end, because if you ask me, it's invariably a disappointment.

Beverley looked thoughtful, 'So I suppose Pablo is my rainbow.'

'Precisely!'

'Sex on a stick has arrived,' a voice shouted from the doorway. We turned around and there was Cam, looking very debonair in a dark brown suit.'

'Good grief, you look almost heterosexual,' I squealed and ran over to him.

'And you are looking pretty fine yourself, Moll,' he spun me around. 'Is that an Armani gown I see before me?'

'You're so observant,' I laughed. I had been waggling it in his face for the past week. It was a bargain buy seven years ago, beautifully cut, dark teal and incredibly flattering. I still loved it as much as the first time I wore it.

'I wish you weren't gay Cam, you and Alex look so good together, and you get on so well, and....'

'Beverley!' I cried in mock horror, 'that would ruin everything.'

'The only reason we get on is because I'm a poof. Ours is a platonic love,' Cam clasped me to his chest and then threw me backwards. Caught off guard, I slipped straight out of his arms and thudded to the ground with a scream. On cue, Mum and Evie arrived to see me sprawled on the floor, unable to speak because I was laughing so much.

'Alexandra, you can't be drunk already?' Mum looked horrified.

'I'm not, I just fell over,' I giggled as Cam pulled me to my feet. More mayhem arrived as Fred, Bart and Bubbles came clomping up the steps wearing reindeer antlers with flashing lights and singing 'Rudolph the Red-nosed Reindeer'.

'I got these on my New York trip last week, fab aren't they?' Bart struck a pose.

'Quite subdued for Sitges,' I laughed, 'but fabulously tacky all the same.'

'I love them,' Evie squealed, 'let me try a pair on.'

Cam and I glanced at each other and grinned. You can take the girl out of America but you can't take America out of the girl.

An hour later we were all bedded in around the table stuffing our faces and shrieking with laughter. The centrepiece of the table was a spectacular ice mountain strewn with *fruits de la mer*. It was wonderful to see everyone all relaxed and happy. It would have been great if my brother and sister were there, and Mel, but they were all committed elsewhere. In an ideal world, I would have loved Pierre to be sitting at the other end of the table, puffing away on his umpteenth cigarette and giggling at his own dreadful jokes but he was now probably tucking into a noisy festive dinner with Juan Carlos's family. As if reading my thoughts, Fred glanced up and winked at me. He mouthed 'Are you okay?' I nodded back and mouthed 'You?' He waggled his hand as if to say 'so-so', then turned his attention back to Bubbles who was building a nativity scene with the remnants of the fish platter.

'D'you think the baby Jesus would have minded being a clam?' she sighed as she put one into an oyster shell and tucked it in with a lettuce blanket.

Cam poured more wine and poked around the table debris for his cigarettes, 'What colour do you think the sky is in her world?'

'Oh most definitely psychedelic,' I fished his Marlboros out from under a lobster shell.

'You look almost contented, Moll,' said Cam, lighting a cigarette.

'I am, I suppose, I mean look at everybody – who would believe we would all be sitting around a table together celebrating

Christmas?'

'You're looking at your own reflection, sweetheart,' Cam smiled.

'Eh?'

'You are the glue that binds us all. Without you this wouldn't have happened.'

'That's a very nice thing to say, even if it's not totally true,' I squeezed his arm and allowed myself a smile. For the first time in a long time, I had a sense of belonging. In less than eleven months my life had changed beyond my wildest dreams. I was looking at a whole table, full of people who, I knew, even after such a short time, would be there for me no matter what. I was obviously getting something right. However bad I seemed to be at relationships, at least I could do friendships.

'Hey, now we've got them all here shall we get our little surprise?' Cam leaned over and whispered.

'Good idea,' we stood up and wandered out to the art room where we had hidden a large piece of hardboard. Everyone was so busy gabbling they didn't even notice us struggling back in with it. I coughed loudly and they all shut up and looked quizzically at us.

'Right everyone, we said that we would name the baby when it was born, and I think as we are sitting here in these beautiful surroundings tonight, junior has definitely arrived and it's time to make a decision,' I nodded to Cam who picked up the piece of wood and leaned it on his chair.

'As you know, Moll and I are a bit prone to sitting up all night talking bollocks, and just lately we have been putting it to good use,' he glanced back at me.

'We came up with a name that seems hugely appropriate, and to help you visualise it, Cam made a mock-up sign.'

'Oh c'mon, shut up and show us,' screamed Bart.

'No, listen first. There was an artistic movement here in Sitges years ago called the *Escola Luminista*. Remember all that wonderful stuff you told me about, Bubbles - all those artists being drawn here because of the quality of the light? Well Cam and I sat on the beach looking at the sunset a week ago and this place just glowed with a pinkish light. It was beautiful. And bearing in mind we're all about creativity in all its many guises and not least of which we have a few clauses in the lease to honour, we thought this might work, as it sort of celebrates the history of the place and pays a little respect to all those artists who have been here before.' Cam swivelled the sign around with a flourish, 'We give to you - *Academia Luminista*!'

They all went quiet, and then Beverley spoke, 'I think it's amazing.'

'So all in favour of *Academia Luminista*, put your hands up now!' Everyone's hand shot up.

I jumped up and down with excitement, 'So we have a name! Let's drink to that.'

As we all raised our glasses I felt the *alma* of the building begin to seep back into its walls. The house was happy.

'C'mon, more food,' Mum stood up along with Evie, and suddenly the table erupted into a flurry of activity. Within seconds the remains of the fish fest had been cleared away – including much to her annoyance – Bubbles' nativity scene. But when steaming plate after steaming plate arrived on the centre of the table, including a huge joint of mustard encrusted beef, crispy roast potatoes and every side dish known to man, she forgot her chagrin and gorged away happily like the rest of us.

Later, after everyone had finished mounting a full-scale attack on a trolley of *postres* that could raise blood sugar levels by just looking at it, we adopted post-pig-out recovery positions in different corners of the Academy. Cam and I snuggled up on a sofa by the tree.

'What would you like for Christmas, Cam?'

'A child.'

'What?' I sat up and looked at him.

'I would love to be a dad, but it doesn't really fit in with the lifestyle does it?'

'Why don't you find a single woman who wants one and get the turkey-baster out?'

'Stop it, I'm being serious,' a single drunken tear slid down his cheek.

'Hey there, I'm sorry. You really mean this don't you?'

'It's the only thing that makes me question my sexuality.'

'You poor bubba,' I cuddled up to him. 'D'you want me to have one for you?'

'Nah, if it's a boy he'll end up looking like Mick Hucknall.'

'You cheeky git, mind you, you've got a point,' I winced.

'That gets you nicely off the hook,' he shrugged.

'If you really wanted me to, I would,' I gasped indignantly. 'We'd make great parents.'

'Moll, I have no doubt that we would but that just isn't in your future and you know it isn't.'

I sighed and nodded. It was true, I had never really been child orientated. My biological clock always had a couple of cogs missing and never really gave me any indication it was ticking away, apart from one occasion. I was lying in Central Park one hot New York afternoon watching a mother taking in the sight of her baby taking his first steps. Suddenly I became aware of the tears pricking the backs of my eyes and the twinge of my ovaries as they looked enviously at my other internal organs that all seemed to be gainfully employed. But that was a single isolated incident, never to be repeated.

'This school is the only baby you need to be concerning yourself with. Bubbles making that nativity scene must have made me a little broody. I just want a little Cam Clam,' he winked. 'C'mon let's go down to El Cabaret and give Simon and Aaron some stick.'

'Hey, if you had more than one you could have a whole Cam Clam Clan. Try saying that quickly.'

We both sniggered and stood up.

'You can't go anywhere yet, we have to open one present each,' Beverley looked like an excited little girl.

Everyone scrambled over to the tree and started grabbing gifts, then something I'd totally forgotten about came back to haunt me. Mum picked up a rectangular box and gave it to Evie, 'You'll wonder how you managed without it,' she said brightly.

Cam nudged me and whispered, 'You're dead.'

I gulped as Evie opened the box to find a bright purple vibrator with silver and pearl beads.

'Let me show you how it works,' my mum grabbed it out of the box and waved it around excitedly. Evie's eyes widened in shock and everyone went quiet. Mum stared at the vibrator in her hand, 'It's only a back massager.'

Bubbles leaned over and whispered into her ear, her mouth fell open in horror and she dropped the offending article onto the floor. 'Alex! I've sent them to everybody, Great Aunt Dolly, everybody!' she shrieked.

I stood chewing my lips nervously, 'Just think of the 'Thank You' cards.'

She looked around the room. Cue mass hysteria.

'It's a very pretty one,' said Evie calmly as she bent down and retrieved her Purple Park Avenue Princess, 'it'll go nicely with my others.'

'Oh my god, I gave one to your sister, d'you think she'll have me committed?'

'I'm afraid so Mum, but I'll make sure you get a nice room with a view.'

'Thank you darling,' and then she burst out laughing. 'If you ask me for your pink one back young lady…' I nodded dumbly as she continued; 'I shan't be giving it to you…not now I know what it's really for.'

I pulled a disgusted face as I struggled with the image.

'I thought I'd get that reaction,' Mum nudged Evie. 'Joke's back on you darling.'

'It certainly is Mother,' I grinned.

Cam bent down and grabbed a small package from underneath the tree, 'For you Moll, it's just a little thing. Don't worry, no batteries involved,' he laughed.

I rummaged around until I found an identical sized present. We both unwrapped our gifts and shook our heads in disbelief as we held up the same Christmas ornament – a brightly coloured bejewelled Harlequin.

'It just reminded me of you,' we both muttered in unison, then hugged each other because we knew even though we wore similar masks for the rest of the world – behind all that bravado we were just a couple of clowns who occasionally let their guard down and cried in private.

We hung our respective Harlequins on the tree and watched them as they flickered in the lights. Just for a fleeting second, I looked up and allowed myself two small painful memories, my dad with a glass of whiskey in one hand and a bauble in the other, singing his head off to dreadful Christmas carols as he decorated the tree. And the other – well let's just say it involves another man and another tree. But before either had the chance to settle and fill me with melancholy, Cam swept me away into the night, where, with both our masks tightly in place, we entertained the troops until dawn.

FORTY FOUR

'How about a Beachcomber and Forager Candelabra Masterclass?'

'Bit of a mouthful,' I grinned at Fred.

'I can't believe we're so busy,' he gestured to the wipe board on the wall. 'Have you seen these bookings? People need us!'

It was the third week of January, and the *Academia Luminista* was officially open way ahead of schedule. My final performance on the shopping channel had obviously struck a chord and our press releases had kick-started a flood of enquiries from the UK. We had been featured in *The Evening Standard*, *The Independent*, and a whole host of travel websites. We had journalists flying over solidly for the next month and *OK* magazine wanted to cover the Hen Weekend we were hosting for Jonella – a page three girl turned pop singer - in the first week of February.

We were making it up as we went along. Championing the simple things in life was echoing the mood of the moment. The art classes were going to be about as back to childhood as you could get, there wouldn't be any pressure to be a master of sophisticated techniques, just an exuberant celebration of colours and textures. We would take clients on inspirational walks around Barcelona and then let them loose in the art room. Fred intended to frame and mount their work as they went along and then hang it on the walls, surrounding his charges with the fruits of their labour. We figured that even the most rudimentary efforts would look spectacular, particularly when bathed in the fantastic light that always streamed in through the windows.

We were encouraging people to be human canvases as well. Bringing out a suitcase full of clothes to customise *à la Bubbles* was a great way to revamp an existing wardrobe, and we were getting loads of enquiries from cross-dressers. Whatever way they wanted to express their creativity, we had it covered. Flights from the UK were cheap and the combination of a couple of days of winter sun and a little Sitges-style 'happiness' seemed to be a tonic that many people needed. We were giving hotels in the town business and were trying to integrate as many Spanish people into the Academy as possible, including a couple of great dancing teachers who had the locals literally lining up for their classes.

'It's unbelievable,' Bev scribbled away on her notepad, 'if we carry on at this rate, we'll need more staff.'

'It'll probably settle down once the novelty wears off,' I smiled, 'but it does make sense to keep this place as busy as possible. Anyhow, don't worry about staffing - one thing you will always find in Sitges is someone who wants to earn some cash.'

'Would you two mind if I went and sorted out the art room for a while? I need to reorganise some stuff,' Fred was already halfway out the door.

'No,' we both sighed as we grinned at each other. Fred was beside himself with his new responsibility and was feeling inspired again, so we just let him get on with it.

'Actually – Alex ...' Beverley looked at her watch.

'Go on, bugger off and leave me to it.'

'It's not what you think,' she squeaked. 'I'm having a cookery lesson with Evie; she's teaching me some traditional Jewish recipes.'

'Then you're going to leg it back to yours and bonk Pablo's brains out?'

'Maybe,' she laughed. 'Hey, you don't want to come do you? Evie would love having both her surrogate daughters hanging on her every word.'

'No, seriously, I'm as happy as a clam here. It's actually worrying me how much I'm enjoying this.' I waved towards the door, 'Go on, shoo, before you're late.'

She bounced out and I watched her walk along the *paseo* towards town. The significance of her relationship with Evie didn't escape me; in fact it brought a lump to my throat. A Jewish woman who had lost her daughter and a Jewish girl who had never had the mother she deserved – you couldn't make up this sort of stuff. In fact with Nieves clucking around after her as well, Beverley was basking in maternal attention and it was beautiful to see. Awash with warm and comforting mother and daughter feelings, impulsively I reached for the phone and dialled Mum's number but all I got was her voice on the answer machine, *'Hello, I'm not here because I have a life. Please leave a message after the tone.'* Taken a bit aback, I spluttered out a message, *'Err, hello Mum, it's Alex, give me a call if you can fit me into your busy schedule – in the meantime I'll try to get myself a life, okay? Love you.'*

I clicked the phone down and shook my head. It was incredible to think that this was the same mother who used to think having afternoon tea at John Lewis was the height of sophistication. The same mum who less than a year ago would have sold her soul to be the first person with a pair of spring sandals from the Per Una collection at Marks & Spencer's.

Ten minutes later the phone rang. I flicked it onto loudspeaker and carried on typing.

'Darling, how lovely to hear from you.'

'Hi Mum, what have you been up to? Not getting smashed I hope.'

'Have you heard yourself lately, you're beginning to sound just like your sister,' a peal of laughter followed and I felt myself bristling as she carried on. 'I've just come back from taking my wonderful grandchildren ice-skating, and I have to say Alex, I was quite good.'

I was suddenly besieged with visions of Mum whizzing around the ice looking like some ageing Jane Torvill in a glittery frock halfway up her arse. 'Erm, what did you wear?'

'Jeans and a jumper, Alex what on Earth is wrong with you today?'

'Sorry, I was just having an 'I want my mummy moment' and you didn't sound like my mummy any more. I'll get over it.'

'Alex, of course I'm your mummy. Oh by the way, I love that vibrator.'

'Let's talk about something else Mum, please ... anything you want – ornaments, topiary, Pavlova, next door's cat, marijuana – just not masturbation. Oh my god, I've just said masturbation to my mum.'

'Calm down Alex! We all masturbate ... I'll have twenty pounds cash back please.'

'You're in the supermarket!' hyperventilation started to kick in.

'Yes darling, I had to run out as soon as I got back, I was worried they would run out of mince.' Horror of horrors, I heard her start explaining things to the cashier, 'Yes it's my daughter, they all think we give up on sex when we've given birth to them.' I heard an explosion of raucous laughter.

'Mum, you're on the mobile.'

'Of course I am; how else would I be talking to you from Asda...Bye bye now, yes she's still on the line, yes, thank you, I'll tell her... Noreen the cashier says that sex gets better as you get older.'

'Can we stop this conversation now? Think of all those brain cells you're killing with all those dangerous radio waves. Why don't you call me when you get back home, it's much cheaper. Tell you what! I'll call you in fifteen minutes. How does that sound?'

'Ridiculous,' she chuckled away merrily. 'You are funny sometimes - worldly and broad-minded in so many ways and yet so straight-laced in others – just like your dad.'

Having spent so many years thinking she didn't understand me at all, it was something of a revelation to realise that she did, but that didn't make this little topic any easier to deal with, 'Mum, with the best will in the world, I think most daughters would have a problem talking about the 'M' word with their mothers.'

'Why Alex? It's natural. I think it should be something mothers teach their daughters.'

'Just call me Frankenstein! I've created a monster.'

'Honestly, Alex, one moment you're mortified because I'm too 'mumsie', and now finally I'm having a little fun and letting my hair down, and that's not right either. I can't win with you.'

'Sorry, Mum, you're right; I just didn't expect you to go straight from Doris Day to Germaine Greer. Maybe it's because you're back in your natural habitat I just expected you to be back to your usual self.'

'Well, while we're on that subject, Alex, I want to talk to you. I've made a decision that might cause a few ripples.'

This sounded serious.

'I've decided to sell up and move to your part of the world.'

I was stunned, and a tad panicky. 'But, Mum, say I don't stay here, say you're here on your own, say you're lonely, say...'

'Alex, I'll be fine, and I'm doing this because I want to. I've met some lovely people and I will be able to afford a beautiful home with plenty of room for the family. Evie and I might even share a house. Your dad and I always wanted to do it one day, and funnily enough, I feel closer to him out there.'

'Mum, how do I put this? You and Evie? I mean, you're not, well, you know...are you?'

'Alex!' The scream said it all.

'Alright keep your hair on, just checking.'

Five minutes later, I put the phone down and sat looking blankly at my computer screen. Was this really happening? Was my mum really going to up sticks and come to Spain? As if echoing my thoughts a voice came from the doorway.

'So your mum's moving over here then?' Fred plonked himself down in front of me and lit a cigarette. 'Did you REALLY think she and Evie were lovers?'

'Did you REALLY eavesdrop the entire conversation?'

'Alex, you are such a stupid cow sometimes,' Fred sighed. 'Did you mean what you said?'

'Which bit?'

'The bit about you maybe not staying here,' his brow furrowed with concern.

'Fred, I'm not going anywhere in the foreseeable future. I was a bit freaked out about Mum coming here,' I shrugged. 'It's a massive move for her, and I'm feeling responsible.'

'You're worried about *being* responsible.'

'Yes I suppose so. I have this frightening picture in my head of

Mum and me sitting in our rocking chairs like a couple of old spinsters, taking in the sea air, sipping sherry.'

'What's so bad about that?'

'It's like something out of a Jane Austen novel.'

Fred raised his eyebrows, 'Alex, the combination of you and a mother who has discovered wacky baccy is hardly *Pride and Prejudice*. Plus the fact, if you've got the sherry out, you'll have to factor Cam into the equation.'

'S'pose so. Fancy coming out in search of Mr Darcy?' I winked at him.

'I'll get my coat, Miss Bennett,' Fred shrieked in a falsetto voice and leapt up.

'You are not going to pull a tall dark stranger wearing that.'

'Why?' Fred zipped up his bright yellow puffa jacket.

'It would look great on an eight-year-old.'

'It was cheap as chips and it keeps me warm. One more word from you and I'll start making derogatory remarks about those stupid ponchos and fluffy boots you insist on wearing.'

'I love my Ugg boots!' I screamed indignantly. 'I bought my first pair in Australia years ago, way before they were trendy. And for the record, my poncho was a gift from an Argentinean gaucho.'

Fred guffawed, 'And that makes them okay does it? I'm going to get you a set of Peruvian pipes, one of those funny little woollen hats, and if this all goes tits up you can start busking for a living.'

'Now that I'd like to see,' a voice came from the doorway along with an icy blast of cold air. We spun around and there was a very drab and jaded Stephan. 'I thought I'd come and check out what all the fuss was about.'

I smiled warily, 'We'll give you a guided tour, won't we Fred?' I was not in the mood for a bitch fight, and hoped that Stephan would keep a lid on his spitefulness if Fred were around.

It seemed to work, in fact I was amazed at how subdued he was. As we went from room to room he gazed quietly around while Fred waxed lyrical about everything from the floor tiles to the light switches. He even managed a half smile when we reached the art room, as it was impossible to remain impervious to Fred's infectious enthusiasm.

In fact by the time we reached the front door to show him out, I was so amazed at his restrained attitude that I felt myself on the verge of inviting him to join us for a drink, but Stephan soon put paid to that little idea. He thanked Fred politely for showing him around and turned to face me.

'Well, Alex, congratulations, it would appear that you have everything a girl could want, well....' He paused and gave a little smirk, 'Maybe not everything? But hey, you can't have it all, dahling,' I leaned back as he put his face close to mine, 'that would be plain greedy now, wouldn't it?'

'I think you should start drinking more water Stephan. A detox does wonders for getting rid of all that poison that builds up in your system,' I hissed through gritted teeth.

'And I thought you two were on the verge of becoming friends,' sighed Fred as Stephan disappeared into the distance.

'That just shows how wrong we can be.' I gave a wry smile. 'C'mon, let's lock up and go play.'

FORTY FIVE

'I can't believe you are persuading me to do this again,' Cam was flinging himself theatrically around the art studio while Bubbles, Fred and I looked on.

There were only two weeks to Carnival and this year the big Sunday Procession was on February 14ᵗʰ – a fact that I was shamelessly using as emotional blackmail.

'But think of what a fantastic birthday present it would be for me and Beverley if you won the Alternative Drag Carnival Queen competition,' I looked beseechingly at him. 'It's not as if it's going to be fixed this time, the town council are running it and insisting that all contestants sing live with a backing track.' I had finally told Cam about how Stephan had literally 'blown' his chances the year before.

'Apparently Stephan is disappearing to Barcelona for singing lessons three times a week,' said Bubbles, 'but he'll still sound like a strangulated cat - you'll walk it this time.'

Cam leaned over the table and studied the initial sketches for the outfit Bubbles and Fred had designed for him.

'It's inspired isn't it?' Fred looked earnestly at Cam.

'Yeah, and who have I got to thank for that?' Cam shot me a menacing glance, 'It's okay for you, Moll, you haven't got to go on that stage and make a monkey of yourself.'

'But we'll be your backing singers,' chirped Bubbles.

'Who exactly?'

'Me, Fred and Bart,' Bubbles grabbed a bright pink felt tip and added some extra detail to the outfit, 'and the song is frigging perfect.'

Cam smirked, 'Okay, give me the song sheet; I'd better start practising.'

I squeaked, 'You'll do it?'

'You knew I would, you crafty cow.'

'Okay,' Fred clapped his hands, 'we've got three weeks, time to get to work, Bubbles. We're going to need twenty metres of pink latex.'

'Let me make a few calls, and then Beverley can bring it back with her tomorrow night.'

'That'll be a nice diversion for her! 'Excuse me kids, Mum's got to go and pick up rubber from the fetish factory.' Beverley was having a few days in the UK with the twins and breaking it to them that she had found herself a boyfriend.

'Maybe she could tell them she's making them a paddling pool?'

'They're at university, Fred.'

'Oh.'

'Right, now we have that sorted, I'm going into Barcelona,' Bubbles stood up and shook out her vintage 1950s black satin and lace frock.

'I thought you were looking a bit over the top for a Tuesday afternoon, what are you up to?'

'I have a date.'

'Who's the lucky lady?' Cam whistled as Bubbles slipped a faux fur cape over her ensemble, whipped out an ornate powder compact and applied a vivid slash of dark red lipstick to her puckered lips.

'It's a guy,' she sighed nonchalantly.

'What?' We all screamed.

'He's a Spanish director who knows one of my ex-clients. He wants me to appear in a short film – a kind of *Basic Instinct* with a mental dominatrix who likes to murder people by sitting on their faces.'

'And you were worried about getting up on a stage and singing,' I nudged Cam and coughed; 'Good luck Bubbles, I'm sure you'll go down a storm.'

'If necessary,' she winked, 'a girl's gotta do what a girl's gotta do,' she rustled past a very stricken-looking Fred and walked out of the door. 'See you guys tomorrow.'

'Just banish the image from your mind, Fred,' Cam shook his shoulders gently and turned to me. 'He's in shock.'

'Anyone want a coffee?' I waved my hands in front of Fred's face.

'She's full of surprises isn't she?' Fred shook his head incredulously, 'I just can't imagine...'

'Don't!' Cam and I shouted in unison.

*

'What freaky people! How in god's name do you hear about these places?' Beverley thudded a huge bag, bulging with pink rubber, in front of Bubbles who had been nursing a massive hangover all day.

'Cos we've led very different lives, Beverley,' she shrugged, 'and now to widen the gap just that little bit further, I'm going to be a movie star.'

'I beg your pardon.'

'Come with me,' I grabbed Beverley's arm and guided her out of the door. 'Bubbles is branching out into fetish movies.'

'We're not doing them here are we?' Beverley sounded panicky, 'Christ! I've been away less than a week.'

'No, no, no, don't worry, it's some perverted Spanish director who seems to think the sight of a naked Bubbles suffocating people between her thighs will guarantee him an appearance at the Sitges Film Festival.'

Beverley's face took on the same traumatised look that Fred's had the day before.

'Plus something else is going on that has been a bit weird.'

'More?'

'Either we have a poltergeist or Cam is better at practical jokes than I give him credit for.'

Over the past few days things had got a little odd. Firstly my poncho had gone missing from its hook in the kitchen. I of course blamed Fred who hated it, but he swore blind he hadn't moved it, so we put it down to a light-fingered local who had been attending dance classes. Then, we came in the day after and there was a new canvas on an easel in the art room with an almost child-like impression of the sea, painted in acrylics, and a half-drunk glass of red wine next to it.

'Last night, Cam and I decided to stay here on the sofas in the reception room to see if we could catch whoever it is but we both fell asleep and in the middle of night I leapt out of my skin because I swear I felt something brush my cheek. Cam was still sleeping – or pretending to.'

Beverley shuddered, 'it must be Cam. Or Bubbles? Ghosts don't drink and paint. Do they?'

I laughed, 'Who knows? But I can usually tell if his lordship is fibbing and I don't think he was. The strangest thing was the smell, it was like the sea.'

'So we have a sea-faring, drunken, poncho-wearing artistic phantom on the loose?'

'Whatever or whoever, it'll all come out sooner or later. Anyhow more importantly, tell me how your trip went. How were the girls?'

'They were a bit upset as Laurence has been winding them up that he wants me back. Apparently all he and Tanya ever do is row.'

'Bothered?'

'Not in the slightest. I wouldn't go back to that life for all the tea in China. But d'you know what? Maybe it's because I'm happy with Pablo, I don't bear the pair of them any malice any more. I don't really feel anything, is that a bit odd?'

'No, just shows what a lovely person you are, and proves you did the right thing.'

'Yeah, and the twins will love Pablo when they meet him, I'll just have to time it carefully.'

'You're really quite serious about this guy aren't you?'

'We get along so brilliantly, well, apart from the occasional row about tomatoes – what is it with that family?' she laughed. 'He worships the ground I walk on, and Alex – I really like that.'

'I'm not surprised, I think we all like a bit of that from time to time.'

'Yours will come along soon, Alex.'

'Mmnn,' I grunted uneasily, 'that would be the last thing I need right now as we have a lot of work to do. For the next three weeks this is officially Carnival Central and we've got Jonella and her hen party arriving this weekend. We have all the bedrooms booked out from Thursday onwards so it will be all hands on deck. Evie is going to keep everyone fed and watered, plus Mum will be pretty busy on the sewing machine. We are hosting a pre-Carnival supper party next Wednesday with canapés and cocktails. I'm fully booked doing make-up for the five days. Fred and Bubbles are running up frocks and various accessories and Tony has been dressing wigs since last week. They're all in the art room if you want a quick peek. The lime green Carmen Miranda is amazing. And most importantly - Cam is going to win the Alternative Carnival Queen Crown this year if it kills us all in the process. Hey! Why don't you be in the backing group?'

'Yeah alright.'

'Say what?'

'I'll do it, why not? I've never done anything daring in my life, I'll do it.'

'Beverley you are a trooper,' I squealed. 'Bubbles!'

'What? Stop screaming,' she peered grumpily around the corner of the art room door.

'You have a fourth member of the backing group. Beverley's going to do it.'

'Well, fuck me, wonders never cease – no offence Beverley – but you might have to let your hair down a little.'

'How far?'

'Trailing in the mud sister.'

'Yay! Will I be wearing rubber?'

'A little bit…'

'Leather?'

'If you want…'

Beverley started jumping up and down like a little girl. Bubbles' expression changed to one of pure wickedness. I had the feeling Beverley's outfit wasn't going to cost us an awful lot in materials. 'Why aren't you going to be in the group Alex? It'll be fun.'

'Because I will have my work cut out back stage. I'll be quite happy supporting you lot,' I smiled.

'Mel's coming over with the kids for Carnival week. They're going to use my apartment and I'll stay with Pablo. You don't mind do you, we thought it was better than causing you and Cam total disruption?'

'Pardon?' I had a 'my-two-friends-are-organising-stuff-without-me-being-involved' control freak moment.

'We had a quick coffee yesterday and she booked the flights there and then. Aren't Blackberry's amazing things?'

'I had an email from her yesterday, she didn't mention it.'

'She probably wanted to surprise you. Sorry - me and my big mouth.'

'She knows I hate surprises. When is she coming?'

'The Friday morning before Carnival, she's taken the day off.'

'Now *that* is a surprise.'

FORTY SIX

Mel walked around the Academy with her mouth open, 'It looks fantastic! The pictures just don't do it justice.'

'Aunty Alex, are they your boobs on the wall – it says *Alex* on the sign?' my God-daughter Chloe looked up at me.

'Erm – yes they are,' I shot a worried look at Mel as Nat came up and had a closer look at the array of gilded breasts that were gracing the stairwell. He turned around and said, 'They're not as big as those. Cor! Are they Jonella's – from the magazines?'

I nodded dumbly.

During her hen-weekend, Jonella had decided that the perfect wedding present for Anton, her Hubby-To-Be, was to have her magnificent mammaries immortalised in plaster and painted gold. Fred obliged and then decided that he would create our very own wall of fame, or should I say – shame.

'Can you have yours done Mum? Look, there's Beverley's,' chirped Chloe.

'Maybe darling,' Mel muttered dismissively, 'although I think Aunty Alex has quite enough boobs, don't you?'

'We thought we might use them as moulds for our silicone breasts,' I looked at Mel who looked suitably confused. 'They're for the cross-dressers. You wouldn't believe the price they're charging on the Internet for them. The funny thing is, when I came in this morning they had all been moved around the wall.'

'Practical joker on the loose huh?' shrugged Mel.

'Well, we think it might be a ghost!'

Mel rolled her eyes and shook her head but before she had a chance to pass comment she was stopped in her tracks.

'Excuse me everybody,' a deep voice with a strong Liverpudlian accent boomed from above. Ken, one of our guests, came trundling down the stairs, his sixteen stone frame encased in a sequinned Union Jack sheath with a huge pair of diamante chandelier earrings swinging from his otherwise bald and unadorned head. 'I'm just going for a wig fitting with Tony, and then I'm seeing you for a make-up run through. Three o'clock isn't it?'

'Sure is, I'll have everything ready.'

'Better get a bloody great cement-mixer babes,' he roared as he disappeared into the art room, where he was met with a loud squeal of approval from Tony.

'We've made you some outfits, guys,' Chloe and Nat were still gawping at each other.

'I'm not wearing a dress,' Nat's voice was full of panic.

'Don't worry,' I laughed.

'Good, cos it's gay.'

'Everything's gay as far as he's concerned, isn't it darling? Yoghurt, Eastenders, grey sweatpants – the list is endless,' Mel ruffled his hair and then jumped back in mock horror as he glared at her, 'Mum, don't touch my hair, I've told you.'

'He spends a whole hour every morning putting gel on it,' piped Chloe.

'And that's not *gay?* C'mon I'll show you what we've come up with.'

We went into the dance studio where we had set up a huge rail with outfits of every type and colour – the only ones that weren't there were Cam's and the backing group's – they were being made in secret at Evie's – no way were we letting the cat out of the bag before the big night.

I rifled through and found a plastic suit carrier with 'Nat & Chloe' written on it. I opened it up and showed them their *Pirates of the Caribbean* outfits, 'Will Johnny Depp and Keira Knightley do you?'

'Cool,' nodded Nat. 'Have I got a sword?'

'Of course, and so have you Chloe.'

They held their outfits up and pranced around in front of the mirror. Mel smiled, 'Good choice Aunty Alex. What am I going to wear?'

'I thought old frumpy Mexican widow for you. I've got you a great moustache.'

'Thanks.'

'You can choose your own. Cam has at least twenty horrendous get-ups, we have more wigs than you can poke a stick at, and your best friend is a make-up artist – you're sorted. Did you remember a pair of black high heels?'

'Nah – I said I would have a quick nip around the shoe shops with Beverley later. You coming?'

'No chance darling, I am up to my eyes in it here. I won't be worth talking to until everybody is safely up on that stage on Sunday night. You'll be okay won't you?'

'Yeah, I'm taking the kids into Barcelona tomorrow, and we're not going until Wednesday so we'll have time to catch up; well, I hope we will.'

'Of course we will stupid, I've told you, after Sunday the pressure is off.'

She shrugged, 'You might still be busy, you never know. C'mon kids, let's leave your Godmother to it. Say 'thank you' to her for sorting out your gear.'

'Thank you, Aunty Alex,' they reluctantly put their things back in the bag. I smiled - they might be teenagers but they were still big kids.

'Someone has eaten half the cake I left in the fridge,' I heard Evie shout up from the kitchen. 'Whoever it is, own up to your crimes. Fred was it you?'

'More ghostly activity?' Mel laughed.

'It's certainly bloody odd,' we walked out into the hall. Tony's head appeared from around the door, 'Ken is ready for his close-up Alex. Ouch!' He squealed in pain as Ken pushed him out of the way and leapt out in a two-foot high red, white and blue wig that nearly went flying as it hit the door frame.

'Ta daaaaaa!! Whaddya think kids?'

'You look like a woman,' grunted Nat.

'Why thank you, sweetie,' Ken ruffled Nat's hair. He flinched and went to say something, then obviously thought better of it.

'Off you go,' I pushed them out of the door and turned back to Ken, 'Okay, something subtle and understated for you then.'

FORTY SEVEN

'That was brilliant!' Tony, Evie, Mum and I clapped rapturously as Cam and the gang took their bows after their first full dress rehearsal.

'We are so going to win this tonight,' laughed Cam. 'This feels so weird,' he squirmed around in his rubber outfit. 'I'm going to lose pounds in this thing – and there's little enough of me as it is.'

'There's little enough of this as it is,' Beverley tried to cover up her bum with the thin strip of fabric that constituted her skirt.

'You look very Xena,' grinned Bubbles, whose own outfit left very little to the imagination.

'You're not as sexy as us.' Bart and Fred were both sporting a pair of silicone 'Jonella's' especially for the occasion and were jiggling them in front of the mirror.

'I can't believe I had a hand in making this,' roared Mum as she helped Cam peel off his costume. 'Who would have thought it?'

'Well, let's get it all off and put away,' I was filled with deep-seated anxiety and hadn't slept a wink the night before.

'Hi there,' we all froze in our tracks as the door opened. We didn't want anyone coming across enemy lines at this stage. Thankfully it was Mel and the kids.

'What is that?' Nat shouted.

'Never you mind darling,' Mel raised her eyebrows at me.

Nat threw himself moodily onto the sofa and grunted the immortal teenage phrase, 'I'm bored.'

'Tell you what, why don't I take Nat and Chloe roller-blading?' Cam grinned, 'We've got a whole cupboard full of skates here, and I could do with some fresh air.'

'That's nice of you Cam,' said Mel.

'Whatever! Just be careful the lot of you. No dramas today pahleese!'

'Calm down, Alex, why don't you go and have a nice long bath, chill out and make yourself look presentable. You won't get the chance later, you'll be too busy looking after everyone else,' Beverley pinched my cheek gently.

'But, there's so much to do…'

'And so many of us to do it - go,' Mum ushered me out of the door. 'See you in an hour or so.'

I went gratefully, if a little reluctantly, out into the sunshine. As I walked down the *paseo,* I heard Cam and the kids clattering down the stairs, and I turned as they whizzed off in the opposite direction. I squinted at the church in the distance. It was eleven-thirty. Another five hours and the madness would begin in earnest. I just wished the butterflies in my stomach would go away. I took a deep breath and tried to calm myself. Everything was going to be okay.

'You look lovely, Alex,' Mum beamed at me as I walked back into the Academy.

'It's just a shirt and jeans, Mum,' I looked at her quizzically. Was I going mad or was everyone grinning inanely at me? They all seemed even more on edge than me.

'I think you just look more rested,' nodded Mel. 'Amazing what a bath and a bit of slap can do.'

'Where's Cam, it's nearly two o'clock?'

'I dunno, he's meant to be back by now,' said Beverley looking at her Cartier watch, 'he promised.'

'He's probably buying Nat and Chloe a pizza or something, I'm sure they're fine.'

I heard the sound of the front door opening, 'There you go, it's probably them now.' I turned around and through the stained glass panels I saw a solitary figure approaching the dance studio. As it got nearer I realised everyone else had gone very quiet and as I looked closer I thought my eyes were deceiving me – they weren't.

'Happy Birthday, Alex.'

I looked around the room; everyone was staring at me expectantly. I looked back at the person standing in the doorway,

'Stan, what the hell are you doing here?'

'We have got to talk.'

'Alex, I'm ready for you,' it was Ken waving at me from the hallway.

'I have a make-up to do,' I marched out of the door and stomped off to my make-up station in the art room, followed by both Ken and Stan.

'Alex, will you listen to me?'

'I'm busy, Stan. Sit down Ken,' I snapped brusquely. 'Same as we did on Friday okay for you?'

'That'd be lovely. Don't mind me, you two, you just carry on, I can always go outside and have a fag if you need five minutes.'

'You stay right where you are Ken.'

'I know how it all looks, Alex. I wanted to explain that afternoon in Barcelona but your phone kept ringing, and then we had that stupid argument.'

'You should have told me right from the start.'

'To be fair, until that day in Barcelona – the subject had never come up.'

'Excuse me! If I remember rightly, YOU wouldn't discuss past relationships. Now I know why.' Ken winced as I slapped a blob of foundation onto his face.

'If you had just let me explain when I called you…'

'He called you?'

'Yes, can you close your eyes please?'

'And she hung up on me.'

'Now that's not very nice, Alex.'

'Ken you need to close your eyes otherwise I'll get make-up in them, and if you keep taking his side, I'll do it on purpose.'

'Alright, alright, but can I just ask one thing?'

'What Ken?'

'What exactly was it he didn't tell you?'

'That he's married,' I yelled and glared at Stan.

'Was married; my divorce was finalised two weeks ago.'

'Really?' Both Ken and I turned and looked at him.

'Cam said there was absolutely no point in contacting you unless

I was divorced.'

'Cam knew about this?'

'Well what's your problem then?' Ken half-opened one eye and peered at me. 'Seems like a grand gesture on his part?'

'They all knew didn't they? That's why everyone's been so weird lately. I'll murder the lot of them.'

'I think I'll come back when you've calmed down a bit, Alex, the thought of you and eyelash glue in this mood is making me panic. Just going for a fag,' Ken zipped out and left the two of us staring at each other.

'Don't be mad at everyone, Alex; they're just trying to help. I know how this looks, but if you would just let me explain ...'

'I'm busy.'

'You're bloody obstinate. I told Cam you wouldn't listen,' he sighed.

I flopped down into Ken's chair, 'How's your dad?'

'He's fine, taking things very slowly, but Miriam is going to keep an eye on him for me, she's...' he hesitated for a second, 'my ex-wife.'

I exhaled loudly and nodded towards the window where I could see Ken's silhouette lighting another cigarette, 'Fire away, he'll be a while.'

Stan leaned awkwardly against the wall and began to talk, while I crossed my arms over my chest and tried to ignore the fact he still looked utterly gorgeous.

'Miriam and I started going out with each other at school, split for a bit when I went to college, then picked up again when I came home to see Dad. I honestly think we would have drifted apart but during my last year at university, I got her pregnant.'

'So you did the decent thing?'

'Of course, but a week after the wedding she miscarried. Then she miscarried again a few months later, and then again a third time the next year. The rot began to set in and we did nothing but argue, so when I got offered a job in The Philippines, I took it in the hope that a change of environment would make things better. It didn't. She hated every moment of it, so we went back home. When another job abroad came along, she wouldn't come, she said she would rather stay in Australia and work locally.'

'And that didn't appeal to you?'

'C'mon Alex, you know it wouldn't have done. We just got into this habit. I'd go off for a month here and a month there. Gradually the contracts got longer and trips home got shorter. If it wasn't work, I always managed to find a charitable cause that needed my attention. She didn't want to upset my dad, or her parents, so we just played the happy couple.'

'How happy?'

'If you're asking about sex, she went off the whole thing after the third miscarriage, so I started to have the odd fling here and there, never asked what she got up to, and before you know it, we had been married twenty-five years.'

''Why did you never call it a day?'

'We spoke about splitting up loads of times but never really got around to it. I think it always suited me because I knew somebody was there for Dad, and she never complained. I paid all the bills and stuff. I suppose she just became a glorified housekeeper.'

'But why didn't you tell me this in the beginning?'

'Because when I first met you, I didn't know where it was going. It could have just been another fling. In all honesty, I felt a bit of a dick about the whole thing. How d'you explain a stupid situation like that?'

'You just have,' I said quietly, 'so what changed?'

'You know what changed. I realised we had something more going for us, so I was plucking up the courage to explain stuff to you when the shit hit the fan.'

'But why the divorce? Why now? What about your dad? Weren't you worried it might upset him?'

'It was he who encouraged me to do it. When it looked pretty critical, we had a heart to heart and I told him about you, and then he opened up about a woman that he once knew before my mum came along. It turns out he only married my mum because he got her pregnant with me. Talk about like father like son, eh? He said he always regretted letting this other woman go - she was the love of his life. When Mum buggered off, he tried to find her but she had married someone else. So he told me to get things sorted with Miriam and chase your tail till I caught you.'

'How did she take it?'

'She was relieved.'

This was all too freaky, 'She's either a saint or an idiot.'

'Or has somebody else,' he gave a wry smile. 'She's been having a long-standing affair with the local estate agent.'

'Good god,' I shook my head.

'It's all a bloody great mess really, isn't it?'

'And then again, you could be just talking a load of bollocks.'

'For Pete's sake Alex, give me a break woman.'

'I don't know Stan, I just don't know,' I put my head in my hands. 'I'm getting along with life just fine without you.'

He came and knelt down in front of me, 'But it was better with each other wasn't it? I know I disappointed you, I know I should have told you earlier, but now I've explained, can you please forgive me? I'm not a bad bloke – honest.' He held out a simply wrapped package, 'I got you a little present.'

I had a million questions running around in my head but before I had the chance to respond, the moment was lost, whipped from right under our noses. The door opened and Chloe ran in sobbing, 'Aunty Alex, don't be mad but Nat tripped Cam up by accident and he's hurt his ankle *really* badly.'

'Where is he, Chloe?'

'He's been taken to the doctors to have it x-rayed, Nat went with him.'

Everyone came running in, 'It'll be the surgery on *Espalter*,' said Fred, 'I'll go.'

'Me too,' squealed Bart.

'I've got a hire car here, c'mon.' Stan stood up and looked at me, 'We'll continue this chat later, okay?'

The moment he left, Chloe – a drama queen in training – totally inhaled the atmosphere, threw herself around my shoulders and wailed, 'We've ruined everything, if we hadn't gone rollerblading this would never have happened.' She looked up at me with big doe-eyes, 'Will I still be able to wear my dress?'

'Chloe you selfish little minx, leave your aunty alone, she has a lot on her mind at the moment,' Mel raised her eyes hopefully at me as she extracted her daughter from my person.

'You're damn right I have. I need to have a little chat with you lot.'

'I think just saying 'thank you' would be nice,' Mum pursed her lips.

Ken walked back in the door, 'Christ! What's happened now? It's like a bloody soap opera here.'

'It's Cam, he's hurt his leg rollerblading, and the way I'm feeling I may just hurt his other one.'

'You're a stroppy bitch, aren't you?' Ken sat down in front of me, 'If a bloke like that flew from the other side of the world to get back with me, I'd be thrilled. He's bloody lovely. You don't want 'im, I'll 'ave 'im.'

'Well said!' Mel glared at me.

'We just thought you'd be pleased,' said Beverley.

'We all agreed he deserved the chance to tell you his story,' Evie gave me a sanctimonious look.

'Don't forget he did hurt Alex,' Bubbles smiled at me protectively, 'and it's none of our business what she decides to do.'

'Thank you, Bubbles.'

'Although I do think you'd be mad not to give it another go.'

'Especially as you still have that smelly t-shirt of his stuffed down the back of the sofa,' Beverley piped up.

'We didn't do this lightly, Alex,' Mel said, 'but as you have said on many an occasions – you are crap at relationships. We didn't want to see another one go totally pear-shaped without giving it a fighting chance.'

'You have no staying power Alex, at the first sign of trouble you go running,' added my mum. 'Life's not perfect darling, and sometimes you have to accept that neither are most people.'

'He was married - let's not forget that little fact.'

'He's not now, so what are you going to do?'

'I don't know.'

'How about finishing my bloody make-up?'
'Sorry Ken.'

FORTY EIGHT

An hour later the boys returned with a hobbling Cam, complete with leg in plaster and crutches.

'I've fractured a bone in my ankle,' he looked at me sadly, and then whispered when Stan was out of earshot, 'am I in trouble?'

'I think if you weren't partially crippled already, you would have been in the next ten minutes, let's put it that way.'

'He rang me in a right state, Alex.'

'When?'

'The day after you put the phone down on him, he couldn't get through to you.'

'That would be because I had his number barred.'

Stan appeared by my side and I thrust my arms behind my back to hide the goose bumps that sprung up the minute his arm brushed mine.

'Anyhow, what are we going to do now? All that work for nothing,' I swiftly changed the subject.

'I'll do it,' said Bart.

'With the best will in the world Bart, that outfit will drown you, it needs someone as tall as Cam,' said Bubbles.

'That counts me out, too,' said Fred, his voice oozing relief, 'backing singing is one thing, but that – no way!'

'We'll have to leave it until next year,' Evie said as she patted Cam reassuringly on the back.

'Stephan wins again,' Cam looked down at his leg. 'I can't believe this has happened.'

'Sorry,' muttered Nat who had been hanging back in the corner.

'It's not your fault, Nat,' Cam cried, 'we were having a laugh. I was the one that was showing off.'

'Now, why doesn't that surprise me?' Fred sighed.

'Don't start, I feel like shit,' said Cam, 'I've ruined it for the lot of you, I'm sorry.'

'I'll do it.'

We all turned and looked at Stan, who nodded and repeated: 'I'll do it. I'm the same height as Cam, a bit bigger but not far off.'

'Are you sure about this? Do you realise what you have to do?'

'Prance around in a frock?'

'Erm, it's a bit more complicated than that. How are you on Beach Boy numbers? Well, tunes, we've changed the words.'

'I have to sing?'

'Yes, and it's not exactly a frock either. Will it fit him Bubbles?'

'It'll stretch.'

'C'mon, come and see what you've let yourself in for,' I led Stan into the dance studio and unveiled his outfit.

'Is that what I think it is?'

'Yep,' everyone else had filed in and was looking at him expectantly.

'Are you going to do it?' Cam grinned at him, 'Or are you too chicken?'

'No one calls me chicken, Fairycakes, of course I'm doing it.'

'Right, everyone, we've only got a few hours to get him up to speed on this,' everyone except Cam scurried off to get things organised.

'Where do you want me first?' A very nervous Stan clapped his hands together.

'We need to remove your body hair, Stan.'

'What?'

'Don't worry, even though I would personally like to rip every last one of your hairs out with hot wax,' I smiled as he winced, 'we'll have to shave you. There's a shower room up stairs on the left, I'll go and get some razors and see you in a few minutes.'

He disappeared and I turned to Cam, 'Are you okay, you must be in a huge amount of pain.'

'I'm okay, but really Moll – are you angry with me?'

I went over and gave him a kiss on the forehead, 'I don't know yet,' I smiled, 'but for the time being, he's only doing this to get back in my good books, and I for one, am going to enjoy every last agonising moment.'

Bart came mincing in, 'Where is our little starlet?'

'Perfect timing, Bart, there is a pile of razors in my make-up kit, could you grab them and take them upstairs to the shower room? Stan needs to be shaved all over.'

'And you want me to do it?' Bart gasped.

'I can't think of anyone better for the job.'

'You really are evil,' wailed Cam, nearly falling off the sofa, 'he'll die.'

'I know,' I smiled, 'a girl's got to have a little revenge.'

To give him his dues, despite the twenty agonising minutes he spent with every crack and crevice of his body being thoroughly scrutinised by Bart, Stan took everything we threw at him with great aplomb and patience. Finally he was sitting in the make-up chair in front of me and he didn't even complain when I produced a pair of tweezers and started plucking his eyebrows.

'You're loving this, aren't you?'

'Yup.'

'We do need to talk, Alex.'

'I know, but not now, I'm just about to plaster you with pink glitter; not exactly conducive to 'Where are we going in life?' conversations.'

'How about I take you out to dinner tomorrow?'

'Tonight might be such a life-changing experience it might not be me you want to take out to dinner tomorrow.'

'Alex,' he growled.

'Okay, dinner it is. Now, have you learned your song?'

'Nearly, have you opened your present?'

'Yes, thank you, it was very thoughtful.' I looked over to the hardback sitting on the window ledge. It was *Passionate Nomad: The Life of Freya Stark* by Jane Geniesse. I had to give it to the lad; he definitely 'got' me.

By ten o'clock everyone was nearly ready. All the other clients had been and gone and were now camping it up at restaurants and bars over Sitges. Mel had found a glittery dress and a wig and was letting Chloe make her up, and I have to say, my little protégée was doing a grand job.

I walked into the dance studio where Stan was being squeezed into his outfit. Cam was still stretched out on the sofa, 'He does make a frighteningly ugly woman doesn't he?'

'Cam, I would watch it if I were you, he might hit you with his handbag,' I chuckled.

Stan nearly lost his footing in his six-inch platforms, 'It's lucky I have a head for heights, how do you walk in these things?'

'I couldn't,' I smirked.

Bubbles pinned the last bits into place and Tony came in with the wig. Finally Stan turned and looked in the mirror, 'Jeez, now *this* would give my dad another heart attack.'

Two absolutely dire rehearsals later, it was time to go. I quickly changed into my blue gingham dress and brown plaited wig and as I buckled up my red sparkling shoes, Cam came hopping over on his crutches, 'Good luck Dorothy, I think you're going to need it.'

I looked up, 'He's dreadful isn't he?'

'He's trying his best.'

'I feel mean letting him do it; I don't want people laughing at him, or any of the others for that matter. Christ, I know how mums feel when their kids are appearing in the school play. I feel sick.'

'Moll, he'll be fine, just put a couple of stiff drinks inside him. He'll get high on the atmosphere – honestly.'

I produced a silver hip flask from my basket, 'I had already thought of that. I wish you could come, are you going to be alright?'

'I'll be fine. Your mum and Evie are staying to fuss over me. Now bugger off.'

'How are you feeling?' Even though Stan wasn't vaguely recognisable through the thick layers of make-up, I could see from his sheer stance alone, that he was nervous. His fists were clenched tightly around a can of beer that he was sucking from a straw as if it were the last drop of liquid on Earth.

'Great,' he lied. 'You look nice. I like the short skirt.'

'Where's Toto?' shouted Fred, adjusting his pink wig for the umpteenth time. Tony had styled their wigs into huge, over-sized buns that jiggled as they moved. The effect en masse was going to be great. Their outfits were comprised of the remnants of the pink latex, strips of pink leather and silver lamé – even Beverley was looking at herself in the mirror admiringly.

'They'll carry you through, don't worry,' I whispered to Stan, and gave him the hip flask. 'This will hit the spot.'

'What is it?'

'Cognac, here, let me open it,' I grabbed the straw from his beer and shoved it into the flask.

He took a deep mouthful and shook his head, 'Phew, that's strong,' then he tried to put the lid back on, but was thwarted in his attempt by the three-inch talons we had stuck on his fingers. 'How do you girls cope?

'We're just multi-talented, amazing creatures - that's all,' I smiled.

'I wouldn't be here if you weren't, Alex.'

A lump came from nowhere and screeched to a halt in my throat. All I wanted to do was throw myself into his arms and apologise for blanking him out of my life so readily, but luckily for me, all I had to do was take one step back and look at him. This was *so* not the moment for a tearful reunion. So I opened my basket and produced a lipstick, 'Come here and let me touch you up,' I winked. 'Anybody else in need of some attention?'

There was a chorus of 'Yes Alex' so I did the final checks before we all waved goodbye to Cam and got into the limousine I had booked to take us to the huge stage that had been set up near the church. We were going to travel in style. If nothing else, we'd do that.

FORTY NINE

By the time we reached the church, the procession had already passed and you could hear the tail end making its way through the streets of Sitges. A huge crowd had stayed to watch the next piece of entertainment. As he looked out the window, I could feel Stan's leg shaking against mine. I thrust the hip flask back at him, 'Time for another swig I think.'

'Oh my god,' groaned Beverley, 'what the hell are we doing?'

'Don't you start,' Stan handed the flask to her.

'Me next,' whimpered Fred, holding his arm out to Beverley.

Even Bubbles and Bart, both of whom usually had a moth-like attraction to the limelight, were uncharacteristically quiet.

'Alex, there are kids out there,' Stan look horrified. 'Are we going to get arrested?'

'They won't know what the hell you are! Don't worry; I doubt very much the police would even get it. Now stay in the car, finish the brandy, practise the song and I'll find out when you are on.' I leapt out of the limo and fought my way to the front of the stage where a number of Catalan dignitaries were seated at a table. I gave them the entry form out of my basket and they pushed a list towards me. The Academy was on last, just after Parrots Bar featuring Stephanie.

'Alex!' I turned around. Mel and the kids were waving and they came over, followed by Tony and Ian.

'How are they?'

My look must have said it all. 'The poor babies,' cooed Mel. 'Pablo and Nieves are over there.' I looked over to the church steps and there they were, blowing kisses excitedly.

Suddenly the PA system made a loud screeching noise that

caused us to jump out of our skins, and there was a loud roar as a presenter I recognised from the local *Maricell* TV station took to the stage.

'Look at all those cameras,' hissed Mel. 'They're bloody filming it.'

'Jesus,' I laughed nervously, 'we'd better not tell them.' Then I had a pang, 'Cam would have been in his element. Mind you, this probably means it's on live,' I sent him a quick text and walked back to the car as the first entry came on stage – a sad little creature in very bad drag, giving it Edith Piaf in what sounded like a Dutch accent. I consoled myself with the thought that at least we wouldn't come last.

As I opened the door, a burst of the criminally bad rendition of *Je Ne Regrette Rien* filled the car. 'Listen to that. Believe me, you have nothing to worry about.' The atmosphere seemed better than when I had left. The now empty hip flask had obviously calmed their nerves, plus the fact Bubbles was puffing away on a huge joint that was involving them all in a passive smoking sort of way.

'This is so Rock and Roll! We got the music, we got the drugs, now all we need is sex,' Stan slurred. 'Can I have Alex with you sex, I mean sex with you, Alex?'

Maybe not everybody was involved passively...

'Bubbles, please tell me you didn't let him have an actual puff,' I looked at her pleadingly as Stan dissolved into fits of laughter.

'Just a couple,' she winced. 'He said he wanted some.'

'And you lot didn't stop him? Shame on you. You know what her weed is like,' I desperately opened all the windows and found him a bottle of water.

Thirty minutes later, it was time to get a still very laid back Stan and very jittery Bart, Bubbles, Beverley and Fred to the stage. Stephanie was due to go on, and when the opening bars of *Diamonds are a Girl's Best Friend* started to peal out, we took our chance to file as inconspicuously as possible past the crowds of people whose eyes were all looking ahead. As Stephanie came out in a cloud of white feathers and diamanté, there was a huge roar.

'I thought you said he couldn't sing for toffee,' Beverley hissed at Bubbles.

I had to admit the singing lessons had obviously paid off and when a team of muscle built guys in gold shorts emerged and held Stephanie aloft, my heart started to sink. By the time we made it to the stage, all we could hear was rapturous applause as Stephanie and her boys took their bows.

Stan seemed rooted to the spot - his nerves had obviously come back. He turned to me and shook his head, 'I don't know if I can do this, Alex.'

'Yes you can, you big Aussie chicken,' a familiar voice rang out.

We turned to see Cam reclining in a wheelchair with Mum and Evie grinning behind him, 'No way was I going to miss this.'

'Where the hell did you get that wheelchair?'

'Isn't it marvellous?' Evie enthused. 'I stole it from the community centre on my way over.'

Cam wheeled himself over to Stan and nudged his legs, 'Okay chick-chick, are you going to win this or not?'

Stan grinned down at Cam, 'I'm going to give it a damn good try, Fairycakes.'

'Quickly, they're introducing you,' I squeaked.

He squeezed my hand and tottered off with the others as the Spanish presenter said something in Catalan.

'That's not an introduction,' Cam suddenly spun his wheels and rolled out onto the stage. He swiped the microphone off the very shocked presenter and shouted: 'And now, all the way from Down Under, we have the incredible, the fantastic, the very, very sexy – Rita Rabbit and the Love Beads who are here to sing their very special version of ... *Good Vibrations* ...'

There was screaming in the audience as they realised what had walked on stage - Stan was essentially a life-sized pink rabbit vibrator with his very own shaking string of 'love beads'. He turned and gave me one last glance as the music started, then the fear evaporated and in his own unique style he started to belt out our improvised words:

I - I love the rubber dress I wear.

And the way all that gel feels on my hair.

I - I hear the sound of a gentle buzz

It's time to send her sailing through the air….

Then the 'Love Beads' literally jumped and vibrated from side to side as they belted out the chorus:

I'm giving it good vibrations

I'm giving her excitations

Good, good, good, good vibrations ...

By the time Stan reached the last verse…

I - I have a set of special beads

That are there - to satisfy - all your needs

I - I know exactly what spots to reach

Just a couple of double AAs – I'm here to please.

…Stan had the crowd eating out of his hand, even those who just thought he was a very funny lady-man in a pink dress.

'He's pulled it off!' Cam had tears of laughter streaming down his face as Stan took yet another bow. 'I don't think I have ever heard anything quite like it in my life! It was like Les Patterson out there, and when he started dancing I thought I was going to piss myself. Look out here he comes.'

'Wasn't I a great vibrator?' He picked me up and spun me around.

'An absolute prize dildo, darling,' I laughed.

The four excited, sweaty, little 'Love Beads' ran out behind him. 'That was brilliant!' screamed Bart. 'They loved us. You were great Stan.'

'So were you lot,' he roared. 'Beverley, I thought you were going to shake yourself out of that costume.'

'I did,' Bubbles looked down at an exposed breast that was peeking out from a strip of latex.

'Can we do it again tomorrow?' Fred had adrenalin coursing through his veins, 'I loved that.'

'You never know, you might be doing it again in a minute if you win,' Cam laughed.

'Whatever! We've won anyway, just by getting out there and doing it,' he shook his head and started laughing. 'That was the biggest buzz,' and then laughed again, 'no, I was the biggest buzz.'

Bart held his arms out and said 'Group hug?'

'Oh for Pete's sake, Bart,' Cam leaned over the edge of his wheelchair and pretended to be sick.

There was a commotion behind us as all the other entrants started to file backstage, including Stephanie who hid his face behind his hand as he whispered something to his entourage who all sniggered. As I stared coolly at him, I felt Stan's arm slip around my shoulders.

I looked up at him and smiled, 'Don't worry; you're more of a woman than he'll ever be.'

'Darling, you say the nicest things.'

'Sssh,' said Cam, 'they're reading out the results.'

One by one, every act was called to the stage and congratulated. Eventually there were only two acts left; Stan and Stephanie. My heart was in my mouth as the presenter turned and beckoned them both on stage. Suddenly, she shouted to the crowd, turned to Stephanie and held her arm aloft. As the audience cheered, I looked at Cam and sighed 'Maybe next time.' He shook his head and nodded back to the stage, 'Look behind you – Stephanie came second – we've bloody won!' he shouted and nearly tipped his wheelchair over.

I let out a yell. The crowd was applauding madly but as Stephanie stalked off the stage and got closer, I saw something I wasn't ready for – his eyes were welling up and he looked totally crushed. 'Isn't this the bit where Dorothy goes back to Kansas?' he hissed as he pushed past me.

I watched him go and looked at Cam, 'That didn't feel as good as I thought it would.'

'Don't let it get to you; lover boy is just about to crucify our ear holes for a second time.'

I glanced back at Stephanie who disappeared into the night, then grinned at Cam, 'D'you wanna come out front and get the full impact?'

'Yeah!'

I grabbed the wheelchair and we careered down the ramp and pushed our way to the front. I looked up at Stan clumsily camping it up as only a straight man can, and realised that after years of wandering this planet alone, my moment had finally arrived - the one you dream of, hope for, hear about but deep down in your soul have secretly given up on. There in the middle of multi-coloured smoky madness, huge spinning glitter balls sending stripes of light bouncing off the sequins and PVC, as he looked down at me and blew a kiss, I knew I was gazing into the eyes of what other people call 'The One'. I suppose given my track record, I shouldn't have even been remotely surprised that my future soul mate was wearing more lipstick than me and at this present moment in time, had less body hair, but then as Stan went to take his final curtsey, I was shaken out of my girlish musings by the sight of him tripping on a wire and the roar of pain as he fell head first into the crowd.

FIFTY

On account of the fact that the two men I held most dear had both managed to fracture their ankles on the same day, for six weeks after Carnival I lived in what can only be described as invalid hell. Newspaper and cigarette runs, bathing duties, finding the remote control, phone chargers, books, hairbrushes, notepads, underpants - plus three meals a day and enough snacks to keep a Multiplex cinema audience munching for a month. Added to which I had to find time to fit work into the equation. It's enough of a challenge dealing with one man with a cold but two men with their legs in plaster? Nurses of the world – I salute you!

Luckily, by the first of April, the end was in sight and I accompanied the pair of them to the surgery on *Espalter* to have their plasters removed. After sitting in the crowded waiting room for what seemed like forever, a gruff looking nurse came out and gestured for one of them to follow her.

Cam and Stan looked at each other, hid their hands behind their backs and counted to three. Cam drew rock. Stan drew paper.

'You lose. Off you go then, Fairycakes, and don't cry when the nasty doctor cuts your leg open by accident.'

Cam hobbled off and I looked at Stan, 'How old are you?'

He put his arm around my shoulder, 'Sorry darling, it's been a long haul for you.'

I laughed slightly manically, 'You can say that again.'

'Well, at least we've had a chance to get things sorted out,' he brushed my hair back from my face and kissed my forehead.

Stan's enforced incarceration had meant plenty of time to talk – and boy had we talked. Stan was 'A Man with a Plan'. He was so determined to make things work between us; he was willing to curb his travels, find work in Spain and live a 'normal' life with me. For my part, I was so determined not to muck this up, that I had found myself nodding a lot, essentially agreeing with everything he said, and not voicing any concerns I had about his total change of lifestyle.

Stan still couldn't get over the fact that after spending a quarter of a century dangling from trees without incident, it was women's shoes that caused his downfall – a fact Cam took great delight in reminding him. Now he was gagging to get out there and start working again.

'I'll be able to start doing some bits and pieces in a few days; it'll be good to get outside again.'

'Stan, aren't you meant to carry on resting your leg, have some physiotherapy and take things slowly? Don't run before you can bloody walk.'

'Yeah, yeah, of course I won't do anything until I'm ready.'

Fat chance - he had already approached the local council about tree surgery work but he had done such a thorough job the previous year, they didn't need his services. So he spoke to Ben, who was only too happy to have such a knowledgeable 'assistant'. I was wary, but Stan seemed okay with it, and as he kept reminding me, it would be good not to have responsibility for a change. He could relax and enjoy a simpler life and spend plenty of time with me into the bargain.

Everything was going to be perfect. That was his Plan.

For the next two months everything did seem to be working out okay. Stan's leg healed remarkably quickly, as did Cam's, who he bullied into regular exercise routines. Stan and Ben worked well together, each benefiting from the other's expertise. Gardens in Sitges were now not only looking fantastic, they were pest free.

Mum had rented out her house in the UK and she and Evie were living in a fantastic old villa on the outskirts of Sitges. Even though they insisted they preferred to be away from the madding crowd, not many days passed without them coming into the Academy, which was fast becoming the little haven of happiness we had intended it to be. No two days were the same as every group of people that crossed the threshold was unique. The one thing that seemed to be guaranteed was the sound of laughter, apart from the melt-down moments that often happened in the kitchen, or as we now called it – Evie's therapy room. This little rabbi had created her own little synagogue. As a result of opening up all this pent up creativity and helping people see themselves as they really were, all it took was a combination of Evie's sympathetic face and a bowl of the *sopa del dia* to unleash the inevitable tears. It was a healing process and old wounds were being exposed. We all knew that when the usually open door was quietly shut, we had to keep our distance. But for the most part it was a riot, and the cherry arrived on top of the cake when Beverley came bouncing in one sunny June morning, clad in a white crop top and jeans and grinning from ear to ear.

'Guess what?' she sat on the edge of my desk.

'Laurence and Tanya have decided to move to the American Mid-West and become evangelist preachers?'

'Wish they bloody well would,' she shook her head vigorously. 'Think again.'

'The entire Hernandez-Cruz family has given up tomatoes?'

'Hernandez-Cruz family very relevant to what I'm just about to tell you,' she started waving her left hand about.

'Oh my god, you don't mean … ?'

'Yes, I'm going to be one of them! You are looking at the future Mrs Hernandez-Cruz!' she screamed. I jumped up and hugged her.

'Congratulations, babes; that is fantastic news. Is that the ring? It's exquisite.'

She was wearing the most beautiful antique pearl and diamond ring set into rose gold, 'Nieves gave it to him to give to me - it was her mother's,' her eyes welled up. 'I wore that other bloody great diamond for years and it meant nothing, but this …' she looked at her hand, 'means everything.'

Bubbles walked through the door, presumably straight out of bed. She was wearing a tatty old pair of jogging bottoms and a grubby vest that would never see white again.

'I'm getting married,' trilled Beverley who was far too

preoccupied to notice Bubbles' unkempt appearance.

'Again? You're a sucker for punishment, aren't you?'

'Bubbles!' I frowned at her.

'Just joking,' a flicker of a smile played across her lips, 'I'll be nicer when I've had coffee.'

'And a shower, Room 4 is empty,' I said chucking the key at her.

Totally unperturbed, she turned and walked out, 'Cheers, I had a bit of a Sitges night. What a blast! At least some of us are still out there doing it for the singletons.'

'God you're such an incurable romantic, Bubbles,' I shouted after her.

'I think she'd like to be,' sighed Beverley sadly.

'Yeah, you're probably right; same goes for a lot of people I suppose.'

'Well at least you have Stan,' she said airily. 'Hey, we're going to go up to a new urbanisation just outside Sitges. The houses all have the most amazing views. Why don't you come with us and have a look,' she gazed down at her ring again. 'I'm sure it won't be long before Stan pops the question.'

At that point a vast chasm opened up between Beverley and me. We may have been born on the same day, but we were opposite sides of the Aquarian coin. The blood in my veins ran suddenly cold. A horrible realisation began to sweep over me. If this lovely man – the one I called The One – did ask me to marry him, I wasn't convinced I'd say 'Yes', and as for moving into an urbanisation and doing the ex-pat thing - I felt sick.

'Are you alright, Alex?'

I turned and looked past Beverley to the *paseo*. Fred and Bart were walking along eyeing up passing joggers. I utilised the distraction. 'Now, here come two boys who love a bit of romance,' I prodded her brown belly, 'and even though it's early, I think a little celebratory Bucks Fizz is in order.' I nipped downstairs deep in thought. What the hell was wrong with me? Maybe it was about time I sought out a good therapist.

As it turned out, over the next few days I was to find out it wasn't just me who was feeling a bit unsettled. It started with a row about scrambled eggs. All I did was mention that I preferred mine softer than he did. I do have to admit at this point that the eggs in question were already on the toast. He had prepared them and I did push them away with *one of those looks*. But however much of a 'little madam' I was being, I wasn't prepared for the reaction that followed and the line I suppose I'd known was coming at some point. Having thrown both plates into the sink, Stan barged back into the lounge and hollered the worst thing possible, namely: 'I got bloody divorced for you.'

Red rag to bull…

'So, are you going to pull that little one out of the bag every time we have a disagreement? Am I going to have to feel eternally grateful because you finally had the guts to end a sham of a marriage? I didn't ask you to do that, did I? I was quite happy here, thank you very much, and now here you are ruining it, as all bloody men do. Every single bloody time…'

The Rant was upon me.

I won't bore you with the entire tirade; let's just say it was lengthy, high on drama queen, low on objectivity and sufficiently bad enough to ensure that for the next three days Stan and I barely uttered a word to each other, and when we did, it was to squabble about anything and everything: - wet towels left on the floor; who had finished the last of the toilet paper; the fact I'd thrown away a newspaper that he wasn't finished with - it was like living in a war zone.

When Cam took me for a coffee and gently announced he felt he should start looking around for alternative accommodation, I was horrified, but he insisted that it wasn't because he was unhappy; he just felt that Stan and I deserved more privacy. And so did he - especially with the summer and its various attractions looming. I argued that we could move into another apartment but he was adamant that it was he who should leave.

Stan didn't seem to take the news of Cam's forthcoming departure well, either. He started to get even grouchier and kept wandering off on solitary walks. The arms which usually offered reassurance and security suddenly stayed resolutely by his side. I found myself continually asking him what was wrong and getting snapped at.

I began to ponder whether Cam was the glue that bound us together. It was certainly down to his sterling efforts that we had got to this stage. Without him, it could well have been just a summer fling. Maybe we needed a third party, a kind of buffer to prevent either of us from having to face up to the fact that we couldn't do relationships? How the hell were we going to fare without him?

Tellingly, it was Cam I chose to discuss it with. Stan was working in a *masia* just outside Sitges, so I went to the Santa Maria to meet Cam for a quick lunch and poured my heart out.

'Oh, Moll, me leaving is not a problem, and you haven't done anything either,' Cam said reassuringly. 'You are just two very independent people getting used to each other.'

'You honestly think that is all it is?'

'Well, there might be a little more to it,' he fished around in his pocket and pulled out a crumpled piece of paper. 'Here's what's probably bugging him. I found it in the bin this morning.'

I took it warily. Our history regarding discarded notes wasn't good. I read it quietly. It was an official letter from the Canadian Forestry Commission offering Stan a one-year contract with immediate effect. Apparently spruce budworms were misbehaving in Quebec.

I was suddenly torn between my selfish desire to have him here with me, and the knowledge that whatever he had planned in his head, he was just going to get more and more frustrated. I'd be kidding myself if I thought this was going to be the only letter; there would be more offers in the future, each one reminding him of the work he was so passionate about. I folded it up and put it in my handbag.

'What are you going to do?' Cam looked at me sadly.

'I don't know.'

'This doesn't have to be your 'out' you know. You don't have to use this as yet another excuse for it not to work.'

'What d'you mean?'

'He didn't throw in the towel; he threw the letter in the bin. Not the act of a man who wants to lose you,' Cam said sternly. 'Don't do what I always do and sabotage it. Try going the extra half-mile for a change. Why do you think Enrique got so frustrated with me?'

'Because he was immature and couldn't handle you?'

'The reason he was so jealous and insecure is because I wouldn't give an inch. He wanted to play house and be in love and I just couldn't deal with it.'

'So he robbed you and beat you to a pulp!' I exclaimed.

'Latino temper, and as you know, I can be quite scathing when I choose to be. That night was no exception. I pushed quite a few buttons and then paid the price for it.'

'You never mentioned this at the time.'

'I couldn't see it at the time, but watching how you are with Stan is like looking in a mirror. You are more petrified of losing yourself than him, and I think he is exactly the same.'

'Where did you learn to be so wise?'

'Same place that you did. Long dark nights of the soul and all that shit,' Cam smiled. 'By the way, when was the last time you two had a romantic evening in?'

'I can't remember.'

'Well, maybe it's about time you did.'

After a bit of a manic morning at the Academy, I made my excuses and went shopping. I bought some beautiful fresh fish and vibrant salad, some of Stan's favourite wine and nipped in to see Nieves, who sent me home with a huge bag of sweet little tomatoes. I stopped off at the local baker and picked up a warm baguette and went home to prepare for the evening. The only way to know what was really going on in Stan's head was to talk to him. This didn't have to be a deal breaker, we were grown-ups who loved each other, weren't we?

Cam went off to the gym and was going straight out with Bart and Fred for the evening. He felt this was one night he should make himself a bit scarce, and for once I didn't argue. By eight o'clock everything was ready, including me. The fish was marinating, the salad prepared and the ultra dry *Petit Caus* was chilling in the fridge. Sex had trickled off at the same rate as our conversations of late, so I chose my outfit with Stan in mind. As he liked simple and elegant, I hoped a hip-hugging white Ghost dress that revealed more than a hint of cleavage would do the trick. But by nine o'clock, there was still no sign of him. I called his mobile and there was no answer, so I had a glass of wine and sat on the balcony. By ten o'clock I had finished the first bottle and by eleven I was well into the second and he still wasn't answering his phone. I lay on the sofa and worried. This wasn't like him.

'Hey, wake up.'

I shot up, the room was in darkness and I was still on the sofa.

'C'mon, Moll, go to bed, you're freezing.'

I looked blearily up at Cam, 'Stan didn't come home,' I whimpered, 'I hope he's okay.'

'He'll be alright. C'mon, it's way past three,' he held my hand and pulled me up. Suddenly there was the sound of a car door slamming outside. I rushed over to the balcony and there was a taxi pulling away, leaving a very shaky Stan staggering towards the building.

'Somebody is going to get his butt kicked,' hummed Cam.

'I'm just glad he's okay. Don't worry - I'll kill him tomorrow. No point now, he won't feel a thing.'

'Hello ladies!' Stan's voice bellowed up from below.

'Ssh! You drunken idiot,' I leaned over the balcony and hissed.

'Are you waiting up for me with your rolling pins?' He tripped over the pavement. 'Hey Fairycakes, you keeping my woman company?'

'I'll go down and get him,' Cam sighed, 'he's not going to manage to negotiate the front door, let alone the stairs.'

Two minutes later, Cam came tottering into the apartment with Stan hanging around his neck. His eyes were bloodshot and he had red wine stains down his shirt.

'Straight into bed with you, I think,' I muttered, ushering them towards the open bedroom door.

'I'm alright,' slurred Stan. 'I am my own man. I can do exactly as I want – or at least I used to be able to.' He toppled diagonally onto the bed and after mumbling a load of unintelligible mumbo jumbo to himself, he passed out.

Cam and I tried to get him out of his clothes but it was futile - he was a dead weight - so we pulled his boots off and left him to it. I looked at Cam, 'He used to be able to do what he wants, eh?'

'He's drunk, Alex.'

'*In vino veritas*. Anyhow, it's not your problem, go to bed,' I kissed him on the forehead and went and sat on the sofa and gazed out into the darkness. The gentle sound of the sea lapping against the sand lulled me into a meditative state. I felt my eyes flicker shut then gave in to the images whizzing through my mind.

FIFTY ONE

The sound of a mosquito buzzing around my face woke me the next morning. I was fully clothed and still on the sofa – a sure sign of a night gone wrong. I stood up and stretched then peered outside. The beach was empty save for a few dog walkers and joggers. I slipped out onto the balcony, disrobed and grabbed some tracksuit bottoms and a vest from the clean washing pile. I looked around and spotted one of Stan's sweatshirts. I pulled it on and padded into the bathroom. After cleaning my teeth, splashing my face with cold water and pulling back my hair into a ponytail, I felt a bit more human. As I grabbed my shades from the hall table I looked into the bedroom. The shutters were drawn and I could hear his gentle snoring. Resisting the temptation to slide onto the bed and snuggle up to his warm back, I slid into my flip flops and closed the front door behind me.

Outside the air was fresh. I contemplated walking to the *Terramar*, but pretty soon the regular jogging crew would be out and I needed a bit more solitude, so I headed past the cemetery towards the nudist beach which was empty and quiet. Maybe here would be a good place to strip bare what was going on? The sand was damp and the wind whipped around my face so I found a little cove in the rocks and huddled inside. As I gazed out to sea the tears started to roll down my face. It just wasn't working; Stan was like a caged animal. It didn't seem right, that considering I was someone who held so close to my heart the idea of living the life you were born to live - that I was now the reason somebody else wasn't. But I didn't want to lose him either.

I heard the sound of footsteps crunching in the sand and froze. They got nearer and as I looked up, I was staring into an unmistakeable face behind the D&G shades – it was Stephan. We hadn't seen each other since Carnival and he was the last person on Earth that I expected, or indeed wanted, to see.

'Hiding away from the world are we?' He leaned on a rock.

'Yep, and that includes you; especially you.'

Much to my astonishment, rather than hit back with some venomous remark, he plopped down onto the sand beside me, 'I followed you here.' He took his shades off and studied my face, 'You looked so sad.'

'So you thought you'd come and gloat?'

'No, I've wanted to talk to you for a while now,' he paused, 'I want to apologise to you.'

'To me? For what?'

'I have been horrible to you since you arrived here, very bad in fact, and though it pains me to say it, you have done some amazing things. I've never seen anyone cause such a shake-up in this town as quickly as you have. The Academy is fantastic! When I went to see it that night, I had intended to talk to you then, but Fred was there and …'

I eyed him warily, waiting for the sting in the tail.

'I was jealous,' he shrugged. 'I couldn't bring myself to say 'sorry'. Everybody loves Alex - you can't put a foot wrong. Me, I get paid to be a bitch, it's how I get by.'

'Well you're a bloody good one I'll give you that Stephan, Stephanie? Whoever?'

'Stephan,' he hung his head and sighed, '... who hides behind Stephanie.'

'We all hide Stephan, why d'you think I'm curled up behind a rock at six o'clock in the morning?'

'My rock.'

'Pardon?'

'This is where I come when I want to think things through.'

'Oh Christ, I've even managed to muscle in on this as well, eh?'

'You're welcome,' he lit a cigarette and looked out to sea. 'I have been in this town since the 80s you know. I've seen so many people come and go - all running from something. Some people work it out but the majority don't. I have wondered from time to time, what was it you were running from, Alex?'

'Normality, convention, a failing career; I came here to sort my life out and break away from the mindless rat race I was becoming absorbed into in the UK. What drew you here?'

'I was brought up in Croatia, or Yugoslavia as it was then. When I was very young and stupid I had an affair with an extremely important man. He was very high up in the military when I met him - wife, children – the consummate family man,' he laughed ironically. 'Amazing what people will risk for a piece of ass. In my innocence, I really thought he loved me. But he was a very ambitious man, and politically things were starting to change. Looking back, I realise he saw opportunities for himself that would have been wrecked had there been any sort of scandal. So one day, without warning, I was given a wad of money and a ticket to Spain with the strict instructions that if I were ever to set foot back in the country, my family would suffer the consequences. I was eighteen.'

'How did you end up here?'

'Homing instinct I suppose. I started out in Madrid and then followed the parties to Barcelona – you've got to remember that before Franco died in '75, the gay community had to be very clandestine and under cover in Spain. I arrived as the whole thing went mad. We were all caught up in this hedonistic, rebellious Cultural Revolution. It was so exciting and so different from my life back home.'

'Wow!' I sighed, 'What a story!'

'Alex, I have a confession that I need to get off my chest. D'you remember the night I gave you the note?'

'How could I forget? My life fell apart that night, although I have to say, at the time, I felt vaguely grateful to you.'

'I wasn't really visiting a friend in those apartments.'

My heart started to pound.

'I saw your man walking home and I followed him. I was going to see if I could – how shall I put it? Persuade him to have a little fun.'

'But why on Earth would you do something like that?'

'To hurt you, Alex, to have one up on you, but I didn't need to. I found that note and realised that this time the girl wasn't going to get the boy. This time the girl was going to know exactly how I have felt, time and time again. All I had to do was be the messenger.'

Relieved as I was, I still choked up, 'But why me, Stephan, I don't understand? I came here with an open heart and I never intended to hurt anyone or tread on anybody's toes but right from the word 'go', you hit out at me. All I ever did was fight back.'

'Because you did inadvertently steal what was mine; or at least what I wanted. He adores you.'

The penny dropped.

'Oh my god, this is about Cam, isn't it?'

He nodded, 'I had always felt there was a common bond of some sort but he's always been a very guarded person when it comes to anything personal. He keeps everyone at bay, and then you arrived, and suddenly Alex and Cam were inseparable. I couldn't get near him any more and the more I saw you out and about together, the more spiteful I felt towards you.'

'But you're not even each other's type are you?'

'Oh Alex, It's not about being lovers. I want him as a friend. I have no friends.'

'And there I was thinking it was all to do with that stupid Carnival.'

'Oh that didn't help. Cam dragging up very badly was always amusing and then you totally changed that. Cam deserved to win last year but I just wasn't ready to give in gracefully. What else have I got in my life? And now this year – beaten by a straight man! Where do I go from here – a washed-up, tired old drag queen without a crown? Well, you certainly showed me, didn't you?'

'I'm sorry Stephan.'

'Sorry? Don't be sorry Alex. You got them both; the type of man I would kill for and the friend I would die for. You deserve it. You are one of life's good people. I, on the other hand, am not. I have never understood why you didn't spread that story about me and Jorges over town – I spread stuff about you that wasn't even true half the time.'

'Oh, don't read too much into that, Stephan, I wasn't being noble, I was holding it up my sleeve in case I needed it.'

'But, *cariña* you didn't use it, did you? No matter how many dreadful things I did, you never dropped down to my level. I think that made me hate you even more.'

'I've never been that keen on you either.'

We both smiled sadly.

'But you are here today crying, which means maybe even when you have it all, things are not always perfect?'

I looked at him mistrustfully.

'Alex, I have just told you things about me that nobody else knows. I have admitted to you that I intended to hurt you and I have apologised. If you don't want to confide in me I totally understand, but please do not let it be because you feel you cannot trust me. I'm as tired of this as you are.'

'It's not working out,' I blurted, 'because me having it 'all', as you like to put it, is at someone else's expense.'

'But Stan loves you?' Stephan's face reflected genuine concern.

'Yes he does, but in a way that's the problem - he also loves his work and he's had a great offer that he's refused. He's only staying here for me and I know he will end up resenting it. How can I sit back and watch him pretending to be happy when I know his passion lies elsewhere? I'm in a no-win situation. I can't just bugger off and let Beverley down. Mum's living here now as well. I love Stan dearly but that doesn't stop me having other people to consider.'

'At what cost to you? Alex, now I see your real issue,' sighed Stephan, 'I think before you start worrying about everybody else, you ought to think about what you really want out of life. That is what you came here for, wasn't it?'

'But Stan …'

'… is a grown man who made a decision to come and live here with you, and from what I understand you didn't exactly hold a gun to either your mum's or Beverley's head either. You are not responsible for them - but you have a responsibility to yourself to lead an authentic life and be who you really are.' Stephan jumped up, shaking the sand from his trousers. I went to get up but he shook his head, 'No stay.' He rummaged in his jacket pocket and pulled out a bar of chocolate that he chucked at me, 'A little sugar to sweeten your own medicine.'

I laughed and looked up at him; he was silhouetted against the blue sky looking like some Egyptian prince.

'I like you better without make-up; you're actually a very handsome man.'

A rare smile spread across his face.

'In fact,' I squinted up at him, 'I think it's about time Stephan stepped out into the sunlight and left Stephanie in the shadows where she belongs. Maybe it's about time that you be who you really are too.'

He held his hand out to me, 'Friends? Or is that too much to ask?'

I put my hand in his and squeezed it, 'I think it's about time you had one.'

He squeezed mine back.

'Stephan, have you ever been back to see your family?'

'My parents both died in the 90s and I've lost touch with my sister. I think she lives somewhere in Dubrovnik. We never got on anyway.'

I smiled at him sadly; then with a toss of his raven mane, he was gone.

FIFTY TWO

I leaned back against the hard rock, ate the chocolate and thought long and hard about what Stephan had said. He was right; I hadn't encouraged Mum or Beverley to come here, or Stan for that matter - I wasn't responsible. So, if I took everyone else out of the equation for five minutes, how authentic was I being? Was I where I wanted to be in life?

I knew the answer already; I wasn't. Despite living in a beautiful beachside paradise with money in my pocket and a man who loved me, a life that most people would give their right arm for, something was still so seriously lacking it was driving me nuts. I had to get to the bottom of it before I started making any grand decisions about the future.

My mobile beeped. It was Mum. One of her young was suffering and she was obviously picking up the vibes? Yeah right! I read the text, *Alex; I've just unpacked a box full of your stuff. If you don't come up and get it soon it's going in the bin.*

Life wasn't giving me any answers, a cold wind was whipping up and I certainly wasn't ready to go home, so I decided to wander up to see Mum and Evie. Little did I know as I huffed and puffed my way up to their house in *Valpineda*, that the powers that be 'upstairs' were tuned in and working in very mysterious ways.

I decided to keep quiet about my dilemma as I couldn't be doing with any drama, so we had a cup of coffee together and they left me to it whilst they went shopping. They had a covered veranda which led onto the garden so I took the box that had been sitting in Mum's loft for years and started to unpack the contents onto the large stone table. There were a few old books I hadn't looked at in ages; all self-help books of some description, obviously all bought during some other attempted period of self-discovery and finding my 'power within'. Well, they hadn't exactly worked had they?

As I started to chuck the unwanted books in the bin, I found a copy of *The Artists Way* by Julia Cameron – *A Course in Discovering and Recovering your Creative Self.* It struck a subliminal chord so I sat down and started to leaf through the pages.

Now I'm sure Julia would shake her head in despair if she knew how quickly I sped read her 12-week course. This wasn't a slow burn approach to releasing suppressed creativity. It was a short, sharp shock that somehow shook me out of my slumbers. Her words punctured my consciousness like arrows. Pretty soon I was so full of 'holes' you could have strained your tea through me. I'd had a mental, emotional and spiritual 'colonic' courtesy of Julia Cameron and I had to share it with somebody so I called Cam.

'Molly where are you?'

'At Mum's. Is Stan awake yet?'

'Nope, he's still out for the count.'

'Serves him right. D'you fancy a coffee at Picnic?'

'Sure.'

'Cam, there's a red bag under your bed, can you bring it?'

'I don't have a red bag.'

'I know, it's mine, I hid it there.'

'What's in it?'

'You'll see.'

Cam was already sitting at the beach bar when I arrived. I plopped myself down next to him. He was nursing the bag, 'I've ordered you a *cortado*. Can I open the bag now?'

'You mean you haven't already?'

'I'm offended, how can you even suggest such a thing?'

'Did you?'

'Of course,' he grinned impishly, 'but what on Earth were you thinking hiding your journals in my room,' he tipped the red notepads out onto the table with a flourish. 'Weren't you worried I'd clean under my bed and find them?'

'YOU clean under your bed?'

'Good point.'

'Would you have a look at them for me now?'

'You're letting me read them?'

'Just have a quick flick through. Most of it is a load of nonsense but I'm intrigued to know your reaction.'

Cam picked one up and went to open it as the coffee arrived. A sudden wave of self-consciousness washed over me, 'No, wait a minute, let me drink this first and then I'll wander around for a while and leave you to it. I don't want to watch your face.'

'Why don't you just go home?'

'Not yet, I need to get my head around something before I see Stan,' I downed my coffee and stood up. 'I'll be back in a while.'

I wandered around the *pueblo* deep in thought. Stan tapped into my nomadic, adventurous side, but when it came to my more artistic leaning, it was Cam who I related to. If anyone would get where my mind was currently heading it was him. I wondered anxiously what he would make of my scribbles. After about an hour, a text came through from him telling me to return. When I arrived at Picnic my journals were sitting neatly in a pile next to a bottle of cava and two glasses. I sat down and looked at him quizzically, 'Well?'

'Firstly Moll, I now know for sure that you are a deranged lunatic with deep psychological issues, you're quite a bitch on the quiet and your 'v's and 'r's look identical,' he popped the cork, 'but I also know why you look so relaxed when you are curled up with a pen in hand and one of these ...' he nodded towards the journals and pushed a glass towards me. 'It's because deep in that little soul of yours you are a writer.'

'Thank you Cam. I really needed to hear that,' my eyes welled up. 'I did have a dream of doing exactly that, but somewhere along the way I forgot to do anything about it.'

'I only skimmed the surface really but from the bits I read, Moll, I can't believe you've never realised this before.'

'I forgot I had a story - well, lots of stories.'

'You certainly couldn't make the majority of this up, that's for sure,' he laughed, 'but why is this so important now?'

I told him about the conversation with Stephan and the book I'd read. He listened quietly and kept nodding to himself. Finally he spoke, 'When you first came here I told you that people come here, heal and move on, or stay and help other people do it.'

'Yes.'

'I never saw you as one of the ones who would stay, not because you're selfish or unwilling to help, quite the reverse. But it stops YOU from shining. I was wondering when you would finally get that pouring all your energy into other people is just one bloody great distraction. You should be out there doing your own thing.'

'Is that why you didn't want to teach at the Academy?'

'Partly; and partly because I would feel like a fraud.'

'You are anything but a fraud, Cam Ferguson.'

He smiled, 'C'mon, you need to head home. I think you're due a little chat with Mr Berringer. Who knew Stephan would have helped you clear your head? Wonders will never cease.'

'He's actually really nice, Cam, and he needs a few friends right now.'

'See, you just can't help yourself, can you? Stop it Moll. You haven't got time to worry about him; you need to make a few decisions.'

'Alright,' I laughed and dialled Stan's mobile. He answered drowsily, 'Hey babes, how much shit am I in?'

'None whatsoever, but we do need to have a little team talk.'

'Come and snuggle in with me, I want a cuddle.'

'I'll be back in five.'

FIFTY THREE

The setting sun was turning everything rosy pink by the time Stan and I eventually showered and dressed – a combination of great sex and reluctance on both our parts to actually initiate The Talk. Stan went and opened the bottle of vintage red we had been saving for a special occasion and I slung a few olives in a bowl and made some bruschetta with the loaf I had bought the night before. As I was rubbing garlic onto the toasted bread, Stan came up and put his head on my shoulder. I turned and kissed him on the cheek. Just looking at his face made my throat constrict and my eyes well up. I didn't want this to be the end.

'Hey, don't cry. Oh shit, I'm sorry I've been a bit difficult lately. It's just that ...'

'I've read the letter.'

'What have you been doing? Rummaging through bins?'

'No, Cam has.'

'That boy needs a new hobby,' Stan joked half-heartedly as he grabbed a plate and led me onto the balcony where Pete's leaves were swaying in the gentle sea breeze. We flopped down into the comfortable chairs and looked at each other, and then Stan spoke.

'Look, it was only an offer Alex. I get them all the time.'

'Would you have gone if it wasn't for me?'

'I suppose so, but ... I'm here now.'

'And bored shitless,' I raised my eyebrows at him.

'Maybe I do need to look for other work,' he slugged back a large mouthful of wine.

'Brilliant, then we can start looking for a nice big house further up in the hills, lots of socialising with the neighbours, dinner parties and barbeques – we'd have the perfect life.'

He looked at me with a bewildered expression on his face.

'But we'd end up killing each other,' I smiled. 'Look Stan, I fell in love with the whole man, not the diluted version I'm dealing with now. I never asked or expected you to give up what you love; you decided to do that in a misguided attempt to give me what you thought I wanted.'

'You don't?'

'No, but I just didn't speak up. I had a strong inkling that it maybe wasn't the best route for us, but I was too afraid of losing you again. And I suppose I just keep looking at everybody in 'happy' conventional relationships and hoping some bloody magic switch will suddenly click and I'd get 'it'. But we're not 'everybody' are we? Our switch isn't the same as theirs?'

'We wouldn't be together if it was Alex.'

'So, look at me straight in the eyes and tell me you think that staying here is going to work for us?'

He looked down and sighed, 'But you have a life here, the Academy, all your friends ...'

'My friends will always be my friends. The Academy has helped and continues to help people find direction and yes, I'm proud of my contribution to it. I loved being part of the whole creative process but my job is done - d'you know how I spent my day yesterday?' My voice went up a few octaves and sounded like my Mum's suddenly, 'I gave a make-up lesson to a painfully shy cross-dresser who wanted to look like Margaret Thatcher!'

Stan tried unsuccessfully to suppress a grin.

'He was twenty-five stone and as hairy as hell,' as he dissolved, I carried on, 'I then spent two hours scouring the Academy for a lost handbag that one of the Spanish dancing clients had supposedly left behind, made the mistake of mentioning 'El Phantom' on her eighth call...'

'El Phantom?'

'The friendly ghost, anyhow, she now thinks I'm loco, as she very quickly pointed out when she called back a ninth time to say that she had found her handbag in the boot of her car. I then had to deal with a Bubbles tantrum as Fred had used something from her store cupboard for a collage he was doing with one of his groups, and process bookings, change people's hotels, and run around the *pueblo* buying up water as our delivery didn't turn up - all the stuff that keeps it running smoothly and ensures that everyone is happy - necessary stuff. But all I keep doing is giving out and I know from previous experience, it will wear me down and I won't be as enthusiastic anymore. I'm not really a natural organiser; I'm good at the ideas bit.'

'You sound like you've been thinking about this for a while,' Stan reached out for my hand.

'Not that long, in fact believe it or not it was Stephan who made me realise a few things this morning.'

'Stephan?'

'Yeah, we bumped into each other on the beach and reached, how shall I put it - an understanding.'

'So, what was this revelation of yours?'

'That in the same way I've been getting a diluted you, you haven't been getting the whole *enchilada* with me.'

'Sounds worrying,' he beckoned for me to sit on his lap, 'so come and tell me about these bits of Alex Chapman I know nothing about.'

When Cam came in from the bar at four am we were still there chatting. Stephan had been right. Whether or not you identify with the term 'soul mate', Stan and I were sufficiently in synch with each other's dreams and aspirations to arrive at the same conclusions and loved each other enough to have the confidence to explore certain avenues. Cam made coffee and came and sat whilst we outlined our plans to him.

'If you two are happy, then I'm happy,' he sighed, 'and I suppose in some weird way it does make perfect sense to me. When are you going to tell Beverley?'

'Tomorrow,' I took a deep breath, 'I hope she'll understand.'

'She's a friend, of course she will,' said Stan reassuringly.

'Once she gets used to the idea of not having you around,' I could see Cam's eyes glistening in the early morning light.

'C'mon time for bed,' Stan stood up and stretched.

'I'm just going to sit here for a while, it's a lot to take in,' Cam poured himself another coffee and smiled up at me. I bent down and kissed him, 'Just be sure you don't fall asleep here. D'you want me to sit up with you for a while?' Cam shook his head.

'You're such a little mother hen,' Stan gave me a gentle tap on the bottom and tweaked Cam's ear, 'Night FC.'

As we snuggled up in bed, I turned to Stan, 'I've just had a great idea.'

'Another one? Alex, please can't it wait until the morning.'

'It is the morning, listen to this.'

He had to admit, it was a great idea.

*

'I'll come back and run courses for you from time to time, we'll email each other and Skype, and …'

'Alex,' Beverley put out her hand to stop me gabbling, 'Stop feeling so guilty. It's not wrong to think about your own happiness. Heaven's above, there's plenty of people out there who think about nothing else.'

'I know, it's just difficult letting people down, and you only got behind this because of me.'

'Bullshit, I did this for me. You'd be letting yourself down if you didn't do this, if …' she paused for effect, '… this is what you want to do?'

'It is. I know it might seem a bit odd to you, but then maybe Stan and I are odd people.'

'You're your own people,' she smiled, 'but I do have one request.'

'Shoot.'

'Pablo and I had two dates for the wedding based on the availability of the church, one was in eight months, and the other was in one month. Will you stay for another four weeks?'

'Beverly I'll stay as long as you need and I will come back in eight months, so don't rush your wedding plans just for me.'

'Yeah, but I will have my work cut out in eight months, I mean, two-month-old babies can be quite a handful.'

'What!! You're frigging pregnant? Congratulations! Wait a

minute, you just said babies, as in plural?'

'Twins again - isn't it amazing? Pablo is beside himself. It's been so difficult keeping it a secret, but it's such a miracle, I just didn't want to tempt fate. You're the first person I've told.'

'Oh my god, well then the last thing you really need is my other little request.'

'Oh no,' she gushed, 'I think it's an amazing idea, and as you have four weeks then maybe you could spend a little time getting a certain little someone up to speed with how we run the place?'

'Of course,' I hugged her, 'thank you for being so understanding.'

'Hey, I'm the happiest I've ever been in my life, and in the same way that you can't keep Stan from what he loves doing, I can't hold you back either. I think you've done your time on the helping other people front. One more thing before you go?'

'Anything'

'Will you be a Godmother to the bumps?' Beverley patted her slightly rounded belly.

'I would be thrilled,' I bounced off in search of Fred. I had a very important job for him to do.

FIFTY FOUR

'What do you think he'll say when he sees that?' Stan and I stood outside on the steps of the Academy which was bathed in a deep pink glow courtesy of the most fantastic sunset I had ever seen.

'I really don't know, but I couldn't leave Sitges without doing this,' I looked over at the large white sign that had been planted into the grass.

Images of Sitges - An Exhibition by Cameron Ferguson – Private Viewing Tonight - Invited Guests Only

I didn't have long to wait for a reaction, as two minutes later I caught sight of him and Stephan walking along the *paseo*. Since I had invited Stephan around to dinner one night and we had laid any previous animosity to rest, he and Cam had been seeing quite a bit of each other. Cam saw me and waved, Stan darted indoors, 'Better go and warn everyone.'

I had told Cam we were having a pre-wedding cocktail party for Beverley and Pablo, so he didn't suspect a thing. As he approached the stairs, I instinctively stood in front of the sign, 'Hello darling, everything ready?' he went to hug me and then craned his neck to look behind me. I stepped back and his face dropped, 'What's this? Moll, what have you done?'

'Just go in, Cam, just go and look,' I opened the door and bit my lip.

'He'll be fine *cariña*,' Stephan nodded as he pushed Cam through the door.

'I hope so,' I muttered as I followed them in.

There was a round of applause as Cam walked into the reception and looked around him. His pictures were everywhere: small sketches cleverly mounted with oversized frames, watercolours, charcoal drawings, bold pictures in bright acrylics. Fred had worked day and night for the past two weeks and his brilliant framing and mounting had enhanced Cam's work perfectly. Everyone stood back as Cam walked silently from room to room taking it all in. Finally he walked back towards me, his face deadly serious, then he grinned, 'Call this a preview? Where's my glass of cava?'

'Just coming Cam,' I clapped my hands together and squealed with pleasure. The relief flooded over me in waves, although I still had one more surprise up my sleeve.

Stan walked over, 'Well done Fairycakes - you can certainly handle a pencil well, that's for sure.'

'I can handle a lot of things well, Stanley, it's just that you won't let me.'

'You'd have a bit of trouble if you started any of that nonsense.'

I laughed and caught Stephan's gaze for a split second. He smiled in acknowledgement.

Later when everyone was leaving, an exhausted but very jubilant Cam flopped down on one of the sofas, 'Beverley looks amazing pregnant, doesn't she? She just glows. She bought five of the watercolours, and so did your mum, who I have to say is being very stoic about your imminent departure. She actually thinks you're doing the right thing.'

'Wonders never cease, do they?' I smiled, 'You sold twenty-eight pictures actually.'

'I don't believe it,' Cam shook his head in amazement. 'Who bought that big one? That had 'sold' on it when I arrived.'

We looked over to the painting of the Sitges church that I had used on the invitations.

'Oh that was bought by someone who couldn't come, but they sent a letter and a cheque of course,' I handed over a blue envelope that had been waiting in my handbag for this moment to arrive.

Cam grabbed it and his face started to crumble as he recognised the spidery handwriting. He looked up at me and gasped, 'You sent an invite to my parents?'

'Yes,' I whispered nervously, 'I found the address in your diary.'

'I agreed she should do it,' Stan had been hovering in anticipation. 'Maybe you ought to read the letter, Cam?'

'I can't do it.' He thrust the letter at me and put his face in his hands. Stephan came and sat next to him.

'Okay,' I cleared my throat and began …

Dearest Cameron

Words cannot express the joy we felt when we received your invitation, even though we realise it was not your decision to send it.

Not a day has ever gone by without wondering where you are, hoping you are well and regretting how things were left between us. I can only, as a father, implore you to get in contact so that this dreadful situation can be remedied.

Your beautiful picture will take pride of place in the house but I hope from the bottom of my heart that you will arrive with it.

I am organising my usual exhibition of local artists in the autumn and would be honoured if you would agree to let me show some of your new work, as your 'A' Level course work is looking a little tired and as good as it is, I think people are getting a little bored of seeing it rolled out every year.

I will totally understand if you choose to ignore this letter, and will respect your wish to maintain no contact with us, but both your mother and I ask from the bottom of our hearts to be forgiven, or at the very least, be given the opportunity to make things right.

Our love and prayers always,

Your very proud parents

Mum And Dad

By the time I reached the bottom of the page, the tears were rolling down my cheeks, and I could hear Cam sobbing quietly. Even Stan was glassy-eyed.

'It's your shout mate,' he patted Cam's back.

'But don't wait until it's too late,' added Stephan quietly.

'I hope I haven't done the wrong thing, Cam,' I looked imploringly at him. 'I just hated the idea of you regretting something for the rest of your life.'

'Don't worry Moll; I would have got around to it eventually.

Don't mind me; it's just the initial shock of realising they still care.'

'Of course they do, Cam, they just made mistakes like we all do.'

'So the Prodigal Son is going to return in a blaze of watercolour glory.' He wiped his eyes but it was a momentary respite. His chest heaved again as fifteen years worth of pain hurtled to the surface.

FIFTY FIVE

'She does make a fantastic fairytale princess, doesn't she?' I stood with Mel and Stan beaming stupidly at Beverley in her pale pink meringue.

'I never knew Bubbles had that kind of dress in her,' Mel shook her head, 'mind you, look what she did with the bridesmaids.'

Bubbles had decided that Beverley's wedding would be a good excuse for a Love Beads reunion, so along with Fred and Bart, who I have to say, were being very sporting about the whole thing, Bubbles was wearing a pink latex halter neck with matching pink wig. Pablo had totally got into the camp spirit and was currently having his picture taken with Fred and Bart, much to the astonishment of his Catalan relatives who were adopting a slightly stand-offish approach to the whole affair - apart from Nieves of course, who was muscling in on every photo possible.

I beckoned Stephan who was hanging back uncharacteristically shyly.

'Are you okay?'

'Yes, I just, well, feel a little uncomfortable being here. It doesn't seem that long ago we were at each other's throats.'

'Oh, Stephan, Beverley and Pablo invited you here; you're going to be taking over from me at the Academy. Trust me, we're all over it.'

Stephan smiled happily and smoothed down the sleeves of his white linen suit. He had been the perfect choice to fill in the gap I was leaving. He was a creative, bohemian soul, his make-up skills were outstanding, but most importantly - Sitges was his spiritual home. The Academy was his calling, not mine. Beverley had been justifiably wary of his suitability but during the past month he had changed so dramatically, it was difficult to associate him with the unhappy and bitter character he'd once been.

'I love that orange shirt, Stephan,' commented Mel, 'only someone with your colouring could look so great in it.'

'It's tangerine,' he corrected her with an acidic flash of the old Stephan, then added kindly, 'but I think you could also wear it, you have a beautiful tan.'

'That's what comes of giving up your job and moving to the country,' she beamed at me. 'It's the best decision I ever made. Why did you never talk sense into me earlier?'

'Like you'd have listened?' I rolled my eyes.

'I've got a bakery,' she squeaked at Stephan. 'I'm going to make everything - cupcakes, fairy cakes, apple cake, bread, muffins. I'm so excited!'

'So I see,' he laughed.

I looked on in amusement; it was like looking at Mel in her early twenties. This change hadn't come a moment too soon as far as I was concerned.

After a series of particularly horrendous cases and the accompanying diagnosis of high blood pressure, Mel decided she wanted out of the legal profession and, in a moment of madness, put her house in Chiswick on the market. Against all odds in a depreciating market, it had sold immediately for nearly eighty grand more than the asking price - a fact that she attributed to the very trendy Soho House lending extra kudos to this already desirable west London location. She had always loved Dorset and had found a beautiful property in a picturesque village. It was a roomy farmhouse with outhouses where John could operate his graphics business, and there was an existing bakery in the grounds. The change had obviously agreed with her. She looked dazzling in a pale turquoise and silver dress with the most exquisite crystal sandals. Gone were the frown lines and sallow skin. She looked years younger and happy. All she had to do now was slow John down a tad. Slightly unnerved by the loss of her mammoth income, he had insisted on taking on extra work.

'For ten years he nags me and now *he's* turning into a

workaholic,' she gave an exasperated sigh. 'He was meant to be here this weekend.'

'Don't worry Mel, it'll all work itself out,' Stan gave me a kiss on the cheek, 'things always do.' I gave him a squeeze back.

'I think Nat is a little taken with Alice and Heidi. He keeps gazing at them when he thinks they're not looking,' I laughed.

'God, I remember those days,' chuckled Stan. 'Bloody terrible they were, too.'

'He's not making a total idiot of himself is he?' Mel cringed. 'He does that stupid monosyllabic grunting thing they all seem to do nowadays. How they communicate with each other is a mystery.'

'They don't talk, they Twitter, text and do Facebook.'

'Bit like you then, Moll?' Cam wandered over swinging his camera. 'C'mon, group shot. Might be the last time we'll all be together for a while.'

'Let me take one of Alex and her two men,' Stephan grabbed the camera and I stood in between Cam and Stan.

'You look lovely, Alex,' said Cam appraising my new outfit, 'look at those boobs.'

'Shut up,' I said bashfully, pulling my pale aqua wrap around my chest to cover the plunging neckline of the matching clingy dress.

'Now what did you have to go and do that for? I was enjoying the view,' Stan punched Cam a little too enthusiastically.

'Ouch, you big lummox, aren't you going to say I look nice?'

There followed a five minute mutual appreciation of the finer points of Cam and Stan's attire from the shoes - which they bought together the day before - to the natty ties and clashing shirts - that they also bought together the day before! Since Cam had been giving this straight guy the queer eye, Stan suddenly had a sense of style. I was keeping my lips firmly sealed, no sarcastic remarks, no obvious commentary of any kind – I didn't want to send a skittish Stan retreating back to his baggy khaki trousers and ancient deck shoes. Or did I?

Finally Stephan took a few shots, and then a voice bellowed out: 'Alex,' it was Beverley. 'Come here and start being a best woman.'

I had categorically refused to be a 'Matron of Honour.'

The reception was of course, at the Academy, and along with all Cam's artwork, pink and white balloons were festooned everywhere. Huge vases of white roses were dotted about and all the brightly coloured curtains had been temporarily replaced with billowing clouds of white chiffon. Evie had worked alongside a caterer to create a decadent feast: fresh asparagus with quails' eggs and saffron butter to start, followed by scallops on a bed of sweet potatoes with coconut and ginger, drizzled with a lime and coriander sauce. Then we tucked into duck breasts with a pomegranate salsa and green beans, and for dessert, my mother – the Confectionary Queen herself - created a special wedding Pavlova with raspberries and rose cream, scattered with edible sugared rose petals. It was all washed down with the best the local *Penedes* wines, and of course, lashings of cava.

Then all too soon, as the coffees were being served, it was time to say a few words. Pablo's best man, another plumber called Ernan, stood up and ricocheted off a one-minute speech in Catalan, which caused the poor fellow to turn a vivid shade of beetroot, but nevertheless everyone cheered and gave him a standing ovation worthy of Nelson Mandela.

Pablo then launched into an amazing bi-lingual feat. One moment he spoke in Catalan and the next his own special brand of English. His bi-lingual platitudes went on for about five minutes, and then he finally wound up by turning to me: 'Wisout her, I would not 'ave met my wife. I have to ask Alex to say somesing, as she is ze best woman of Beverley.'

I stood up, painfully aware that I had a volcanic eruption of emotion just bubbling under the surface. I decided to keep it very short and began in a slightly shaky voice:

'Looking around the room is absolute testimony to the fact that no matter what life chucks at you, there is always a different life out there for you if you are brave enough to take that leap.' I looked across the room to where Mum was sitting with Evie, Cam and Stephan, she nodded and dabbed at her eyes with her napkin. 'It was on the first day I met Beverley that I chose to go on the little adventure that led me here, and she was there again on the day I decided to make Sitges my home, so it seems fitting that she herself has found happiness in this magical little town with its very magical people. Whatever the future may hold, I know I'm leaving her in safe hands, amongst good friends and married to a good man. So I would like you to join me in raising a glass to the bride and groom, their families and their future health and happiness ... to Pablo and Beverley!'

The room erupted into cheers as I sunk into my chair and buried my face tearfully in my napkin. Stan's arm came straight around me.

Cam raised an eyebrow then said, 'Are you two really alright?'

We nodded and snuggled in closer to each other, 'It's a happy sad day,' I sniffed.

'I'd say,' muttered Stan.

FIFTY SIX

I wandered outside for some fresh air, and as usual, there was Caveman sitting on his rock, almost like he was standing guard over the Academy. Suddenly I noticed something. If I wasn't mistaken he was wearing my poncho - the little bugger. I marched over towards him. He was smoking a cigar and looking out to sea. As I approached him I almost expected him to run off but he turned and faced me, his dark eyes glinting mischievously.

'El Phantom,' I stood with my hands on my hips.

'*La Reina del Cava*,' he cocked his head to one side and grinned, 'or should I say, The Cava Queen?'

'You speak English?' I was astounded.

'I speak many languages,' he gave a deep throaty laugh, 'but I prefer to listen.' He took a long dramatic drag of his cigar and blew a gust of smoke towards me. 'The beauty of people thinking you are crazy is that they assume you cannot understand or even hear what they are saying.' His stare was so intense, I felt myself shiver. He touched my poncho, 'You would like this back?'

'No, you might as well keep it,' I replied. 'You painted the picture too I assume? Moved the boobs? Ate the cake?' He laughed. I was fascinated. The smell of the sea hung all around him and his long grey hair was encrusted with sand. He was like some strange Merman. 'You visited the night I slept there, didn't you?'

'Yes. Your friend, who was there, is a very gifted young man. I like his paintings very much.'

'How do you keep getting in? We lock the place up every night.'

He raised an eyebrow at me and grinned, then tugged at my poncho, pulling it off one of his leathery brown shoulders. Hanging around his neck on a piece of string and gleaming in the dying sunlight was a bronze key identical to the one we used for the kitchen door.

'Where did you get that?'

'It's mine,' he shrugged.

'Look, I don't know where you found it but maybe you should give it back now? A joke is a joke, but you can't just keep wandering in and out and pinching whatever takes your fancy. What happens if someone catches you?'

He leaned forward on his knee and gestured for me to come a little closer. As I bent down to listen, he whispered, 'The house is mine.'

'Yeah right!'

He jumped off the rock, 'Alex why do you doubt me?'

My face still registered disbelief as he carried on, 'Ask your friend Nieves, she knows all about my father's bastard child,' he nodded towards the Academy, and sure enough, there was Nieves watching us from a window.

'She's not your ...?'

'Mother, no,' he smiled, 'but she was my mother's best friend. She is very kind to me. Where do you think she is going every time she walks towards the cemetery with that basket of hers - to feed the dead?'

'But why on Earth do you live in a cave if you own that place?'

He smiled and re-lit his cigar with a battered old Zippo. 'My father came from a very wealthy family in Barcelona. He made money selling art but always fancied himself an artist. So he bought the house as a summer retreat for him and all his artistic friends. My mother was an artist's model. That's how she met him. They had an affair and I was the result. He died when I was still young and left me the house in his will. Nobody knew about me until that point. Such a scandal! There were legal battles contesting the will for years. My mother never had any peace and spent the rest of her life fighting for a house that we never lived in. It killed her in the end. She died of cancer, ironically just before she won our case. I was sixteen.'

'So did you ever live in the house?'

'No, I travelled around the world for twenty years before I came back here. No-one even knew who I was, except Nieves of course.'

'The cave?'

He laughed, 'My father and mother used to swim there for their secret liaisons. I was conceived there.'

'Wow!'

'She and I used to go there all the time, so when I came back I spent a night there. That night turned into weeks and then I decided I liked the simplicity of it so I stayed. I used to have a romantic fantasy that one day a woman would literally emerge from the sea. We would live in my cave, and later I would reveal to her that I was the owner of a magnificent house and we would live there happily ever after.'

'And?'

'I never met such a woman,' he looked at me and winked.

'Don't you get lonely there?'

'Oh I have many visitors as I'm sure you have heard about,' he gazed out to sea. 'That made me feel a little crazy in the beginning, but you get used to it. Spirits are not so scary. I have seen far stranger things in my life ...'

I could have stayed there all night and listened to his stories but the sound of footsteps crunching across the sand brought our conversation to an end.

'There you are, woman,' Stan appeared at my side. 'You okay?'

'Why wouldn't I be?' I turned to Caveman, 'This is Stan.'

'So you are the man depriving us of our Cava Queen?'

'Eh?' Stan looked confused.

'He means you're taking me away,' I smiled and looked back at Caveman, 'but with the greatest respect in the world, I'm taking myself away. But before I go I have to thank you for loaning us your house. We are all grateful. It has made many people happy.'

'You saw the beauty in it. That would have made my father happy,' he smiled. 'It is Nieves you have to thank for that by the way. She is a tough nut to crack when it comes to people, but she assured me the house would be in safe hands.'

'And now Beverley is part of her family - amazing really.'

'Wait a minute, you own the Academy?' Stan looked even more bewildered.

'It's a long story Stan, I'll tell you later. It's time we went back in. Would you like to come?' I looked at Caveman, 'Maybe a little glass of cava to celebrate?'

He shook his head, leaned down behind the rock and pulled out a half-full bottle of the very same cava we were serving and took a huge gulp.

'You've already helped yourself I see,' I had to laugh.

He wiped his mouth with the back of his hand and burped, 'It would have been rude not to toast the beautiful bride.'

'I didn't catch your name, mate?' Stan held his hand out.

'Eduardo,' he shook Stan's hand solicitously, 'Eduardo Güell.'

I held out my hand which he took and immediately kissed, 'I would prefer it if what we have just discussed is kept a secret. I am happy with my life the way it is and would not want things to change. I put the property in what I consider to be the right hands but there are many people who may consider it a betrayal. We Catalans have been oppressed and suppressed so many times throughout history, it makes us a little too insular and suspicious, and like so many people on this earth, we have been seduced by greed. '

'Well, now there will be two Catalan children who will hopefully inherit the stewardship of the property, Eduardo,' I paused and smiled, it was strange to call him by his name.

'Yes, and Nieves is the closest to family that I have, so it seems fitting that things have worked out this way. But, I am sad you are leaving.'

'I need to go for a while, but not forever.' I slipped my arm around Stan, 'We both do.'

'Good luck to both of you and maybe one day when you return, I will show you my home.'

'We would love that,' Stan responded, 'kind of fancy a home like that myself.'

'I don't think Alex could live in a cave,' Eduardo's stare bore into my soul. I suddenly felt so intensely scrutinised it was getting uncomfortable. 'We must go, bye for now Eduardo, and thank you once again.'

He bowed and smiled a knowing smile, then suddenly looked past me and said 'Okay, I will tell her.'

I wasn't prepared for what came next.

'Your father wants you to know that you are doing the right thing and don't worry, he will watch over your mother. She has a present for you that he knows you will appreciate.'

My mouth dropped open in disbelief and despite myself I spun around, and then looked back at Eduardo who shrugged, 'He is always with you. He loved the water too, didn't he? You look very much like him by the way.'

'I do,' I faltered as what felt like a gentle breeze passed across the back of my neck, followed by an incredible sense of warmth. Tears sprung to my eyes, 'Eduardo, is he happy?'

He smiled and nodded, 'He is at peace, now go and see your mother; she is looking for you.'

Stan and I turned and wandered back to the Academy. 'Now that was weird,' he said shaking his head. 'You okay Alex?'

'Yes,' I sighed, I was still reeling from the shock of what had just passed, but felt strangely comforted.

Stan nudged me in the ribs, 'I think our Caveman has the hots for you.'

'You idiot,' I looked back and there he was gazing at us. I felt a sudden rush of sadness envelope me, 'I've always been lucky enough to be surrounded by friends and family, even if I haven't always appreciated it as much as I should sometimes. I feel for him being as alone as he is. Mind you ...' I grinned, 'taking *him* home to the NADs and announcing that I was moving into his cave would have been worth it just to see the look on their faces.'

Stan chuckled, 'Hey, here comes trouble.' I looked up and there was Mum marching towards us.

'There you are, I've been looking everywhere for you.' She was carrying a package. I turned and looked at Eduardo once more; he smiled knowingly and started to walk away.

Stan kissed me on the forehead, 'I'll go in and give you some time with your mum. She's all yours Mrs C,' he shouted as he wandered back over to the Academy.

I sat down on one of the benches and Mum plopped down beside me, 'What a lovely day it's been Alex. I don't think I've ever been to such a happy wedding.' She gave a long sigh and added, 'Of course I had hoped it might have been you and Stan tying the knot, but I suppose that was just a little too much to hope for.'

I went to answer, but she waggled her finger at me, 'I'm not nagging you Alex, you don't need to justify yourself.'

'D'you believe I'm doing the right thing?'

'Does it really matter what I think?'

'Yes, Mum, it does.'

'For what it's worth, yes I do believe you and Stan are doing what's best for you. I'm going to miss you of course, but the most important thing for me is your happiness, and I think you've found yourself a man whose feet are as itchy as yours.'

I hugged her; I was going to miss her like hell. 'Mum, thank you.'

'What for Alex?'

'For proving to me that it is possible to get younger as you grow older.'

She chuckled, 'Well this old dog has certainly learned some new tricks, and for that I have to thank you.'

'Can I have my present now?' I gestured towards the package on her lap.

'How do you know it's for you?' she smiled.

I explained the last part of my conversation with Eduardo.

She looked out to sea, 'That doesn't surprise me one little bit. I told you I felt closer to him out here, and he probably finds you quite entertaining to follow around I'm sure.'

I laughed.

She handed me the package and watched with amusement as I pulled open the paper and gasped. There were my childhood journals, the very ones I used to take with me on my Saturday jaunts – bright red books covered with scribbles and strange collages of magazine cuttings and pictures. 'I thought these were long gone,' I murmured as yet again I felt myself welling up. As days went, this was turning into an emotional rollercoaster. I glanced through them marvelling at my childish handwriting and very evident multiple personality disorder. One minute I was an Indian princess, the next I was a spy. But they were awash with memories and brought back so many parts of my childhood that had been long forgotten, 'I don't know what to say Mum, I can't believe you kept them.'

'Your dad kept these in his bedside cabinet for years, I'd often catch him having a flick through and laughing to himself.'

'I'm not surprised; I really was quite mental wasn't I?'

'You had a vivid imagination Alex,' she laid her hands on mine, 'you still do darling.'

'Thank you for giving me these now Mum; it's like some kind of omen.'

'Just go and do your best Alex, it will be more than enough.'

I snuggled up close to her and we sat watching the waves crash onto the sand until dusk started to fall, then headed back into the Academy where everyone was on the dance floor. I smiled as I caught sight of Nieves moving effortlessly to the Latin beat that flowed through her veins. She looked up and summoned me with a click of her fingers. I happily joined the *fiesta* and lost myself in the music.

Finally at around three am it was over. Stan and I walked back along the *paseo* enjoying the warm sea breeze. I took it all in as I slipped my arm through his. The sounds and sights of this beautiful chameleon-like town that changed its mood from hour to hour, from season to season, I had loved every different facet and knew it would always hold a special place in my heart, but now it was time to go. I glanced at Stan's profile and smiled. Wherever life was going to take me, I knew he was going to be a part of it. Exactly what that journey was going to entail remained a mystery to me, but that was the beauty of it. Almost as if he were reading my thoughts, Stan hugged me closer and looked down, 'You sure about this, Alex?'

I   nodded,   'Yep,   it's   time   to   go.'

FIFTY SEVEN

'How many bags sir?'

'Just the one.'

As Stan lifted his suitcase onto the belt I momentarily floundered and gripped his arm.

'You can come with me, you know. It's not too late. I can go and get you a ticket right now,' he raised his eyebrows at me, 'a couple of months in the middle of nowhere might be very inspiring for you.'

'No, I'll be fine, honestly,' I laughed at him. 'You might love the idea of just a few million trees for company, but it just ain't me darling.'

'I'd give it a go, just think of all those lumberjacks and mounties,' Cam's voice piped up from behind us.

'They'd eat you for breakfast, Fairycakes.'

'What a lovely thought,' Cam sighed. 'Look, I think you two could do with a little space so I'm going to bugger off and daydream about great big men in checked shirts.' Cam held out his hand to Stan, 'Time to say goodbye Bug Man.'

'Homophobic Stan has come a long way, Cam,' he laughed and gave him a hug.

'Damn right he has. You look after yourself out there, no falling off trees,' Cam smiled. 'I'll be on my mobile, Alex,' he turned and walked away quickly.

'Coffee?' Stan grabbed my suitcase and laptop bag, 'C'mon woman, stop looking so glum, you've got loads to look forward to over the next couple of months. The time will fly by.' He walked towards the café with me trotting half-heartedly behind.

We sat down nursing our drinks staring at each other.

I attempted a weak laugh, 'We are doing the right thing, aren't we?' My previously unquestionable logic was wavering in the face of reality.

'I bloody well hope so.' He levelled his clear green eyes at me. 'What a pair eh?'

'We just have to do different stuff at the moment. At least we've been honest. There are lots of people out there who spend their entire lives avoiding get it all out there in the open.'

Boy had we been honest. That night on the balcony before Cam came home, we had left no stone unturned. We knew that we were both nomads at heart, the only thing that was lacking was my sense of purpose, and that had to be addressed before we could even think about travelling together. In the same way that Stan was getting frustrated in Sitges, I would never be content merely trailing around behind him. Neither of us wanted or needed a 24/7/365 partnership, so we resolved to find a way to make our relationship work and whichever way we looked at it, the only option that worked for both of us was the one we were taking now.

I felt the excitement bubble up just at the thought of what I wanted to do. I had sent a few excerpts from my recent journals to various agents and had a few meetings planned in London over the following couple of weeks. It was looking very positive, and during this period of trying to establish this new direction for myself, I was going to stay with the one person who would keep me focused – Mel. There would be no procrastination with her. She had been waiting years for the opportunity to instil a little discipline into yours truly.

Stan slid his hand across the table and grabbed mine, 'When I get my first stretch of leave, you and I are going to do something very special. I want you to meet me in Oz so you can meet my dad, and we're going to visit some islands in Polynesia where you can swim with whales, but now,' he downed his coffee, 'it's time for me to go.'

We jumped up and hugged, he kissed my hair and whispered 'Don't you dare meet some slick city publisher and forget me.'

'Like I could do that,' I kissed him. 'Anyhow, I think they're all menopausal women, but while we're on that subject, Stanley Berringer,' I leaned back and raised an eyebrow at him.

'Don't you worry, I prefer having something to look forward to than something to feel guilty about,' he kissed me again.

'That was the right answer; now promise me you'll load Skype...'

'...and Facebook. Yes Boss, I'll do it.'

'Good boy, now go before I start trying to climb into your hand luggage.'

With a small lump in my throat and a single tear in my eye, I watched Stan walk through Departures and then went off to find Cam, who was waiting for me at the BMI check-in desk. 'You look surprisingly okay. I was expecting a sobbing mess,' he looked at me quizzically.

'I'm fine darling, have you checked in yet?'

He pointed at his suitcase on the floor and shook his head, 'Wanted to make sure we were sitting together – are you sure you don't mind coming with me?'

'Not at all, it'll be good for you to have a bit of back up, just so long as you don't try to pass me off as your girlfriend.'

'Now that would rather defeat the object, wouldn't it?' Cam had spoken to his parents on the phone and apparently his mother wasn't in the best of health, so he had decided there was no time like the present to make the journey back to Scotland. We were going to spend a few days together in Edinburgh before we continued on to see his parents. Then with the ordeal over, he was going to fly back to Spain to make a start on the many commissions he had received since the exhibition, as Beverley had given him his own studio in the Academy.

'I wouldn't mind Alex, you know - if you wanted to change flights and go with Stan.'

'Cam!' I looked at him incredulously, 'I'm fine honestly. We both are. Stop fretting.'

'You're going to miss each other.'

'Of course I'm going to miss him you idiot, but a month or two isn't a long time. He'll be doing what he loves, and in all honesty, I need a little 'me' time. I can concentrate on getting a book deal.

Then, I can work on my laptop wherever in the world I want to be.'
I smiled as I suddenly had a flashback of my dad's face looking
down at me as I used to run away each Saturday morning. But
despite my cheerful demeanour, I could tell by the way Cam was
frowning he still wasn't convinced. 'Cam I promise you, if the
spruce budworms put up a bit of a fight and he does have to stay in
the Canadian forest for months on end, I'll find the nearest bit of
civilisation and base myself there. I'll write, he'll come home at
weekends and we'll be fine. Then we'll see what other
opportunities arise and go from there. We just want to remain a bit
open to whatever the future may bring.'

'You're a bloody pair of commitophobes!'

'We ARE committed to each other Cam. We just don't have to
live in each other's pockets to prove that. I have beaten myself up
for years for being a failure at relationships and having no sense of
direction. Now I have a relationship that suits me and I know what
I want to do with my life – surely that's a good thing?'

'It is Moll,' he hugged me. 'I just don't want you and him to go
tits up. I love you both too much for that.' He looked down at my
feet, clad in bright red satin *espadrilles* – a present from Nieves,
'Remember to click your heels occasionally and come home will
you?'

'Can you imagine the trouble I'd be in with Mummy if I didn't?'

My phone beeped. I took it out of my handbag and read the text.

'By the look of that soppy grin on your face, I'd say that was
lover boy,' Cam smirked.

'Yeah, he misses me already.'

'Ooohhh … it would have been such a fairytale ending if you
and Stan had disappeared off into the sunset together,' Cam wailed
theatrically.

'Enough! You soppy old romantic! There'll be plenty of
spectacular sunsets in Stan's and my future. But what's all this crap
about endings? Ending to what exactly?' I laughed, 'Real fairy
tales don't have endings Cam, just infinite possibilities. Anyhow, if
you would excuse the pun, this is merely another chapter,' I stroked
his cheek, 'for all of us.'